By K.C. WELLS

NOVELS

LEARNING TO LOVE
Michael & Sean
Evan & Daniel
Josh & Chris

COLLARS & CUFFS
An Unlocked Heart
Trusting Thomas

Published by DREAMSPINNER PRESS
http://www.dreamspinnerpress.com

TRUSTING THOMAS

K.C. WELLS

A COLLARS & CUFFS STORY

Dreamspinner Press

Published by
Dreamspinner Press
5032 Capital Circle SW
Ste 2, PMB# 279
Tallahassee, FL 32305-7886
USA
http://www.dreamspinnerpress.com/

Trusting Thomas
© 2013 by K.C. Wells.

Cover Art
© 2013 Cover photo by Terry J Cyr.
Cover design by Paul Richmond.
http://www.paulrichmondstudio.com
Cover content is for illustrative purposes only and any person depicted on the cover is a model.

ISBN: 978-1-62798-328-0
Digital ISBN: 978-1-62798-329-7

Printed in the United States of America
First Edition
October 2013

For Will Parkinson,

My friend and ally.

And, apparently, my psychically linked twin.

This one is just for you.

"Thank you" doesn't cover it.

Not by a long shot.

My thanks to James Masters
for his wonderful list, which became Thomas's rules.

100 Things a Dom/Master Should Know
Published by James Masters at Smashwords
Copyright 2012

And to Max Vos
for the inspiration for a certain ritual.
Thank you.

Prologue

One week before New Year's Eve

THEY certainly know how to throw a great party, I'll give them that.

Steven Drummond gazed at the festivities with mixed feelings. The Christmas party at the BDSM club, St. Andrew's, was in full swing and everyone was having a good time. *So why I am feeling pissed off?* Steven shook his head and drained his glass of wine. That would be his one and only drink tonight. He glanced at the young man by his side. David couldn't keep his eyes off the group of subs who had congregated near a table that groaned under the weight of party food. Steven snickered. He knew *exactly* what David was thinking.

"Boy?"

David immediately turned his head. "Yes, Sir." David focused on Steven's chest, and Steven swelled with pride. The young man had the makings of an excellent submissive.

"You may join the other subs, if you'd like." Steven didn't fail to notice the flash of joy in those expressive blue eyes. "I know I can trust you to behave as you should."

David beamed. "Thank you, Sir. I won't let you down." He moved gracefully to join the others, who greeted him effusively. David laughed as they surrounded him, joking and giggling.

"Is that your new sub, Steven? He's looking good."

Steven turned around to greet Alan Marchant, his friend since Alan joined the club six months ago. Steven liked him straightaway. There was a no-nonsense air about him, and he had a nice manner with the subs.

This praise of David delighted Steven. "He's going to be a damn good one," he admitted with a satisfied smile.

Alan smirked. "That proud gleam in your eye looks good too." He glanced around the club. "St. Andrew's has pulled out all the stops for this do." He gave Steven a searching glance. "I take it their money worries have all been sorted out, then?"

Steven scowled. It was no secret the club had been through three changes of management in the last year, and he fervently hoped there would be no more. True, the place definitely looked better, and someone had certainly spent a lot of money. The recent changes were not all to the good, however, as far as Steven was concerned. He looked at the men standing around. He recognized a few of the Doms, but there were a great many new faces.

"I find myself wondering if the entrance procedures are as rigorous as they once were," he muttered as he spied a familiar face among the crowd. Not for the first time, he wondered who had vetted Curtis Rogers's application. The man had been a member for about six months, give or take, and after seeing him with one or two of the subs, Steven had voiced concerns. He felt Curtis was too rough. But he'd been told in no uncertain terms his suspicions were unfounded.

"I know what you mean," murmured Alan, his gaze alighting on Curtis. "No *way* is that man a trained Dom."

Steven gave Alan a sardonic grin. "My best friend trains Doms," he said as Alan tilted his head. "He has strict rules he drums into every Dom who passes through his hands." He returned his gaze to Curtis. "And *that man* would fail every single one of them." He scowled. Thomas would have run Curtis out of the club in a heartbeat. Steven had spoken with Curtis on a number of occasions, and his opinion of the man had not improved.

Curtis approached a table where a slender, pale young man knelt, leashed to the chair leg. In direct contrast to the laughing, happy subs who chatted with David, this boy kept his head bowed. His shoulders were hunched and everything about his body language screamed misery. Hands hung limply by his sides. Steven had the impression the lad had folded in on himself, shutting out the outside world.

Steven itched to know more about him.

"I'll be back in a moment," he murmured to Alan, who arched his brows when he saw the object of Steven's focus and then nodded once in acknowledgment. Steven walked as casually as he could toward the table, straining to hear what passed between Curtis and his sub. As he neared them, he was able to pick up their conversation.

"Straighten up, boy," Curtis hissed. "Shoulders back. Are you trying to shame me *again* in front of all these Doms, you sorry excuse for a sub? Christ, I swear, every time I bring you here, you act up." He towered over the kneeling sub, who straightened immediately, but apparently not quick enough for his master. Curtis aimed a blow at the kneeling submissive, sending him sprawling with a loud thud as he connected with the hard wooden floor. "Now get up and stop looking so fucking nervous!"

Steven inhaled sharply. He watched the sub struggle to right himself. And it was then he saw the bruises. There were lots of them. On his arms. Half hidden by his shirt. His face. Christ, the boy was a mess. He trembled, his gaze darting agitatedly between the floor and Curtis.

Steven regarded the men surrounding this scene. No one moved or spoke. That brief glance decided him. He would not renew his membership at the end of the month. He couldn't be part of a club where such unwarranted violence toward a sub went totally unheeded. But right now there was a more pressing problem, and Steven needed some advice.

He walked back to Alan, wrinkling his brow. Alan watched him approach with widening eyes.

"What the hell did the sub do, exactly?"

Steven shrugged. "Beats me. Nothing that warranted being knocked to the ground, that's for sure." He half turned, trying to spy Curtis with his peripheral vision. The boy was kneeling once again, eyes downcast, while Curtis talked animatedly with another young man.

"That's Curtis's new sub," Alan explained under his breath.

Incredulous, Steven gazed at Alan. "He has two subs?" Alan nodded, looking beyond Steven to where Curtis stood. Steven's lip curled. "This isn't right. He shouldn't be taking on another sub, not when he treats his existing one so poorly."

"Sir?" David touched Steven's arm tentatively. Steven hadn't heard him approach. The sub's expression was troubled.

Steven straightened. "What is it, David?" He kept his voice calm. David was clearly flustered.

"Sir, I have to talk to you. It's important. Is there somewhere we can go, somewhere more… private?"

Steven thought for a moment. "Come with me." He led the way to one of the private rooms near the bar, and David followed him inside. Steven closed the door and leaned back against it. "Okay, David, talk to me." David's breathing was ragged, his cheeks flushed. Something was wrong.

"Sir, I was talking with one of the subs, a guy called Christian. He was telling me about his master's other sub, Peter. He was telling me his master likes to…." David swallowed nervously.

"Go on, boy," Steven encouraged him. David breathed deeply.

"Sir, it seems his master beats Peter—a lot."

Steven was unsure what to say. His sub was reasonably new to the lifestyle. He could have no conception of what it was to be a pain slut. He pondered how best to explain it.

"David, some submissives like a lot of pain." He got no further. David's eyes met his, and Steven jerked in surprise at this unaccustomed behavior. David gazed earnestly at him.

"No, Sir, forgive me, but that's not the case here. Christian made a comment that concerned me. He said, 'I didn't think Peter was a pain slut, but Master says he is. As much as he gets beaten, I guess he must be.'" David shivered. "It just didn't sound right, Sir."

Steven thought fast. "Do you happen to know his master's name?" His heart sank as he asked the question. All of a sudden he had a bad feeling he knew what David's reply would be.

David nodded slowly. "It's Curtis Rogers, Sir." He shuddered, clearly upset by the situation. Steven put his arm around the boy's shoulders, feeling the tremors that rippled through him. He pulled David against him.

"Easy there," he murmured. "I need to speak with my friend for a moment, and then we're going home. All right?" David nodded and seemed to calm himself. "Good boy. And thank you for telling me. You did the right thing." He waited until David was once more in control of his emotions and then led him from the room. Alan was hovering outside, concern evident in his expression.

"Everything okay?"

Steven gave him a brief nod. "I'm going to take David home now. And then I think I need to make a phone call. That best friend of mine that I mentioned earlier? He runs a BDSM club. I need his advice here, Alan, before I step in and do something stupid."

Alan regarded him thoughtfully. "Then by all means, take some advice. And let me know what you decide to do." He clasped Steven's hand firmly. "If you need anything, you have my number." Steven gave him a look of gratitude before turning to his sub. David watched the two men solemnly.

"Come on, boy. Let's go home."

"SO WHAT do you think I should do?" Steven asked. He stood by his lounge window, looking out over the Manchester city center skyline. Two days had passed before he had the opportunity to call his best friend, Thomas Williams. Christmas obligations had taken precedence, unfortunately.

Thomas's snort reverberated in his ear. "I know you, Steven. You want to dash in there on your white horse and rescue the sub in distress, don't you?"

Steven pulled a face. "Am I that obvious?"

There was a brief silence at the other end. Finally Thomas spoke, his tone earnest.

"Steven, you don't know what's going on. You don't have all the facts. You've been given the tiniest glimpse into this boy's life—and it's not enough." He paused, giving Steven time to mull over his words. "Is there any way you can get to see Peter in his home? See how Curtis treats him when they're away from the club?"

Steven thought quickly. "I could always call round there to inquire if Curtis is going to the New Year's Eve party. Apparently, they're going to have a sub auction—for charity—and I don't know if he's aware of it."

"Are you well enough acquainted with Curtis to do that? What I mean to say is, would your appearance at his home arouse his suspicions?"

Steven considered Thomas's question. It was a valid one. "We've spoken on a number of occasions," he admitted, "so I'm not exactly a stranger. I could ask if his subs will be going, as if I'm checking on numbers or something." The excuse sounded lame, even to his ears.

He heard Thomas expel his breath. "If you insist on checking this out further, you'd better make it an excellent performance. From all accounts, Curtis Rogers isn't a man I'd wish to cross."

That got Steven's attention. "What have you heard?"

Thomas cleared his throat before speaking. "Only rumors, if I'm honest. It seems Mr. Rogers is mixed up with some pretty undesirable elements and has his fingers in too many pies, shall we say—some of which are probably illegal."

The more Steven heard about Curtis Rogers, the more he disliked the man.

"That settles it. I'm going to call round there." He spoke decisively.

"Fine—but get back to me, please, once you've seen him." Thomas coughed once. "And Steven? Don't do anything until you've talked to me. I mean it." Steven knew that authoritative tone. He'd seen many a submissive and Dominant quake when on the receiving end of it.

"I promise." Damn, the man knew him *far* too well.

STEVEN pulled up outside Curtis's gate and paused with the engine still running. His jaw dropped. Whatever Curtis did for a living, it must pay very well. The house was a palace compared to Steven's three-bedroom city-center apartment. A long, sweeping gravel driveway led to a large building that could only be described as ostentatious. Two cars stood in front of the double garage, and Steven estimated their combined worth to be nearly two hundred thousand pounds. He spent a moment admiring their sleek lines. He was a sucker for a fine automobile.

Swinging his car off the road and into the driveway, Steven drove toward the house. He parked across from the two cars, exited and locked his Volvo, and approached the front door. Before he could ring the bell, the huge, ornate wooden door opened slowly. Steven recognized Christian from the party.

"Good afternoon. Is your master at home?"

Christian nodded and stepped aside to let Steven enter. "Come this way, sir. I'll inform my master you are here." He led Steven into a light, airy hallway featuring a large, opulent staircase. After opening a door to his left, he directed Steven to enter. Steven found himself in a large lounge with an inglenook fireplace dominating one wall and three leather sofas arranged around it. "Please take a seat, sir. My master will join you shortly."

Steven sat on the nearest sofa, eyeing the paintings and various ornaments. Curtis had spared no expense, it seemed. The Christmas tree in the window stood at least nine feet tall. Its branches were hidden from view by the vast amount of baubles that adorned it.

"Admiring my interior decorator's handiwork?"

Steven rose to greet Curtis, who eyed him speculatively. Curtis was dressed casually in jeans and a sweater. He approached Steven with an outstretched hand, his lips pursed.

"What brings you to my neck of the woods, Drummond?"

Steven shook his hand, feeling surprisingly nervous all of a sudden. He went through his prepared story.

"Yeah, I'll be going to the party," Curtis said. "Christian here is up for auction." He indicated the sub with a brief flick of his hand. "He should raise quite a bit for charity, don't you think? A good-looking boy." He leered at Christian.

"I should think so," Steven murmured noncommittally. "And are you going to auction your other sub too?"

Curtis scowled. "At this rate, Peter won't be allowed to go. We'll have to see. Speaking of which…." Curtis walked to the door and opened it, then shouted into the hall. "Peter! Where's that tea?" He looked back at Steven, his scowl deepening. "That boy… I swear he's more trouble than he's worth." He returned to where Steven stood and gestured to the sofa. "Sit, Drummond. The tea will be here shortly… if that boy knows what's good for him." Curtis's eyes narrowed. He fixed Steven with a steely gaze. "Was that your only reason for coming round?"

Steven thought on his feet. "Well, if I'm honest…." He glanced around the room. "I heard at the club you got a great new house." He gave an embarrassed shrug. "I was curious to see how the other half lived." He held his breath, hoping to appeal to the man's vanity.

Curtis puffed up, his chest swelling, and Steven heaved an internal sigh of relief.

"Ahh, *now* I understand!" Curtis beamed. "Gorgeous, isn't it? Cost me a pretty penny too."

The door opened, and Peter entered, carrying a tray laden with a silver teapot, cups, saucers, a milk jug, and sugar bowl, plus a plate of cookies. He approached the waiting men hesitantly. As he neared the low coffee table, he stumbled slightly, slopping the milk onto the tray. He looked immediately toward Curtis, and Steven had trouble repressing the shiver that ran down his spine. The fear in those eyes....

"You stupid—" Curtis took one step toward Peter, and the sub flinched, leaving Steven in no doubt he expected to be struck. He cowered, squeezing his eyes shut, awaiting the blow that never came. Curtis caught sight of Steven's face and straightened hurriedly. "Put down the tray, and then get that cleaned up." His jaw clenched, Curtis enunciated every word carefully, but there was an underlying tone that chilled Steven. Peter's face was white as he left the room in a hurry, then soon returned with paper towels to mop up the relatively small amount of spilled milk.

Steven took this opportunity to study the boy. He estimated Peter to be in his midtwenties. The bruises he'd spied at the club looked worse in the light of day. They encircled the boy's slender wrists, rising under the long-sleeved shirt he wore. But the bruising on the boy's face.... Peter glanced up fearfully at him before hurriedly lowering his gaze, and Steven tried to put as much reassurance into his returning glance as possible. Curtis's attention was fixed on the sub.

"You can go now," he gritted out. Steven watched Peter's speedy exit; he'd never seen a sub move so fast to get out of a master's presence. Curtis poured Steven a cup of tea, and Steven helped himself to the milk. He didn't want to drink tea, damn it. He wanted to get out of there. He wanted to ring Thomas. Steven sat back and made polite conversation, trying not to steal glances at the clock on the mantelpiece. His skin felt as if it were crawling. The first thing he'd do when he reached his apartment would be to take a long, hot shower. He needed to get clean.

"I'M TELLING you, it felt... wrong." For an articulate, intelligent man, Steven had difficulty identifying his emotions. Before calling Thomas, he'd sat at his dining table staring off into space, his thoughts totally fixed on the sub. The more he thought about it, the more he became convinced Peter was being mistreated. The deciding factor had been Peter's facial expression. There was not the merest hint of joy or even happiness in that expression. Rather, the haunted, fearful look in Peter's eyes refused to let go of Steven, hours after he'd gotten out of there.

He heard Thomas's patient sigh at the other end of the phone.

"Okay, you've sold me." Thomas sounded resigned. "What do you want to do?"

That was the easy part. Steven knew *exactly* what he wanted to do. The problem would be how to get his best friend and former trainer to agree.

"I'm going to get him away from Curtis."

Thomas let out a dry chuckle. "*That* much I'd already surmised. My question is… how?"

Steven took a deep breath. Now for the tricky part.

"I'm going to go to the New Year's Eve party and see if he accompanies Curtis. If he's there, I'll distract Curtis somehow. There's a friend of mine who might help with that part. And when the opportunity presents itself, I'll make my move."

"And if he's not there?"

"Then there's only one other place he'd be… at home. Which is where I'll be heading."

Thomas fell silent for a moment. Steven braced himself for what he knew was coming. Sure enough….

"What makes you think Peter will be in a position to answer the door? *And* if he is, do you really think he will let you waltz in there and take him? What if he doesn't want to go? What do you do then?"

"*I don't know*, all right?" Steven winced. He didn't mean to shout, but he was playing it by ear here. "My bigger problem is, what I do with Peter if I manage to get him out of Curtis's clutches."

The pause at the other end seemed heavy. "What do you mean?" Thomas's tone was suddenly cautious. Yeah, no one could ever accuse Thomas of being slow on the uptake. The man's mind was as sharp as a razor.

"He can't stay here, Thomas. I couldn't train David *and* care for an injured sub. David's needs come first. And Peter would need a lot of care."

Steven closed his eyes, and that pale, bruised face swam behind his eyelids. "So I was thinking of bringing him to you." He held his breath, waiting for the outburst from his friend. He didn't have to wait long.

"And what makes you think *I* can look after him?" Thomas's voice rose.

"Thomas, you don't have to be at that club of yours 24-7, do you? You don't have a submissive of your own. You live alone—unless that's changed?" He waited for Thomas to jump in. Silence. Steven plunged ahead. "Okay, then you're in a much better position than I am to look after him." He fell quiet, secretly urging Thomas to agree. The silence continued for a few moments. Steven began to worry.

Thomas cleared his throat. "You're a pain, Steven, do you know that?" Steven held his breath. "Very well. Ring me on New Year's Eve and keep me fully apprised of the situation. I mean that, Steven. I don't want to receive a phone call from Greater Manchester Police informing me you've been arrested for breaking and entering, as well as kidnapping."

Steven let out his breath in a long exhale. Thank God.

"I promise. I'll let you know what's happening every step of the way."

"There'll be times when you might not be able to reach me. We've got a collaring ceremony taking place that night, and I'll be involved." Steven couldn't miss Thomas's quiet sigh. "I'll keep my phone on me, okay? If you can't get through at first, keep trying. I mean that, Steven." The authoritative edge to his voice was once more in evidence.

"Understood." Steven couldn't stop his smile. "And thank you, Thomas."

"I must be mad," Thomas murmured. "What the hell am I letting myself in for, I wonder?"

"It'll just be for a little while," Steven said. There was a gruff noise from the other end.

"We'll have to see about that, won't we?"

O̲ne

New Year

"PETER'S definitely not here, Sir," murmured David. Steven straightened.

"You're sure? You've looked everywhere?" He heard every word, in spite of the music booming through the speakers. Everyone was talking, laughing, dancing….

David dipped his head once. "And I also overheard Christian talking. I might have misunderstood, but I'm sure he said something about Peter being in a cage tonight."

Steven went still. "You're sure he said 'cage'?"

David nodded, his eyes wide. "He didn't *really* mean Peter is in a cage… did he? I mean, he shouldn't be in the cage if his master isn't present." Steven's heart swelled. David remembered everything he was taught. Not for the first time, Steven thought how proud he was to have David as his submissive.

"Liste\n to me, boy." He cupped David's chin, lifting it so the sub was forced to look at him directly. "Curtis Rogers is not a Dom, all right? He has *no right* to call himself Peter's master. And we are going to get Peter away from him so he can learn what it means to be a submissive, if that's what he wants."

David's gaze never wavered. He nodded slowly, swallowing.

"Then I need your help."

David composed himself quickly. "What do you need me to do, Sir?"

19

Steven gave him a quick grin and kissed his cheek. "Good boy." David's blush was delightful. "I need you to keep a lookout for me. I'm going to find Curtis's car keys, because hopefully there will also be a set of house keys attached." His grin widened as David inhaled sharply. "Come on, then. Let's go to the parking bay."

Dom and sub made their way through the throng of partygoers toward the back of the club, where the boys who did the valet parking were sprawled on chairs, drinking Cokes. The back door was open, despite the chill winter's air: the boys were smoking. Steven turned to look at the wall behind him and saw a board with many hooks laden with keys, all neatly labeled.

"Right," he whispered to David, "you go strike up a conversation. Keep them talking for about five minutes, then meet me outside the club. Okay?" David nodded and headed for the three boys. Steven hurried to the board and searched rapidly through the myriad bunches of keys until at last he spied Curtis's name. With a triumphant smirk he grabbed the set of keys and cast a darting glance toward his sub. David was chatting animatedly with the boys, who were laughing and joking with him. *Good boy.* Steven glanced at his watch. Ten thirty. Plenty of time to get to Curtis's house, grab Peter, take him to Thomas, and then get back here to replace the keys. At least he knew Curtis would be staying put until midnight. The sub auction wasn't due to happen until just before twelve.

Abruptly, Steven's heart began to race. Okay, so maybe what he was about to do was slightly illegal. Hell, who was he kidding? It was *damned* illegal, but he kept telling himself the end justified the means. Peter couldn't stay with that brute a second longer. He needed rescuing.

THE house was virtually in darkness.

"Shouldn't we be worried about an alarm, Sir?" David peered out anxiously through the car window.

Steven shook his head. "He's not likely to have set the alarm if Peter is inside, is he?" Well, Steven fervently *hoped* the alarm wasn't set. "Come on, let's have a look around."

As silently as possible, the two men got out of the car and walked up to the house. The only light visible came from a lamp softly glowing in the large front window and the wall light next to the front door. Steven peered at the window. No sign of Peter. Then he reasoned: *As if Curtis would leave Peter where he could be seen.* He motioned to David to follow him, and they took the path that led along the side of the house until they arrived at the huge expanse of a garden. Steven glanced at the windows again. A faint light shone from deeper within the house. He took out his phone and activated its flashlight function to examine the lock on the back door. After glancing down at the keys in his hand, he let out a quiet whoop of triumph.

"We're going in."

Stealthily, they crept inside. They found themselves in a large kitchen filled with shiny appliances and black marble work surfaces. "Head for the light," he whispered and went toward the open kitchen door. The light came from a room off the small hallway.

"Master? Christian? Is that you? Who's there?"

Steven stiffened at the sound of Peter's voice, which quavered. He edged his way carefully into the room... and stopped.

In the corner sat a cage about four feet high and three feet wide. Peter raised his head from his curled-up position on the floor of the cage. His wrist and leg restraints were connected by chains to a thick loop of steel suspended from the roof of the cage, allowing him little movement. A bottle of water sat beside him. He wore a thin pair of sweatpants and an equally thin T-shirt. His feet were bare.

Peter's eyes grew round as he saw the two men approach the cage.

"I-I remember you," he whispered, his gaze alighting on Steven. He glanced at David, who smiled kindly at him. Instantly, Peter froze. "You have to leave! He could be back any second!"

Steven gave the small room a cursory glance. A set of keys hung from a nail on the wall... ones just about the right size to be the keys for Peter's restraints. He grabbed them and opened the cage door. It wasn't locked: no need—Peter wasn't going anywhere. Clumsily, Steven fumbled with the restraints, his hands shaking.

"You're coming with us," he said firmly. Peter shook his head, aghast.

"I can't! I can't leave my master!"

"Boy, I don't have time to wait. We need to get you out of here now."

Peter trembled violently. "You don't understand," he whispered. "I can't leave him—he won't let me. He's my master. He would beat me if I tried to leave."

"Then we're going to get out of here before he comes back." Steven stared at Peter. "Will you come with me?" Stubbornly, Peter shook his head. "Then I will just have to carry you out." Peter howled in protest as Steven pulled him gently from the cage and then hefted him up over his shoulder. At five feet eleven and with well-defined musculature, thanks to his hours spent in the local gym, Steven had no problem carrying the slight sub. All the fight promptly went out of Peter, and he sagged against Steven, a deadweight.

David led the way out of the house and locked the door behind them.

"Sir, if you want to go in the back with Peter, I can drive, as long as you give me directions."

Steven gave his sub a fond look. "That's okay, David. I'll strap Peter into the front seat, and then I'll drop you outside the club. Can you get the keys back to the parking board?" David nodded. "We'll wait outside for you. Then we'll take Peter here to Master Thomas's house. Once Peter is safe, you and I can go home. You did really well, David. As a reward, you're sleeping in my bed tonight… when we eventually get to sleep, that is."

David beamed with pride, and his sharp intake of breath and happy grin spoke volumes.

Steven chuckled. He'd always planned on fucking the boy tonight—nothing like letting the New Year in with a bang—but he wanted to go to sleep with his submissive in his arms. And judging by the contented expression on David's face, his sub wanted that too.

First things first, however. While David was returning the keys to their rightful position, Steven would ring Thomas. Better warn the man they were on their way—with a houseguest for him.

THOMAS WILLIAMS was pacing his lounge floor. He couldn't help it. Ever since Steven's phone call, he'd been restless. The call had arrived a short time before midnight. He couldn't believe Steven had actually gone through with it. He glanced continually at the clock above the fireplace. When he knew Steven was finally on his way, via St. Andrew's club, Thomas had slipped out of Collars & Cuffs after leaving a brief note for Leo. Despite his present anxiety, the thought of his business partner caused Thomas to smile. When he'd last seen Leo, he'd had his arms around Alex, the two men lost in their own world as they kissed lovingly. No *way* was Thomas about to interrupt.

22

He rubbed the back of his neck and tried to ignore the churning in his belly. Catching sight of himself in the gold-framed mirror above the fire, he grimaced.

"You're getting too old for this shit." He shook his head. What was he thinking? He was fifty-five, nearly fifty-six, far too old to be taking on the responsibility of a new submissive. Training subs was a game for a younger man, he reasoned. Then he caught himself. He *wasn't* training Peter, for God's sake. He was simply giving the boy breathing space, helping him along the road to recovery. That much, he could do. What Peter did after that would be entirely up to him.

Thomas examined his reflection. His hair was totally gray, but, thank God, it was still full and thick. The club lawyer, Peter Willoughby, was bald, and it somehow seemed right for him. Thomas shuddered. The thought of going bald filled him with horror. Because once *that* happened, it really would feel as though he was getting old. He leaned closer, peering at the mirror.

"You don't look too bad for your age, Williams." Thomas shook himself. Such introspection and vanity wasn't like him, but he put it down to the present situation, which had him rattled. The uncertainty of it all was what put him out of step. He hadn't a clue what to expect when Steven eventually walked through his front door. Steven had described Peter's condition, and Thomas thought the first order would be to let the boy sleep. From the sound of it, Peter was in dire need of some care and attention.

Footsteps outside—his visitors had arrived. Thomas hurried to the front door. Steven and his sub had Peter between them, supporting his arms on their shoulders. Thomas gave a quick glance along the quiet, deserted street. Not a soul to be seen. He held the door wide to allow them entry and then directed them into the warm lounge. Steven eased Peter down onto the sofa and then straightened. Thomas inspected the boy. Peter was tall, maybe five nine, but he was painfully thin. His clothing gave no protection against the cold winter's night, and he shivered constantly. Longish, straggly brown hair framed a pale face. Peter's eyes were closed. What was all too evident, however, was the bruising. Thomas scowled and let out what could only be described as a low growl. *No one* deserved to be treated in this way. There was no excuse.

Peter's eyes opened wide at the sound, and Thomas cursed himself when he saw the fear in those green eyes, which were almost the same shade of green as his own. They were a lovely shape, framed with dark lashes. They'd be even more beautiful without the shadows that surrounded them. Peter stared up at him with his lips pressed tightly together, as if he didn't trust himself to speak.

"You're safe here, Peter." Thomas spoke quietly, making his voice as soothing as possible. "My name is Thomas Williams. I'm going to be taking care of you for a while." He waited.

Peter shook his head. "I-I can't stay here. He'll come looking for me. And when he finds me...." Peter shuddered and closed his eyes. "He says I can't leave him—ever." He sagged back even further into the sofa.

For a moment, Thomas considered this statement. Why would Curtis tell the boy he couldn't leave? Something here required investigation, but this was not the time. He turned to Steven. David stood slightly behind him, watching Peter. Thomas noted that David had said nothing. Steven was obviously training him well.

"Okay, you've done enough for one night." Thomas gave Steven a wry smile. "Thank you for delivering Peter, but now you two need to get out of here. Do you still have some partying to do?"

Steven said, "No, as far as I'm concerned, the party's over. But we have some celebrating of our own to do—don't we, David?" He waggled his eyebrows, and David let out a smothered giggle.

Ah, *that* kind of celebrating. Thomas couldn't help smiling. "Off you go, then," he said, ushering them toward the door. Steven stopped for a moment and grabbed him in a fierce hug. Thomas smiled. He was very fond of Steven. The man was an excellent Dom, but an even better friend. "I'll be in touch," he said quietly.

Steven nodded. "You can also expect two applications crossing your desk soon. I'm changing clubs. And I might be bringing another Dom with me."

Thomas nodded. With everything he'd heard in recent months about St. Andrew's, it didn't surprise him to hear Steven might want out of there.

"I look forward to receiving them. But just so you know... you will receive the same rigorous grilling *everyone* gets who wants entry to my club."

Steven laughed. "I wouldn't have it any other way." He clasped Thomas's hand firmly. "Thank you, Thomas. Really." Thomas merely nodded. Steven glanced at David. "Come on, boy, let's go home and get you in my bed."

David's slight gasp of embarrassment and flushed cheeks were a pleasure to encounter. Thomas watched them as they got into the car and drove off. He closed the door and bolted it securely before returning to the lounge to check on Peter. His heart gave a slight stutter when he caught sight of him. Peter was asleep, clearly exhausted from the evening's activity. Thomas gazed over his inert form. Okay, time to see what other horrors awaited below the clothing. Time to bathe his houseguest.

He slipped his arms under the sleeping boy and lifted him, cradling him easily. Christ, there was nothing to him. He pulled Peter against his wide chest, feeling him stir in his sleep. A low, troubled moan escaped the boy's parted lips, and Thomas made soothing noises. Peter's eyes opened, and for a second he regarded Thomas fearfully.

"Hold on, lad." Thomas kept his voice low. Peter reached up and around Thomas's neck, pushing his face into the soft fabric of Thomas's thick shirt. "That's it. Good lad." Carefully, he carried Peter into the hallway and up the wide staircase. The boy was so light, he was no great burden to carry. Thomas reached the upper landing, heading straight for the bathroom. Once there, he placed Peter into a wicker chair and stepped back. Peter slumped with his chin lowered to his chest, bereft of all energy, letting his hands hang limply over the arms of the chair.

Thomas had thought to put the boy in the shower, but seeing him in this state changed his mind. He turned on the faucets, filling the large Victorian-style tub rapidly. Steam soon filled the air. A thought occurred to him, and he reached into the cupboard below the washbasin for a bottle containing lavender bath oil. He sometimes took a bath to wind down after a hard night at the club, and the lavender soothed him, often lulling him into sleep in the tub. He poured a capful into the warm water and then brought his attention back to the fatigued boy.

"Okay, lad, let's get these clothes off of you." Peter's eyes flew open, and it was all too easy to read the panic there. The boy shuddered. Thomas held out his hands, palms up. "Easy, lad. I'm simply going to bathe you. You're in no state to be left alone right now. And to be honest, you are not the first person I've bathed—not even close."

Peter's face turned ashen and he hugged himself. His gaze darted to the door behind Thomas before returning to stare at Thomas's outstretched hands.

He gripped the arms of the wicker chair so tightly his knuckles went white. He began to shake uncontrollably.

Thomas gazed at Peter without blinking. "Peter. You have to trust me, all right?"

Peter fixed him with a panicked stare for a few moments longer. His chin trembled. Then, to Thomas's relief, he nodded once. Thomas gave him a half smile.

"Good lad." He tugged at the hem of Peter's T-shirt and pulled it up and off, trying not to stare at the dark smudges that marred Peter's chest. A thin leather collar lay around his neck. Thomas went to unfasten it, and Peter reached up instinctively to prevent him. Thomas waited, saying nothing, and Peter lowered his hands. Thomas removed the collar and dropped it with the T-shirt onto the floor. After unfastening the cord around the boy's waist, he slipped the sweatpants past Peter's slim hips, down to his ankles, and removed them completely. Now nude, Peter immediately covered his genitals. Thomas said nothing but held out a hand to the boy. After a moment's pause, Peter slipped his hand into Thomas's and grasped it tightly. Thomas helped him to stand, then supported the lad as he climbed carefully into the tub. It was then Thomas caught sight of Peter's back, and he had to bite his lip in an effort not to cry out.

What was before him was a crisscrossed map of scars, some old, some clearly new. They spread out across his shoulder blades, reaching down as far as the swell of his arse. It was obvious no one had tended to the boy; some of the newer scars seemed infected. Thomas would need to treat these injuries before he let the boy sleep. He could only guess at how Peter had suffered at the hands of his former master.

Peter sat in the tub, staring vacantly. He brought up his knees and wrapped his arms around them, hugging them. Thomas knew a defeated submissive when he saw one. This lad had no fight left in him. He picked up a soft washcloth and the bottle of bodywash. Peter no longer looked at him. Thomas shook his head. If he ever got his hands on Curtis Rogers….

"I'm going to wash you now, Peter." He spoke quietly, careful to let Peter know what was going to happen so the boy didn't jump out of his skin. He poured a generous amount of bodywash onto the now-damp washcloth, then gently wiped the lad, moving the soft lather over his body. Peter closed his eyes. His only reaction was to shiver when Thomas reached his back. Thomas winced. "I'll see to your back once we're done here." He gently disengaged one of Peter's hands from around his knees and handed him the washcloth. "If it makes you feel better, lad, *you* can wash your cock, balls, and arse." Peter glanced up at him warily, and Thomas nodded. Drawing in a deep breath, Peter knelt up in the warm water and proceeded to clean himself. Thomas looked away. He wasn't in the least bit embarrassed, but he figured it would put Peter at ease to know Thomas wasn't watching him.

"Done, Sir." The two words took Thomas by surprise. He turned back to the boy. Peter held out the damp cloth with his eyes lowered, and Thomas took it and placed it behind him in the washbasin.

"Okay, lie back and get your hair wet so I can shampoo it." Peter obeyed in silence, lowering himself carefully into the water, wincing as his back came into contact with the surface. "Easy, lad. This won't take long." Peter raised himself up on his elbows, and Thomas opened the shampoo, poured himself a handful, and then gently lathered it into Peter's hair. Peter closed his eyes again, and Thomas tried to make the movement as soothing as possible. He slipped an arm under Peter's shoulders and lowered him back down, then swirled the water over his hair to remove all traces of shampoo.

"Up you get, lad." He helped Peter to stand and reached for a thick bath towel from the radiator. After wrapping it around the lad, he pulled the tub's drain plug and then held out both hands to help Peter step gingerly from the tub. "Can you sit on the edge of the tub, Peter? I want to look at your back."

In silence, the boy wrapped the towel around his hips and then perched on the edge, half turning so Thomas could clearly see the extent of the damage. From the bathroom cabinet, Thomas removed a tube of antiseptic cream and some cotton wool. Carefully, so carefully, he patted Peter's back dry with another warm towel and then wiped the cream into each separate wound, taking his time. Peter didn't make a sound, sitting there with his back straight, staring off into space. Now and again he stiffened, and Thomas eased off and waited until the boy relaxed once more. He handed the boy a smaller towel and indicated his hair. Peter rubbed at his head until the hair was virtually bone dry while Thomas worked at his task. Once finished, Thomas put the cream to one side, stood, and grabbed a dark-blue toweling robe from the back of the bathroom door. He held it open, and Peter slipped his arms into the sleeves, then wrapped it around himself and tied it tightly. He grabbed his clothes from the floor.

"Follow me, lad." Thomas led him into the spare bedroom, next door to his own. He'd already made up the bed after Steven had first called. Thomas pulled back the cover and duvet. "In you get." Peter placed his clothing on the chair and climbed into the bed, and Thomas pulled the duvet to cover him. Peter curled up on his side immediately, facing away. Thomas regarded him for a moment. He couldn't begin to imagine what thoughts were passing through Peter's head right now. He only knew there was a long way to go before Peter's fears gave way to trust. He listened as Peter's breathing changed and the boy slipped quickly into a deep sleep.

Thomas left the bedside lamp lit and walked as silently as possible from the room, pulling the door to but not closing it completely. He padded quietly downstairs and went into the lounge and closed the door behind him. He glanced at the clock: almost one in the morning. Leo would still be at the club. After poking the logs on the fire, he settled into his large, squashy armchair and reached for his phone. His call went to voice mail.

"Leo, I know it's late, and the party's probably still going strong there, but would you and Alex come round here in the morning? There's something I need to tell you. It's nothing to worry about, but it is important. Make it after nine, okay? I'm tired out and heading off to bed. I'll have breakfast ready for you both. How's that? Thanks, Leo. See you in the morning."

He hung up the phone and then cast a longing glance at the brandy decanter. Right now a small glass of brandy sounded like a great idea, but not with Peter upstairs. Thomas wanted to keep his wits about him tonight. He didn't have a clue how Peter would pass the night, but he wanted to be alert for any eventuality. He had a feeling he might be having quite a few alcohol-free days in the not-too-distant future.

Two

Misunderstandings and Decisions

"COME on in, you two." Thomas stood aside to let Leo and Alex into the warm hallway and hurriedly closed the door behind them. In spite of the hours since he'd last seen them, the happy expressions they'd worn at the party were still in evidence. Suspiciously so. "Er... anything you want to tell me?" He arched his brows and fixed Leo with a searching gaze. Leo gave a casual shrug, but Thomas caught the brief flick of his eyes toward Alex, who flushed bright red. Both men looked tired but contented, and Thomas decided to leave the matter there. Doubtless Leo would let him know at some point.

"All right, Leo, go into the lounge and enjoy the fire. You'll soon warm up." He glanced at Alex. "And you, pup, can help me in the kitchen with the coffee. Breakfast won't be long." Alex let out a giggle. Yeah, something was *definitely* up. He crooked a finger and beckoned Alex to follow him. Alex gave Leo a last longing, backward glance. Thomas chuckled. "He's not going anywhere." Alex laughed at that. Thomas led him into the large kitchen and directed him to the coffee machine. Maybe he could get Alex to divulge something. Then again....

LEO HART stretched out his long legs toward the welcome heat of the fire. Living in a Victorian house had its advantages. He'd love to have an old-fashioned fireplace like this in the apartment, but it simply wouldn't fit in with his decor. He closed his eyes, enjoying the warmth, the sound of the crackling logs, the slow tick of Thomas's grandfather clock. Everything combined to create a sense of peace that pervaded the room. He loved spending time in Thomas's house. He could hear Alex's laughter in the kitchen. His lover was in such a good mood. A slow smile crossed Leo's face. They'd gone home from the party and spent a good hour working out a contract. Alex wanted to formalize their D/s relationship, and Leo was delighted to oblige. Of course, once the details were sorted, Alex had wanted to celebrate. However, their "celebrations" carried on into the early hours, neither man wanting to call a halt to their coupling. All in all, it was a wonderful way to begin a new year. Leo's smile increased as he thought back on their negotiations. The new year promised to be very interesting indeed.

A slight noise caught his attention, and he opened his eyes to look toward the doorway. A pale, slender young man stood there, bundled up in a blue robe, rubbing his eyes sleepily. Leo stared in astonishment. Who the hell was this? The young man spotted him, and Leo watched him stiffen. He clearly hadn't expected to find Leo there. Leo stood, and the young man's eyes widened. Hell, Leo sometimes forgot that, at six three, he could be a daunting figure. He hastened to put Thomas's guest at his ease.

"Good morning. I'm Leo Hart, Thomas's partner. Thomas invited me round." A look crossed the boy's face. Leo could swear the boy looked disappointed—and saddened. He sighed dejectedly and his shoulders slumped. With shuffling footsteps, he crossed the room and slowly lowered himself to his knees before Leo. He reached with trembling hands to grasp the buckle of Leo's belt and began to open it. *What the fuck?*

"SO ARE you going to tell me why you're looking so happy this morning?" Thomas teased as he peered into the oven, where cooked bacon and sausages were warming. Alex let out another delighted giggle. Thomas had to smile. Alex had changed so much since their first meeting back in June. Mind you, so had Leo. The two men were obviously good for each other. He hadn't seen Leo this happy in a long while. In fact, in the two and a half years since the death of Leo's former lover and submissive, Gabe, Thomas had often thought never to see his business partner happy again. He glanced toward Alex, who was pouring out the coffee into large mugs and smiling to himself. "Not going to tell me, huh?" He chuckled.

Trusting Thomas

Alex met his eyes for the briefest moment before lowering them hastily, smirking. Thomas shook his head. The lad did *not* like making eye contact, which was probably just as well, seeing as he was now Leo's submissive. Thomas was glad things seemed to be settling down between the pair, even if he'd had to step in—twice—to sort out Leo's messes.

"Thomas? Could you get in here, please?" Leo's call reached him from the lounge. It held a note of agitation that made both Thomas and Alex look up in surprise. Thomas put down the oven cloth he held and walked into the lounge, with Alex close behind him. Thomas came to a dead stop. Peter was on his knees before Leo, who held him firmly around the wrists. Leo's belt was unfastened. Peter simply knelt there with his head bowed, but Thomas could see the boy was shaking.

"I see you've met my houseguest, Peter," Thomas said dryly.

Leo's face was a picture of embarrassment. "Your 'houseguest' was apparently all set to give me a blow job," he muttered. Thomas quirked his eyebrows. The lad hid his face against Leo's belly. As Leo gazed down at him, his expression changed. He let go of Peter's wrists and gently helped him to his feet.

Thomas addressed the lad. "Peter, why would you do this?"

Peter blinked. "Isn't that why you brought your friend round here? So I could service him?" His voice quavered.

Thomas was horrified. For a moment he was too shocked to speak. What had this poor boy been subjected to?

"No, Peter. That's not what's going to happen. I would never ask that of you. Ever." He spoke quietly but forcefully. He wanted there to be no misunderstanding. "Why would you think I expected you to do that?"

Peter lowered his chin. "That's how I was taught, Sir," he murmured. Thomas gaped in frank bewilderment. His previous thought returned to prod him. What the fuck had Curtis Rogers done to this boy? Thomas needed some thinking space—and he needed to talk to Leo.

"Peter, I'd like you to go back to bed for a little while. I'll fetch you downstairs for some breakfast once my guests have left. Okay?" Peter answered with a small nod, without making eye contact.

Thomas turned to Alex, who was watching the scene openmouthed. "Alex, would you please take Peter upstairs to his room? He'll show you where it is." Alex nodded, his gaze fixed on Peter. A thought occurred to

Thomas. "And, Alex? You might want to have a chat with him before you come back down. See if he can tell you what just happened here." Alex gave another nod of assent and walked up to the lad and took his arm.

"Come on, Peter," he said pleasantly. "Let's get you back to bed, shall we?"

Thomas gave him a look of approval. Smart boy. Peter was plainly agitated, and perhaps Alex might be able to work out what was going on in his head. Peter looked down at the hand resting on his arm and then at Alex's kind expression. His chin dipped twice abruptly, and he allowed himself to be led from the room.

Leo exhaled loudly. "Want to tell me what's going on now?"

Thomas sighed. "You're going to need some coffee first." He walked back into the kitchen, picked up two mugs, and brought them into the lounge. Leo was still standing in front of the fireplace, staring down in disbelief at the spot where Peter had knelt. Thomas handed him a mug and then sat in one of the two armchairs that bracketed the fire. Leo eyed the mug. "Sit down," Thomas began patiently, "and I'll tell you what I know."

For the next ten minutes, Thomas relayed everything, from Steven's initial phone call to the dramatic way in which Peter had been taken from his home. Leo whistled.

"Your friend Steven is either very brave or very reckless. What if he'd got caught?"

Thomas looked down at his half-empty mug. "I don't think that occurred to him, to be honest. Or if it did, he pushed it aside. He was hell-bent on rescuing Peter." Thomas glanced up at the ceiling. "And now that I get a glimpse of what the lad's been through, I have to say I'm glad Steven stepped in."

"So what are you going to do with him?"

Thomas gave a shrug. "In the first instance, I'm going to take care of his physical needs. The boy needs feeding up, for a start. And his back needs some attention. Secondly, I'm going to give him some breathing space until he decides what he wants to do next."

Leo shook his head. "I'm not sure you know what you're letting yourself in for with this lad. From the look of things, he's going to be needy. Do you have the time to deal with that?"

Thomas gave a faint chuckle. "That's why I called you round here. If I'm going to do this, I'll need to free up some time. You might have more hours than usual at the club. Would that be a problem? And you'd have to take more stints as Dungeon Master, or else choose another reliable Dom to take my place. Personally, I'd recommend Jonathon. I think he's more than up to the task."

Leo gazed thoughtfully into the flames. "You really mean to do this, don't you?"

Thomas nodded slowly.

"Then of course you should do it. I owe you, anyway." Thomas cocked his head, and Leo gave him an appreciative look. "You were there for me when Gabe died. You picked up the slack all those times I couldn't even drag myself from my bed. You stepped in every time I rang up and said I couldn't face coming to the club. What kind of partner—or friend—would I be if I wasn't there when you needed me?"

Thomas let out a sigh of relief and got up from his chair, his arms open. Leo observed him for a moment and then sighed, lifted his long frame from his chair, and walked into Thomas's arms to be hugged firmly. His breath tickled Thomas's ear. "You've been hugging me a lot lately," he murmured.

"Don't spoil the moment," Thomas whispered back, chuckling. He didn't relinquish his hold on the taller man. Leo was like a son to him. In the fifteen years since they first met when a green twenty-two-year-old approached him in a BDSM club and demanded to be trained as a Dom, Leo had worked his way into Thomas's heart. Leo's parents were dead by that point, and Thomas took it upon himself to provide him with a father figure. He considered himself lucky to have a business partner who was also one of his closest friends.

ALEX pulled the duvet over Peter, then dragged a chair closer to the bed, sat on it, and put his feet up on the bed. Peter wouldn't look at him.

"Peter, you can talk to me." Silence. "Peter? It's okay. Do you want to talk about what happened?"

Peter shook his head. "You wouldn't understand." He closed his eyes, and Alex was convinced he was fighting to hold back tears.

Alex chuckled. "Maybe I'd understand better than you think. That tall hunk you were about to blow is my boyfriend—but he's also my Dom." *Now* he had Peter's attention.

"Your… your Dom?" Alex nodded. "You're a submissive?"

Alex grinned. "Yep. We started dating before I found out Leo was a Dom—which is a whole different story, by the way—and then I decided I wanted to know more about being a sub. Do you have a Dom?"

His words seemed to flick a switch in Peter. He leapt, naked, from the bed and began searching for his clothes in a panic. He slipped his hand briefly under the mattress and then started looking for his clothes once more. Alex watched, perplexed, his eyes widening as he caught sight of the bruises on Peter's body and the scars across his back. *What the fuck happened to him?* He didn't have time to think further on it, as when Peter's search proved fruitless, he went into full panic mode.

"I have to get out of here. I have to go back." He was shaking, his eyes wild. And he was breathing so rapidly, he had to be hyperventilating.

"Whoa there," Alex said soothingly. "You need to calm down, all right?" He didn't touch Peter, afraid of how he would react. He could only watch helplessly as Peter finally collapsed onto the bed and curled up into a tight ball. Sobs racked his thin body, sobs that tore at Alex's insides. Alex grabbed the edges of the duvet and pulled it over Peter and then sat beside him on the bed, rubbing his back with gentle strokes through the duvet. It must have been about ten minutes or so before he began to see an improvement. He listened as Peter's sobs decreased little by little, until at last he lay silent, his breathing more even. Alex didn't let up with his gentle back rub, however, as it seemed to be having a hypnotic effect. Alex was content to sit there, feeling Peter grow steadily calmer, until at last he opened his eyes and stared at Alex.

"Do you enjoy being a submissive?"

Alex stopped midstroke. He hadn't expected so forthright a question.

"Yes," he replied simply. A faint smile twisted his lips. "Actually, I love it. I'm only just discovering what it means to be a sub, but Leo is a great teacher." Peter's eyes were filled with such an expression of curiosity, Alex felt compelled to ask, "Downstairs, before…. Why would you think Thomas would want you to blow Leo?"

Peter shrugged, glancing away. "That's what I was trained to do. That's what *submissives* do."

"Peter, can I ask… what do you think a submissive is?"

Peter sighed. "A submissive is there to be available at all times, ready for whatever the master desires." It sounded as if he was reciting a well-worn litany. He spoke in a dull, lifeless monotone. "If the master wants to inflict pain, the sub accepts it, without complaint, to whatever level the master sees fit. A submissive can be punished at any time, without explanation, if the master feels punishment is required. A submissive should keep his body ready to accept penetration whenever the master desires it and be prepared to service the needs of anyone the master invites to use the submissive's body."

Alex had heard enough. He laid his hand on Peter's arm. "Was all this in your contract?"

Peter stared at him, clearly puzzled. "Contract?"

Alex felt the hairs on his arms rise. "Didn't your master sit down with you and go through a contract? You know, discuss what activities you were prepared to try and those you weren't? Go through his expectations of you and, more importantly, what you should expect from him?"

Peter shook his head.

"What were your safewords?" That same perplexed expression was etched across Peter's face. Alex's anger started to boil. No safewords. No contract. "So let me get this straight. Basically, this guy didn't give you a contract, gave you no choice as to what happened to you, didn't give you a way to stop things if it got too much, used you as a punching bag and fucked you whenever he felt like it, as well as inviting round his friends to fuck you too?"

Peter caught his breath, his eyes suddenly overly bright. He gazed miserably at Alex, and Alex took a deep breath, reining in his fury.

"Listen to me, Peter," he began in a low, firm voice, "that man is not your master. A master doesn't treat subs like that. What you've just described to me is so far removed from my experience, it's…." How to show Peter what he meant? Slowly, hesitantly at first, Alex told Peter of his relationship with Leo. He told him about the club and what he'd seen there. He spoke of his best friend, Pietro, who had been collared the previous night by Pietro's Dom, Miles. He told Peter all he'd learned so far about being a submissive.

Peter's eyes never left his throughout the whole long monologue. He sat up, hugging his knees, clearly engrossed. When at last Alex finished speaking, Peter stared at him in silence for a moment. Alex could almost hear the cogs turning in his brain.

"I want that," Peter whispered. "That's what I've always wanted. I-I just thought that wasn't the way things happened. Mas... *Curtis* never gave me an option." Alex beamed with pride. It was a good first step if Peter stopped referring to Curtis as his master. "But... how do I go about it?"

"Leave that to me," Alex advised, pulling back the duvet to let Peter slide under it and rest his head on the bed's firm pillows. All of a sudden Peter looked so very tired. Alex covered him and then sat beside him on the bed. "You've got some thinking to do about where you go from here." Peter nodded. "So lie here quietly for a while. Thomas will come and get you when it's time to get up." He smiled gently at the pale young man, who was undoubtedly older than himself. "I get the feeling you and I will meet again. Then we can talk some more, if you'd like."

"I'd like that." Peter gave a half smile that transformed his face. Alex grinned and grasped Peter's hand tightly before exiting the room, leaving him staring up at the ceiling, obviously deep in thought.

THOMAS stood to collect Leo's empty mug as Alex appeared at the lounge door. Biting at his lower lip, he flicked his gaze from one man to the other, clearly unsure how to voice whatever was in his head. In a flash, Thomas realized what lay at the heart of Alex's internal conflict.

"Alex, do you want to speak your mind?" Alex heaved a sigh of relief, giving him a grateful look. He nodded eagerly.

Leo pulled a cushion from behind him and dropped it at his feet. "Come sit here, boy."

Alex hurried forward and dropped to the floor at Leo's feet, leaning back against his legs and closing his eyes as Leo ran gentle fingers through his hair. Thomas watched the two men reconnect. It was as though calm flowed through those fingers. Thomas could almost see Alex's anxiety retreat. "Okay, talk to us."

Alex's gaze settled on Thomas, although, typically of Alex, he couldn't bring himself to look Thomas in the eye. "Peter is a mess," he said frankly.

He related his conversation with the young man. Thomas was appalled as he listened to Peter's view of being a submissive. Steven's suspicions proved correct: Curtis Rogers was certainly no trained Dom. Peter rose in his estimation, however, when Thomas learned that, despite all he'd been through, the lad still wanted to know more about being a submissive.

With a start, Thomas realized his attention had wandered. "I'm sorry," he apologized. "Did I miss something?"

Leo chuckled. "I think you need more sleep, old man." Thomas merely gave him a look to convey his opinion of Leo's choice of phrase. Leo stared back unrepentantly. "But you might need to rethink your plans in light of this. First of all, I feel Peter would benefit from professional help."

Thomas gazed at him with interest. "Do you have someone in mind?"

Leo nodded. "Laura Herne. She's an excellent psychologist and perfect for our needs." Thomas murmured in agreement. Alex raised his head to glance inquiringly at Leo. "She knows all about the D/s lifestyle," Leo explained.

Thomas chuckled. "She should—she's a sub." Alex's eyes widened, and Thomas laughed. "Yes, pup, doctors can be submissives too. I've come across Laura a few times. She has a nice way about her. Yes, good choice, Leo." Leo bowed his head once in acknowledgment. "You said 'first of all.' What else did you have in mind?"

Leo hesitated.

"Come on, lad, not like you to be reticent. Out with it."

Leo took a deep breath. "I think you should train him."

Thomas caught his breath. The first thing to cross his mind was his earlier thought. *I'm too old to be training submissives.* But as soon as the thought resurfaced, he berated himself. *That was before you met him.* Peter clearly needed help. And what was more important, he *wanted* that help.

Leo obviously sensed his initial doubts and plunged ahead.

"Thomas, you've trained both Doms and subs. Show Peter how a Dom should be, how *you* train a Dom to be. Let him see what he should expect when he finally finds a master of his own. And then train him how to be a submissive. Go through the basic training. But I'd only do that once he's healed—physically, at least—and ready for more." Leo paused, watching Thomas.

Thomas stared into the flames, considering Leo's words. Finally he let out his breath in a steady exhale.

"You're right, of course. The boy needs training."

"I think it's a great idea." Alex's voice was low but brimmed with approval. "You're just what he needs, Thomas." Abruptly, he paled. "I'm sorry. I didn't mean to be disrespectful."

Thomas spoke quickly. "Alex, it's fine. I said you could speak your mind. Right now I'm Thomas Williams, your boyfriend's business partner. Okay?" He leveled a firm look in Alex's direction. Alex didn't seem convinced, but he nodded briefly. Thomas winked at Leo before continuing. "Of course, you speak to me like that in the club and you'll be over my knee in seconds, getting your arse spanked."

Alex gulped nervously. Both Doms laughed at his reaction.

Both Leo and Alex's stomachs chose that moment to grumble loudly. Thomas gave his guests an apologetic look.

"Right, breakfast time. The sooner I get you two fed, the sooner Peter and I can have our first conversation." As he stood and led the two men into the warm kitchen, he reflected momentarily that life may have just gotten a whole lot more complicated than he'd planned.

Three

Let's Begin....

PETER cried out as the whip connected with his back.

"Please, Master, no more!" Even as he uttered the words, he knew he'd made a mistake, one for which his master would punish him harshly. His instruction hammered through Peter's brain. *Never beg me to stop.* The whip descended with more severity, but he couldn't hold back his cries of agony. Not that his master minded *those*. Indeed, the more Peter screamed in pain, the more his master seemed to like it. Peter clawed at the sheet beneath him, desperate to get away from the anguish inflicted on his back. His master's face contorted in an expression of evil glee as Peter's screams grew ever louder and more desperate. As the whip sliced through the air and lashed his body, Peter's tears fell readily. *God, please, no more*, he prayed silently, though there was no hope in him of a reprieve. *Why should this time be any different from the last?*

With an agonized howl, Peter sat bolt upright in his bed, awakened with a jolt from his nightmare. Tears fell freely down his cheeks. Harsh sobs rent the air as he struggled to catch his breath. A hand touched his arm and instantly Peter went still, fearing the worst. He stiffened and squeezed his eyes shut, awaiting his master's wrath.

"Easy now, you're safe, you're safe."

The words were soothing and low, the voice kindly. Peter cautiously opened one eye and found the gray-haired man who'd bathed him leaning low over him, regarding him sympathetically. That hand barely moved on him, its contact fleeting but enough for Peter to know there was no malice in the man. Not at this moment, anyway. In a rush, he remembered his shameful actions downstairs. Surely he would be punished now.

"Peter, you're awake. It was only a dream."

Peter struggled to remember the man's name. Thomas something. With both eyes open now, he met Thomas's concerned expression.

"That's it, lad." Thomas's voice was full of encouragement. Peter took several gulps of air in an effort to compose himself. Thomas held out a cotton handkerchief, and Peter took it gratefully, wiping away his cooling tears from his eyes and cheeks. Thomas withdrew his hand.

Thomas sat on the edge of the bed, clasping his hands loosely, observing him in silence. Peter was used to silence—it was usually the prelude to his master venting his anger. But this was different. There was a calm about this man that seemed to pervade the room. Composed at last, Peter straightened and expelled the remnants of the nightmare with a final exhalation.

"Good boy." Thomas reached behind him, grabbed Peter's sweatpants and T-shirt, and handed them to him. Peter realized with a shock they had been cleaned and dried. They were warm, with a smell about them that reminded him of laundry days as a child. The scent comforted him.

"Put those on and come downstairs." Thomas got to his feet and stood beside the bed, gazing down at Peter with obvious concern. "I have breakfast ready for you, and then we can talk." He glanced briefly at the clock beside the bed. "Maybe brunch would be a more accurate description."

With a chuckle, the older man left. Peter glanced around his room, seeing it clearly for the first time. The bed was a good size, with a warm brushed-cotton duvet and several thick pillows. An armchair stood beside the bed, where that boy—Alex?—sat earlier. In the corner of the room was an old-fashioned oak wardrobe and matching chest of drawers, and between them stood a full-length, freestanding mirror. An old-fashioned writing desk in dark, polished wood stood against another wall, and in front of it an office swivel chair that somehow stood out as incongruous in this room. The curtains at the window were heavy and lined, a rich cream color that complemented the magnolia walls with their heavily sculpted wallpaper.

Peter liked the room. There was a pleasant feel to it, and the same sense of calm that had hung around Thomas pervaded the room. It was then that he noticed for the first time some new items at the foot of the bed. Thick woolen socks lay there, along with a folded sweater that seemed much too large for Peter, but he was glad to see it all the same. His thin T-shirt afforded little protection from the cold. Hurriedly, Peter got dressed, putting on the socks first. His shoes had been left behind, along with all his other meager belongings. As he slipped on the T-shirt, he felt the skin pull slightly on his back. Such discomfort had become a part of life, something to be endured in silence—he'd learned quickly that Curtis didn't like it when he whined. He remembered Thomas treating his back the previous night. Right now something else was causing him discomfort: he desperately needed to pee. As he emerged from his room, he spotted, with relief, the bathroom to his right. He ducked in and used it. Mission accomplished. Now to find out what on earth he was doing here.

The house was quiet as he slipped downstairs, caressing the varnished oak balustrade as he descended the polished wooden stairs. Everything indicated this was an old house, possibly Victorian. The steady, slow tick of a grandfather clock in the wide, airy hallway was yet another reminder of his childhood. His gran had possessed such a clock. He loved to listen to it, the rhythmic sounds reminiscent of summer days spent with his gran.

"In here, Peter."

He followed Thomas's voice and entered a large kitchen toward the back of the house. Wooden cabinets glowed warmly in the sunlight, which streamed through a wide window. Beyond, Peter could see a garden with trees and shrubs, their branches stark and bare. In the middle of the room stood a wide wooden table with six chairs around it. Pale-yellow walls and lemon-colored blinds created a sunny, inviting room.

Thomas had set the table for one and was in the process of dishing out a cooked breakfast. Peter's stomach grumbled loudly, and his mouth watered at the smell of bacon, sausage, scrambled eggs, and baked beans. Slices of toast already stood in a rack on the table, along with a glass of orange juice. Wow. Peter couldn't remember the last time someone had made him breakfast.

"Don't let it go cold, lad. Sit yourself down and tuck in. When did you last eat, anyway?"

Peter considered this. He'd had a light meal the previous night before Ma— before *Curtis* and Christian had left for the club's New Year's Eve party. And with the mood Curtis had been in, he'd been lucky to have that. Thank goodness Christian had snuck him a bit more food. But then he remembered Curtis's parting *gift*. He'd fucked him so forcefully that Peter had screamed in pain. Shudders rippled through him as the memory seized him. He pushed away from the table, wanting nothing more than to draw up his legs and hug his knees, to fold in on himself.

Thomas's manner changed. He reached across and patted Peter sympathetically on the arm. "Don't think about that right now. Just eat."

Peter was dizzy, and he was aware of his racing heartbeat. *For God's sake, calm down. What is there to fear in this sunny kitchen?* He knew his reaction was unreasonable. Peter inhaled deeply as he tried to reconnect with the earlier feelings of calm he'd experienced in Thomas's presence. *That's it, breathe. Breathe.* After several long seconds, he felt calm flow through him once more. His gaze fell upon the full plate before him. He sat down and started to attack his breakfast hungrily. Thomas poured himself a cup of coffee and stood with his back to the window, watching as Peter's breakfast disappeared.

"I don't usually eat like this at breakfast time," Thomas admitted. "But it's New Year's Day, and I had friends over. Normally, breakfast is muesli and toast, but I think it's nice to do this once in a while." He chuckled as the last of the toast vanished. "I think you needed that, lad."

Peter gave a half smile as he drank the last of his juice. Considering the strangeness of his present situation, he couldn't believe how at ease he was feeling, compared with his panic only a short time ago. He struggled to put his finger on the cause. It could only be Thomas. There was something about him that seemed to demand calm. The atmosphere in the quiet house was nothing like home. And just like that, the warm feeling in his belly disappeared, to be replaced with a churning sensation. His chest tightened. Curtis wouldn't let this go. Curtis would find him, and when he did….

Thomas pulled out the chair facing him and sat down, placing his half-empty cup on the table. He stretched out his hands, palms down, and stroked the polished surface, seemingly deep in thought. Several moments lapsed before he spoke.

"Is there anything you'd like to ask before we start?"

Start? Start what? Peter's mind raced. Yeah, there was one basic, fundamental question that had been plaguing him ever since two strangers had come into his home and basically kidnapped him.

"What am I doing here?" His words came out more abruptly than he'd anticipated. In fact, he couldn't believe he'd had the nerve to say them.

Thomas nodded. "Good question." He cleared his throat. "Steven Drummond, the Dom who brought you here, is a very good friend of mine. He spotted you at his club and had reason to believe you were being abused by your master. Was he correct?"

Peter's throat seized. He wanted to say yes, to pour out all he'd been through at the hands of Curtis Rogers, but fear coursed through him. If it ever got back to Curtis…. However nice Thomas seemed, he was a stranger. And clearly a Dom. Peter was not prepared to trust anyone right now, especially another Dom.

"No," he croaked.

Thomas didn't react at first. He merely regarded Peter with an expression that was almost sympathetic, as if he actually understood *why* Peter answered the way he did.

"Okay," Thomas began, his voice low and pleasant. "I'm sure you have your reasons for denying the abuse. But I need to know the truth, Peter, if I am going to be able to help you. Because if it's not true, then I can help get you back to your master." Those green eyes locked on him, and Peter felt powerless to break away. "So I am going to ask you a few questions. You don't have to answer them. But when I have finished, if—in your heart—you can say yes to *any* of them, then I need to know. Do you understand?"

Peter nodded numbly and then waited, unsure of what would follow. Listening wouldn't cost him anything.

Thomas folded his hands. "Did your master ever scare you and make you feel fearful?" His voice was quiet but firm.

Peter gulped. Oh hell.

"Did you think you could never do anything right or please your master?"

Peter's chest tightened, and his breathing became more erratic.

"Did your master ever hit, push, or choke you, pull your hair, or slap you while he was angry? And were these acts nonconsensual?"

Peter began to feel dizzy. Bile rose in his throat.

"Did your master yell at you or tell you that you were worthless or no good? And I am not talking about what took place during a scene here."

Despite his racing heart, Peter latched onto one word. *Scene.* What was a scene? Thomas's uncanny knack of asking just the right questions was unnerving him tremendously. How could he know exactly what to ask?

43

Thomas's voice grew quieter. "Did you believe you had to tiptoe around your master to prevent an outburst of anger?"

Oh God, yes! Peter gazed at Thomas with eyes full of misery. The question went right to the heart of Peter's daily existence in that house. The words were there, on the tip of his tongue. All he needed to do was simply open his mouth.

"Last question." Thomas spoke in almost a whisper. "Did your master ever ignore or refuse you the right to use a safeword?"

There was that word again, the one Alex had used. *Safeword.* Peter had felt far from safe with Curtis. This one word resonated within him. Peter's heart was urging him, despite his initial misgivings. *Trust him.*

A sob burst from him. He couldn't have held onto it if his life had depended on it. And fast on its heels were more violent sobs, which racked his body, leaving him breathless and weak. He had to say something. *For God's sake, tell him,* a voice screamed inside his head.

"Yes!" he cried out. Tears flowed down his cheeks and he trembled uncontrollably. "Oh God, yes, *all* those things!" No sooner had the words left his lips than he felt a sense of relief flow through him, which made him weep all the more violently. He'd finally admitted it.

IT TOOK all of Thomas's strength of will not to leap from his seat and move around the table to hug the boy. His heart ached when he heard the abject misery in Peter's plaintive cries. But he knew such a reaction would not help the sub. He needed to be strong now, although hearing the boy's admission tore at his insides.

He reached for the kitchen paper towels, and after tearing off several pieces, he held them out across the table. Peter took them with a shaking hand and wiped his tears as his sobs finally died away. Thomas waited until Peter was calm once more. His confession seemed to have done him good, however. He sat straighter in his chair and breathed more evenly. Thomas tried not to look at the bruising around those slender wrists, or the bruises on his arms. His throat tightened. Best not to let the boy see his reaction.

"You did well, Peter," Thomas acknowledged, noting immediately how his words affected the sub. Peter relaxed noticeably, and the tension across his shoulders eased. Here was a boy who would surely flourish when given

44

plenty of praise and encouragement. "I run a BDSM club in the gay village. One of my roles there is training Dominants and submissives. I train subs so that when they find a Dom who best fits their needs, they are ready to serve. They know what is expected of them, how to behave, et cetera." He leveled a forthright stare at Peter. "Did your master ever train you like that?"

Peter said nothing, but his look of misery was very telling. His hands twisted in his lap and he rocked slightly in his chair. That previous tension was back with a vengeance. Thomas forged ahead.

"I'm going to take that as a no. I spoke with Alex after your conversation, and he indicated you were keen to learn more about being a submissive. So I'm going to train you. But I warn you—your training might not be what you expect at first. For one thing, I want you to see a psychologist."

He noted the stricken expression that crossed Peter's face. "Why do I need to see a psychologist?"

Thomas pondered for a few seconds before replying, trying to word his response. "Peter, I don't know all you've been through with your former master. But judging from your reaction just now to my questions, I would say you have some... issues that need to be worked through. Would you agree with that?"

Peter nodded, albeit reluctantly.

"Now don't worry about this. Dr. Herne is a really good psychologist, but there's one thing in her favor that makes her perfect for you. She understands the D/s lifestyle—and from your perspective of it."

"She's a submissive?" Peter's wide stare was really sweet. It brought a chuckle to Thomas's lips.

"Yes, lad. You'll be among friends. As for your training, you'll need to sign a temporary contract."

"Alex mentioned contracts," Peter admitted. "What... what will it contain?"

"At this stage, I'm going to keep things nice and simple. For my part, I will agree to provide for all your needs—accommodation, food, clothing." He glanced at Peter, who seemed almost lost beneath the sweater that was plainly too big for him. "And we'll start by getting you some new clothes." Peter blushed fetchingly, but then the color slid from his cheeks. "What is it, Peter?"

"What will you expect me to do in return for all this?" Peter's voice was flat.

Thomas cursed inwardly to see the light die in Peter's eyes. In that instant he knew what Peter was thinking. *Damn Curtis Rogers.* "All I expect of you, lad, is that you accept my rules and agree to abide by them. Right now, I am more concerned about getting you into a routine than training you in how to be a submissive. So I will be giving you responsibilities. Starting with cooking."

"Cooking?" Peter's expression of surprise was delightful.

"Can you cook?" Thomas hoped he hadn't made a big mistake here. He didn't want to end up with food poisoning. To his relief, Peter gave a shy smile. He'd take that as a big yes. "Great. Well, starting from Monday, you will be in charge of the cooking in this house, which will also include washing up and keeping the kitchen clean and tidy. I don't know what sort of cooking you're used to, but I tend to eat very healthily. I can't stand processed food, so there's usually lots of fresh meat, fish, and vegetables on my shopping list. I will also expect you to make fresh bread. I'll provide you with a cookbook that covers anything you might possibly want to prepare, and you'll work out a list of what meals you'll be preparing ahead of time, so you can put together a shopping list."

Peter paled. "Will you expect me to go shopping?"

"No, lad." Peter's palpable relief at hearing his reply puzzled him. The boy clearly didn't want to go out in public. It was as if he feared Curtis would come after him, though why Curtis would go to such extremes over a missing submissive, especially when he had recently gained a second, was beyond Thomas. Not for the first time, Thomas thought this required investigation, but not now. "I'll make sure the shopping gets done. The local supermarket is used to delivering to my door. Just make sure the list is ready."

Peter's chin dipped twice.

Thomas got up from his chair and collected the empty plates and glass, then placed them beside the kitchen sink. He turned back to Peter, who focused on him warily.

"Cooking will be the first of your responsibilities. Each week for the next ten weeks or so, I will add a new responsibility. But there is a routine I want you to get used to straightaway. Most days I will be at the club, although my hours there will vary. But sometimes I work until late, so you will be here alone. I will expect phone calls from you every day at specified times. You will simply be ringing to check in with me so I know everything is all right." He paused, making sure Peter was still focused. "If I do not hear from you, I will worry. And when I get home, there will be a punishment. Is that understood?" He kept his voice firm and low but with no hint of menace. The boy didn't need that. Besides, it seemed the mere word "punishment" was enough. Peter shuddered.

"Yes...." Peter hesitated. "How should I address you? Master?"

Thomas shook his head vehemently. "Submissives who are members of the club get to use that particular honorific. You'll use it when you address your Dom, but only after the two of you have been together for quite a while. For now, 'Sir' is perfectly adequate. And from now on, that is how you'll address me. Understood?"

Peter bowed his head once. "Yes, Sir." He spoke in a hushed tone.

"Alex spoke with you about what it means to him to be a submissive." Peter's eyes glittered. *Aha.* "You obviously entered into an arrangement of sorts with Curtis Rogers because you wanted to explore the D/s lifestyle. Are you sure you still want to pursue this?"

Peter's brow knitted. "Sir, why would I not want to pursue it?"

Thomas let out a soft sigh. "Because, lad, maybe what you have been through has changed your mind. That would be understandable in the circumstances."

"No, Sir." Peter jutted out his chin. "I want to continue." His voice dropped. "Especially after I talked with Alex."

Thomas nodded approvingly. "Very well. But there will be no scenes, no D/s training until you've read and agreed to my rules." Peter tilted his head, clearly puzzled. Thomas leaned back against the sink. "Peter, when I train a Dom, I make him learn one hundred rules." He chuckled to hear Peter's sharp inhalation. "These are my rules for ensuring he leaves me knowing how to treat a sub. When I've finished training you and your contract comes to an end, we'll find you a Dom. But you need to know what you can expect from him, how you should be treated. So from now on, you're going to work through ten rules each week. When you aren't carrying out your responsibilities, I want you to be reflecting on them, thinking about what they mean to you. At the end of each week, you're going to write me an essay outlining your reactions to those rules. I expect you to be honest."

He paused to give Peter time to digest his words. Peter sat there with a thoughtful expression, seemingly taking it all in. The lad was doing better than he had anticipated.

"For the time being, I will take you to your appointments with Dr. Herne and fetch you home afterward, until such time as we agree you're able to go there alone." The shudder that rippled through Peter definitely gave Thomas cause for concern. Maybe it was time for a few questions. "Tell me about Curtis's new sub."

"Christian?" Peter's mouth dropped at the corners. "He hasn't been with Curtis very long. He was all right. He wasn't mean to me or anything." He stiffened slightly and added as an afterthought, "Sir."

"Why would Curtis need another submissive?"

Peter shrugged. "I got the impression I was getting too old for him. Christian's only eighteen, and I'm twenty-six." He let out a dry chuckle. "What is it with you guys being hung up on age all the time?" No sooner had the words left his mouth than he paled, clearly horrified at his boldness. Thomas wasn't offended. It was the first time he'd seen Peter show some spirit, and to be honest, it gladdened his heart. Curtis hadn't destroyed him entirely, then.

Thomas chortled, mainly to let Peter know he wasn't in trouble. Peter's shoulders sagged with relief. "Was there a sub before you?"

Peter nodded. "Ethan, Sir. But I think he went on to another master. He must have, because one day everything of his disappeared from the house." He shivered. "Then it was just me."

Thomas changed the subject. "Do you have anything you'd like to ask me, lad?"

There was a moment's hesitation before Peter gave a slow nod. More hesitation.

"Sir, will you... will you want to fuck me?"

Ever since Alex had related their conversation, Thomas had been expecting this. He had no way of knowing how Peter felt about the way Curtis had abused his body, but he knew he had to make things clear from the start.

"I don't have penetrative sex with submissives when I train them," he said at last. Peter blinked rapidly and sucked in a deep breath. He clearly hadn't anticipated that. Thomas smiled inwardly, wondering how his next words would be received. "But part of your training will be to develop your self-control. So while you are under my roof, there will be no masturbation. And you're not allowed to come." Blinking gave way to a wide-eyed look of absolute amazement. "Not unless I give you permission." Peter sagged back into his chair, letting out an unsteady breath. Thomas grinned wickedly. "I'm not a monster, boy." His tone held amusement. "But you'll have to earn that particular reward."

Peter gave several rapid nods.

"Peter, your life here will be focused on learning and developing routines. There will be rewards when you please me and punishments when you don't. If any of that isn't acceptable, this is your last chance to back out." He reached on top of the fridge and pulled down a contract he'd placed there before Peter entered the kitchen. Moment of truth. He placed the contract carefully in front of Peter, who stared at it, swallowing. "I'd like you to take this away and read it. This is a simplified contract that states all those things we've discussed. If you are happy with our roles, and you agree to accept my rules and abide by them, then sign it. We will review it again after three months." Thomas folded his arms. Enough talking. It was up to Peter now.

Peter gazed at the one-page document in silence, his breathing even, his whole demeanor composed. That was a good sign. Thomas observed him, glad to see him taking his time. At last Peter raised his head and met Thomas's gaze.

"Thank you, Sir. May I take it to my room now and read it?"

Thomas was relieved. At least the boy was thinking clearly. He'd been prepared for Peter signing the contract blindly, but the fact that he wanted to consider it carefully was encouraging.

"Yes, lad, that's fine. I'll await your decision."

Peter stood and picked up the contract. "Thank you, Sir." He waited.

Thomas realized he was awaiting permission. Either Curtis had ground it into him, or else Peter was a naturally polite young man. Thomas looked forward to finding out what made this boy tick. Provided he got the opportunity, of course.

"You may go, lad."

Peter gave a brisk nod and left the kitchen. Thomas watched his exit thoughtfully. The lad was an undiscovered country crying out to be explored. Thomas found himself hoping he got the chance to do just that.

PETER sat on his bed, resting against the padded headboard. He winced at the contact with his back. The contract lay on the bed beside him. It made for straightforward reading, and it contained exactly what Thomas had said. There didn't seem to be any catches Peter could find. There was no mention of BDSM, simply an agreement that Thomas would provide for his needs and that Peter would agree to abide by his rules. Now all he had to do was decide.

Peter was under no illusions. Curtis *would* pursue him. No doubt in his mind about that. Peter knew far too much, and as such he was a threat. When Christian had appeared, Peter swiftly realized that something was afoot. He had no clue what Curtis was planning, but he knew it didn't bode well. Curtis needn't worry—there was no way Peter was about to tell anyone what the man was up to. That was far too risky. He had his own suspicions as to what had happened to the previous sub, Ethan, but that's all they were—suspicions. There was no proof. And keeping quiet about Curtis's activities had kept him alive so far.

Peter closed his eyes. In his mind he saw Thomas: gray hair; green, twinkling eyes; kindly expression. He dimly remembered being carried upstairs in the man's strong arms, nestled against that wide chest. And those gentle hands that had tended to his back. Everything in Peter was telling him to trust Thomas. Peter wanted to. Badly. But after four years with Curtis, trust was a commodity in short supply. His mind went back to the conversation in the kitchen. Thomas wasn't going to fuck him. The sheer relief when he heard those words had been hard to restrain. After seeing what took place in the private rooms of St. Andrew's, Peter had been astonished to hear Thomas didn't have sex with his subs. Didn't *all* Doms fuck their submissives? The more Peter heard, the more he wanted to know about this man.

He got up from the bed, taking the contract with him, and went to the writing desk. He opened it and found an elegant pen. Sitting at the desk, Peter stared at the document. The heading *Collars & Cuffs* was emblazoned in red, the only splash of color on an otherwise pristine white surface.

You know what to do. Peter's hand trembled as he picked up the pen. *Do it.* Still he hesitated, trying to ignore the voice in his head. *Remember how Alex described his life?* You *want that.* You always *wanted that.* That did it. Exhaling shakily, Peter steadied his hand and signed his name with a flourish of black ink.

Trusting Thomas

He dropped the pen onto the desktop and sat back. *I hope to God I'm doing the right thing.* Thomas's face rose unbidden in his mind. Despite his fears, Peter latched onto one thought, repeating it like a mantra in his head, as though the mere process of doing this would make it become truth.

I can trust him. I can trust him. I can trust him.

K.C. Wells

Four

Week One

PETER put down his pen with a sigh and stretched his back, reaching high above him with his fingers laced together, palms up. Thank God *that* was over. He regarded the fruits of his morning's labor with relief.

Thomas had given him a dark-blue ring-bound notebook for the purpose of writing his weekly essays. But his first task had been to write down what led him to his present situation. Peter could see why Thomas might find such a thing useful; he knew next to nothing about Peter. So he'd sat down this morning to put together a description of how he met Curtis, and his life after that point. And it had taken him *hours*. Not that Peter's life had been so eventful. No, what had taken time were the frequent pauses where he had to stop and *breathe* or else be undone by the painful memories that threatened to overwhelm him. Things he'd long forgotten came back to poke and prod him with thin, spiteful fingers. Pain he'd pushed aside was suddenly there once more, raking sharp talons down his spine. But Peter persevered. And now that it was finished, he had no intention of ever reading it again. The mere act of writing it had somehow been a cathartic exercise. Writing down each remembered horror had taken some of the sting out of it, made it just that little bit less painful. No, it was enough that he'd completed the task. If Thomas wanted to read it, that was fine.

He glanced at his watch and let out a hiss of breath. It was nearly time to make his eleven o'clock call. Thomas left the house early that Monday morning, and Peter had started work on his task straightaway. It was a good thing he noticed the time. There was no *way* he wanted to miss his first call. He scrambled down the stairs, trying not to fall in his haste, and hurried into the lounge. The phone stood on a little cabinet with a padded seat built into it, and Peter sat down and grabbed the slip of paper that bore the number of Thomas's club.

Anxiously, he dialed the number and waited for it to connect. After only two rings, someone picked up the phone.

"Well done, boy. You remembered." Thomas's voice was deep and firm, and somehow Peter knew he was smiling. Warmth flooded through him.

"Thank you, Sir." Peter couldn't hold back his smile. Thomas was pleased with him.

"By the way, the clothes I ordered online on Saturday were delivered here this morning. So when I get home, you'll have new clothes to try on."

Much to his chagrin, this news left Peter excited, like a little boy anticipating Christmas morning. *It doesn't take much to make* me *happy, does it?* Thomas had shown him what he was ordering and asked for his opinion. To be honest, Peter would have said yes to whatever Thomas wanted him to wear. Since their conversation in the kitchen, he'd been filled with a sense of hope that his life really had turned itself around. He knew he was deliberately pushing his fears to one side, but the sense of euphoria that flowed through him temporarily submerged all the worries about Curtis. Peter couldn't get over the difference a mere few days had made to his life.

"Peter?"

With a start, Peter realized his mind had wandered. "Sorry, Sir. I zoned out for a second there."

"Then you probably missed what I said. I didn't want you to feel uncomfortable in the house on your own for the first time, so you'll be having a visitor."

Peter's heart beat faster. He knew it was irrational, but he couldn't help his body's reaction. "A v-visitor, Sir?"

Thomas's voice was soothing, calming. "It's okay, boy. Breathe." *How had he known?* "That's it, listen to my voice and breathe deeply. You're safe, Peter." Peter hung on to his words and inhaled, keeping his breathing even.

After a few seconds he felt calmer. "Good boy." Thomas's praise settled on him, surrounding him like a warm blanket.

"I'm all right now, Sir." Peter straightened. He knew Thomas couldn't see him, but it felt good to get his posture right.

"You remember Alex, from a few days ago?"

Had it really only been a few days? "Yes, Sir."

"Alex will be calling round to see you. In fact, he should be there any minute." There was a moment's pause. "I'm looking forward to tasting your first meal, Peter. Do you have everything you need?"

"Yes, Sir." Peter had sat down with the cookbook on Sunday afternoon and worked out his menu for the week. Once Thomas showed him where everything was kept and what supplies were already available, it hadn't taken him long to put together a shopping list.

"Good." Peter could hear Thomas's approval. "In that case, I'll let you go. Don't forget your call at three."

"I won't forget, Sir." Peter spoke fervently. He wouldn't let Thomas down.

"I look forward to hearing from you then. Have a good time with Alex." Thomas hung up, and Peter replaced the handset. If Alex was going to appear, the least Peter could do was make sure the kettle was on. He went into the kitchen. His feet made virtually no sound on the wooden floor in his thick socks. He'd no sooner clicked on the kettle than he heard the doorbell. Silently, he made his way to the lounge window and peered through the blinds as surreptitiously as he could. Yes, it was Alex standing outside, shivering slightly. Peter hurried to the front door and unbolted it.

"Good morning. I take it Master Thomas told you I was coming?" Alex stepped into the warm hallway, held his hands out over the radiator, and then sighed with pleasure. "It's freezing out there!"

All of a sudden Peter was tongue-tied. He watched as Alex removed his thick jacket and hung it on a hook near the door. What should he say to him?

Alex regarded him for a second or two. "Peter, it's okay to be nervous, all right? But think about it. Thomas wouldn't let me anywhere near you if he didn't trust me, would he?"

Peter gave himself a mental kick up the backside. He knew Alex was right. It was just a matter of convincing his stupid brain of that fact.

"I'm sorry," he said quietly. "Would you like some tea or coffee?"

Alex's eyes lit up hopefully. "I don't suppose Thomas has any green tea in the house?"

Peter smiled. "I'm not sure. Let's go see."

The two young men went into the kitchen, and Peter headed for the cabinet above the kettle. There were various boxes of different teas in there, and Peter hunted through them. A triumphant sound escaped him as he pounced on a box near the back of the cupboard. "Green tea with vanilla—will that do?" Alex's wide grin said plenty.

Peter had never tried green tea. He sniffed cautiously at the tea bags and then dropped two into waiting mugs. Alex glanced around the kitchen.

"This is a really nice kitchen."

Peter had to agree. It wasn't as sterile-looking as Curtis's kitchen. The wooden cabinets gave the room a lovely warm feeling. He poured boiling water over the teabags and let them infuse for several seconds. While he waited, he looked around. There were plenty of work surfaces in a deep cream marble, all uncluttered. Peter liked that. He found he couldn't think straight with too much clutter. Someone had really given this kitchen a lot of thought.

"Should be ready now." Alex's words brought Peter back into the moment. He gave Alex a sheepish look, embarrassed to be caught with his mind wandering. He seemed to be doing that a lot today. He squeezed out the tea bags and handed a mug to Alex before pushing the sugar bowl toward him. Alex waved his hand. "Nah, I'm sweet enough." He winked. Peter reddened.

They sat down at the wide table, and Peter hurriedly reached for coasters.

"So, have you settled in yet?" Alex sipped carefully at his tea.

Peter nodded. "Though it will be better when I have some clothes." He glanced down at his T-shirt and sweatpants. "Sir ordered me some. I'll get them tonight." He thought back on Thomas's shopping list. The man had been very thorough: jeans, T-shirts, shirts, sweaters, underwear, and even sneakers. At first, Peter's mind reverted back to his earlier suspicion. Why would Thomas do all this for him and not want *something* in return? Then he recalled Thomas's reaction, the horror in his eyes he'd tried to hide when Peter had voiced that very thought. Ashamed, Peter pushed the memory from his head.

Alex glanced at the notepad on the worktop, next to the cookbook. "You're going to be doing the cooking, is that right?" Peter nodded. "Have you done much cooking before?"

"I lived with my grandmother for a while before I—" Peter didn't want to think about moving in with Curtis. He shuddered and then composed himself. "She taught me to do some basic stuff. But over the past few years, cooking has simply been a matter of heating up ready meals. Curtis—" He shivered. "Curtis lived on processed food."

Alex pulled a face. "Tell me about it. It was one of the reasons I had to get out of my parents' house. The junk they used to eat…." He opened the notepad and glanced at Peter's scrawl. "So what's on the menu tonight?"

Peter found himself relaxing in Alex's presence. The younger man seemed quite laid-back and self-assured, and Peter was relieved when Alex didn't press him for details of his life with Curtis. There was no way he would share what he'd been through. Everything was still far too raw.

"I'm going to make spiced parsnip soup." The recipe looked simple enough. "I thought about making some fresh bread to go with it."

Alex's eyes lit up. "Ooh, fresh homemade bread. Can I help?"

Peter wavered for a second, about to say yes. But then he reconsidered. It was *his* responsibility. Thomas was trusting *him* to carry it out.

"Thanks for the offer, but I'd like to do it myself, if you don't mind."

Alex's slow smile of approval warmed him. "I think Thomas would like that. Can I at least stay and keep you company while you do stuff?"

Peter had no problem with that. He opened the cookbook to the page he'd marked with a slip of paper and began assembling his ingredients so he had everything to hand. He'd found a plastic container labeled "bread flour—six seeds" in the tall cabinet that contained foodstuffs, and thought it might make some really tasty bread. Dried yeast sachets were tucked in next to the container.

"Have you made bread before?" Alex inquired.

Peter shook his head. "I'll be honest. I'm a bit nervous. What if the bread doesn't rise?" He chewed at his lower lip.

Alex glanced around the kitchen and found an AGA cooker, a heavy, cast-iron heat-storage stove. He grinned. "Not going to be a problem. As long as you have somewhere warm for the bread to rise, it'll be fine. You could sit the loaf tin on top of the AGA. Just make sure it's not too warm."

Peter's brows lifted. "You sound like you've done this before."

Alex chuckled. "I work in an Italian restaurant. Luca always makes his own bread." He moaned softly. "His ciabatta is to *die* for."

Peter laughed, feeling much more at ease. He reached into a lower cupboard, pulled out kitchen scales, and proceeded to weigh out the ingredients. His large glass mixing bowl was soon full of flour, butter, and yeast. Once the warm water had been added, Peter began using his hands to combine the contents of the bowl into dough. Alex's gaze followed his every movement, and as the dough began to cling to Peter's fingers, Alex giggled.

"You need to sprinkle a little flour over the dough so it doesn't get too sticky."

Peter let out a low growl. "I think we passed *sticky* a while back—this stuff has the consistency of *glue*." He'd somehow managed to get dough onto everything. He wiped at his brow in exasperation. Damn—now there was dough in his hair, on his nose, in his eyebrows....

Alex's giggle morphed into a full-blown guffaw. "Oh man—just look at you! It's the Pillsbury Doughboy!" Peter couldn't hold back his glare, and Alex quickly covered his mouth with his hand. All this served to do, however, was to muffle his laughter. "Do you want a hand?" Peter could just about make out the words.

"Yes!" The word came out with more desperation than he intended. Alex dipped a spoon into the flour container and sprinkled it lightly over the dough. Peter did his best to fold the flour into the now extremely sticky glop in the bowl, but the flour went *everywhere*. Peter glanced in quiet desperation at the recipe. He grasped the bowl firmly and upended it, intending for the dough to end up on the table, ready for kneading.

The dough had other ideas. It hung there upside down, refusing to leave the bowl. *What the hell?* He shook the bowl. No reaction. Reaching into the bowl, he clawed at the mixture, trying to pry it from the sides and grimacing when it got under his fingernails. Eventually an amorphous blob slumped onto the table.

Peter and Alex stared at the gooey mass for a second or two.

Alex said, "So, now you knead it, right? So it might have been a good idea to flour the table *before* you emptied the dough onto it?" Alex's eyes danced with amusement.

Peter groaned. "You might have *said* something!" Frowning, he stuck his hand into the flour container, grabbed a handful of flour, and dumped it over the sticky mass. He then proceeded to pummel the dough, gingerly at first, but with more vigor as it became pliant.

"Hey, take it easy—what has that poor bread ever done to you?" Alex was laughing. Peter glanced up at him. Alex mimed how to knead the dough correctly, and Peter followed his hand movements. He sighed with relief as the dough began to resemble the picture in the cookbook.

"Okay, now stick it back in the bowl, cover it with a damp cloth, and leave it to prove on the AGA." Peter patted and pulled the dough into a rounded ball and helped it back into the bowl. He held a clean tea towel under the tap, wrung it out, and then laid it over the receptacle. He placed his precious dough safely to one side on the AGA and eyed the kitchen table in horror. Large bits of dough clung to its surface. This was going to take some clearing up.

"I do believe there's more on the table than there is in the bowl."

Alex's comment, accompanied by a wicked chuckle, was a declaration of war.

Peter slowly hooked his finger into a particularly large clump of dough and pulled it free from the table. He regarded it solemnly for a moment, then raised his head—and flicked it at Alex. It landed with startling accuracy on Alex's chin. Alex's eyes widened.

"Oh, so it's like *that*, is it?" Grinning, he scraped some dough from the table and flung it at Peter. Peter sidestepped neatly and it hit the kitchen door and stuck. "Hah! Lucky move. Next time I won't miss."

The two men raced to the table and began picking up every bit of dough they could find. And then the battle commenced. Peter conserved his ammunition and flicked tiny pellets at Alex, laughing as it landed with astonishing accuracy. Alex's aim wasn't as good, so his dough bullets ended up on the floor, worktops, Thomas's shoe….

Oh. Fuck.

The battle came to an abrupt halt as both men suddenly noticed Thomas standing in the doorway, staring at the scene. Peter's heart jolted in his chest. He froze, not daring to look Thomas in the eye. Beside him, he was aware of Alex doing exactly the same thing.

"I thought I'd bring the clothes home so you could put on something warmer." Something in Thomas's tone made Peter look up, and when he did, he could have wept with relief. Thomas was trying not to laugh. Peter could see him straining with the effort.

"I'm going to go back to the club now," Thomas said slowly, "and when I get home this evening, you two will have cleared up this mess until the kitchen sparkles. Is that clear?" His gaze passed over both men.

Peter nodded, gulping. Alex hadn't even raised his head, but Peter detected his brisk nod. Thomas surveyed the kitchen one more time before retreating. Peter listened as the front door opened and closed. At last he took a breath. He looked at Alex. Alex looked at him. And all of a sudden both men were laughing, with tears running down their faces. Peter's sides ached from it.

"I… can't remember… the last time I laughed like this," he managed to stammer out.

Alex wiped his eyes. "Me neither." He glanced around at the detritus of their battle and sighed. "Oh well, cleanup time."

Twenty minutes later the kitchen was once more looking clean, with not a scrap of dough to be seen. Both Peter and Alex had gone over the room carefully, anxiously searching for any elusive bits, but they appeared to have found it all. Peter made some more green tea, and they sat at the table, sipping slowly, listening to birdsong from the garden.

"I could get to like this," Peter admitted, indicating his tea with a brief nod.

Alex beamed. "It's good, isn't it? I like it with jasmine too." He sipped the fragrant tea. "So, apart from cooking, what else will you be doing with your days?"

"Reading through Thomas's rules for Doms." Seeing Alex's confusion at this, Peter explained what Thomas wanted him to do. Alex's mouth dropped open.

"I'd *love* to see those. I think that would be fascinating. Can I?"

Peter hesitated. Then he figured there was nothing wrong in it. Doubtless, Leo had a copy of his own. He nodded. "They're in my room." He stood, pushing back his chair, and Alex followed suit. As they went into the hallway, Peter glanced down at some boxes that were stacked at the foot of the stairs. "These must be my clothes."

"I'll give you a hand to take them up to your room." Alex picked up two of them and Peter the third. Alex grunted. "How much stuff did Thomas buy for you?"

Peter grimaced. "He bought everything. I mean, you're looking at all the clothes I possess right now." Alex nodded somberly. They entered Peter's room, and both men dropped the boxes onto the bed. Alex winked.

"So do I get a fashion show when you try this lot on?" Peter flushed and Alex chortled. "I take it that's a no. Well, at least I can help you unpack it all. The bread needs time to prove, so we might as well use the time wisely." He waited for Peter's reaction.

Peter acknowledged his suggestion with a dip of his head, and Alex immediately attacked the box with a gleeful sound, ripping the brown postage tape from its seams. Peter couldn't help but warm to him. Between them, they removed all the clothing from its various packaging and discarded the box, placing it at the foot of the bed. This was repeated with the next two boxes, until clothing was piled high on the bed.

Alex glanced around the room. "Do you have hangers?" Without waiting for Peter's reply, he opened the doors of the oak wardrobe, letting out a triumphant cry as he saw inside. "Bingo! Plenty of coat hangers. Let's get hanging, then." Peter sorted the clothes into two piles, items for the wardrobe and the rest for the chest of drawers. Alex brought a handful of hangers and placed them on the bed, and they spent the next ten minutes or so hanging up Peter's new shirts, jeans, and trousers. Underwear and socks were safely stowed in the top drawer, and T-shirts and sweaters were folded neatly and placed in the second.

At last the bed was clear of clothing, and Alex grinned. "Peter, you have clothes."

Peter smiled. It gave him a comforting feeling to know he was being taken care of like this. Then he realized that drinking two cups of green tea in quick succession had its consequences.

"You'll have to excuse me for a minute," he said, blushing. Alex nodded, and he quickly exited the room.

ALEX started to dismantle the cardboard boxes, flattening them, getting them ready for the recycling collection. His gaze landed on the opened writing desk and the blue notebook sitting there. Curiosity finally got the better of him. He quietly crossed the room and flipped open the notebook, then skimmed down the handwritten paragraphs. His eyes widened.

I begged Curtis not to do it, but he simply pushed the broom handle into my arse. No lube. I couldn't help it. I screamed. He withdrew it, and it felt as though my insides came away with it. And then he roughly shoved it into me again. And again. I remember pulling at the straps that held me down. I can still hear the laughter of the three men who stood around the table, watching him do it, egging him on. That hateful voice cackling before he said, "Oh fuck, now he's bleeding." And when I screamed out in pain, one of the men hit me on the jaw before thrusting his thick cock into my mouth with such speed and force that I was choking from it. "That's the way to shut him up." I couldn't shut it all out—their shouts of derision, the splashes of hot come on my back as they jerked off.... Mercifully, I passed out soon after that.

What the...? With a shock Alex heard Peter flush the toilet, and he hurriedly shut the notebook. He moved swiftly to the other side of the room and continued dismantling the boxes. Peter came back into the room and smiled when he saw what Alex was doing.

"Thanks for that. Sir is apparently really keen on recycling."

Alex struggled to retain his composure. Right now he felt thoroughly ashamed of himself for peeking into what was clearly a very private document, but more than that, he was filled with horror at what he'd read. He couldn't look Peter in the eye. *Come on, Alex, get it together. Because otherwise, he's going to notice....* With a supreme effort he smiled at Peter.

61

"So what's next on your to-do list for today?" He kept the words light and cheerful, but the effort it took to accomplish this was enormous.

Peter glanced at the clock beside his bed. "It's too early to start preparing the soup, but it is lunchtime." He gave Alex a shy look. "Would you like to have lunch with me?" There was a hopeful light in his eyes that Alex couldn't ignore.

"Sure," he said with a half smile. "What's for lunch?"

Five

Regrets—and First-Night Nerves

LEO looked up from his folder at the sound of a quiet knock on the open office door. Alex stood there with his head lowered. A quick glance at his lover's posture was all Leo needed to tell him something was wrong.

"Alex? What is it? What's happened?" Leo got up from his desk and walked swiftly to his submissive. Alex kept his eyes down, and Leo realized the boy was trembling. "Talk to me, boy." Leo spoke urgently in a low voice. "I thought you were spending most of your day off with Peter. Is he okay?"

Alex's voice shook slightly. "I left him cutting up vegetables for dinner tonight." Suddenly he drew in a sharp breath. "Damn! I asked him if I could look at Master Thomas's rules, but I forgot."

"Never mind the rules—what's wrong?" Leo pulled Alex to him and held him close, noting his slumped shoulders, chin dropped to his chest, cheeks that burned. Alex stiffened in his arms and tried to pull away, but Leo held on. He pressed his lips to Alex's ear. "I've got you, boy. You're not going anywhere until you tell me what's wrong."

Alex sagged against him, burying his face in Leo's white shirt. "I don't like myself very much right now, Sir," he mumbled. Leo stroked his hair.

"Did something happen at Thomas's house?" Leo kept his voice low. After a moment's hesitation, Alex nodded. "Can you tell me about it?" This got a shake of his head. "Why not?"

63

Alex lifted his head and focused on Leo's chin. "I saw something I wasn't supposed to see. I can't talk about it." The abject misery in his voice tore at Leo's heart.

"Was what you saw so bad?" Leo was dismayed to see tears welling up in Alex's pale-blue eyes. Apparently yes. He pulled Alex close. "What do you need, boy? What can I do to take whatever this is away from you?"

Alex froze. "Make it stop hurting, Sir. Make the pain go away."

Leo knew exactly what to do. "Come with me." He spoke with authority and saw his words take effect. Alex straightened, and an expression of utter relief spread across his face.

"Yes, Sir."

Leo led the way out of the office toward the private rooms. Jonathon was coming out of room three with Dillon, his sub. Both men looked tired but content. Leo guessed it had been a good scene. He stopped Jonathon with a light touch on his arm.

"Jonathon, are you all right to man the office for a while? Thomas is in the group room, and I need to do something urgently."

Jonathon gave Alex a brief but searching glance and then looked at Leo. "Sure thing, Leo. Take as long as you need." Leo gave him a grateful look, grasped Alex's arm, and led him into room four.

"Strip, boy, now."

In silence, Alex peeled off his clothing and shucked off his sneakers. Leo picked up the house phone and checked that it was working and manned. By the time he put down the receiver, Alex was standing naked in the middle of the room.

Leo began to remove his own shirt slowly, making sure Alex was focused on his movements.

"I'm going to take the pain away, boy. But to do that, you're going to give up all control. You won't be able to move. All you'll be able to do is take what I give you—and feel." He slipped the shirt over the back of a chair and walked to the bed. He pulled up the straps that were located at the four corners of the bed, each one ending with a leather cuff.

"Get over here on the bed, facedown." Alex moved slowly and stretched out on the bed. Leo pushed a pillow under his chest, effectively lifting his upper body from the bed. "Arms toward the headboard, boy." Leo fastened cuffs around Alex's wrists, adjusting the straps so he was held tightly. He then pulled at Alex's ankles until he lay spread-eagled, and then secured them in a similar fashion. Leo reached under him and tugged at his cock and balls so they were exposed. Alex didn't utter a sound but lay there, quiescent.

"I'm moving to the cupboard, boy." Leo went to the equipment cupboard that every private room possessed. He peered at the array of instruments it held, searching for one specific item. He grabbed a riding crop and returned to the bed.

"Turn your head toward me." When Alex complied, Leo held out the riding crop, making sure Alex saw it. He smacked its tip into his palm a few times, noting how Alex's eyes widened at the sound. The distinctive snap as it struck Leo's palm had Alex swallowing.

"I'm not going to blindfold or gag you, boy. I need to hear you, all right? And before I begin...." He paused, locking eyes with his boy. "What are your safewords?"

"*Pasta* and *chianti*, Sir." Alex spoke in a whisper. Leo had a fair idea of the emotions running through his submissive in that moment. They had only shared one scene involving flagellation, using a tawse, and that was a brief introduction at best. Alex had responded well, but the present situation required something more, something to take his boy out of himself. To his credit, Alex was trying to maintain his composure, but Leo could see the strain he was under. Time to begin.

"Ready, boy?"

Alex nodded, still fixing his gaze on the crop. Leo clambered onto the bed and, bending low, he kissed Alex on the lips before moving to whisper in his ear. "I love you."

The tension across Alex's shoulders eased perceptibly. "I love you too, Sir."

Leo got off the bed and took up a position to the side. Slowly, he traced the riding crop along Alex's back and buttocks and lightly touched his exposed balls with it. Alex shivered. Leo ran the crop from the top of his buttocks down to just above the backs of his knees. He returned to stroking the crop over the lower half of his buttocks. Ready.

"I'm going to start out with a light touch, and then it will build slowly. I'll stop now and then so you can have a few moments' respite. If it gets too much, use your safewords. We won't go further than you can handle. Okay, boy?"

Alex dipped his chin once but then apparently realized Leo wanted verbal confirmation. "Yes, Sir." His voice was steady.

Leo began to strike him, the first strokes soft, covering the entire buttocks and the backs of his thighs, letting him grow accustomed to the feel of the crop against his body. He paused to reach over and stroke Alex down his spine, caressing his arse before resuming his stance, ready to increase the intensity. This time he landed a couple of sharper strokes across his buttocks.

ALEX caught his breath at the first of the sharper taps across his arse. Leo alternated between light and sharp taps with the crop. That harsh swish became more frequent. Alex focused on the sensations in his body, awaiting each new stroke, his breath hitching as the whipping continued. Every now and then Leo would pause, bending low to kiss his back, shoulder blades, neck, buttocks—tender kisses, a constant reassurance of Leo's love. And then the strokes would resume, building into a battery of sharp strikes that seemed to reverberate throughout his body. Alex lost himself in the rain of blows as he concentrated on the physical sensations that began to blot out the frantic tumbling of his thoughts, until all he could do was *feel*.... He let go, exulting in the liberating experience.

Alex was suddenly aware that the blows had stopped, as Leo's bare chest pressed lightly against his back. Leo's breath was hot against Alex's ear.

"I am so proud of you, boy. You did really well." Leo's hands soothed his body with firm caresses. Little by little Alex slipped back, growing more aware of his surroundings. His heart soared to hear his master's praise, but his body ached to feel a more intimate connection between them.

"Sir." It was only one word, but with it Alex tried to convey his urgent need. He wanted. And judging from the way Leo's breath caught, his master wanted too. Alex heard the rasp of a zip lowering and then the snick of a lid being opened. Coolness trickled down his crack, and then Leo pushed two fingers into Alex's arse with an urgency that betrayed his own needs. Alex tilted his arse as best he could, pushing back on those fingers, desperate for what was to come. Leo's fingers disappeared, to be replaced with the slow press of Leo's bare cock against his hole. "Oh, yes, Sir!"

He held his breath as Leo pushed into him, not pausing until he was buried balls deep. Alex could feel the zip against his cheeks and the smoothness of the leather pants Leo still wore. He was aware of Leo's hands grabbing his hips forcefully, lifting them as Leo began to plow into him. The zip rasped his flesh with every thrust. Leo went deep, punctuating each thrust with grunts of pleasure. Restrained as he was, Alex could barely move. He could only lie there and take it, exulting in every groan wrung from Leo as he neared climax.

Leo's hand reached around to tug at his cock, and Alex suddenly found himself teetering on the edge of orgasm. Leo stiffened, and Alex felt heat within him as his master shot his load deep inside.

"Mine!" Leo's triumphant howl pushed Alex over the edge, and he came, erupting over the bed, his body trembling with the severity of his climax, bowled over by its force. Leo's chest, damp with perspiration, pressed against his back. And then Leo began kissing him. Their mouths met in a collision of lips and tongues as Leo claimed him again and again.

"Love you, boy." The words were music to Alex's ears. He lay beneath Leo, shaking, reveling in the feel of his master's strong arms around him, Leo's lips pressed to Alex's hair, cheek, neck, murmurings of praise and love flowing constantly from his tongue.

"Master." The heartfelt whisper slipped from him even as Leo's seed slipped from his body in a slow trickle, a delicious reminder of both their coupling and Leo's recent decision to forgo the use of condoms. There would only ever be the two of them. Leo's arms tightened around him, and then Leo was releasing him from his bonds, kissing his wrists and ankles, before once more taking Alex in his arms, holding him close. Alex was relaxed, his mind at peace as Leo held him, no words between them but the soft murmurings of lovers. He had no idea how long they lay together, entwined in each other's arms, but finally Leo rolled onto his side and rested his head in his hand, gazing down at Alex, and the glimmer of concern reappeared once again.

"Feeling better?"

Alex nodded. "Thank you, Sir."

"Can you give me any clue what upset you so much?"

Alex considered the question for several seconds. "I... I can't tell you exactly, Sir. It's not my place to share what I read." Leo's brow wrinkled, and Alex could have kicked himself for letting that much slip. *Oh well, time to come clean.* "Peter was writing a diary, Sir."

..

..

. . .

..

Leo's brow cleared. "Seems like Thomas has already started some kind of training." Alex suddenly recalled Leo making him do just such a thing back in November—and that Thomas had made Leo do the same thing when he trained him, all those years ago.

Leo speared him with an intense look that made Alex squirm. "I take it Peter doesn't know you read his diary."

"No, Sir." He gazed up at Leo, his cheeks hot. "I'm sorry, Sir, I just snuck a peek when he was in the bathroom. I guess curiosity got the better of me." He lowered his gaze. His chin hit his chest, until Leo slipped a finger under to lift his head.

"Thank you for telling me, boy. And I'm proud of you for not betraying Peter's secrets. Whatever he wrote is between him and Thomas, should he choose to read it. Sometimes, the act of simply writing things down can provide release. I hope that was the case for Peter." Leo kissed the top of Alex's head. "It's forgotten. Okay?" Alex was aware of Leo's intense gaze.

"Yes, Sir. Forgotten." Alex hoped the diary brought Peter some peace. Even though his glimpse had been brief, what he'd read made his heart ache. What that poor young man had been through didn't bear thinking about. Alex was thankful for whatever circumstances had brought Peter to Thomas. Maybe now, with Thomas's help, Peter would have the chance to heal.

THOMAS let himself into the house as quietly as possible. Peter had called right on time at three and said that everything was going well, but Thomas was curious to see how dinner preparations were coming along. He sniffed the air eagerly as the smell of freshly baked bread wafted through the house. Earlier, he'd had to get out of the house as fast as possible. It wouldn't do for Peter to see him laughing at the state of the two boys covered in flour and bread dough.

He entered the kitchen to find it sparkling clean and extremely tidy. A saucepan sat on the AGA, and Thomas could hear the faintest bubbling as something simmered. Whatever it was smelled damn good. Peter had already washed up and put away whatever he'd used. Thomas couldn't resist peeking into his breadbox. A delicious-looking loaf sat there, and he had to fight the urge to slice off a piece right then and spread it with butter. Thomas could never resist homemade bread.

But of Peter there was no sign. Thomas was about to leave the kitchen when something caught his eye. On the stone tiles of the kitchen floor, he found a single drop of blood. He glanced around quickly, looking for more, but every surface was wiped clean. And now the lad's absence was suspicious.

"Peter? Can you come into the kitchen, please?" Thomas heard a rumble above as Peter moved his chair. His bedroom door opened and the boy came down the stairs, seemingly taking his time. He appeared in the doorway with his hands behind his back, dressed in a new pair of jeans, a red sweater, and thick socks on his feet. Peter was pale and fidgety and kept his head lowered.

"Hands by your sides, lad, if you please."

With an air of extreme reluctance, Peter slowly brought his hands from behind his back to hang limply. The left hand was wrapped up in what looked like several layers of kitchen paper towel. The blood was impossible to miss. *What on earth...?*

Thomas beckoned with a finger. "Come here, boy." Peter shuffled forward and Thomas simply held out his hand, keeping his gaze on the bloodied wrappings. Peter bit his lower lip and slowly lifted his hand, placing it in Thomas's upturned palm. Carefully, Thomas peeled away the layers of kitchen paper until the boy's hand was revealed, along with a deep cut across his middle three fingers. Peter stared at the floor.

"Care to tell me what happened here?" Thomas kept his tone even.

"I... I cut myself while I was preparing the vegetables for the soup," Peter whispered. His voice trembled. "I'm sorry, Sir. I couldn't get it to stop bleeding, and then I couldn't find the Band-Aids."

Thomas arched his brows. "Band-Aids? It strikes me that you need more than a Band-Aid on these, boy!" No sooner had the words left his lips than Thomas regretted them. Peter started to shake. Thomas softened his voice. "Easy now, Peter. It looks like you've got the bleeding under control at least. Let's get these cuts seen to before we do anything else." He released his hand and went to the cupboard next to the sink. "For future reference, my first-aid box is in here." He pulled out a distinctive green box with a white cross and opened it. He found the box of Band-Aids, a bottle of antiseptic wound wash, and some cotton wool.

He wiped over the cuts with the wound wash, noting how Peter held himself rigid, trying not to wince. Once the blood was removed, Thomas could see all was not as bad as it had first appeared. The cuts weren't too deep, but they were clearly causing the lad some discomfort. Thomas put a dab of antiseptic cream onto three Band-Aids and then wrapped them around the injured fingers. On a whim, he lifted Peter's hand and laid a brief kiss on each finger.

Noting Peter's expression of utter confusion, Thomas let out a dry chuckle.

"That's what my mother used to do whenever I cut myself. Healing kisses, she used to call them. I figured your poor fingers needed a bit of extra help." He released Peter's hand and cleared away the detritus, finally putting the box back in its usual resting place. He pulled out a chair and sat, indicating with a flick of his hand for Peter to do the same. Peter perched awkwardly on the chair, looking decidedly ill at ease.

"When did this happen?" Thomas kept his voice low. Having seen Peter's reaction when he raised his voice, he wanted to do all he could to keep the lad calm.

Peter swallowed. "Just after Alex left at two thirty, I began chopping up the vegetables." He sounded subdued. "I intended to make the soup ahead of time and then have it simmering for when you came home."

"So you'd already cut yourself when you rang me at the club?" Peter nodded miserably. "Why didn't you tell me?" Peter's chin dipped to his chest, and he mumbled something that Thomas didn't catch. Thomas placed a finger under his chin and lifted Peter's face. "Look at me, boy." The words were whisper soft. "Say that again."

"It wasn't important." Peter's words pierced the near silence of the kitchen.

Thomas was momentarily at a loss for words.

"How can you say that? Of course it was important. You hurt yourself."

"But I don't matter, Sir."

Thomas caught his breath. That simple statement brought him to a swift understanding of his new submissive. The boy thought himself worthless. Of no value. To anyone. Thomas's chest constricted as he regarded the boy's calm acceptance of his last statement as though it were fact. Well, that was something Thomas would have to change—with time.

He made sure Peter was looking at him. "Boy, you are of value. You matter—to me."

PETER was confused. Everything in him screamed that Curtis had been right, that Peter was a worthless piece of human garbage, as the man had told him on many occasions. He'd heard the words so often, he'd come to accept them. Yet Thomas sat there, telling him the exact opposite, and what's more, telling him with sincerity underlying every word. How could he matter to Thomas? He'd only known Peter for a few days, and apart from that long talk the first morning in the kitchen, they'd barely had more than three conversations. Peter tended to keep to his room, except during mealtimes, and Thomas hadn't pushed him.

"You matter, Peter. To me." There he went again, saying it like it was true. Peter rubbed his hand through his hair, blinking rapidly. This didn't make sense.

Thomas leaned forward, grasped his hand, and pulled it down into his lap, laying his hand over it as if to keep it there.

"I don't care if you don't believe me right now. The important thing to realize is that I'm going to keep reminding you of it every day—until you *do* believe it." There was no getting away from those green eyes, which locked on him. Thomas clearly believed everything he was saying. That much was obvious. Peter couldn't break away, couldn't tear his eyes from the man.

After a few seconds of intense scrutiny, Thomas finally lowered his gaze, and Peter inhaled shakily, gratefully drawing air deep into his lungs. There was definitely something about the man that affected him.

"I don't know about you, but I'm hungry." Thomas's serious expression morphed into a look that was considerably lighter. "And I can't wait to try the soup—not to mention that bread, which looks fantastic." His eyes gleamed.

71

"However did you manage to keep from trying a slice or two? It was calling to me the minute I came through the front door."

Peter's chest swelled.

"I wanted to wait until you came home. It only seemed fair that you try it first."

Thomas shook his head with a chuckle. "No, lad, that's the cook's privilege. In future, you get to try whatever you make, when you make it. And especially if it's homemade bread." He got up and opened the breadbox and removed the loaf. "So, shall we try it?"

Peter gave a shy smile. "Why not?" He picked up Thomas's solid ash breadboard from the work surface and handed it over before going to the fridge to collect the butter. When he turned back to the table, Thomas held up the bread knife, and a grin stretched across his face.

"Just one thing, lad. *I'll* be doing the slicing."

THOMAS was relieved to see Peter trying not to smirk. That was better.

He sliced off the end of the loaf. The bread had a lovely consistency and smelled divine. Right on cue, Thomas's stomach growled. He winked at Peter.

"Want to share the crust?" Peter's eager expression said more than words, and the boy took the crust and swiftly spread it with butter, sliced it in two, and handed him a piece. Thomas bit into it and gave a low moan of pleasure as the flavor burst upon his tongue. Peter's blissful expression said it all. Thomas devoured his piece in three bites.

"Delicious." He smacked his lips and then gazed at Peter. "This was the first time you made bread?"

Peter's cheeks were tinged with pink. "Yes, Sir."

Thomas couldn't resist. "And to think, we might have ended up with an even bigger loaf if you and Alex hadn't thrown so much of it at each other." He held his breath, waiting for Peter's reaction. The boy's jaw dropped, and then, fortunately, he saw the humorous intent. A giggle escaped him, and Thomas felt relief flood through him. As early days went, this one seemed to have got off on the right track in spite of the odd hiccup. They had plenty of time to acclimatize to each other, to get to know each other's foibles, but Thomas knew one thing for certain. Never again did he want to see the lad doubt his worth. He would strive to make Peter realize he was valuable. Thomas would see to that.

K.C. Wells

Six

Crossroads

PETER had intended to take his dinner up to his room to eat alone, but the look on Thomas's face when he spied the table set for one made it clear this was not an option. And it hadn't been so bad. The two men ate in silence, apart from the odd appreciative sound from Thomas as he enjoyed the soup and bread. Thomas had been full of praise for the spiced parsnip soup, and Peter glowed with pride.

Peter washed the bowls and plates, half listening to the strains of classical music that filtered through from the lounge. He had no idea what he was listening to, but it soothed him. He paused in the middle of wiping the breadboard to listen to the music, moving gently. German voices soared in beautiful harmony.

"Do you like it?"

Startled, Peter jumped. Thomas had made no sound as he approached. Internally, Peter berated himself. *Fancy jumping like a frightened rabbit.* He glanced over his shoulder to where Thomas was standing in the doorway, leaning against the doorjamb and watching him. Fortunately, there was nothing in his expression that spoke of pity.

Peter stood still, trying not to feel self-conscious, although his cheeks were hot. He cleared his throat. "It's lovely, Sir. What is it? I'm not very knowledgeable about classical music." He turned back to his task, conscious that Thomas had stepped into the kitchen and was walking toward the sink.

74

Peter breathed deeply, doing his best to keep calm. *He's not Curtis. You're safe here.* No matter how many times he repeated the words to himself, he struggled to overcome his body's default setting. Thomas was a Dom. Experience had taught Peter one thing—he couldn't trust a Dom, no matter how much his heart told him Thomas was different. Peter needed to listen to his head for a change.

"It's Cantata 140, "Wachet Auf," by Bach. It means, 'Sleepers awake.'" Thomas took the now dried board from his hands and put it back where it belonged on the work surface. "You don't mind if I lend a hand? Call it my thanks for the delicious dinner."

Peter tried his best to smile. "I'm glad you enjoyed it, Sir."

Thomas stepped closer. "You did well, boy." He took hold of Peter's left hand. "But I'm glad to see you're keeping your hand dry. Even if rubber gloves are *extremely* unbecoming."

Peter glanced at the bright-orange glove he wore. "Yes, Sir, but very sensible." Praise had been such a rare commodity in his life that it felt strange to be on the receiving end, but Thomas's words, though few, meant a lot to him. They gave him a warm feeling inside, which helped to ease the fluttery sensations in the pit of his stomach.

"What would you like to do when you've finished?" Thomas asked, taking the dried plates and stacking them in the cupboard. "I was going to read in front of the fire. You may join me, if you wish."

Peter gave him a grateful glance. "Thank you, Sir, but I'd like to go to my room and get started on those rules, if I may. Besides, I was thinking about having an early night. I know my first appointment with Dr. Herne is tomorrow morning." And there was no way he could envisage spending an entire evening in Thomas's company. His gut clenched at the thought.

Thomas's eyes gleamed with approval. "Good idea, lad. In which case I will say good night to you now, in case I don't see you again this evening. Happy reading." Thomas gave him a warm smile and exited the room.

Peter surveyed the kitchen one last time. It was spotless. Satisfied with what he'd accomplished, he poured himself a glass of water and was about to head up the stairs when a thought occurred to him. He went to the door of the lounge and peered in. Thomas was sitting in one of the big, squashy armchairs in front of the fire with an open book in his lap. At that moment he appeared lost in thought with his eyes closed, concentrating on the music.

Peter hovered in the doorway, unwilling to enter the room. He coughed nervously. Thomas opened his eyes.

"Did you want something, Peter?"

"Yes, Sir. I… I wanted to make myself a cup of green tea. Would that be okay, Sir?"

"Peter, you don't have to ask every time you want something. This is your home now."

Peter wasn't about to argue with him. It didn't feel like his home. He waited.

Thomas let out a patient sigh. "Peter, go make yourself some tea." His eyes closed once more.

"Yes, Sir. Would you like some?"

Thomas opened his eyes and smiled. "That's a lovely thought. There's some chamomile tea in the cupboard, though. I'd prefer a cup of that to green tea." His eyes glittered with amusement. "I see Alex has already won you over to the delights of his favorite drink."

Peter flushed. "Yes, Sir." He retreated back into the kitchen and put on the kettle. In the china cupboard he found a delicate porcelain cup and saucer that seemed perfectly suited for chamomile tea. Once the kettle had boiled, he poured the water over the teabags and let the tea infuse as he stared at the pattern on the china, a simple painting of country roses. He carefully carried the cup and saucer to Thomas.

Thomas's eyes lit up when he saw the cup. "Beautiful choice, boy. That cup belonged to my grandmother. She had an entire set at one time, but this is all that remains. It's also my favorite." He took the cup and sipped the tea. He raised his gaze to Peter's face. "Thank you, Peter. Good night."

As Peter reached the door, Thomas spoke. "How is your back today?"

"It's fine, Sir. Thank you, by the way, for taking care of me the way you did. It feels much better now." Peter was gratified that Thomas had thought to ask. "Good night, Sir." He left the room, collected his glass and cup of green tea, and went upstairs. After placing them on the bedside table, he switched on the lamp, which cast a warm glow around the room. From the desk he retrieved the plain folder Thomas had given him two days previously, containing his rules for Doms. Peter hadn't looked at the list yet. He'd wanted to be more settled in before he began in earnest, but the way things were going, that might be a while yet. Maybe he'd just better get on with it.

Trusting Thomas

Peter pushed several pillows into a pile and sat back against them, making himself comfortable. He sipped his tea and opened the folder. The list was a couple of sheets long. He took a deep breath and read the first rule.

Respect is key to any D/s relationship, as is trust from both sides.

Peter lowered the sheet to the bed. Trust. Respect. His thoughts immediately returned to that night four years ago when he'd ventured into his first BDSM club. He'd been so apprehensive—scared to death if he were honest. He'd watched a few BDSM clips on the Internet and had read a couple of novels on the subject, all of which brought him to that particular moment in time. He knew he craved what he'd seen and read, to the point where it was all he could think about.

The club was noisy, packed with people of all shapes and sizes, who wore a *hell* of a lot of leather. Peter was looking around nervously, unsure of what to do next, when a tall, muscular man appeared at his side, a man with eyes that seemed to see right into Peter's very soul.

"You need, boy." Those simple words jolted him. *How can he see so much, so quickly?* All Peter could do was nod helplessly. The man took his arm.

"I'll take care of you. Trust me."

Peter reflected on Curtis's words now with the value of hindsight. The man had homed in on him with all the speed of a predator spying its prey. Had Peter given out signals somehow? Had he seemed *that* vulnerable? He only knew that Curtis had taken him from the club before he'd had the chance to talk to anyone else. Curtis took him to his home, and all the while promises fell from his lips like autumn leaves. Promises to take care of him, train him, make him his submissive. And look where it had got him.

Peter shuddered, trying to force the memories from his mind. Any trust he'd ever had in Curtis had been shattered. And as for respect…. He picked up the list and glanced at the next rule.

Never punish a submissive out of anger and rage

Peter wanted to laugh out loud. He remembered the times when Curtis had taken a whip or a cane to him because one of his deals had fallen through and he'd wanted to vent his anger. Or the times when one of his "associates" had complained about Peter's performance. Curtis had called it "sampling the merchandise." *Merchandise.* The associate, however, hadn't been pleased and made sure Curtis knew it. And Curtis in turn had made sure Peter felt the full weight of his wrath. Peter's back was a canvas to Curtis's rage. He stretched, feeling the skin tighten across his back. His scars were a permanent reminder.

He put down his cup and read through the next rules. The words were beginning to slide into each other. *A Dom should listen to his submissive, should love unconditionally, be mindful of a submissive's feelings, a Dom should not intentionally harm his submissive….*

With a sob he threw the list onto the floor. He grabbed a pillow and curled up around it, sobbing into it, his hot tears soaking into the brushed cotton. He cried unrestrainedly, and he knew these tears had been a long time coming. He also knew why he was crying. Pain filled him, pain at the thought of everything that bastard had put him through during the last four years. But there was sorrow too. Thomas's rules showed him what might have been, had Curtis not gotten to him first. They hinted at a world where he would have been cherished, valued, listened to… loved. His tears fell as Peter lost track of time, finally releasing everything he'd kept bottled up tight inside for the last few years.

His sobs eased off eventually, and he sat up, his breath hitching. The rules lay on the floor where he'd tossed them. He picked them up and placed them on the bed. Peter inhaled deeply. He was at a crossroads. But which way to turn? Down one road lay his bitter memories. He could cling to them, keep them fresh in his mind to serve as a warning never again to trust another as he'd trusted Curtis. Another road led to the future, a road that twisted and turned, affording no glimpse of what lay ahead. But these rules filled Peter with hope. If this was what Thomas expected of every Dom he trained, then there had to be a Dom out there who would cherish him.

Peter wiped his eyes angrily. It was about time he kicked Curtis out of his head as best he could. Maybe seeing a psychologist was a good idea after all. The state Peter had been in during the last few years, he'd hate to get a glimpse of what was going on in his head. His guess was that it would be messy in there. Curtis was out of his life now. He knew he'd never be entirely free of his memories, but the least he could do was try to put them behind him. His feet were now on an altogether different path. And he knew exactly which path he would take. The one that gave him hope.

THOMAS paused at Peter's half-open door, listening. The regular sounds of his submissive's breathing brought him peace. Peter was finally asleep. Earlier, he'd left the lounge to find a book in the next room, only to be confronted with the sound of sobbing from upstairs. Those sobs tore at his heart, and he wanted with every fiber of his being to go to Peter and hold him, comfort him. There was so much pain, so much heartache. Thomas had stood there, tears pricking the corners of his eyes as he listened to his submissive sob his heart out. *I promise you, lad, I will do my best to help you heal.* Thomas clenched his fists. *And if Curtis Rogers ever crosses my path, that will be a day he will regret for the rest of his life.*

PETER wiped his eyes with the tissues Dr. Herne had thoughtfully provided when their session started. He inhaled shakily. The previous night's tears had left him wrung out, and he'd fallen asleep almost the instant his head hit the pillow. That morning he awoke refreshed, however. He'd been apprehensive about his first appointment, but Dr. Herne had quickly put him at ease. It helped to know nothing of their sessions would be revealed without his permission.

"Feeling better?" Dr. Herne sat in her chair next to his, leaning forward. Her warm hazel eyes were focused on him. She pushed her auburn hair away from her face and curled it behind her ear.

Peter nodded. "Yes, thank you. And you were right about the tissues."

She smiled. "I've been doing this for a while, Peter. I know what to expect." She sat back, glancing down at the notes in her lap. "I'm very pleased with how this session has progressed. It's given me a good idea of the work ahead of us. I'd like us to meet three times a week, initially: Mondays, Wednesdays, and Fridays. Okay?"

Peter gulped. "Three times a week? Seriously?"

Her expression was sympathetic. "Peter, you're going to have to trust me on this, all right? We have a lot of things to work through. Today was surely an indication of that, wasn't it? And we've only just got started." She focused her gaze on him. Reluctantly, he nodded. She beamed. "That's a good start. Try to work on the relaxation techniques I showed you when you find yourself getting worked up. And remember, Peter. The memories won't ever leave you entirely. They will become less painful and less frequent with time. Right now, they're fresh and raw. But you *will* come through this, I promise you." The expression in her eyes softened. "And Master Thomas will look after you."

Peter shook his head. "It sounds so weird, hearing you call him that."

Dr. Herne chuckled. "I wouldn't dare to call him anything else. That man is a legend."

Peter stared. "Legend?"

She smiled. "Master Thomas has been a Dom in this city for a great many years. He's acknowledged by those in our lifestyle as an excellent trainer of both Doms and subs. You will learn a great deal from him, and he won't steer you wrong. I've always thought it odd that he's never had a submissive of his own, though."

"Never? Why not? You mean, he just trains them and then passes them on to someone else?"

She shrugged. "Maybe he's never found the right sub. His life seems to revolve around his club, and that must take up so *much* of his time. I'm not even sure if there's ever been anyone in his life." Her cheeks flushed. "And me talking about Master Thomas like this feels *so* wrong, so I'm going to stop right there."

"Especially as he's sitting right outside that door," Peter added with a grin. Dr. Herne's eyes widened. "And he has excellent hearing." He couldn't resist teasing her. The session had been better than he'd hoped. She'd got him talking about his life with Thomas, and although this had been awkward, Peter had to admit he felt better for it. Enough to tease the good doctor, apparently.

Dr. Herne shook her head. "You are going to be trouble, aren't you?" She laughed. "I think these sessions will work out just fine, Peter." She looked at the clock on the wall. "Okay, our time is up. I'll see you on Friday this week, all right? And then next week we'll get into the pattern I mentioned." They stood, and Peter clasped her hand gratefully. There was something about the psychologist that made it impossible not to warm to her. He'd never been so relaxed meeting someone for the first time. He knew the sessions would be tough, he had no illusions about that, but he felt much better about them. At least he didn't have to explain about his lifestyle. That was *definitely* a bonus.

Thomas got to his feet as Peter entered the doctor's waiting room. Thomas shook her hand.

"Good to see you again, Laura."

It amused Peter to see his doctor blush and lower her gaze. "Master Thomas."

Thomas laughed. "No, not here. Here I'm plain Thomas Williams."

Dr. Herne's eyebrows went skyward. "You could *never* be described as plain, Sir." Her admiration of Thomas was evident. Her cheeks remained tinged with pink as she turned to Peter. "Until Friday?"

Peter dipped his head once in acknowledgment, and Thomas opened the outer door of the office for him. As they walked along the corridor leading to the thickly carpeted stairs, Thomas kept his hand on Peter's arm, as if reassuring him of his presence.

"You don't have to tell me anything of your sessions. I hope you know that." Thomas spoke earnestly. "That's between you and Dr. Herne."

"Yes, Sir." Peter was pleased to hear Thomas say it, however. As they descended the stairs, he cast a surreptitious glance in Thomas's direction, reflecting on Dr. Herne's words. Why didn't Thomas have someone in his life? There was no sign of another person's presence in his home. He glanced once more. Thomas was tall. Not as tall as Leo, but then Leo was six three. The man was wide across the chest, but his waist was trim. No middle-age paunch there. Thomas obviously took care of himself. His gray hair made him look very distinguished, but Peter had to admit, Thomas's eyes were incredible. They were a lovely clear green, not unlike the color of his own eyes, and very expressive.

"And what planet are *you* on?"

Abruptly, Peter realized Thomas was addressing him. "Sorry, Sir,"

Thomas let out a dry chuckle. "I was only asking if you had everything you needed for dinner this evening. I was going to take you home and then go to the club for a meeting. If you need anything, I can have it delivered." He held open the door that led out onto the street, and Peter took a deep breath before stepping out into the sunshine. It was a beautiful morning, bright and crisp, but that didn't matter. His heart raced. *Come on, it's not far to the car. Get a grip or Thomas will notice.* Peter's hands were suddenly clenched tight.

"I have everything I need, Sir." He struggled to keep the words even, tremor free.

"What a polite young man!" Peter looked to his right to see who had spoken. A white-haired woman, easily in her seventies, was gazing up at him with shining eyes. She was standing beside the shop next door. "It's rare these days to see a son being so polite to his father." She beamed at the pair.

Thomas gave her a courteous nod. "Ma'am." He met Peter's gaze. "Come along... son." They walked toward the car park. Peter saw Thomas biting back a grin, and to his surprise, despite his internal panic, he found himself doing the same.

"An easy mistake to make, I suppose." Thomas's voice shook slightly with amusement. Then he glanced keenly at Peter. "Though we look nothing alike."

"No, Sir." Peter should have been feeling good. He'd had a good night's sleep, and his first session with his psychologist had been relatively painless in spite of a few tears of frustration. Dinner was already planned, a simple ham and cheese omelet with green beans and sautéed potatoes. And he had the whole day to begin his weekly essay concerning the first ten rules. If he could bring himself to look at them again. He tried to ignore the fluttering in his stomach. *Not far now. You're nearly there.*

He concentrated on getting to the car park as fast as possible, but as he gazed across St. Ann's square, he glimpsed a familiar figure. Curtis was walking slowly across the square with one of his associates, his face contorted in a scowl. All of a sudden, Peter felt as if there were no air left in his lungs. He wheezed, trying to breathe. *Please, God, don't let him turn this way. Don't let him see me.* The world began to gray out, becoming fuzzier. Dimly, he could hear Thomas's voice, as though through cotton wool.

"Peter. *Peter.*" Peter couldn't drag his eyes away from Curtis until he turned the corner and was out of sight. Peter collapsed in a heap at Thomas's feet, his legs suddenly unable to bear his weight.

Strong arms slipped under his to lift him up. An arm moved around his waist, holding him tight.

Trusting Thomas

"I have you, boy." Thomas's voice, much more distinct now, spoke next to his ear. Peter sagged against him, bereft of energy. "We're nearly at the car park. Hold on."

Within a minute they arrived at the pedestrian entrance to the car park. Thomas had parked on the first level, fortunately, and he helped Peter to the car.

"Can you stand while I get the car open?"

Peter dragged several deep gulps of air into his lungs. He bobbed his head once. Thomas opened the passenger door and helped Peter into the seat, reaching across him to secure the seat belt. He came around the front of the car and climbed in, then reached into the glove box, took out a bottle of water, and opened it.

"Drink this. Lucky I always keep a bottle in the car." He handed it to Peter, who took it eagerly. "Small sips, please."

Peter drank steadily, feeling the panic recede now they were no longer in the open air. He sagged into the seat, his eyes closed, his breathing less erratic.

"Okay, boy, talk to me. What happened out there?"

Peter opened his eyes and looked at Thomas, who was regarding him with concern.

"Curtis. I saw Curtis, Sir." He couldn't keep his voice from trembling. That much he could share. There was no way he was telling Thomas why he'd been panicked even before the sighting. Thomas already thought him weak. No sense reinforcing that opinion.

Thomas paled. "Did he see you? Think, lad."

Peter shook his head. "No, Sir. He never saw me." Of that Peter was certain. Because if Curtis had seen him, he wouldn't have walked away. He would have headed straight for Peter, public place or not.

Thomas exhaled. "Thank God." Peter tilted his head, puzzled at his reaction. Thomas met his gaze. "I don't want you worrying about Curtis Rogers. Is that understood?"

Peter shuddered. Thomas tapped the steering wheel. "Let's get you home, boy."

Peter let all the tension whoosh out of him on one long, shaky breath. Home. The word sounded better all the time.

THOMAS put together a simple lunch of bread and cheese. Peter plainly wanted to protest, but the lad was obviously still shaken by his experience. One look at his trembling hands was enough for Thomas. He made Peter a cup of tea with two spoons of sugar. His mother had sworn by sweet tea for shock. He watched as Peter drank it down.

"You'll be making our dinner this evening," Thomas stated firmly. "But right now you need someone to take care of you. And that's me." He locked eyes with the lad. "No arguments."

Peter lowered his eyes to the table. "Yes, Sir." The words were almost a whisper.

They ate in silence. Thomas was itching to know more about Curtis. Why was the lad so afraid of him? Because that had been stark fear etched across his sub's face in the square, no question about it. Thomas could only hope that the boy's sessions with Laura would prove useful. Peter needed to confront his demons. One demon in particular.

Seven

Crime and Punishment

THOMAS sat alone in his office at the club in his comfy leather chair with his back to the desk. Below in the street, he could hear the people walking through the gay village, chatting animatedly. He supposed a district comprised entirely of gay clubs and bars was something of an anomaly, and Manchester was rightly proud of Canal Street and the village. It was lunchtime, but already the bars were alive with visitors. Music pumped out into the street. Thomas's mind was not on the scene below, however.

"Penny for them?"

Thomas swiveled his chair to face the door. Leo leaned back against the doorjamb with his arms folded, his gaze fixed on Thomas.

"Nah, they're not worth that much," Thomas said with a half grin. Leo crossed the room and planted himself in the worn leather chair facing Thomas, lifting those long legs and propping his feet up on the desk. He smirked, as if daring Thomas to say something. Thomas wasn't about to give him the satisfaction. It was *their* desk, after all.

"I beg to differ. I've been standing here for the last three minutes, and you were oblivious the whole time." Leo nodded toward the coffee machine behind Thomas. "Care to pour me a mug, please?"

Thomas grabbed two mugs, poured out the aromatic brew, and then reached into his mini fridge for fresh milk. He leaned across the desk and handed Leo a mug before settling back into his chair and warming his hands on the mug. He stared absently at the desktop.

"Are you going to make me beg?" Leo huffed. "Something is clearly troubling you. Out with it, man. And while we're on the subject, why are you here? I thought Saturday was your day off. Shouldn't you be home with Peter?"

Thomas took a sip of hot coffee. He regarded Leo in silence for a second or two and then squared his shoulders.

"Peter isn't settling in. He's nervous. He's skittish. He jumps out of his skin if I enter the room quietly. He appears scared all the time. He spends every night in his room. God, he'd *eat* up there if I'd let him!" He scowled. "I've been very patient with him, Leo, really I have. But he won't let me in."

Leo put down his mug and removed his feet from the desk. He folded his arms, his expression thoughtful.

"Thomas, it's been, what, a week? That's no time at all. Do you have any idea yet what he went through with Curtis?" Thomas shook his head. "Have you read the diary you asked him to keep?"

Thomas stared at him in surprise. "How do you know about that?"

"Alex saw it. Never mind that, Alex *read* a bit of it. And no, I don't know what he read, because he wouldn't tell me. I only know it was bad. Maybe *you* need to read it, though." Leo chuckled. "And as to how I know about it, hell, we both know a diary is a useful tool for a sub. I know it was useful for me." He winked.

Thomas tried to smile, aware of Leo's attempt to lighten his mood.

"I feel as though I'm failing him. I want him to relax a little, to feel at home, but it's just not happening." The overwhelming emotion that gripped him was sadness. Peter needed something that Thomas clearly couldn't provide.

"Then you need to read the diary," Leo stated firmly. "Find out more about his past. Maybe that will give you an insight into how best to proceed."

"He doesn't trust me, Leo." Thomas felt that simple statement went to the heart of the matter.

"Trust is something that only comes with time, my friend. You're going to have to be patient. Have you ever worked with a damaged submissive before?"

"No."

"Then maybe you need to talk to Laura Herne." Thomas opened his mouth to retort, but Leo interrupted him. "Not about Peter's case. About how you should be dealing with someone who's obviously been through something traumatic. Those scars on his back that you told me about. The bruising. Surely they tell you something."

Thomas sagged back into his chair. Leo had a point. Talking to Laura was an excellent idea.

"And you're not failing him, Thomas." Leo's voice softened. "You're there for him. You're caring for him. He will let you in eventually. There will come a point when he has to trust you. Just make sure you're ready when that moment arrives."

Thomas silently sent up a prayer of thanks that Leo was in his life. The man was a rock.

"Thank you," he said at last. "Seriously."

Leo waved his hand dismissively. "You've done much more for me in the past. Besides, you shouldn't be wasting time talking to me. Have you noticed the time? It's twelve thirty and your sub hasn't rung."

Thomas glanced at his watch. Peter hadn't rung, and he hadn't noticed. Something was wrong. In a panic he sat bolt upright, grabbed his phone, and speed-dialed his home. After several rings, it connected. Peter said nothing, but his breathing was audible. Thomas realized this was the first time the boy had taken a call.

"Peter, it's me." He spoke quickly, unable to miss the relieved sigh that followed his words. "You didn't ring me at eleven, boy."

Silence greeted him. Thomas waited for a sign that his sub was okay.

"Oh, Sir," Peter whispered. "Sir, I'm so sorry. I… I was writing in my room, and I lost all track of time." Relief swept through Thomas. The boy was all right. He sucked in a deep breath, suddenly aware that his heart was hammering.

"That's okay, Peter. Do you remember me saying I would worry if you didn't call?" Shame filled him. *But I wasn't worried, was I? I didn't even realize he hadn't called.*

"Yes, Sir." The words were barely audible.

"Do you also remember what I said would happen if you forgot?"

More silence. Finally the boy spoke. "You said there would be a punishment when you got home." Thomas heard the quaver in his voice.

"Yes," he said simply. "Don't think about that now. Have you eaten?"

"No, Sir."

"Then make yourself some lunch. You won't need to call me at three. I'll be home early today, in about an hour. I'll see you then. Okay, boy?"

"Yes, Sir."

"Good-bye, Peter. I'll see you in an hour." He disconnected the call and sat back into his chair, puffing out his breath. Peering into his mug, he saw he still had some coffee left. He picked it up and drained the last precious drops.

"Now that's cruel."

Thomas glanced up in surprise. "How so?"

"What do you think that boy is going to be doing for the next hour, Thomas? He's going to be sweating buckets, just thinking about what punishment you've got in store for him."

"And then maybe next time he won't forget."

Leo shrugged.

Thomas barked out a laugh. "You've done the same thing. Left a sub to stew for a while."

Leo's eyes met his. "Yeah, but not a sub like that boy. Peter already has too much going on in that mind of his, if you ask me. He doesn't need more stress."

Thomas pursed his lips. The man had a point. And Thomas had an idea.

"What are you and Alex doing tonight?"

Leo's brows lifted. "No plans beyond cuddling up on the couch. He's finishing work at five. Why?"

Thomas thought quickly. "Come to dinner. It's been nearly a week since Peter saw Alex, and I think he's been on his own too much. The only other person he's seen apart from me is Laura Herne. I think it would be good if he could spend more time with Alex." He gazed imploringly at Leo. "Please, Leo? Jonathon is Dungeon Master tonight, and Miles will be here."

Leo cracked a smile. "Just let me ring my boy." He got up and left the room. Thomas stared at the clock on the wall. Leo was right, of course. Peter would spend the intervening time panicking about his punishment. *Damn the man for being right. I need to talk to Laura Herne.* This whole situation was like walking in a minefield. Every step needed to be considered, every action thought through. And if Laura could help him, so much the better. But it would be worth it if Peter came through it all a healed young man, ready to serve a Dom and enjoy his life as a submissive.

Leo poked his head around the door. "Alex said yes. Well, to be more accurate, he said, 'Yay! No cooking for me tonight!' It was his turn to cook. I hope dinner will be suitably delicious to make up for me missing out on Alex's garlic chicken."

Thomas came to a swift decision. "I'll make sure of it. In fact, I'm leaving now. If we're going to have guests, I need to give Peter enough notice." And besides, he wanted to get home as fast as possible. Leo was right. Peter would probably be in a mindless panic by now.

He grabbed his leather jacket from the hanger behind the office door. "I'll see you both at the house at six thirty, eating at seven, okay?"

Leo gave him an impatient look. "Yes, fine, now go and see your boy."

Not my boy, Thomas thought ruefully. He pushed the thought aside. He had a punishment to mete out. One he was already regretting.

THE first thing that struck him as he came through the front door was the eerie silence. There were no sounds in the house apart from the quiet ticking of the grandfather clock in the hallway.

"Peter?" No answer. Thomas glanced briefly into the lounge and the kitchen. There was no sign of the boy. He raced up the stairs, where he pushed open doors and peered around them. No Peter.

Thomas was starting to panic. Where the hell was the boy? He flew down the stairs, his heart thumping. *"Peter!"* He stood in the hallway, running his fingers through his hair. Had he left? Thomas thought not. On the two occasions Peter left the house for his appointments, there had been no mistaking the fear in his eyes, the tremors that coursed through his body, the ashen face. Friday's session was even worse, because after Tuesday's experience, Peter clearly expected to see Curtis appear around every corner.

A slight sound echoed in the hall. Thomas stilled immediately, straining to hear. There it was again, the faintest whimper coming from the hall cupboard. Cautiously, Thomas grasped its round brass handle and pulled the door open. He peered into the darkness. To his dismay, he found Peter lying in a tight ball on the floor amid the boots, shoe polish, and boxes, with his arms wrapped tightly around his knees and his eyes locked on Thomas. The fear in those eyes....

Thomas reached toward him, only to have Peter flinch. A low cry escaped him.

"Please, Sir, please don't hurt me. I'm sorry, Sir, I won't forget again, I promise."

Thomas's heart lurched in his chest. So much fear in every syllable. He crouched down slowly, making sure he stayed in Peter's line of sight. He kept his voice soft, his movements measured.

"Peter, I need you to come out of there, okay? I'm not going to hurt you. Please, boy. You've got to trust me." He held out his hand, moving as close to the boy as he dared, so as not to spook him. There was a long silence. Peter regarded him fearfully. "*Please*, Peter." Thomas could only wait.

A shaking hand finally edged its way toward him, and Thomas held his breath. He turned his hand palm up and let Peter's hand slip into his. *Thank God*. Thomas wrapped his fingers gently around the trembling hand. Peter was cold.

"Come on, boy, it's freezing in there. Let's get you into the lounge and get a fire started." Talking could wait until the lad was warm again. "Come on, Peter." To his relief, Peter sat up, shivering. Keeping tight hold of the boy's hand, Thomas helped him to his feet, difficult as that was in the confined space. Peter stepped into the hallway, his face pale, his body shaking. Fear still lurked behind those green eyes, which never left Thomas. Peter's wary expression tugged at Thomas's heart.

"Good boy." Thomas kept his words deliberately quiet. He didn't want to startle the lad. "That's it." He ushered the trembling young man into the lounge, where he spied a throw over the back of the sofa. He grabbed it and wrapped it around Peter. The expression on Peter's face made it clear he hadn't expected this sort of treatment. Thomas guided him to sit in one of the two armchairs and then set about lighting the fire as swiftly as he could, twisting paper and laying kindling, piling on small logs until at last a bright fire burned behind the grate. Thomas glanced across at Peter. The lad was staring into the flames. The light was reflected in those expressive eyes. He hadn't relaxed into the chair, however. The rigidity of the boy's spine told Thomas much.

"I'm going into the kitchen to make us both a cup of tea. Okay, boy?"

Trusting Thomas

Thomas could have sighed with relief when Peter gave a slow nod of assent. Hurriedly, he dashed into the kitchen and prepared two cups of tea, choosing green tea with vanilla for Peter. When he returned to the lounge, Peter had curled up in the chair with his feet tucked under him and the throw snuggled around him. *Better.* Thomas handed him the cup and then sat in the chair facing him. He didn't speak. It was more important that Peter become calmer. The boy sipped his tea, his eyes rounding as he tasted it. He glanced across at Thomas with a grateful look. Thomas merely dipped his chin once and concentrated on drinking his tea. The slow ticking of the clock was a comforting sound, along with the crackle of the flames. The logs spat occasionally.

Peter stretched down and placed his cup on the floor. He sat back, his eyes still fixed on the fire.

"Better?" Thomas finally risked speaking.

Peter nodded. "Yes, Sir." He hesitated, clearly wanting to say more. The trembling in his body had eased, but Thomas knew it wouldn't take much to spook the lad.

"What is it, boy?"

Peter straightened in his chair. "Sir, I need to know. What is my punishment?" Brave words, but Thomas noted the trembling lower lip, the nervous swallowing. The boy still reeked of fear.

"Very well." Thomas stood, went into the next room, and grabbed a writing pad and pen from the desk. He returned to the lounge and handed the pad and pen to Peter.

"Write this down, please."

Looking utterly bewildered, Peter opened the pad and waited with pen poised above the paper.

"I will not forget to ring Sir at the appointed times," Thomas dictated. Peter wrote down the line and then looked up expectantly. "That's it, lad. Now write that line out until you've filled both sides of one sheet of paper." Peter bit his lip and blinked rapidly, clearly confused. "Get it done, lad. We'll talk once you've completed that particular task."

Peter's expression cleared. Thomas knew the boy was now thinking there was more to come. Which was exactly what Thomas wanted him to think. The two men sat in silence, Thomas contemplating the flames, Peter writing neatly, carefully on the pad balanced on his covered knees. Time was marked by the slow ticking of the clock. And as Peter wrote, he relaxed back into the chair.

At last Peter lowered his pen. "Finished, Sir." He held out the pad.

Thomas stood up and took it from him, then tore the sheet free of the pad. He regarded it solemnly and then ripped it in half. Peter's shocked gasp rang out loudly in the quiet room. Thomas tore through both halves. Again. Again. When the sheet was rent into small pieces, Thomas tossed them onto the fire. He met Peter's wide-eyed look of astonishment.

"Punishment over."

Peter's mouth dropped open. He sucked in a quick breath. "That's it?"

Thomas nodded, his gaze never moving from Peter's face. "Now," he began briskly, as though nothing had happened, "I'm sorry to tell you tonight's dinner plans need to change. We're having guests, Leo and Alex. That's why I came home early, to see if I needed to go shopping." He looked at Peter expectantly. "What had you planned on cooking?"

Peter stared at him. Thomas waited patiently for his boy's brain to catch up. Several seconds passed. At last Peter cleared his throat.

"I was going to make lasagna and garlic bread, Sir. With fresh fruit and yogurt after."

Thomas's stomach chose that moment to growl, a reminder that he'd had no lunch. Come to think of it, had Peter?

"Did you eat lunch like I told you?"

A guilty expression stole over Peter's face. "No, Sir. I... I was too nervous to eat."

Thomas had suspected as much. "Right, then it's time we both ate. Come on, lad. Let's raid the fridge." He headed for the kitchen, listening to make sure Peter was following. Right now Thomas's chest felt tight. In his head he was kicking himself. He'd never considered how Peter would react to being punished, and to find the boy in so much fear of what he'd do filled Thomas with self-loathing. He was trying to keep things as light as possible, and he could only pray Peter got back quickly onto an even keel.

Thomas brought together bread, butter, sliced chicken, and salad vegetables on the table, and began to assemble a couple of substantial sandwiches. He became aware of Peter hovering in the doorway. The boy had lost his pallor and seemed much calmer. Thomas put a sandwich on a side plate and placed it in front of a chair.

"Sit down, lad. Get that eaten."

Peter scraped back the chair, and after regarding the plate in silence for a second or two, he sat and eagerly tucked into the sandwich, rolling his eyes back.

"Good?" Peter simply nodded. Thomas couldn't help but smile as the boy demolished the food, seemingly enjoying every bite. It vanished in no time. Thomas put away the ingredients and sat to eat his sandwich, while Peter took the board and utensils to the sink to clean them. By the time everything had been wiped and put away, Thomas had finished. Peter sat watching him, his expression neutral. Thomas would take *neutral* over *scared to death* any day.

He gave a satisfied sigh. "Okay, about dinner. Do you have enough ingredients to make lasagna for four people instead of two?"

"Yes, Sir." Peter glanced at him shyly. "I intended to make double the amount and freeze the rest for another night. And I already have the bread in the freezer." The boy appeared to be over his shock, but Thomas wasn't entirely convinced. Peter needed to relax. He racked his brains.

And then it came to him. "Excellent! Well, if you have everything in hand, it would be a shame to waste the fire. I was going to sit and read, maybe put some music on." He gave the boy a keen look. "Would you like to curl up on the sofa under the throw? Just for a while, until it's time to start preparations for dinner." He watched the boy's face, ready to take back the suggestion if he showed the slightest discomfort.

To his surprise, Peter accepted it calmly. "Yes, Sir, I... I would like that."

Something had shifted. What, exactly, Thomas had no idea, but there had clearly been a change in Peter's head. Okay, so the boy wasn't totally relaxed, but he looked a thousand times better than how he'd appeared in that damned cupboard. Thomas led the way back into the lounge and picked up the throw. Peter stretched out on the sofa and laid his head on a cushion, and Thomas placed the throw over him. He went to the record deck and peered at the shelves above, which contained his LPs. Leo often made fun of the fact that Thomas insisted on keeping them rather than replacing them with CDs. They'd had many a heated debate over the merits of LPs versus CDs, neither man budging an inch.

Thomas selected some piano music, figuring the situation called for something lighter than the cantata he'd played earlier in the week. Soon gentle melodies filled the room. Thomas picked up his book from the table below the window and then sat in his chair, stretching his legs out toward the fire. Surreptitiously, he gave a quick look in Peter's direction. The boy's eyes were closed, his face relaxed. Smiling to himself, Thomas began to read.

ALEX pushed away his plate with a groan.

"I couldn't eat another thing!" He patted his belly appreciatively. "That was absolutely delicious, Peter. And that garlic bread was yummy!"

"I'm going to have to second that," Leo added, mopping up the last of the sauce with a piece of garlic bread before popping it into his mouth with a flourish.

Peter cast shy looks around the table. It was very nice to have his efforts appreciated. Thomas was rather quiet throughout the meal, and Peter was concerned at first that he'd done something to annoy him. Then he dismissed it. When Thomas had awoken him at four with another cup of tea, the man showed no sign of being annoyed with Peter. In fact, it was as if the whole thing hadn't occurred.

Peter was at a loss to explain the afternoon's events. Thomas's punishment had blown him away. Peter had only experienced Curtis's form of punishment, and that man had only one weapon in his arsenal—pain. In spite of Thomas's previous treatment of him, Peter had assumed all Doms meted out the same punishments. It seemed he would need to rethink his ideas. Thomas was proving to be nothing like Curtis.

"A wonderful meal, lad." Thomas finished his dinner with a contented sigh. He caught Peter's eye. "You did well, boy." He glanced at Leo. "I haven't eaten so well in years. This week has been fantastic. It's a pity you weren't able to try Peter's bread." He winked at Alex. "Once it was baked, that is."

Alex's cheeks reddened. "Yes, Sir."

Thomas addressed Peter. "I really don't have room for fruit and yogurt, but I would love a cup of coffee, if you would oblige."

"Yes, Sir. I'll put the machine on and then sort out the dishes."

"Can I help?" Alex gave Peter a wink. "Let the old guys sit and let their dinner settle?" Peter gasped, waiting for a reaction from Leo, but the Dom merely grinned, his eyes sparkling. Peter hadn't spoken with Leo since he'd arrived, beyond a brief greeting. He didn't know him, and despite Alex's account of how Leo was with the sub, he couldn't entirely relax around him. The man was a *Dom*, for goodness' sake.

When Leo and Thomas exited the kitchen, Alex beamed.

"Well, looks like I'm in for a spanking tonight when I get home."

Peter was horrified. "Leo's going to spank you?"

"Only if I'm really, *really* lucky." He gave Peter another wink. "Of course, first comes the spanking. I'll be coming after, hopefully."

Peter's face was suddenly red hot. Alex was talking so shamelessly about his sex life.

"Are you always like this?" he asked.

Alex burst into a peal of laughter. "Have I shocked you?" Peter tried to shake his head. Alex placed a hand on his arm. "It's Leo's fault. The man brings it out in me, I swear. I never used to be like this. I was always quiet and introverted."

Peter gazed at the bright-eyed young man before him. He couldn't imagine Alex being introverted. And then something struck him.

"Wait a minute. You *like* being spanked?"

Alex's eyes glazed over. "Oh, man, when Leo spanks me, it's like there's a direct connection to my dick." Peter could feel his cheeks flaming. "Trust me, when I'm lying across his knee, my cock like a rock between his thighs, and that hand lands on me again and again…." He shuddered. "I don't like being spanked, I *love* it." He winked. "The problem is, Leo got wise to that pretty swiftly. He doesn't use it as a punishment anymore. If I want a spanking, I have to push him a little. Like that comment tonight about the old guys? He knew *exactly* what I was doing."

Now Peter understood the sparkle in Leo's eyes. But there was something he wanted to know.

"So how does Leo punish you?"

Alex looked thoughtful. "To be honest, I haven't had that many punishments. When Leo first mentioned spanking, the first thought in my head was how quickly I could get him to spank me, 'cause I *really* wanted to experience it. Well, you can see how *that* worked out." He snickered. "He once made me go all night without coming. And my God, that was torture! He was going all out to turn me on—prostate massage, jerking me off, even fucking me—and I wasn't allowed to come." A shiver ran through him. "When I went to bed that night, God, I ached."

"How was Leo the next morning?" Peter couldn't begin to imagine the willpower Alex must have needed to stave off his orgasm.

Alex chuckled. "The next morning? Leo woke me with a blow job." His eyes met Peter's. "That's the thing. Once you've done the punishment, it's forgotten. And the fact that you took their punishment well? Yeah, Doms really like that." He tilted his head. "Why the questions? Has Thomas punished you?"

Peter was gratified to see a look of concern in those pale-blue eyes. Quickly, he related what had happened that morning, although it was a cut-down version. There was no way he was going to tell Alex why he'd been so afraid. Alex didn't need to know about his life with Curtis. Peter would be happy if no one ever knew—except for Dr. Herne and Thomas. If Thomas ever decided to read his diary, of course.

Alex listened and then smiled. "I'm still only getting to know Thomas, but I have to say, I really rate the man." A guilty look stole over his face. "Like right now? I feel I should call him *Master* Thomas, and he isn't even in the room."

Thomas's voice rang out from the lounge "I'd hate to cross a desert with you two! Coffee? Please?" They could hear Leo chuckling.

"Ooops." Alex bit his lower lip, his cheeks tinged with pink. "We'd better get that coffee on, or Leo might decide to take a paddle to my ass tonight, instead of his hand." He went to the coffee machine. Peter stopped him with an outstretched hand on his arm.

"Thanks for this chat, Alex."

Alex beamed. "No problem whatsoever. Actually, I've been thinking. Would you like to make this a regular thing? You and me getting together? 'Cause I'd really like that."

"I'd love that." Despite his embarrassment, he really enjoyed the frank chat with the other sub. It seemed to Peter that every time they talked, he learned something new. And it would be good to get to know Alex better.

Alex regarded him earnestly. "I think you and I could become good friends. What do you say? Could you use a good friend right now?"

Peter grasped Alex's hand tightly. "More than you could imagine."

K.C. Wells

Eight

Week Two—Developments

"WHAT'S this about you clocking off early today? Where do you think *you're* going?"

Thomas didn't need to look up from his notes to know Leo was joking, despite the stern tone he tried to affect.

"Haircut." Silence greeted his words. He glanced up to find Leo regarding his hair critically. He waited, sure there was more to come.

"You don't need a haircut," Leo said at last.

Thomas let out a patient sigh. "Not me—Peter. I wanted to take him last week, but I never got around to it." He looked up at the clock on the wall. "And if you don't let me finish, I'll be late. I want to send off these acceptance letters before I go." More new members. Business was looking good.

"Ah, you've reminded me. We received three applications via e-mail this morning. Have you had a chance to look at them?" Thomas shook his head. "Well, you might want *me* to go through the vetting for one of them."

Now he had Thomas's attention. "Er, since when do you vet applicants? That's *my* province, lad."

Leo grinned. "When one of the applicants cites one Thomas Williams as his referee, that's when." Thomas tilted his head. "The application is from Steven Drummond. Isn't he that mate of yours who liberated Peter?"

Aha. Steven had finally had enough of St. Andrew's. "Ah, I see. Yes, Steven and I go way back. He used to teach with me at the university. Yeah, you'd better do that one. Who are the other two applicants?"

"Steven's submissive, David Foster, and another Dom, Alan Marchant."

Thomas recalled Steven saying he might bring someone else along. "Fine. I can do the other two. Unless you want to do all three? Hmmm?" Leo hated paperwork with a passion.

Leo growled. "Don't push it, old man. I'm letting you have the afternoon off, after all."

Thomas snorted. "*Letting* me? Watch out that I don't take a paddle to your rump, lad." His wide smile belied his words. He loved this playful banter, which occurred on an almost daily basis.

"Thomas, have you got a minute?"

Ben Winters, the barman, stood poised at the doorway. His brow was wrinkled.

Thomas waved him in. "Come on in, Ben. You've just saved Leo from getting his ass spanked." Both Ben and Leo snorted. Thomas liked Ben. He was a good man, solid and dependable. Thomas was training him to be a Dom, although his training had been put on the back burner recently, since Peter's arrival.

Ben approached the desk, his manner apprehensive. Thomas had never seen the man look flustered. "What's up?"

"There's a couple of guys out here at the bar, asking questions. They're wearing green wristbands." That told Thomas the men were probably checking out the place, not here to play.

"Questions? What kind of questions?" Leo was regarding Ben intently.

Ben rubbed his bearded chin. "That's what's odd. They started out asking if we usually got lots of new members. Then one of them started asking if we'd recently taken on a new submissive. Even had a description of the sub. I have to say, it doesn't sound like any of ours."

"How did he describe the sub?" Thomas suddenly had a sinking feeling. Ben swiftly relayed the description, and Thomas's gut clenched. He'd just described Peter. A thought occurred to him. "Are they still here?"

Ben nodded. "I got Elliott to take over for me, said I was going to change a barrel. They were sitting at the bar." His warm brown eyes were anxious. "Thomas, this guy gave me a bad feeling."

"Are the cameras on in the bar?" Another nod from Ben. Thomas clicked away on his keyboard, bringing up the bar on his monitor. "These two?" Ben came around the desk and glanced keenly at the screen. "Yeah, that's them." Two men in smart dress were drinking, looking around the club incessantly. Ben pointed to the man on the left. "He was the one asking all the questions."

Thomas picked up his phone and clicked on the camera icon. After zooming in on the two men, he took a photo and then attached it to an e-mail. He sent it and dialed Steven's number.

"Hi there." Steven sounded delighted to hear from him. "I take it you got our applications. You're not going to give me a rough ride, are you?" Thomas could hear him chuckling.

"Steven, I've not got time to chat right now. This is really important. I just sent you an e-mail. I took a photo in the club bar just now. Can you identify either of the two men in the attachment?"

Steven reacted quickly. "Opening it now." His tone was brisk. Thomas heard him suck in a breath. "Oh shit, that man on the left... that's Curtis Rogers."

Thomas had suspected as much. All of a sudden there was a rolling sensation in the pit of his stomach.

Steven was still speaking. "I was going to ring you. Apparently, he's been going around a few clubs asking questions, so my sources tell me. I've had some reliable friends keeping an eye on him since... you know. He's looking for Peter, isn't he?"

"He just gave my barman a perfect description." Thomas groaned. "Hang on a minute, Steven, would you?" He turned to Ben. "Get back to the bar. Don't give him any reason to be suspicious." Ben dipped his chin and headed for the door. "And, Ben? Act as normal as you can around this guy, all right?" Ben inhaled deeply and then nodded. "Good man. Let me know when they've gone, and if they ask any more questions." Ben exited the office.

Thomas returned to his call. "What happened after the New Year's Eve party? Did he suspect you had anything to do with it? Seeing as you'd been round there?"

"If he did, he hasn't said anything. There's been an odd mood at the club this week, though. Quite a few people looked really agitated. Something's going on, and I was starting to get a bad feeling. I guess that's what made up my mind to apply to Collars & Cuffs."

"Steven, do me a favor. Keep away from Curtis, and anyone else he associates with, okay? That man is bad news."

"Sure thing." There was a second or two of silence. "How is Peter?"

Bless the man's heart. "Peter has a long way to go. But we'll get him there. *I'll* get him there."

Steven's voice positively bubbled with gratitude. "Thank you, Thomas. I'm so glad he has you looking out for him. I look forward to hearing from you soon."

"Count on it." After a brief good-bye, Thomas finished the call. He stared at the monitor, focusing on Curtis. The man was finishing his drink with a last look around. He nodded to his companion, and the two men got up from their seats with a brief acknowledgment to Ben. Thomas switched views to the reception cameras and watched as the two men handed over their wristbands and left the building, both frowning. He pushed out a long breath.

"I take it they've gone?" Leo perched on the edge of the desk. Thomas nodded absently. "And that was Curtis Rogers?"

"Apparently." *What have I got myself mixed up in here?* Thomas didn't like this. Not one bit. He glanced at his watch. "Hell, time I wasn't here." He got up and went to collect his jacket from its hanger.

"Thomas, do *me* a favor, please? Keep an eye out today when you're with Peter getting his haircut. Stay safe, old man." Leo may have spoken gruffly, but there was no denying the love underlying his words. Thomas acknowledged him with a warm look.

"I'll do my best, lad."

PETER looked at the front of the salon across the road from where Thomas had parked his Nissan Primera. The street wasn't busy, thank goodness.

"Have you been here before, Sir?" Peter brushed the hair out of his eyes. It had been this habitual action that had first alerted Thomas to the need for this appointment. It was clear Peter wasn't going to ask him. When Thomas casually mentioned the hair appointment after breakfast that morning, Peter's face glowed warmly. He seemed touched that Thomas had noticed. Thomas had spoken as though it wasn't a big deal, but Peter had reacted as though Thomas had done something very special. *God, has no one ever cared for this lad?* Peter's initial pleasure quickly morphed into another much stronger emotion. It was most noticeable when it came time to leave the house. The boy had trembled. Thomas was dying to know what lay at the heart of his behavior. Hopefully one day all would become clear.

"Me personally? No, lad. I usually go to a nice, old-fashioned barber's around the corner, where the guy who cuts my hair only cuts to one style and has one speed—*really* slow." Thomas could have sworn he heard the faintest suspicion of a chuckle from Peter. "I'm not kidding. It can take him nearly half an hour to trim my hair, and let's face it, boy, there's not *that* much to cut, is there?" Although his hair was thick and full on top, Thomas kept the sides and back short. It made life a lot simpler, and if the truth be told, he liked his regular visits to Chris's barber chair. The man was entertaining, and Thomas had been going there for longer than he cared to remember.

"I asked around the club, and a couple of the subs recommended this place. They said specifically to ask for Darren, so come on, lad, let's get in there. *Darren* is waiting for you." He emphasized the name with a waggle of his eyebrows. This time the chuckle was definitely there. Thomas felt an acute sense of relief. Maybe Peter was finally beginning to relax in his presence. God, he hoped so.

They got out of the car, Thomas locked it, and they crossed the road. Thomas's eyes flicked constantly from left to right, on the lookout for anyone who resembled the two men from that morning. Peter looked distinctly nervous. Thomas pushed open the door, holding his arm protectively around Peter's shoulders as he guided him through the warm salon. The interior was definitely more fashionable than his humble barber's shop. Large posters showing male models with very modern hairstyles adorned the walls. There were rows of mirrors, gleaming washbasins in the corner, and a buzz of chatter. Virtually every seat was occupied. It certainly appeared to be a very popular establishment.

"Do you have an appointment?"

Trusting Thomas

The young man behind the desk addressed Thomas, although he was regarding Peter's hair with a look of mild surprise.

"Appointment with Darren at three. Booking in the name of Williams." Thomas tried hard not to take an instant dislike to the young man, but his disdainful expression was making that very difficult.

Apparently, he wasn't the only one. A tall, slim man appeared, his blond hair flicked across his brow. He fixed cool blue eyes on the receptionist, who visibly shrank under the weight of his intense gaze. Thomas was impressed. To gain such a reaction from a mere stare.... The blond stranger turned to Thomas and Peter, extending a slim hand.

"I'm Darren. I take it your young friend here is my three o'clock?" His voice was firm, masculine. He appraised Peter's hair with a critical eye and then smiled. It transformed his face. "I know exactly what I'd like to do with his hair, sir." Darren may have been discussing Peter's hair, but he addressed his words to Thomas. *Interesting.*

Peter looked like a rabbit caught in the headlights of an oncoming car. He blinked and swallowed profusely. Darren's manner changed instantly.

"Come and sit down, and I'll talk you through what I'd like to do." He spoke quietly but with authority. Peter couldn't tear his eyes away, nodding as Darren led him toward the one remaining empty chair. Thomas followed.

"Your jacket?" Darren waited while Peter slipped the jacket off and handed it over. Darren simply held it out and cast a quick glance in the receptionist's direction. "Paul? Hang up this gentleman's jacket, please." Thomas bit back a smile. The receptionist couldn't move fast enough, sliding from his chair and across the floor to grab the jacket before whisking it to the coat rack behind his desk. Thomas caught a glimpse of an amused twinkle in Darren's blue eyes. For a second the two men regarded each other. Yeah, Thomas *definitely* liked Darren.

Darren took a black, silky robe from a hook beside the mirror and flicked it expertly around Peter, then tied it at his nape. He glanced at Thomas in the mirror and then went to the back of the salon where a single chair stood near the door. He picked it up easily, brought it forth, placed it next to the wall, and then indicated with an outstretched hand that it was for Thomas. Thomas was grateful. From that vantage point he would be able to see not only the boy and Darren, but also the street outside. The morning's event had left him decidedly nervous, and Thomas was not about to relax entirely.

Darren planted himself behind Peter, regarding him in the mirror with pursed lips while running his long, slim fingers restlessly through the boy's hair, pulling it this way and that. Peter's gaze darted between Darren in the mirror and Thomas. This was clearly a new experience for him.

Thomas appraised Darren. The man was roughly five eleven, slim, and obviously someone who took care of himself. He was lean and toned. Thomas estimated him to be in his late twenties, possibly early thirties. Confidence radiated off him.

"I'm thinking short layers, sweeping toward the face at the sides, a feathered fringe just off the eyes, framing the face softly. But yes, keeping the hair out of his eyes—which are incredible, by the way. It would be a shame to have anything hide them." All the time, Darren directed his words to Thomas. Peter listened intently, flicking his gaze intermittently between Darren and Thomas.

Darren stood to one side. "All right, then. Let's get you over to the wash station and shampooed." Peter stood, and Darren led him to the corner.

At the shampoo station he settled him into a chair with his neck resting in the hollow of the basin. Thomas watched Peter's eyes close as Darren massaged shampoo into his hair. His fingers moved dexterously, almost sensually. Thomas could see the boy relaxing into the chair, letting his hands go limp in his lap. It gave Thomas an idea. Maybe a head massage would make an appropriate reward in the future. It wasn't something he'd ever attempted before, but a little research on the Internet might prove useful. There was no disguising Peter's reaction. The boy was totally at ease under Darren's expert handling.

With a start, Thomas realized he'd zoned out for a second. Darren gently rubbed Peter's head with a dark towel and then guided him back to his cutting chair.

Thomas was fascinated by the speed with which Darren snipped and cut. His hands were constantly moving. Peter was focused on the mirror, his gaze never leaving Darren as the man concentrated all his attention on his work. After drying Peter's hair, Darren made a final few critical snips here and there. He turned to Thomas.

"Well, what do you think?"

Trusting Thomas

Thomas couldn't believe the transformation. Peter's hair looked silky soft, sweeping onto his cheeks and forehead in short layers. The new haircut served to accentuate the changes in Peter that Thomas was seeing now for the first time. Peter looked nothing like the ashen-faced young man who arrived at his home that night. His face was less drawn, his eyes brighter. There was color in his cheeks and a healthy bloom to him that hadn't been there before. Had Thomas never really *looked* at the boy? Peter clearly loved the new look. He seemed unable to drag his gaze away from his reflection.

"You've done a fantastic job," Thomas murmured quietly. "Hasn't he, lad?" Peter's shy nod of agreement was a pleasure to behold.

Darren's eyes sparkled. "Praise from you, sir, is praise indeed." Thomas arched his brows, and Darren winked. "Your reputation precedes you, *Master* Thomas." His voice was hushed. "I would have known you anywhere. Some of my customers have been known to get very talkative in my chair, especially when their *masters* are not around."

Thomas's brow wrinkled. "Hmmm, not entirely sure I approve of that. I will be speaking with your customers when I next see them. But I'm not going to embarrass you by asking you to repeat what they said."

Darren was quick to jump in. "Nothing derogatory, I assure you. In fact, they spoke of you in glowing terms. And their… lifestyle certainly sounds fascinating."

That made up Thomas's mind. He reached into his wallet and pulled out a business card. He held it out to Darren, who took it and perused it with interest.

"If you ever decide to look at this lifestyle from *my* side of the fence, I would be pleased to show you around the club. I think you would find it educational." Instinct told him the man had all the makings of a fine Dom. Whether he would be interested in pursuing such a path would be up to Darren.

Darren regarded him thoughtfully. "You know, I may take you up on that offer." He looked over his shoulder. "Paul? The gentleman's jacket, please?" He frowned as he watched the receptionist's movements. "Honestly," he muttered under his breath, "sometimes I think that boy needs a damn good spanking."

Thomas snorted. "My thoughts precisely." His eyes met Darren's, and he winked. "My palm was itching."

Darren laughed, a rich, natural sound that rolled out of him. He shook Thomas's hand and then helped Peter into his jacket. Peter had been quietly watching the interplay between them.

Thomas went to the desk and paid the receptionist, who was trying not to look him in the eye. Darren walked them to the door.

"It's been a pleasure to meet you," he said simply, addressing Thomas, and then regarded Peter with a kindly expression. He caught Thomas's eye and lowered his voice. "And I will definitely be seeing you again."

"I look forward to it," Thomas said earnestly. He had a good feeling about Darren. He placed his hand on Peter's arm. "Come on, lad. Let's go home."

THOMAS paused outside Peter's bedroom door, listening to the steady sound of the boy's breathing. Peter was fast asleep. Silently pushing open the door, he entered the room and then walked to the bed. The lad lay on his side, breathing easily. Thomas wondered how far off the nightmares were. Peter didn't generally sleep well. Thomas had heard him tossing and turning on several occasions, and a couple of times he heard him muttering in his sleep, sounds that didn't speak of happy dreams. *What will it take, lad, to give you a peaceful night's sleep?* He glanced toward the open desk and could just make out the shape of Peter's notebook. He hadn't read Peter's first essay on his rules. Making as little sound as possible, he picked up the notebook and slipped from the room, gently pulling the door to behind him.

The fire was still burning well. He settled back into his armchair, then cast a longing look in the direction of his brandy decanter. It had been a while. His mind made up, Thomas got up and poured himself a small glass. He returned to his chair and leaned back. He sipped the brandy, enjoying the warmth it created inside him. After a few minutes spent contemplating the flames, he reached down and picked up the notebook. He opened it at the front, pausing as he looked at the neat handwriting. *Do I want to read this part?* Thomas was definitely of two minds. Writing down their thoughts often brought some release to submissives and helped them to focus, but more often than not, he didn't read what they wrote. Part of him wanted to focus on where Peter was going, not the journey that had brought him to Thomas's door. He couldn't deny, however, he was curious to know what the boy had gone through.

After several minutes of consideration, he decided to start with the essay. The diary would still be there at a later date, if he ever decided it would be a useful thing to read. A more profitable use of his time might be to talk with Laura Herne, and he resolved to call her in the morning from the club.

He flicked over several pages, found the essay, and began to read. One paragraph caught his eye.

> *The one thing that struck me most about these ten rules was that a submissive is someone to be listened to, someone whose feelings matter. I doubt if Curtis ever gave a single second's thought to my feelings. Was I his submissive or his slave? I'd read about the relationship between master and slave long before I met him, but surely there are rules for how a Dom treats a slave too. All I know is, these rules have made me doubt whether Curtis ever had any training at all. At the same time, however, they give me hope. Okay, I accept that I will be punished at times. I'm human, therefore fallible, and I'll make mistakes—but maybe from now on, I'll know what I'm being punished for. I can't see you, Sir, lashing out at me because you had a bad day. Taking a whip to my back because something went wrong at work. I can't see you ever intentionally harming me, Sir, even though I've only known you a relatively short time. And I really liked rule nine. Be mindful of the submissive's feelings. I've already seen this rule in action, Sir, every day. You care about how I feel.*

> *So as I wrote before, these rules bring me hope. I'm starting to realize that if I eventually find a Dom who lives up to just the first ten of your rules, I'll be looking at a very different life. I can't wait to read the rest, to find out what else lies in store for me.*

Thomas closed the notebook and let his gaze be drawn to the dancing flames. There was a positive note to the essay that made him think Peter had gotten something worthwhile out of his reading. Part of him still itched to read the first pages, but he resisted. He didn't want what he might read there to color how he saw Peter. He would rather discover the boy for himself.

Nine

Surprises

"GOOD morning, Sir."

Peter kept his voice low as he placed a cup of tea beside Thomas's bed, along with the morning paper. It had taken a few days to get used to this new responsibility, but he liked waking Thomas like this. He'd had to get used to getting up earlier, but he didn't mind that. It was peaceful to stand in the kitchen while he prepared the tea. The only sounds he could hear were the clock and the birds singing out in the garden. He had already set out Thomas's bowl of muesli on the kitchen table, and the bread was ready for the toaster.

He waited until Thomas stirred before drawing back the bedroom's heavy curtains. At this time of the morning the sun hadn't risen yet, but the sky was paler than when Peter had first opened his eyes. Waking up hadn't been difficult this morning. His dreams had seen to that. Thomas was a lump under the duvet, with only the top of his head visible.

"Morning, boy." Thomas pushed down the duvet and emerged yawning, his eyes still looking sleepy. But Peter liked it that those eyes sought him right away. Thomas smiled as he reached for his tea. The appreciative noises he made were gratifying. "You make a great cup of tea, lad. Perfect to wake up to."

Peter bowed his head, aware that Thomas was more alert all of a sudden, focusing on him with a keen glance.

K.C. Wells

"What's wrong, boy?"

Peter held his breath. Damn it, the man missed nothing.

"You had a bad night, didn't you?"

Peter clamped his lips shut. He had no intentions of sharing last night's dream with Thomas. It was enough that he'd awoken in a cold sweat, shivering as the vestiges of the nightmare finally ebbed away. He'd been with Thomas for nearly four weeks now, and he was still praying for a night of unblemished sleep. Most mornings, he awoke not feeling completely rested, aware that his sleep had been disturbed, but some nights were worse than others. Some nights he couldn't shake the dreams, no matter how hard he tried.

Thomas patted the bed. "Sit down, boy. I want to talk to you." He was wide-awake.

Surprised, Peter sat and regarded Thomas in silence, wondering what was coming. Thomas was watching him, a thoughtful expression on his face. Peter knew his eyes had dark half circles under them. He'd seen them in the mirror that morning.

Finally, Thomas spoke. "Peter, what you've started here is a process of recovery. Unfortunately, recovery doesn't happen overnight. It's a process that builds upon itself. Yes, you're making steps, and this is good, but you also have to realize that for every two steps forward, there might be one step back. For every two good days, there may be a night of nightmares waiting for you around the corner. I know it's disheartening, but you have to focus on the forward movement." Thomas held out his hand, palm up, and Peter took it. "You wrote recently about hope. Well, you have to cling to that hope. You have to believe that all things are possible, even a night of unbroken sleep, because it *will* come, boy, I promise you."

In that moment, with Thomas's hand clasped warmly around his, Peter believed him.

"One day you will see things differently. One day you'll awaken to sunshine, not just in your room but in your heart, and you'll be able to step out of the shadows, to become the person you were meant to be."

Oh, Peter loved the sound of that. He *longed* for that.

"So celebrate your successes, lad, and concentrate on the steps forward, but accept that there will be steps back too. They are *not your fault*." Peter could hear the emphasis. Thomas's face suddenly creased into a smile. "And

110

now you need to get out of here so I can get my shower and then my breakfast. Besides, we have to discuss your new responsibility." His eyes twinkled.

Peter got up, and Thomas handed him the empty cup. He left the room, dwelling on what Thomas was going to say. He loved doing the cooking. It gave him such a sense of satisfaction to see Thomas appreciate his efforts. Okay, so there had been the odd hiccup. The cheesy oat burgers he'd attempted to create one night had turned out to be more like cheesy oat *rocks*. His own fault for not following the recipe. The mixture had seemed too sloppy, so he'd added more oats... and more... and more.... What emerged from the pan was definitely not a success. Thomas had taken one bite and his eyes had gone wide. He tried valiantly to chew the thing, but there was no way he could eat it.

But Peter remembered what he'd read. All right, so the rule was aimed at Doms, but its truth still applied. *When in the wrong, don't be afraid to admit it*. He'd apologized profusely to Thomas, revealing what he'd done with the recipe and fully expecting to be punished. At least by this point, he knew the punishment would be fair. He was learning. Thomas had regarded him in silence for a second or two and then asked casually if there were any cans of baked beans in tomato sauce in the house. Stunned, Peter nodded, only to find himself a minute later preparing two plates of beans on toast, covered in grated cheese. And it had been really tasty. Since that night, however, when Thomas would inquire what was for dinner, now and again he'd ask with a grin if they were going to have cheesy oat burgers. Peter had blushed the first time, but by the second, he'd accepted the ribbing with good grace.

Thomas came into the kitchen and sat down. Peter saw him take in the tidy, clean kitchen and his breakfast laid out for him. Thomas looked pleased, and Peter's chest swelled.

"Sit down, lad." Peter obeyed and waited. "I've decided you're ready to tackle your next responsibility. As of today, you are in charge of the laundry." Thomas paused. "I take it you've used a washing machine before?"

"Yes, Sir." He fought back the urge to roll his eyes. That would be unspeakably rude. But damn it, he was twenty-six, not six. Then he reminded himself that Thomas had no idea of his upbringing. "I used to do my own washing at home, before—" He broke off. He didn't want to think about that now. "That shouldn't be a problem, Sir."

"And does that also mean you're happy doing the ironing too?"

Ah. Ironing. Never his strong suit. Curtis had forbidden him from going anywhere near the iron once he'd burned a hole through Curtis's favorite shirt. Peter gulped. The ironing too?

"I… I will do my best, Sir." That was as far as he was willing to go right then. He couldn't miss Thomas's look of amusement. It wouldn't have surprised him to learn Thomas could read every thought in his head. The man continually surprised him.

"I only ask because, speaking from past experience, young men and irons don't tend to go well together." His eyes gleamed. "Consider it a challenge, boy."

Peter swallowed. *Oh well… at least I'll get to see what other punishments Thomas has up his sleeve*, he thought in dismay. Because it wouldn't be long before he cocked something up. That much, he was sure of.

PETER'S reaction hadn't gone unnoticed. Thomas chuckled to himself. He could almost smell the apprehension rolling off him in waves. The responsibility would be good for the boy. He'd coped admirably with the cooking, and Thomas made sure to praise him every day. It was slow, but he could see Peter beginning to accept the praise a little easier as each day went by. At least he'd stopped getting embarrassed about the oat burger digs. Thomas had almost been relieved when Peter had produced the indigestible burgers. He was starting to think the boy was secretly a chef and had somehow duped him. *Mistakes help build character,* Leo always insisted. Yeah, but mistakes also made for humorous situations, and Peter definitely needed more humor in his life.

Thomas ate his breakfast swiftly. Leo had done a stint as Dungeon Master last night, and Thomas wanted to get to the club early and make sure everything was shipshape by the time doors opened later that morning. Leo, Jonathon, and Miles were all taking it in turns to monitor the group room. Thomas appreciated how the three had taken over some of his duties since Peter's arrival. It was rare for him to work a full day lately, but it meant he could spend more time with the boy. To their credit, not one of the three Doms uttered a word of complaint, even though they were all spending a lot more time at the club. Pietro, Miles's sub, was a trainee chef. He didn't get many nights off from the restaurant, but when he did, he'd taken to spending them at the club. The pair had only gone through their collaring ceremony a mere three weeks ago, so Thomas couldn't blame Pietro for wanting to be near his master. Dillon, Jonathon's sub, usually spent quite a few nights a week at the club, so no change there. And as for Leo and Alex....

Thomas wasn't sure what effect these extra nights of work were having on his business partner's love life, but he was trying to soften the blow by having the pair round for dinner once a week. Also, Peter had approached Thomas the previous week and asked if it would be all right for him and Alex to meet up regularly during the week. Thomas was delighted. Watching the two together, he realized Peter needed a friend, someone to confide in, and Alex was a good choice.

He found Peter in the utility room, checking out the washing machine. The boy took his responsibilities seriously.

"Got everything figured out, lad?"

"Yes, Sir." Peter already had a basket of laundry and was busy sorting colors from whites.

"Good boy." He liked the blush of pink that tinged Peter's cheeks. "I have to go to the club, but I'll be home for lunch. Do you have a shopping list ready for me?"

"Yes, Sir." Peter hurriedly dropped what he was doing and followed Thomas into the kitchen, where a neatly written list was attached to the cork notice board behind the kitchen door. He handed it to Thomas, who tucked it carefully into his wallet. Peter showed no signs of wanting to step beyond the front door on his own, and Thomas couldn't blame him, considering his reaction to seeing Curtis. Thomas hadn't told him of Curtis's visit to the club. Thomas didn't like hiding this from him—he always insisted on the truth with his subs—but the boy didn't need more fear in his life.

THOMAS had gone to the club. The kitchen was clean and tidy. The washing machine was loaded and humming quietly downstairs. Peter curled up on his bed with his list of rules on the bed beside him.

The more he read, the more he wanted to learn. He often wondered why Thomas had decided on this approach. Why not begin training him as a submissive straightaway? Why give him all this responsibility? And then he read something:

A relationship of trust must form, before a D/s relationship can form.

And suddenly his view of life in the house shifted. *That* was what Thomas was doing. He was giving them time to develop a relationship. Okay, so, strictly speaking, Thomas wasn't going to be his Dom. He was, however, going to train Peter to be a submissive. That called for trust, a very rare element in Peter's world. But he knew enough to know that trust was something you built slowly.

One rule made him smile.

Do not be afraid to please your sub. He's in this with you.

He liked that.

THOMAS hobbled into the office, trying not to wince with each painful step. He could hear Miles running behind him. Thomas tried to lower himself gingerly into the first available chair, but his back protested.

"Thomas, are you all right?" Miles was at his side with hands outstretched, as though to catch Thomas if he should fall.

"Oh, quit fussing, It's just a twinge, that's all." He caught his breath as his back spasmed. Oh hell. Maybe not just a twinge.

"What were you thinking? You shouldn't have tried to move the St. Andrew's cross on your own!"

"Well, I couldn't leave it as it was!" Thomas growled. He knew his anger was better directed at himself, because Miles was correct. "But seeing as that new Dom, Martin, gave it such a strong tug that it came loose from the wall, I had to make it safe. And that meant moving it." Another spasm of pain tore through him, and he winced once more. There was nothing to do but go home. Thomas struggled to his feet, reaching for his jacket.

"What are you doing?" Miles stared at him incredulously. "You should be taking it easy. Sit still."

"I want to go home," Thomas insisted.

Miles snorted. "Yeah, and I can *really* see you driving in that state, Thomas." He glanced at the wall clock. "Give me a sec and I'll drive you."

"What about my car?"

"Forget about your car. Leo can bring it round later. Right now it's more important to get you home in one piece." Miles stood his ground, arms folded. Thomas groaned. There was no getting away from the man. Which was exactly why Thomas could depend on him.

"Fine," he gritted out. "Take me home."

NO SOONER had he stepped into the hall than he heard Peter's door open, and the boy came flying down the stairs. Peter's eyes grew round. Thomas wasn't surprised. He was shuffling like an old man.

Thomas waved a hand at him, ignoring the stab of pain that followed the movement.

"It's nothing. I pulled something in my back at the club. Nothing to worry about."

"Forgive me, Sir, but that's not how it looks to me." Peter jutted out his chin.

God, another one. Any other time and Thomas would have been proud of the boy, but not at that precise moment. Not when pain dogged his every step.

"I'm going to take a shower," Thomas said. "Maybe the hot water will help." He looked up toward the first floor. There was just the small matter of negotiating the staircase....

"Lean on me, Sir. I'll help you to the bathroom."

Bless the lad. Thomas gave him a look of pure gratitude and rested his arm around Peter's shoulders, trying not to overbalance the boy. Peter staggered slightly but held him upright and guided him up the stairs, pausing every few steps until finally they reached the landing.

"Get into your robe, Sir, and I'll set the shower running." Thomas gave him a nod and hobbled into his room. Every movement seemed to exacerbate the torment in his back as he struggled out of his clothes. And as for putting on his robe….

A gentle knock on the door. "Sir, the shower is ready."

Thomas pulled open the bedroom door and shuffled past Peter into the bathroom.

The water was hot, and he braced himself against the tiles, letting the full force of the spray hit his back as he groaned aloud. He stood it for as long as possible, and then he had to move as stiffness set in. The warmth eased the ache in his muscles but not by much. Grumbling to himself, Thomas pulled a thick towel from the rail and patted himself dry. He wrapped it around his waist and headed for the bedroom, but when he pushed open the door to his room, he stopped dead.

Peter had pulled back the duvet and laid towels over the bed. He was standing beside it, peering at a bottle. He straightened as Thomas stepped into the room. Peter wore a T-shirt and his sweatpants.

"What is all this?" Thomas gazed in amazement.

Peter smiled. "This is what I do, Sir. Or should I say, what I did, before—" He broke off. Thomas watched as a brief expression of pain crossed Peter's face. He took a breath and met Thomas's gaze. "Sir, I trained as a masseur. Would you care to lie down and let me help you?"

It wasn't often that Thomas was caught off guard, but damn, the boy was full of surprises.

"It will be a pleasure," Thomas said, walking over to the bed. He hesitated. "What should I do with…?" He gestured to his towel. Peter blushed.

"Sir, keep it on if you wish. I would understand if you felt uncomfortable with me—"

Thomas interrupted him. "This is your area of expertise, lad. Tell me how you want me. And no, I won't be uncomfortable, not in the slightest." The look of relief that crossed Peter's face was unmistakable.

"Lie facedown, Sir, and then I'll undo the towel and drape it over you. Your chest needs to rest on the pillow." Thomas obeyed, wincing as he stretched out on his front with his head turned toward Peter, who placed a folded towel under him, supporting his neck, and another supporting his ankles. He felt Peter's hands reaching around him to unwrap the towel, which he then folded in half and draped over Thomas's arse.

"You're honored, lad." Thomas winked. "You're the first submissive ever to see my arse."

Peter's cheeks were scarlet. "Thank you for the honor, Sir. I won't tell a soul."

Come to think of it, Thomas couldn't remember the last time another man had laid eyes on his derriere. The thought left him reeling. *When was the last time someone held me, touched me... needed me?* Another spasm of pain racked his body, and the thought was driven from his head.

"I need to know where it hurts, Sir." Peter moved his hands over Thomas's back, prodding carefully, intently watching Thomas's reactions. When he nudged his lower back and felt the shudder that rippled through Thomas, his face changed. "Okay, I'm going to start massaging the muscles here slowly. Sir, it will feel worse as I work on it, so be prepared. But you should feel some relief when I'm done."

"I'm in your hands, lad," Thomas murmured as Peter opened the bottle and poured a good quantity of the viscous liquid into his palms. "What's that you've got there?"

"Baby oil, Sir. I found it in the bathroom under the sink. It will have to do as a massage oil, as it was the nearest thing I could find to it."

Thomas chuckled. "I had no idea it was under there. I hope it doesn't have an expiration date. It might have been there for a while." Thomas couldn't recollect buying it. Warm hands slid over his lower back, expertly massaging the aching muscles. Peter didn't waste time getting down to business. Thomas let out a low moan as he worked his hands first in slow circles over the area, then pressed his knuckles into the flesh, but never applied too much pressure.

"You can press harder if you need to," Thomas grunted.

"No, Sir, I can't," Peter said decisively. "I have to be careful when working on the lower back. Your organs aren't protected here by your ribcage." He alternated between palm circles and knuckles, and Thomas's back grew warm.

Thomas was impressed. Peter exuded confidence, moving his hands dexterously with no sign of nervousness whatsoever. And though the muscles still ached, the pain receded.

"Does that feel better, Sir?" Peter murmured, pressing his thumbs in, working the flesh in deep circles.

"Boy, I can't tell you how much better that feels." Thomas felt his body relaxing into the mattress. The lad was a genius.

"I'm not finished yet, Sir." Peter stopped his ministrations and moved to Thomas's head, then dropped to his knees. "If you would rest your forehead on the pillow, I'm going to finish off with a full body massage. It will make you feel relaxed." His eyes pleaded with Thomas. "Let me do this for you, Sir?"

Thomas gave a brief nod before complying with Peter's instructions.

"It would be easier with a massage table, Sir, as I would be able to reach your shoulders less awkwardly. So I'm going to kneel astride you, Sir." Thomas heard the whisper of cotton sliding over skin, and suddenly Peter knelt over him, straddling Thomas's arse with his bare legs against Thomas's warmed skin. Those competent hands slid over his shoulders, a totally different sensation compared to his previous manipulations. Thumbs pressed lightly on either side of his spine, the touch truly wonderful. Thomas began to lose himself in the massage, reveling in the sensations released in his body as Peter worked his magic. Hands slid lower, so gently over the area already worked on, and Peter shifted backward, lowering the towel to press knuckles into the swell of Thomas's arse, now with pressure firmer than the light caresses on his upper back. Peter moved his hands in circles that grew wider, pressing more firmly into the muscled cheeks.

Thomas realized Peter had synchronized his movements with Thomas's breathing. Peter removed the towel completely and pushed up from where the curve of Thomas's arse met his thighs, rolling the flesh expertly, then slid to skim his flanks lightly before returning to knead his buttocks once again. And in that instant another realization hit Thomas—he was hard. His cock lay trapped against the bed, but as Peter pushed at his arse cheeks, Thomas couldn't help the tiniest thrust of his hips. The movement slid his dick over the towel beneath.

Fortunately, Peter chose that moment to clamber off and move to the side of the bed, where he worked Thomas's thigh muscles, kneading the flesh and pausing only to apply oil now and then. But Thomas was painfully aware of his erection and the fact that the demands of his body seemed to be overruling his head. The slow movement of those expert hands took on a whole new dimension as Thomas was submerged in a world of sensation, and his dick grew harder at the now erotic, slippery slide of palms against skin— until softly spoken words pierced the fog that had enveloped his brain.

"Turn over for me, please, Sir?"

Oh hell.

Ten

Rebirth

PETER obviously sensed his hesitation. "Is something wrong, Sir?"

There was no way of hiding it.

Thomas sighed. "No, lad, nothing's wrong." Peter pulled the pillow from under his chest, and Thomas turned carefully onto his back. His dick pointed up into the air, a seven-inch exclamation mark rising from a bush of dark and gray pubic curls, neatly trimmed. He avoided Peter's gaze until the boy touched his hand timidly.

"Sir? Just so you know? This happens a lot." Peter was blushing, and in that instant Thomas realized his blush was not embarrassment at seeing Thomas's erection, but at witnessing his discomfort. The boy pulled his sweatpants back on over his underwear and—bless him—simply oiled up his hands and slid them over Thomas's chest, moving in wide circles, brushing his thumbs lightly over Thomas's nipples, making Thomas catch his breath. His traitorous cock was now pointing toward his chest. God, his dick was so hard it ached. Peter's hands caressed down his abs and worked deeply into the crease where groin met thigh. Thomas had to struggle to suppress the moan that fought to escape his parted lips. *Damn, that feels good.* What had started out as an innocent back rub was now arousing him, undeniably.

Peter paused and then moved his oiled hand unmistakably in the direction of Thomas's cock. In a flash, Thomas grabbed his wrist before he reached the thick shaft. Peter flinched at the sudden movement, staring at Thomas with a startled expression.

"Peter, what are you doing?" Thomas kept his tone even.

"This… this was how Mas— how Curtis expected the massage to be completed, Sir." Peter's voice quavered.

Thomas released his wrist and sat up, then reached for the towel and covered his erection.

"No, lad, we aren't doing that."

Peter blinked. "You don't find me attractive, do you, Sir? Is that it? Is it my scars?" The boy turned away from him, clearly unable to maintain eye contact and with the faintest suspicion of a sob in his voice. *Oh, hell.*

Thomas pulled the boy to him, urging him to sit next to him on the bed. Peter's eyes glistened. Thomas clasped Peter's hand. His skin was soft and silky because of the oil.

"No, Peter, that isn't it at all. You've been reading my rules. What do they say about how a submissive is viewed? Yes, I know there are Doms out there who may act like Curtis. When *I* train Doms, it's with the understanding that a submissive is giving them a gift. A submissive should be cherished. What Curtis did to you goes against everything I teach Doms *and* subs."

Peter lowered his head, but Thomas was having none of it. He lifted the boy's chin with his hand and cupped his cheek.

"You are beautiful, boy. Inside *and* out. When you believe that, it will be the greatest gift you can give to me, because it means I will have trained you well." He withdrew his hand and gazed at the boy, willing him to see the truth underlying his words.

For what seemed like an eternity, Peter regarded him in silence before acknowledging him with a dip of his head. He stood and picked up the bottle of oil.

"I'll go and put on some coffee, Sir. I'll have it waiting for you when you come downstairs." And with that he left the room, pulling the door shut behind him.

Thomas listened to Peter's footsteps as he went downstairs, followed by sounds that told him Peter was sorting out the coffee machine. He lay back on the bed and slipped his hand beneath the towel. He grabbed hold of his dick and squeezed it firmly. The one thing that had shocked him more than anything wasn't Peter's intention to jerk him off, but the fact that he'd wanted the boy to do it. He'd grabbed the lad's wrist out of concern, but there was still that part of him that wanted to feel the boy's hand around his cock, flogging it, tightening around it, squeezing it. Thomas pulled at his dick, which was once more like silk-covered steel, and closed his eyes. He stroked himself faster, and his breathing sped up as he felt the first tingling in his balls that signaled approaching orgasm.

Thomas grunted harshly as he shot his load over his chest and abs. He lay back on the bed, panting and shuddering. *When was the last time I thought of someone doing this for me?* Thomas had no answer. He wiped himself with the towel and sat up once more, focusing his thoughts on the boy downstairs. He hoped to God this didn't set the boy back. It would have been so easy to allow Peter to continue, but letting things progress in that direction would throw off everything he'd been trying to accomplish. He wanted to keep Peter centered. Besides, Thomas's selfish desires didn't come into this. He had a job to do. He had a sub to heal—and train.

PETER rubbed the back of his neck. *How long does it take to get dressed?* Despite Thomas's words, Peter's stomach was churning and his chest felt tight. *Will he treat me the same?* Peter was filled with shame when he thought on what he'd been about to do. What the hell had come over him? He'd been feeling good, massaging Thomas's back, watching the man virtually melt into the mattress. And it had been a while since he'd massaged anyone. It made him feel useful, like he was really helping Thomas. How could he ever have thought Thomas was anything like Curtis? Hadn't the man proved himself, over and over again? Self-loathing filled him. Curtis might not be his master anymore, but he still managed to fuck up Peter's life, be it in his dreams or memories.

And as for what had been running through his mind while he was massaging Thomas, the less he thought about that, the better.

"I never said thank you, did I?"

Peter gave a start. Thomas was standing by the door, watching him.

"I'm sorry I made you jump, lad."

"It's okay, Sir. I was miles away." Peter hurriedly grabbed the mug from the table and filled it with coffee. Thomas pulled out a chair and sat, his movements considerably easier than when he'd arrived home a short time ago. He sipped his coffee and leaned back against his chair, focusing on Peter.

"Thank you, boy. My back feels so much better. You obviously have healing hands."

Peter's chest swelled with pride. "I'm glad I was able to help, Sir."

Thomas regarded him thoughtfully. "I don't intend going back to the club. I think I'll spend the rest of the day taking it easy." He put down his mug. "There *is* something I'd like to do, however. I think we're long overdue for a conversation, don't you?"

"Conversation?"

Thomas nodded. "How is your reading coming along? Are you ready to write your next essay yet?"

"Yes, Sir. In fact it's nearly finished." Peter had been working on it when Thomas had arrived home.

"In that case, how about we go into the lounge for a chat?"

He stood up, and Peter realized it wasn't a request. Thomas went into the lounge, and Peter followed, trying to ignore the fluttery feelings in his stomach. Thomas sat in his usual armchair, and Peter sat on the sofa, bolt upright.

Thomas let out a chortle. "Sit back, lad, relax. This isn't the Spanish Inquisition."

Peter tried to smile, but his nerves had definitely got the better of him. He leaned back against the seat cushion and willed his body to relax. Thomas seemed at ease. Peter envied him. It had been a long time since he'd felt anything like that.

"Peter, you've been with me for nearly five weeks. How do you feel you are settling in?"

Peter thought carefully before answering. *Should I tell him the truth?* It was probably a moot point. The man seemed to be able to read his mind. Besides, the way Thomas had welcomed him into his home and provided for him…. The least Peter could do would be to tell him the truth.

"I'm happy here, Sir. Really. I love cooking for you, serving you." He hesitated.

"I sense a 'but' coming at this point."

Peter inhaled deeply. "I still have nightmares. And even on the nights when I don't, I wake up the next morning feeling tired." He lowered his gaze. "He's in my head, Sir. I can't seem to shake him." There. He'd said it.

"How does that make you feel?" Thomas leaned forward, regarding him intently.

Peter lifted his chin and met Thomas's gaze head-on. "Like you've given me a chance at a new life, and I'm failing you."

A look of sorrow crossed Thomas's face for one fleeting moment, and then it was gone.

"You haven't failed me, boy. Quite the opposite." Thomas looked away, and Peter wondered what was going through his mind. Thomas suddenly straightened and met Peter's eyes.

"This *is* a new start for you. Maybe we need to focus on that."

Something was going on in Thomas's head; that was for sure. Peter waited expectantly.

"Okay, lad, I want you to go to your room and finish your essay. I have to make a few phone calls. I'll call you when I'm ready." Thomas's smile was reassuring.

Ready for what? Peter didn't have a clue. But Thomas looked pleased with himself. *I guess I'll have to trust him.*

THOMAS waited until he heard Peter's bedroom door close and then got out his phone.

"Good morning. I'd like to speak with Darren, please. This is Thomas Williams." He hoped the man could help him out. The idea had come to him as soon as Peter mentioned a new start, and it had been hard to hide his excitement from the boy.

"Mr. Williams, don't tell me…. You need a haircut, right?" There was an underlying note of amusement to Darren's voice. "I'd *love* to get my hands on that gorgeous hair of yours."

Thomas laughed. "Actually, no. I need your help with something."

"I'm intrigued."

Swiftly, he outlined his requirements, mentally crossing his fingers. He needed to do this as soon as possible. To his relief, Darren was receptive.

"Wow, that sounds… interesting. Let me have a look at what we have already booked in for later today." Thomas could hear the rustle of pages turning. "You're in luck. Can you be here in an hour? I know it's short notice, but the room will be available after that."

"Perfect." Thomas could have danced.

"Just one thing. You want me to do this? Because, on reflection… it should really be you, don't you think? I could supervise if you like. Have you ever done this before?"

"No. But the more I think about it…. Yes, you're right. It should be me. Would that be a problem?"

Darren reassured him on that score. "Then I'll see you in an hour. Will anyone else be present?"

Thomas had already thought about that. "Yes. Is that okay?"

"Not a problem." They exchanged a few words, and Thomas finished the call. One down, one to go. He speed-dialed the next call.

"Leo? I need your help."

PETER put down his pen and reread his last paragraph. It had been difficult to concentrate with his thoughts returning constantly to Thomas's last words. What was the man up to? Who was he calling, and what did it have to do with Peter? He forced himself back to the task in hand. Two rules stuck in his mind.

A Dom should care about his submissive.

A Dom's job is to nurture and teach.

His thoughts went immediately to Curtis. Peter had been so hopeful at first. Curtis seemed perfect. He'd promised to take care of Peter, to teach him. Yeah, right. The only thing Curtis had taught Peter was that his voice, his opinion, his feelings didn't count. By the time Peter had worked this out, he'd already seen way too much, and by then it was too late. His life had changed irrevocably. If Curtis prior to that moment had seemed hard and unfeeling, that was as nothing compared to the man who emerged once Peter had seen what went on. He'd never revealed to Curtis the extent of his knowledge of the man's "business" dealings, but there was always an underlying fear that somehow Curtis knew.

Peter shivered. He wanted more than anything to trust Thomas wholly, to place himself in the Dom's hands and know it was safe to do so. But always there were the memories of Curtis lurking in the back of his mind, insidious memories that poisoned every positive thought Thomas engendered in him. True, the nightmares were less frequent, but what Peter yearned for was the ability to block Curtis from his mind. He wanted to latch on to something new, something much more powerful that would sustain him when the night terrors gripped him and memories threatened to overwhelm him. But that was as far as his thoughts took him. He had no idea what it was he sought, but he prayed Thomas would be the one to show him.

A firm knock on the door.

"May I come in?"

Peter liked that Thomas asked. He never once entered without first asking permission, making it clear to Peter that the room was his space. "Come in, Sir."

The door opened, and Thomas stood there, wearing his leather jacket and carrying Peter's woolen jacket over his arm.

"We're going out, lad." He held out the jacket.

"May I ask where we're going, Sir?" He swallowed. Going out. Again.

Thomas smiled enigmatically. "You may ask. That doesn't mean I'm going to tell you." Peter's physical reaction must have betrayed his surprise at this statement. Thomas's voice softened. "You'll have to trust me, boy." That hand was still outstretched toward him.

Peter got up from the bed and walked to the door. He took the jacket.

"I trust you, Sir." He willed himself to believe his own words.

Thomas tilted his head. "But not wholeheartedly." Peter opened his mouth to protest, but Thomas waved his hand. "It's all right, lad. You're not at that point yet. Hopefully what's about to happen will help you." He turned and descended the staircase.

Peter couldn't stop the shiver that rippled through him. Whatever Thomas had planned, it was obviously important. He took a second or two to compose himself and then followed the man downstairs. Inside his head, he pushed aside the small voice that reminded him Thomas was a Dom just like Curtis. It was about time he started listening to a different voice. One with a different message.

PETER was confused when Thomas parked the car and he realized they were once more outside the salon.

"Sir?"

Thomas twisted in his seat to face him. "Remember what I said, boy. You need to trust me." He locked eyes with Peter, who was unable to look away. "Right now, you need to come with me. I'll explain everything once we get in there."

The moment of silence that followed seemed to stretch out until Peter found his courage and grasped it with both hands.

"Yes, Sir."

The look of approval in Thomas's eyes filled him with warmth. "Good boy." The words of praise settled on him, making him feel better. "Now let's get in there."

Once the salon door closed behind him, Peter breathed more easily.

Darren was waiting for them by the front desk. He shook Thomas's hand and dipped his head to acknowledge Peter. "Good to see you again. Everything is ready. Is anyone else going to arrive?" Peter's ears pricked up at that part.

"Yes. Can they be directed upstairs when they get here?"

Darren nodded before turning to his receptionist. "Paul, would you see to that?"

"Certainly, Darren."

Darren led them through a door behind the desk, which revealed a narrow, carpeted staircase. Peter followed the two men upstairs, his heart hammering. Inside his head, he kept up his mantra. *Trust him. Trust him.* It went a little way to relieving the nerves, but not much. At the top was a small landing with three doors leading off it. Darren opened one door and stood aside to let them enter. Peter found himself in a white room that contained a massage table, a washbasin, and a tall white cupboard. A Chinese paper screen, printed in delicate shades of beige and gold, stood against the wall. The room was warm.

"This is our treatment room," Darren explained. "We do full body massage, among other things." He turned to Thomas. "Will this do?"

Thomas looked around. "This is perfect, Darren."

Peter turned around when he heard a slight cough behind them. His eyes grew large as he saw Paul in the doorway, accompanied by Leo and Alex. *What the hell...?* Paul gestured for them to enter. Alex grinned when he saw Peter.

"Thanks for coming at such short notice." Thomas clasped Leo's hand. "And, pup, behave yourself." His eyes sparkled. Alex put his hand to his chest in mock indignation, but Leo flashed him a look that clearly said much. Alex put his hands down by his sides and became still.

Peter was bewildered at this turn of events. Fortunately, Thomas took control. He gave a look to the other occupants of the room and they all fell silent, moving to flank Peter, but all eyes were on Thomas.

"Peter, when we talked this morning, you mentioned me giving you a new start, and it got me thinking. You're about to undergo something that will symbolize this new chapter in your life." He took Peter's hand. "Under Darren's supervision, I'm going to shave you."

Peter was dumbfounded. *All this for a shave?* But Thomas wasn't finished.

"I'm going to remove all the hair that covers you, from the top of your head down. The only bit I'll not touch is your eyebrows, but everything else goes. When I'm finished, a new Peter will have emerged. One who is breaking free of his former life."

Peter couldn't breathe. *All* his hair? And then it hit him. Darren, Leo, and Alex would be watching.

Thomas nodded as though aware of what had just passed through his mind. "Leo and Alex are here for *you*. To support you. As witnesses, if you like, of this new stage in your life." He regarded Peter, his expression kindly but serious. "Do you understand why I'm doing this?"

In that instant, memories flooded through him. Peter saw himself being used, surrounded by men who waited for their turn, not one of them giving a damn about him. He was only there to be struck, beaten, fucked. He gasped as his body recalled the feel of the whip against his skin. He could feel those powerful hands that held him down and stretched him wide while others plowed into him, ignoring his cries, which were then silenced by a palm across his mouth or a gag.

"But I'm not that boy anymore!" Peter fell to his knees with a cry that was loud and full of torment. He squeezed his eyes shut and tried to force the images from his mind. He trembled as hands touched him. He flinched, readying himself for the next blow—which never came. These hands weren't holding him down, but rubbing him softly, gently. His mind reeled in confusion as strong arms suddenly enfolded him. His face pressed against the comforting warmth of a wide chest. Slowly, Peter opened his eyes. Thomas held him. Peter could feel him shaking. Peter closed his eyes once more and concentrated on the feel of Thomas's arms wrapped around him.

He could feel Thomas's heart beating strongly. Peter found himself breathing in time with Thomas, and the simple act of focusing on their respiration was strangely hypnotic. Peter's heart began to beat at a steadier rate. He opened his eyes. Thomas loosened his grip, and Peter sat back on his haunches. Thomas slipped his hands under Peter's arms to help him to stand, but he didn't withdraw them. Instead, he held Peter steady. Peter gazed into Thomas's eyes, and the depth of emotion he saw there floored him. There was no judgment there. No look of disgust. He couldn't see the others, but he heard the hitches in their breathing.

"That's it, lad. Breathe."

Peter focused on Thomas's voice and took deep, even breaths. He thought about what had just happened. Thomas had defeated his panic. He recalled the moment when Thomas had taken his hand and led him from the cupboard. And then he reflected on Thomas's question, which he'd almost lost sight of in the panic that had overwhelmed him. Why would he want to do such a thing? Peter couldn't deny it—he *loved* the idea of breaking free from the painful memories that bound him. Memory was such a powerful thing. Yet Thomas had helped him create new memories. Perhaps these would serve to counteract the past.

And then it hit him. What Thomas was giving him.

"You're giving me the chance to leave the past behind. You're giving me something I can focus on when the voices in my head get too loud. Something powerful." Peter wanted that. He *ached* for it.

Thomas looked at him intently, and Peter glowed to see the look of pride in those expressive green eyes.

129

"Yes, boy. That's exactly what I'm giving you."

Peter took a calming breath. "Then yes, Sir. Do it. Please, Sir."

THOMAS couldn't have been prouder of him in that moment.

"Then let's begin." He struggled to maintain his composure. This was something new for him too, and he knew it would be a powerful, emotional experience for both of them.

"Sir, may I ask something?"

Thomas gave the sub his full attention. "You may, boy."

"Sir, what made you think of doing this?"

Thomas smiled. "When we came here for your haircut, you looked so fresh and new afterward. And this morning, it occurred to me that this was something you needed, all over."

Peter cleared his throat. "I like the idea, Sir, even if the thought of being bald is a little scary."

Thomas gripped his hand. "Remember what I said this morning. You're beautiful."

He could see the tension ease in Peter's body as his words took root. It was time.

He gave Leo a nod, and the man stepped forward, carrying a bag. Thomas had briefed him over the phone. Leo addressed himself to Peter, his voice firm.

"Peter, Alex and I are here for *you*. We're all going to undress you. Think of it as us stripping away your old life. And when Thomas is done, we will dress you again. I've brought a new set of clothes. Something for your first day as a new man, our birthday gift to you." Leo glanced at Darren. "Darren is here as a witness to your rebirth, as it were."

Thomas let go of Peter's hand and moved behind him to remove his jacket. Leo and Alex moved to his sides. The three men slowly undressed him in silence. Peter stood in the midst of them, his breathing more even as each piece of clothing was removed to finally reveal his nude body. Leo gathered up his clothes and stepped back, but Alex wrapped his arms around the boy and hugged him. Peter stiffened but then relaxed, put his arms around Alex, laid his head against Alex's chest, and closed his eyes.

Alex whispered in his ear, saying words clearly audible in the quiet room. "So proud to be here for this, for you." He released Peter and stepped back to join Leo.

Darren stepped forward with a bowl of warm water and set it on a folded towel already laid out on the table. He uncovered a straight razor, and Peter's eyes grew wide. Darren met Thomas's gaze.

"Have you ever used one of these?" He unfolded the blade and touched it carefully. "These things are incredibly sharp."

Thomas noted Peter's brief swallow. He placed his hand on the sub's shoulder.

"Peter? Are you all right?"

Peter nodded. He looked Thomas in the eye. "Yes, Sir. I trust you."

Thomas smiled and turned to Darren. "Yes. In my youth I had a beard for a while. But I'll be careful." He smirked. "And besides, you're here to advise me, aren't you? Did you bring the shaving gel?"

Darren held up the can. "And a pair of clippers, already charged up. I'll cut the hair as short as possible to make it easier for you to shave his head. Shall I start?"

Thomas nodded. He pulled a chair forward, and Peter sat. Darren removed the hair clippers from his pocket and proceeded to cut away Peter's dark-brown hair, leaving only stubble in its wake. Thomas dipped the cloth Darren had brought along into the warm water and wiped it over Peter's head. He squeezed some of the blue shaving gel into his hand and worked it into what little hair remained. Thomas dropped the cloth into the water and picked up the razor. He locked eyes with Peter.

"Ready, boy?"

Peter lifted his head high. "Ready, Sir."

K.C. Wells

Eleven

Into The Fire

WITH slow, careful strokes, Thomas ran the blade over Peter's scalp, only going over each area once to prevent it from burning the tender skin. With each stroke of the razor, Thomas's confidence grew. Peter didn't flinch.

At last his head was smooth. Thomas wrung out the cloth and wiped down the skin, removing any vestiges of gel. He could see Peter's hands twitch, as though he wanted to reach up and touch his head, but the lad refrained from doing so. Thomas ran the blade over Peter's jaw, leaving it smooth. Peter held himself still throughout.

"Good boy," he murmured, and Peter's cheeks flushed. "Stand up, please, arms high."

Peter got to his feet and lifted his arms above his head.

Darren stepped forward and spoke quietly. "Thomas, would you like me to apply the shaving gel?"

Thomas considered this and then looked him in the eye. "Thank you for the offer, Darren, but no. It's very kind of you, but to be honest, this is something I need to do for my boy. I promised him I would help him, and that is what this whole ritual is for." Darren nodded and withdrew.

Thomas smiled as he saw Peter's eyes grow shiny with unshed tears. He knew how powerful this was for the young man and that it was something the two of them needed to share.

Thomas prepared Peter's armpits with the shaving gel and then pulled the flesh taut and scraped away every hair, wiping as each new area of nude skin was revealed. Next came his chest and stomach. The boy had only a smattering of downy hair there. Below his navel, a sparse happy trail led down to a neat bush of pubic hair from which sprang the boy's half-hard, six-inch, uncut cock. With great care, Thomas worked in silence, scraping the razor's bright blade over each bit of skin. Peter stood upright, breathing evenly. Thomas sensed the change in him. The boy was totally focused on him; he could almost have been in subspace.

Before venturing lower, Thomas worked on Peter's arms and back. He took great pains to move with extreme care. Fortunately there were only a few random hairs here and there across his shoulder blades. Thomas had been nervous at the thought of shaving the skin that bore Peter's scars.

"I need you to lie down on the table on your back, lad." Peter complied in silence. "Now spread your legs wide. I'm going to shave your balls." Peter's eyes flickered once, and he swallowed, but then he became still once more. Thomas moved the razor with infinite care, aware of Darren's watchful eye the entire time. Once his balls were free of fuzz, Thomas wiped the warm, damp cloth over the wrinkled, soft skin.

"Onto your front, lad, and draw your knees up under you, wide apart." Once Peter was in position, Thomas worked the gel into the boy's arse cheeks and crack. Something occurred to him. "Peter, I need both hands if I'm going to work as safely as possible. I'd like to ask Darren to spread you for me. Is that okay?" He looked toward Darren to check this was okay with him too. Darren gave him a brief nod.

There was a split second of hesitation before he caught Peter's whispered reply. "Yes, Sir. That's fine."

Darren took up his position and carefully pulled the cheeks apart. Thomas stroked the razor over the taut skin, taking special care around his hole. When Peter's arse was as smooth as a baby's, Thomas wiped him down, and then Darren released him. Thomas then got Peter to stretch out once more while his legs were shaved.

At last the task was finished. When Peter got off the table and stood before Thomas, his skin glowed. The boy was smooth and pink from head to foot. Darren took away the bowl and returned with fresh warm water and a clean cloth. He handed Thomas a bottle of liquid soap. Thomas proceeded to wash the boy from head to foot, taking his time with the cleansing ritual. He picked up a fresh towel, which Darren had thoughtfully placed on the table, and patted the lad down, drying his skin with care.

Peter's gaze never left him as Thomas completed the final task, that of smoothing a silky moisturizer over his entire body, rubbing it gently into his skin from the head down.

"You're anointing him," Darren said in a hushed tone. Thomas gave him a quick glance. Astute man. Peter seemed to be in a trance when Thomas finally stood before him.

"How do you feel, boy?"

Peter glanced down at his body, running his hands over his chest and belly. He reached up to stroke the soft skin where his hair had once been.

"Oh, Sir." There was awe in his voice. Suddenly Thomas had a lump in his throat. The boy was so beautiful, caught in that moment. Leo and Alex came forward with Peter's new clothes, and the three men dressed him in silence.

Peter looked down at the sand-colored chinos and white shirt that now adorned him. "Thank you so much." He smiled at Leo.

Alex leapt forward to seize him in an enthusiastic hug.

"That was amazing. You *look* amazing!" His exclamation proved to be the catalyst for an abrupt change of mood. Peter laughed, wrapping his arms around Alex, returning his hug. Alex chuckled. "I can't resist!" He planted a smacking kiss on top of Peter's now-bald head. All the men laughed. Leo put his arm around Peter's shoulders and squeezed briefly.

"I am very pleased to greet the new Peter," he said with a wink. Peter blushed.

Darren watched the scene with bright eyes. Thomas could tell the man had been genuinely affected by what he'd witnessed. But right now it was time for him to hug his boy. Their first hug.

He held his arms wide. "Come here, boy."

Peter didn't hesitate. He walked into his arms and Thomas hugged him tightly, overjoyed as the lad reached up to return his embrace.

Thomas whispered close to his ear, "I am so very, very proud of you." They stood like that for a moment. Thomas was conscious of Peter's heart beating strongly.

"Thank you, Sir." Thomas heard the tremor in his voice. He didn't say anything but held the boy close, enjoying the connection.

THOMAS put his keys down on the hall table and watched Peter walk slowly into the kitchen. The boy had hardly said a word the whole journey home. Now and again he reached up to touch his bare head, as if to verify that it had really happened. Thomas didn't know what was going through the lad's mind, but he was clearly mulling something over.

He followed Peter into the kitchen and was not surprised to find the boy staring at his reflection in the kitchen window. Thomas chuckled to himself. He'd guided Peter through the salon with instructions that he wasn't to look at his reflection until they got home—and that included the mirror on the sun visor in the car. He wanted Peter to have time to assess his new look. Peter's eyes had pleaded with him briefly, but then he'd nodded. Thomas's heart swelled with pride to watch the lad walk through the salon, eyes front, in total obedience.

"It's time, lad. Do you want to see?" he asked softly. Peter turned to face him and flushed. Thomas chortled. "Of course you do. Come with me, boy." He held out his hand, and Peter took it, allowing himself to be led into the lounge. Thomas stopped as they entered the room and loosely covered Peter's eyes with his hand. He positioned him in front of the fire and then removed his hand, listening to Peter's gasp of surprise as he caught sight of himself in the mirror above the fireplace.

For several long seconds Peter said nothing. He turned his head to the left, then the right, unable to tear himself away from the new man who looked back at him.

"Well, what do you think?"

Peter met his gaze, his eyes wide with surprise.

"I don't look like me anymore," he said. He turned back to the mirror. "I like that." A slight smile crossed his face. And then abruptly his expression grew more thoughtful.

"What is it, boy? What are you thinking right now?"

He turned Peter to face him. The boy bit his lower lip.

"Out with it, lad. Talk to me."

After a second or two of hesitation, Peter spoke. "Sir, it's about my clothes."

Thomas had been thinking about this himself. "Do you want me to return all the clothes I bought for you? I know I bought them for the old Peter." He spoke sincerely, determined to make the boy see how seriously he viewed what had just taken place. "We can buy you new stuff."

Peter shook his head vehemently. "No, Sir, that's not necessary. They're still new, as far as I'm concerned. But I would like to do something with the clothes I was wearing the night I came here."

Now Thomas understood. "Tell me."

Peter lifted his chin higher. "I want to burn them, Sir." His eyes pleaded with Thomas. "Can we do that? Please?"

Thomas was over the moon. He wanted to punch the air and give a cry of elation. He clamped down on his emotions, however, and simply beamed at the lad.

"Yes, boy. I think that's a wonderful idea. There's a fire pit in the garden that I use for cooking in the summer when I have barbecues. We can use that. Go fetch them, and I'll get the starter fluid from the garage. That'll get it burning."

Peter left the room in a mad dash and thudded up the stairs. Thomas grinned. The lad was evidently taking his rebirth very seriously. He thought the idea an excellent one, all the more so because it had come from Peter. He went through the kitchen to the back door, which lead into the garage. In the garage, he opened the wall cupboard and took out a bottle of starter fluid. A rush of icy cold air hit him as he opened the outer door to the garden. He shivered.

"Sir, you'll need this." Peter came up behind him, wearing his jacket and Thomas's beanie, which he'd evidently found. He held out Thomas's thick winter jacket, which was kept in the cupboard under the stairs. Thomas smiled at this thoughtful action.

"Thank you, lad." He winked and indicated the beanie with a nod. "We'll need to get you one of those." He slipped on the jacket while Peter grabbed the sweatpants and T-shirt he'd arrived in and closed the kitchen door behind him. They went into the garden. Peter hadn't been out there— with the present temperature, there'd been no occasion to do so—and he looked around at the large garden with interest. Thomas loved the garden in

136

the summer, but right now it was stark and bare. At the center of the garden was the fire pit, set into a circle of small cobblestones and surrounded by curved stone benches. The grill, which usually sat atop the pit, was safely stored in the garage, away from the rain.

"Throw them in there, lad."

Peter dumped the clothing into the pit. Thomas squirted starter fluid liberally over it and reached into his pocket for the matches he'd brought from the cupboard. He held them out to Peter.

"Do you want to do the honors, boy?"

Silently, Peter took the matches. He removed a single match, struck it against the box, and once it was burning, dropped it onto the alcohol-soaked clothes. With a *whoomph*, they caught. The flames flared up and then died back. Peter reached into his jacket pocket and fished something out.

"What have you got there?" Thomas couldn't see what lay in Peter's closed hand.

Peter's eyes met his. "Curtis's last hold over me." He opened his hand to reveal a thin collar. Thomas's mind went immediately to that first night when he'd bathed the boy. Peter must have taken it to his room that night. Thomas's eyes glittered with approval.

"Do it, boy."

Peter threw the collar onto the fire. They watched as the leather blackened in the flames, curling with the heat. In silence they stood, gazing down at the flames until at last they died away, leaving only the charred remains of Peter's former life. Peter shivered.

Thomas held out his hand. "Come on, boy, let's go inside and get warm."

Peter gave the remnants one last look and then took Thomas's hand.

"Yes, Sir."

PETER went over in his head a list of tasks to be completed. The new week had brought with it a new responsibility. From today, it was his job to clean the house. His days were definitely becoming fuller, and Peter loved it. Structure, organization, routine. This was how Peter had lived his life BC— Before Curtis. He was starting to feel more grounded. He especially loved how each day was to start from now on. Thomas requested to wake up with his usual cup of tea and paper, but now stipulated that Peter should kneel beside the bed in silence until Thomas acknowledged him.

This was the first morning for the new routine, and Peter placed the cup of tea and newspaper beside the bed as usual before lowering himself onto his knees with his hands clasped in front and his head bowed. He heard rather than saw Thomas's first stirrings as the man became aware of his presence. At last Thomas sat up and reached for what Peter had started to call "Sir's wake-up juice" in his head. His Sir really needed that first shot of tea into his system. Thomas sat back, leaning against the headboard as he sipped his tea. Peter kept his eyes lowered and his back straight, determined to do the man proud. Finally Thomas spoke.

"Good morning, boy."

"Good morning, Sir." Peter raised his chin.

Thomas regarded him with a contented expression. "Well done." He reached out and stroked Peter's head, a single gentle movement.

Peter's chest swelled. Sir was pleased. He pushed aside his feelings of delight, however. He could reflect on those when he had time to himself. Right now he had a job to do.

"Sir, I've put out your dark-blue suit and pale-blue shirt for today. You did say you were conducting interviews today, so I thought you'd want to look smart." A thought crossed his mind, and he continued hurriedly. "Not that you don't always look smart, Sir, because you do."

Thomas snickered. "Quit while you're ahead, lad." He glanced at the clothing Peter had placed on the ottoman. "They look perfect. And yes, I'm interviewing new members today, two of whom you are acquainted with." Peter stiffened momentarily but then relaxed. He had to stop doing that. He should know by now that Thomas wouldn't have said anything if he thought it would cause him distress. He waited for Thomas to continue. Thomas eyed him for a second or two, and Peter was sure the man knew what was going on in his head. Fortunately, Thomas said nothing, but there was that knowing tilt of his head that spoke louder than words.

"Who might that be, Sir?"

"My friend Steven Drummond, your white knight. And his sub, David."

Peter hadn't given the two men much thought recently. He would always be grateful that Steven had stepped in the way he did. Maybe one day he'd get the opportunity to thank the man in person.

"What do you have planned for today, boy?"

Thomas's words cut through his internal meanderings. He pulled himself together.

"I have laundry to sort out, and then I'm going to clean downstairs." He'd been shocked to see a fine layer of dust in the lounge under the sofa and intended to give the room a thorough spring-cleaning, even though it was only the tail end of February. Spring was still a way off.

"And will it be a whites wash?" There was an amused twinkle in Thomas's eye. Peter groaned internally. Was he *ever* going to live that down? Once he'd managed to miss *one pair* of white socks, which had somehow snuck their way into a colored wash, and they ended up an interesting shade of pale blue.

Thomas was clearly trying not to laugh. Peter didn't really mind. The atmosphere in the house had improved greatly since his "rebirthing" ritual, as he thought of it. That day had been unforgettable. Peter still got shivers when he brought it to mind. What made it all the more powerful was the effect it continued to have on his life. In those moments when the niggling little voice in his head whispered nothing but poison, Peter went to his room and sat quietly on his bed, closed his eyes, and deliberately focused on that day. He pictured the room. Thomas's look of intense concentration as he shaved him with such care. His reaction when he first caught sight of his reflection. Tossing Curtis's collar into the flames. Little by little the voice receded, until Peter could hear it no longer. It was a powerful memory, one that Peter clung to in the dark when he would awaken damp with sweat from yet another dream in which Curtis et al had given him their own special brand of attention.

"How is this week's essay coming along?"

Thomas's question brought him back to the present. Tonight would be their night for discussion. Peter had thought of a few questions to put to him, things that had been on his mind lately.

"It's coming along well, thank you, Sir. I'm looking forward to our chat this evening." He rubbed at his head where it itched, its smoothness now marred by the emerging new growth.

Thomas chuckled. "Don't scratch, lad. Besides, do you know how long hair takes to grow?"

Peter nodded. "I looked it up. Half an inch a month." He rubbed his scalp once more.

Thomas locked eyes with him. "Boy." Peter lowered his hands reluctantly. Thomas glanced at the clock beside his bed. "Okay, lad, time for me to get up and go do some interviews."

Peter knew that was his cue to leave. He got to his feet and, after collecting Thomas's cup, left the room.

THOMAS pushed back his chair with a contented sigh.

"I swear, boy, your cooking just keeps on getting better and better." He glanced down at the plate, on which there was not a single trace of his dinner remaining. He snorted. "I think you can tell I enjoyed that."

Peter's cheeks glowed. The boy had done him proud with a dish of chicken in a white wine sauce, accompanied by brown rice. The smells had tantalized him as soon as he opened the front door, making his mouth water. Peter got up from the table and removed the plates to the sink before switching on the coffee machine. It wasn't long before the wonderful aroma of freshly brewed coffee pervaded the kitchen.

"How about you pour us both a cup of coffee and bring them through to the lounge?" Thomas said as he stood, pushing his chair back into position. "Then we can have a talk." He waited for Peter to acknowledge his words and then went into the lounge. He glanced around the room in satisfaction. The polished surfaces gleamed, the mirror was smear-free, and the carpet looked like new. The boy had really gone to town on his cleaning. Thomas wasn't an untidy man by any means, but he knew cleaning had not been high on his list of priorities. It was enough that the place was tidy whenever Leo came round. Now and again Thomas would be seized by the urge to clean the house from top to bottom, but such occasions were few and far between.

He listened to the sounds from the kitchen as Peter washed and cleaned up after the meal. There was a chill in the air that night, and Thomas decided to light the fire. The log store next to the fireplace was fully stocked, and the basket on the hearth was filled to the brim with kindling. Peter had seen to everything. Quickly and efficiently Thomas got a fire going, so that by the time Peter came in bearing two cups of coffee, it was burning away merrily.

Peter curled up on the sofa and pulled the throw over his lap, snuggling it around him. He picked up his cup and warmed his hands on it. Thomas seated himself in his favorite squashy armchair and gazed at the boy across from him.

"Was there anything particular you wanted to ask? Something that maybe came to mind during your reading?"

Peter nodded and then sipped his coffee before speaking. "There *is* something I've been thinking about ever since my first conversation with Alex and then with you." He gazed into the flames, and the firelight cast a warm glow on his face. Thomas was pleased to see the changes in the boy since that time. His face had filled out slightly, and that gaunt, drawn look was no longer evident. His eyes were brighter, and there was a light in them that transformed his face.

"Go on, lad," Thomas said encouragingly.

Peter took a long drink of his coffee. "What's a safeword?"

Aha. Thomas had wondered how long it would be before questions like this would arise.

"A safeword is a word of your choosing for use in a scene."

Peter's eyes lit up. "And that was another question. You mentioned scenes in our first conversation. What is a scene?"

His questions told Thomas a lot about Curtis's methods—or lack of them, not that he hadn't already guessed as much.

"A scene is a specific time period where you explore different aspects of the D/s lifestyle with a Dom. Your Dom would probably decide beforehand what aspect you would be working on, and it would usually be something that you had both agreed upon in your contract."

Peter sat in rapt attention. "So what is a safeword and why would I need one?"

"A safeword is your mechanism if things get too much for you, or if you want to slow things down. Because once you utter your safeword, everything stops."

"Really?" Peter's eyes were wide.

Thomas fixed his gaze on the boy. "Absolutely." His tone was firm.

Peter seemed to consider this. "But that sounds like *I'm* the one in charge. That doesn't seem right."

Thomas beamed. "That's *exactly* right, boy. Contrary to what you might think, the submissive is the one with all the power." He could see from the tilt of Peter's head that the lad was confused. "You haven't seen a normal contract. It contains a complete list of activities that can take place in a scene. *You* decide which activities you are prepared to participate in. Those are your soft limits. They might include things you've never done before but you might want to try. Some of them might even be things that scare you, but there's a part of you that wants to give it a go."

Peter was engrossed. "What else?"

"There will also be things that turn you off completely, stuff you know right away that you wouldn't even contemplate. Those are your hard limits. You make a list with your Dom of your hard and soft limits, so he knows right from the outset what you are prepared to try." Peter was nodding. "You also have a safeword for when things get too much and you need to take a moment before continuing. Some subs stick with *red* and *yellow*. Red is 'stop,' yellow is 'give me a minute.'"

"So what did that rule mean?" Peter looked down as he tried to remember. "'A safeword should be in effect no matter how comfortable a sub is.' Why would a sub *not* want a safeword?"

Thomas sighed. "Peter, there are Doms out there who don't play by the rules, just like there are subs who think they don't need limits. A sub might try to please his Dom by taking whatever the guy throws at him, regardless of how much it hurts him. Such a submissive might say he doesn't need a safeword. Any Dom worth his salt would insist on it. Safewords protect *both* of you."

Peter became still, staring at the fire. Thomas had a fair idea of what was passing through the boy's mind at that point. Curtis had never given him the option. Curtis had given him no choice but to accept what was done to him, no matter how much pain it put him through.

"Are you all right, boy?" he asked quietly. He waited a few seconds before Peter raised his head to meet his gaze.

"Yes, Sir." He pushed out his breath in a long exhale. "Right now I'm thinking I'm a very lucky boy." He gave Thomas a half smile. "I've got you as my Dom."

Trusting Thomas

It warmed Thomas inside to hear the lad say the words, but there was a small voice in his head that whispered to him. *But you're* not *his Dom. You're just training him to get him* ready *for his Dom. He's not yours.*

Thomas looked at the boy who sat opposite him, staring at him with shining eyes. For the first time, he wondered what life would be like if Peter was really his. Just as quickly, the voice was back. *He's nearly thirty years younger than you, old man. What would a beautiful young sub of twenty-six want with a Dom* your *age?* Thomas couldn't ignore the words, try as he might. Damn voice had a point. There was no sense thinking that way. It would only lead to disappointment.

Twelve

Gut Instinct

THOMAS got to Laura Herne's office just in time to see Peter emerge from the inner door, closely followed by the psychologist. The boy's eyes were red and he'd clearly been crying. Laura smiled when she caught sight of Thomas.

"He's okay," she assured him. "We had a breakthrough today, that's all." Peter gave her a watery smile. "You did really well, Peter." She patted him kindly on the shoulder.

Peter straightened and met Thomas's gaze. "I need to go to the bathroom, Sir. I won't keep you waiting." He wiped his eyes with a paper tissue.

"No hurry." Thomas waved his hand. Peter went off in the direction of the bathroom, sniffing.

"Is there anything I need to know?" Thomas inquired.

Laura expelled her breath in one long, steady push. "Oh boy."

"Laura, what is it? Anything you can share without breaking patient confidentiality?"

She glanced quickly toward the bathroom door before answering. "What has he told you about Curtis Rogers?" She spoke in a low voice.

"Very little. He wrote a diary entry about his life with Curtis when he first came to me."

"Have you read it?" Thomas shook his head. "I didn't think so, in which case I'm glad he confided in me. He told me about seeing Curtis not far from here a few weeks ago. I gather he was quite distressed."

"To put it mildly," Thomas said dryly. He tilted his head. "He spoke to you about his life with Curtis?"

"Oh yes." Laura shivered and then seemed to snap out of it. "Don't get me wrong. It wasn't talking about Curtis that upset him. The fact that he was able to do it proved very emotional for him, that's all. There's been a change in Peter. I'd like to say it was down to our sessions, but I can't take all the credit." She regarded him shyly. "I think it's you. Whatever you're doing, Sir, keep doing it."

There was a glint in her eyes that Thomas almost missed. He had been thinking about the diary during the last few days, and this latest development made up his mind to ask her opinion.

"Laura, in your opinion, do I need to read his diary?"

She reflected for a few seconds. "If you've come this far and made this much progress without reading it, I'd say leave it alone. Besides, why run the risk it might alter how you see him? If he's able to talk to me about what's happened to him, that's good. *One* of us should be aware of his past." She hesitated and glanced quickly toward the bathroom door. "I will say this. Be careful. You need to keep your eyes and ears open when you're out with him."

He wanted to ask more questions, but Peter returned at that point. He'd washed his face and seemed calmer. Whatever Peter had told Laura had certainly made an impression. The fact that he only saw Laura twice a week now had led Thomas to believe the boy was making progress. If Laura saw today's events as a breakthrough, then hopefully things were looking even better.

"Let's go home, boy."

LUNCH was over. Peter half expected Thomas to go to the club, seeing as he'd taken the morning off to go with him to his appointment, but Thomas showed no sign of wanting to go. Instead, he seemed deep in thought. He wandered out into the garden, pulling his woolen jacket tight around him, with the dark-blue ribbed beanie on his head.

Peter watched him through the kitchen window, wondering what was going on in his head. It occurred to him briefly that Laura Herne might have revealed something from their session, but he dismissed it. Patient confidentiality wouldn't allow her to do that. He was amazed she'd managed to get so much out of him, but once he'd started talking, it had proved difficult to stop it from flooding out of him. Laura had been wonderful. She'd listened to his outpourings with her usual calm manner, without comment or judgment. However, despite her professionalism during their previous sessions, she hadn't been able to hide her anger. Peter recognized the source of that anger. Laura was viewing Curtis's actions through the eyes of a submissive.

When Peter had become too drained to relate any more, Laura switched to asking about his life with Thomas. Her eyes had shone when he spoke of the ritual Thomas had organized.

"I had wondered about the hair," she said with a wink. Peter's cheeks heated up. He'd felt relaxed enough to share something intimate with her, and she'd put his mind at ease. It didn't take away the problem, however. That he would have to deal with on his own.

Peter snapped out of his reveries when the back door opened and Thomas entered.

"Peter, I have a task for you," he said simply, pulling off his beanie and removing his jacket. He placed them on a chair.

Peter gave Thomas his full attention. "Yes, Sir?"

Thomas crooked his index finger. "Come with me." He led Peter to the room next door to the lounge. Peter hadn't been in there, as Thomas kept it locked. Dying of curiosity, Peter peered around the opened door.

"Come in, lad." Thomas stepped carefully into the room, which was difficult, because there was little room to maneuver. Everywhere Peter looked there were boxes, crates, and packing cases, all containing the same thing—books. Along every wall were wooden bookcases that reached to the ceiling. A large sash window overlooked the back garden. Bookcases framed the window at its sides and above, but beneath the window was a wide seat, fitted with a thick seat pad. Numerous cushions lined the cozy little space. Peter fell in love with it immediately.

"Welcome to my library." Thomas was smiling. "I had the bookshelves made and fitted some time ago, but I haven't had the chance to unpack the books."

Peter gazed around in awe. "You have a *lot* of books, Sir." He couldn't hold back his grin.

"I haven't asked before, but this seems to be the perfect moment. Do you like reading?" Peter's eyes lit up, and Thomas laughed. "Well, I guess I have my answer." He glanced around at the myriad containers. "Yes, there are a lot of them. The product of a lifetime teaching English." He turned back to Peter. "I want you to sort out my library, boy. But I warn you, it's a huge undertaking. The books need to be cataloged too."

"Really, Sir?" Peter breathed. Spending time unpacking books, maybe leafing through them, arranging them…. Peter had died and gone to heaven.

Thomas was watching him, eyes bright with amusement. "Have I just given you your dream job, lad?" Peter blushed.

"When can I start, Sir?" He couldn't wait. His fingers itched to get into the books.

Thomas beamed delightedly. "No time like the present, I suppose." He gestured to the boxes. "Have at it, lad." He glanced at his watch. "I could go to the club for an hour or two, while you get started." He fixed Peter with a firm stare. "You *will* remember that you have dinner to prepare, won't you?"

Peter gave a guilty start. Dinner had been the last thing on his mind. Thomas chuckled.

"Why do I have the sudden feeling that I've just presented you with a *major* distraction?"

That brought Peter to his senses. There was no *way* he'd let Thomas down. He'd have to show a lot of self-discipline where the library was concerned. Thomas left the room, and Peter looked around. *Where do I start?* The simplest idea seemed to be to get the books out and make a start on categorizing them, dealing with one box at a time. *Oh, just* start*, why don't you?*

Peter opened his first crate.

THOMAS opened the front door and sniffed. As the aroma of beef stew greeted his nostrils, he admonished himself silently for doubting the lad. One or two hours at the club had turned into three or four. There had been a lot to go through, and Thomas had suffered a mild attack of the guilts for burdening his partner and fellow Doms. So he'd locked himself in the office and worked his way through the pile of administrative paperwork that had built up.

He walked to the kitchen and glanced through the glass door of the oven at a casserole dish containing stew and dumplings. Perfect for such a cold day. Detecting the smell of fresh bread, he sneaked a peek into the breadbox. *And* a loaf of whole wheat bread too.

"Dinner smells good, lad!" he called out.

"In here, Sir." The library. Now *there* was a surprise. Thomas entered the room and found Peter sitting in the window with books piled high around him. He looked up as Thomas approached. The boy looked thoroughly content.

"I'm sorry, Sir, but I've not got very far today. I've only managed to go through one case. Did you have any idea how you'd liked these categorized?"

Thomas glanced at the book on top of the nearest pile. "Most of these are fiction. There are some textbooks and travel guides, but they make up a very small percentage. The fiction can be arranged by author." He picked up the book and examined the blurb. "I haven't read this one in years." He opened it at the front page and skimmed through the opening paragraph. After a few minutes of reading, he became aware of Peter clearing his throat. He looked up. Peter regarded him with distinct amusement.

"Now you know why I haven't got very far today, Sir. I kept doing what *you're* doing right now." The faintest suspicion of a smirk played around his lips.

"Maybe that's enough books for today, boy."

Peter nodded eagerly and carefully extracted himself from his little nook. "I'll go check on the dinner, Sir." He scooted out of the room. Thomas couldn't help but smile. The boy seemed relaxed and happy. Maybe it was about time Thomas rewarded him. After all, he was making progress with Laura Herne, and he had virtually taken over the running of the house. Thomas racked his brains for a suitable reward.

"Peter, what kind of movies do you like?" he said as he walked into the kitchen. Peter closed the oven door, sending the heavenly smell wafting throughout the room.

"Dinner will be in twenty minutes, Sir. What was the question?"

"Films, lad, films," Thomas repeated patiently. "What type of films do you like?"

Peter rubbed his neck. "To be honest, Sir, I haven't seen many films recently." His face fell, but as Thomas watched, he made a visible effort to pull himself together. His expression grew brighter. "I loved the *Star Wars* series. Not the newer ones. The originals."

Thomas couldn't believe it. The remastered DVDs were among his favorites. That settled it.

"How about after dinner, we sprawl out on the sofa and watch Episode IV? What do you say? Think of it as a reward." The look of gratitude on Peter's face brought a lump to his throat. Thomas swallowed. It gladdened his heart to see the boy looking happy. "That settles it. And I might even have some popcorn in the cupboard." Peter's eager look made him wish dinner was already over.

"READY!"

Thomas heard Peter's quiet whoop of delight from the kitchen. He snickered. Maybe he'd left it far too long before rewarding the boy. Thomas switched on the DVD player and the surround sound system, wanting to give Peter the whole cinematic experience. A couple of lamps gave the room a warm glow, and the fire was already burning behind the grate. Thomas couldn't believe how cold it was. Winter seemed endless, and spring, although technically only a week or two away, showed no signs of putting in an appearance.

Peter appeared in the doorway, carrying a large glass bowl filled to the brim with buttered popcorn. The smell was heavenly. Maybe not having dessert had been a good idea after all.

They sat on the sofa, and Thomas pulled the heavy chenille throw over Peter's knees.

"Better?" The boy nodded, snuggling it around him. Thomas placed the bowl between them, and both men dug in straightaway as the movie started. Thomas watched the familiar words scroll their way up the screen and let out a sigh of contentment. *When was the last time I did this*? For the life of him he couldn't remember. He relaxed into the seat cushions with his feet propped up on the thickly cushioned footstool he kept by the sofa. Bliss.

He couldn't miss Peter's low sigh. He gave a quick glance at the boy. Peter's expression said it all. There was no disguising it. Thomas rejoiced inwardly to see him so relaxed.

About a third of the way into the movie, the popcorn was gone. Thomas removed the bowl to the floor and sat back. To his surprise, Peter leaned up against him and laid his head on Thomas's shoulder. Thomas opened his mouth to say something, but one glance at Peter's face stopped him. The boy looked so comfortable there that Thomas didn't have the heart to move him. What was more surprising, however, was how good it felt to have him so close. Carefully, so as not to disturb him too much, Thomas draped his arm around him, and Peter snuggled up closer.

The boy may have been engrossed in the movie, but Thomas lost his focus. His thoughts were on the lad next to him, whose head now rested against Thomas's chest. Damn, this felt good. He could feel the warmth of Peter's body through the layers of clothing, and that felt good too. But he couldn't ignore the voice that suddenly clamored inside his head. *You're supposed to be his trainer. Nothing more.* For the first time, this felt like something more. He tried to push away the insistent thought, but it clung tight. A glance at Peter showed him the boy was totally at ease. He's *clearly comfortable with the situation. Why aren't I?*

Because this is not what you do.

But why not? Why the hell not?

And he envisioned closing a door, mentally locking out the little niggling voice until it grew more and more faint and finally fell silent. Thomas glanced down at Peter as he leaned into him, oblivious to Thomas's internal struggles. *I just want to enjoy this time with my boy.*

Your *boy?*

Yeah, even through a locked door, that one was audible. Damn it.

"HOW'S the library coming along?"

Thomas looked up from the Collars & Cuffs reference forms he'd been reading through at his office desk to see Leo standing by the bookcase, coffee mug in hand. Thomas put down the reference forms and stretched, feeling the muscles pop in his back. Time for another massage, maybe.

"It's looking really good," he admitted. "Peter's not rushing it, I must say. So what if he spends more time reading than he does sorting?" He grinned. "He's happy."

Leo let out a dry chuckle. "And you're letting him? Wow, *you've* changed, old man. The Thomas *I* knew wouldn't have stood for that sort of thing. A sub enjoying himself? Unthinkable." He winked. "Though I have to say, whatever you're doing must agree with you. You're looking better these days."

Thomas cocked his head. "Better? What do you mean? How did I look before, then?" He was genuinely puzzled. "And what do you mean, *whatever I'm doing?*"

Leo was quick to react. "Now, don't take it like that," he huffed. "You looked fine. It's just that now, you look… better."

Thomas wasn't letting him off the hook *that* easily. "Not buying it. Come on. Be specific."

Leo fell silent and fixed his eyes on the desk, clearly deep in thought. At long last he looked up and met Thomas's gaze, his expression serious.

"You've always been someone who seemed unruffled, calm. Somebody who reacts well in a crisis. Unflappable." Thomas nodded in agreement. "But if I'm honest? There's been something missing."

"What?" Thomas wanted to know. All of a sudden it seemed of vital importance.

Leo's eyes met his. "Joy."

Thomas was dumbfounded. Of all the things Leo could have said, this was the most unexpected. "Joy?"

Leo gave a slow nod, never once breaking eye contact. "You're happier."

Thomas's mouth dropped open. *Was* he happier? He tried to do a quick mental assessment, but Leo interrupted his thoughts.

"Don't analyze it, just accept it. He's good for you." Leo folded his arms. He glared at Thomas, as if daring him to comment further.

Thomas was nonplussed. Had Peter made *that* great a change to his life? It was the first time Thomas had shared his home with a sub; that much was true. *Had* it made such a big difference? The boy seemed to have become a natural part of his existence, almost without him noticing. One thing did strike him. Thomas looked forward to going home these days. He hadn't realized how much he'd come to dread going back to the silent Victorian house after a long day at the club, with no cheery voice to greet him, no face to light up in a smile when he came through the door, no other human being pleased to see *him*.

With a shock, it occurred to Thomas that he'd been lonely.

Leo watched him closely, as though privy to this revelation. He walked around the desk, poured out a mug of coffee, and handed it to Thomas. Thomas stared at the mug as if unsure what he was looking at.

"Drink," Leo ordered him, the faintest smile twisting the corners of his mouth. Thomas gave Leo an amused glance and then took a long drink. Leo eyed him with smug satisfaction. "You know I'm right, don't you?"

Thomas opened his mouth to retort, but the words died on his tongue. Yeah, Leo was right.

"You don't have to look so goddamned pleased with yourself about it, though," he said gruffly. Leo's gleeful expression was too much to bear. "Forget about me for a minute. I have something more serious to discuss with you."

"What is it?" Leo sat down in the chair facing Thomas.

Thomas held up the reference form. "We may have to refuse this application."

Leo's eyes widened. "Really?" Thomas could understand his reaction. Usually reference forms were a mere formality, but something about this one disturbed him. "What's the problem?"

"Can't put my finger on it, exactly. Call it a hunch, but there's a lot the club owner isn't saying about this Dom, if you get my meaning. We know the kind of comments people usually make, right?" Leo nodded. "Well, there's very few of them in here. I spent years wading through reference forms whenever the department took on a new member of staff, and you get pretty adept at reading between the lines."

"So you think he's being economical with the truth?"

"Maybe. But my gut tells me there's something not quite right."

Leo snorted. "I'll go with your gut every time, old man." He took the reference form from Thomas and skimmed it. "Hmm, I see what you mean. If you wanted to be really sure, you could give this guy a call. See if he'd be willing to tell you more over the phone."

Thomas considered this. "Actually, that's a good idea." He reached for the phone, and Leo made as if to stand. "And you can stay right there," Thomas added, fixing him with a look. Leo dropped back immediately into his seat. Thomas got through to the club owner and asked a few pertinent questions. He listened in silence for the most part, making occasional noises of agreement. When the call was finished, he replaced the receiver and sat forward.

"Well?" Leo demanded impatiently.

Thomas looked up. "It seems our applicant here is being investigated by his club. The owner doesn't have enough proof to kick him out, but he feels the Dom is trying to jump ship before he's pushed. He's been worried for a while about things subs have been telling him, and he thinks some of them may have been threatened. Again, he can't prove it, because no one is willing to step up and tell him that's what's going on."

"Then no," Leo said decisively. His eyes narrowed. "I say go with your initial instincts, Thomas. They haven't let you down yet."

Thomas nodded. "I agree." He leaned back into his chair. "I had a long talk with Steven Drummond over the phone the other day, by the way. Now that he's no longer a member of St. Andrew's, he was giving me the lowdown on what's been going on over there. I tell you, it all sounds highly suspect."

"In what way?" Leo sat bolt upright.

"Lots of new money pouring into the club. Now, a fresh injection of cash is not necessarily a bad thing, but he's worried about the source. He's been doing some fishing, and it appears one of their Doms has been pumping money into the club since he first arrived." He paused. "And the name was familiar." He locked eyes with Leo.

Leo let out a long, low whistle. "Curtis Rogers."

"Uh-huh." Thomas's forehead creased. "I'm glad we got Peter away from him, although the more I hear, the more I become convinced this isn't over yet. Curtis turning up here, for instance. No, there's something going on."

"Do you think Peter knows anything about it? What does that gut of yours tell you?"

Thomas let out a long-drawn-out sigh. "If I'm honest? Then yes, he knows. But whatever it is, he's not saying. And for the moment I'm happy to leave it like that." He swiveled in his chair and glanced down into the street. "He'll tell me when he's ready. I'll just have to be patient."

"And hope Curtis doesn't find him in the meantime," Leo added.

Thomas shuddered. He hoped to God it didn't come to that, but if it did, Thomas would fight to protect his boy. *And before you say anything, he* is *my boy,* he silently informed that pernicious inner voice of his. *Damn it, he's mine.*

The voice was silent. It didn't have to say a word.

Thirteen

Rewards

THE kiss was sweet, the caresses sweeter. And Peter was in heaven.

Warm, soft lips pressed against his neck, and a wet tongue darted out to flick at the hollow of his collarbone. He mewled as adventurous fingers discovered his nipple and tweaked it. He whimpered as that wonderful mouth kissed across his chest to lick and then suck the now-taut nub of flesh.

"Don't stop," he begged in a whisper, lifting his hips from the bed in slow motion, the muscles across his stomach tightening as pleasure rippled through him. Those lips tantalized him, pressing against his skin, moving lower now. A tongue snaked out from between parted lips to lick his abs before circling his navel.

That wicked tongue paused, and a chuckle reverberated through him. "Stop? Why would I do that?" The deep voice rolled over him, as sensual as the fingers that caressed him. Peter wanted to touch his mystery lover, but one tug at his wrists told him he'd been tied to the bed. "You can't get away. You're mine." And then the kisses resumed, edging closer to his dick, which was filling, lengthening, until at last those lips touched the soft skin of his cock and Peter groaned.

He pushed up with his hips, trying to get more of that eager mouth, those sensuous lips, wanting nothing more than to push his cock deep into hot wetness and feel that agile tongue trace a slippery line down to his balls.

"You want me to suck your dick, boy?" The mystery voice taunted him. "Is that what you want?" Lips hovered above the head of his cock; warm breath wafted over it. So close.

Peter cried out, unable to take any more. "Oh, God, *yes*!" he cried just as his cock was sucked into a hot, wet cavern and then deeper still as his lover swallowed his length. Throat muscles tightened around him.

Peter awoke as his cock erupted onto the sheet below him, pumping out come in spurt after spurt. Frantically, he grabbed hold and squeezed, trying to stop the last remnants from making an appearance, but the damage had been done. The bed was sticky and damp. What was worse, he'd just broken the first instruction Thomas had ever given him. The words echoed in his head. *You're not allowed to come. Not unless I give you permission.* Oh fuck.

He rolled onto his back and lay there, shaking. A quick glance at the alarm clock told him Thomas would be waking shortly. Peter had enough time to strip the bed and remake it with a clean sheet before Thomas got up. That didn't alter the fact that he'd come without permission. And there was no way he would lie to Thomas. He'd have to tell him.

Peter stared up at the ceiling, replaying last week's conversation with Dr. Herne in his head. Up until that point, he'd been talking about Curtis. She'd changed the subject. Peter had told her in one of their first sessions about Thomas's no masturbation/coming rule, and Laura had wanted to know how he felt about that. *Duh.* When he'd first arrived at the house, jerking off had been the last thing on his mind. In fact, he'd begun to worry he'd never get hard again. *Yeah, but that changed, didn't it? Once you got your hands on Thomas....*

He closed his eyes, trying to shut out the voice in his head, but the little shit wasn't giving up that easily. He saw himself kneeling astride Thomas, smoothing his hands down his back, kneading the man's supple flesh. When Thomas began to push his hips ever so slightly into the bed, Peter realized with something of a shock that Sir was aroused. And he wasn't the only one. Laura's words came back to him.

"YOU got an erection?"

Peter closed his eyes tight. "Yes," he whispered. He couldn't look at her.

"Peter, open your eyes. Please."

Slowly, he opened them, only to gaze out her window. The noises from the busy city-center street below filtered through the double-glazed panes.

"Peter, why does it bother you that you got an erection? Surely, after what we discussed early on, this is a good thing. You're starting to react normally again. Having erections is normal."

At last he turned to look at her. "You don't think it's awful that massaging Sir gave me a hard-on?"

Laura chuckled. "With the way he looks? Sweetie, I'd have been surprised if you didn't have one. Think about it for a minute. He was naked. Oiled up. You were kneeling astride him in what, your underwear?" Peter nodded. "You had your hands all over him. If that didn't arouse you, I'd be worried."

"But...." His words trailed off. How to make her understand. "But he's Sir." He tried to convey so much with that one word.

Laura's brow cleared. "Ah. Peter, do you think it's wrong to have sexual feelings about your Dom?"

At last. "Yes!" he blurted out. He lowered his head, and shame coursed through him in a hot rush.

Laura left her seat and knelt before him, taking his hands. She waited patiently until he raised his gaze to meet hers.

"Peter, do you know how many subs have feelings just like yours? Hell, I fell in love with my first Dom. Okay, so it was more like falling in lust, as I came to realize later on, but I'm telling you this to show you it's perfectly normal." She stared at him fixedly. "Think about it. Apart from our sessions and your weekly get-togethers with Alex, this man is your whole world. Of course you're going to think about him. The massage just opened the gate to those feelings."

He considered her words. It was true he hadn't felt any of this prior to that day.

Laura wasn't finished. "But I think there's more to it than the massage. Something else that has made you see Thomas in a different light. Any idea what that might be?"

Peter knew exactly. It was the ceremony. Everything changed for him that day. Thomas had done all that for him. He'd shown Peter he was there for him. That, more than anything, made Peter realize he could trust Thomas. What was more, he knew now that he needed Thomas.

All of a sudden it struck him. "Oh God," he uttered.

"Peter, what is it?" Laura leaned forward. He could hear the note of concern.

"I'm going to lose him."

Laura's brow wrinkled. "Lose him? What do you mean?"

He stared at her, unblinking. "Sir is training me for another Dom. And once he's finished, he won't be my Sir anymore." The thought devastated him.

Laura spoke gently. "Is that the first time it's really hit you?" He nodded. "But now that it has, you need to confront it, to face the fact that you're attracted to your Dom. This won't go away, Peter. You just need to decide how you're going to deal with this attraction." She paused. "And yes, you also have to prepare yourself for the day when it's time to move on."

Peter couldn't think about that now. He wouldn't think about it. Because the thought of losing Thomas was like a vise around his heart.

THOMAS opened his eyes to find Peter kneeling silently beside the bed, his eyes downcast.

"Good morning, boy."

"Good morning, Sir." To his surprise the boy's usual shy morning smile didn't materialize. Peter held himself stiffly, not making eye contact. Thomas pulled himself upright, wincing at the ache in his back. Nowhere as painful as before, however. *Let's face it, I'm getting old.* The fact that it was his birthday in a month's time didn't help matters. Fifty-six. He tried to tell himself that it was not age, but his aching muscles weren't listening.

And of course, Peter noticed.

"Sir, what's wrong? Is it your back again?" An anxious expression crept into his eyes.

Thomas waved his hand dismissively. "It's nothing, lad." He peered intently at the boy's face. "Going to tell me what's bothering you? Because I know *something* is." He waited. In the silence that followed, he became aware of the rumble of the washing machine from downstairs. "Isn't it a little early for doing the laundry?"

Peter's cheeks were red. "About that, Sir." He hesitated.

Thomas didn't jump in but waited. He picked up his cup of tea and sipped it, relishing both the burst of flavor on his tongue and the much-needed jolt of caffeine to his system.

"Sir, I… I had a wet dream. And when I woke up, I—" Peter broke off abruptly, clearly too embarrassed to continue.

Aha. "Were you masturbating? Tell me the truth."

"*No*, Sir," he stressed. "I wouldn't do that. You said not to. Please, Sir, believe me."

Thomas held out a hand to stop him. "It's okay, boy, I believe you." Something crossed his mind. He tilted his head. "Is that the first time you've come since you've been here?"

Peter nodded miserably. His chin dropped to his chest.

Thomas thought quickly. He wasn't about to punish the boy. If anything, he was proud of him. He could have not mentioned it and washed the bedding once Thomas left the house. The fact that he hadn't spoke volumes. And another thing. If that was his first wet dream since his arrival…. Maybe the lad's body was at last getting back to normal. Thomas was concerned that Curtis's treatment may have had a lasting effect on the boy.

It amazed him that Peter had gone this long without coming. He thought of the number of times over the years during training that a sub had begged to be allowed to come. Peter hadn't done that. Not once. Thomas assumed the boy was working through his issues with Laura. He hadn't pushed it, figuring he'd wait until Peter finally said something.

What concerned him now was how to deal with this. His first instinct was to reward the boy for his honesty. But how to go about it? As he sat up, his back protested the movement. *Of course. Perfect.*

"Boy, I'll be honest too. Right now my back is in need of your specialized services. So I have a proposition for you. We're going to go downstairs and have breakfast, after which you will make whatever preparations you need in here to perform a massage. And as payment for your services, I will reward you."

Peter's lips parted. Whatever he'd been expecting, that plainly wasn't it.

"You're… you're not going to punish me?" Those guileless green eyes grew large and round.

Thomas shook his head. "No, lad. It wasn't deliberate. But once we start training, we may need to work on that." He winked, and Peter blushed fetchingly. "So, is my proposition acceptable?" Peter nodded eagerly. "Then downstairs with you, and make sure the coffee's ready for when I get there."

Peter scrambled to his feet. "Yes, Sir." *There* was the smile that greeted Thomas every morning. Peter was out the bedroom door in seconds. Thomas laughed quietly to himself. The idea of the massage had come to him suddenly, a way of rewarding the lad for his honesty without actually telling him that was the case. However, his motives weren't entirely selfless. The thought of Peter's oiled hands gliding over his body was a pleasant one. Part of his anatomy obviously felt the same way. Thomas tossed back the duvet and glared at his stiffening cock.

"And *you* can forget it," he said sternly under his breath, addressing the shaft, which jerked up as if in reaction to his words. He shook his head. Talking to his dick now. Never mind getting old—senility must be setting in.

PETER was tired and sweaty. He'd pulled out all the stops with the massage, making sure every bit of Thomas had been attended to with equal care. Thomas's little grunts and sighs told Peter he was doing a good job. By the time Peter had finished, he'd thought Thomas would have to be poured into his clothes, the man was so relaxed. That thick, erect cock was once again in evidence, however, and it had taken all Peter's strength of will not to wrap his hand around it and gently pull at it. The man was temptation itself.

Thomas lay with his eyes closed, no hint of embarrassment about him. Peter took advantage of this state of affairs to gaze at his Dom unseen. He loved the concave dip of his belly, the wide pecs with their tiny, bronzed nipples that begged to have a tongue flick at them. Thomas's thighs were muscled and firm, and Peter had worked the quads hard, digging his fingers and knuckles into them, knowing how good it would feel once the massage was finished. His eyes were continually drawn to Thomas's erect shaft, which pointed up toward his abs. With a shock Peter noted a glistening bead of precome at the head. Peter's trainers at college had warned him this was a normal reaction, but it didn't stop him from yearning to taste the clear drop of fluid.

His dick stiffened just as Thomas cleared his throat. Hastily, Peter grabbed a towel, held it in front of his hardening length, and then straightened. He hadn't had time to put on his sweatpants, and he certainly didn't want Thomas spying the bulge in his briefs. *How the hell could I explain* that?

Thomas opened his eyes. A smile played about his lips.

"That felt marvelous. What am I saying? It *feels* marvelous."

Peter's chest swelled. Sir was pleased. He grabbed a new towel from the chair beside him with one hand and gave it to Thomas to cover himself. Peter stood back, waiting. Thomas swung his legs out and stood up, wrapping the towel around his waist and securing it. He appeared not to notice Peter's state of undress.

"Thank you, boy. That was quite wonderful." Peter bowed his head in acknowledgment. "I'm going to have a shower and then go to the club for the rest of the day. I assume you will be working in the library?" Thomas had already told him how pleased he was with the library's progress. Peter worked methodically and slowly but surely the boxes were being emptied and made ready to be stored down in the cellar.

"Yes, Sir." Peter collected the oil and towels from the bed and went toward the door.

"You're forgetting something, boy." Peter halted, turning toward him. "Your reward?"

Peter *had* forgotten. He was intrigued by the gleam in Thomas's eyes. "Yes, Sir?"

"You may jerk off."

Peter stilled. Thomas's words were totally unexpected. "S-Sir?"

Thomas grinned. "You heard me. Now off with you so I can get showered. And Peter? Make it a good one. Who knows when the next time will be?"

Yeah, that gleam was definitely wicked. Sir was enjoying himself.

PETER didn't know if Thomas was deliberately taking his time in leaving the house this morning, or if it was simply that time was dragging because Peter kept watching the clock. All he knew was that when Thomas eventually walked out the front door with a wicked grin plastered over his entire face, the door had barely shut after him before Peter was racing up the stairs.

Bed or shower? Peter couldn't make up his mind. His cock was a solid rod in his jeans. The hard-on that had appeared thanks to massaging Thomas's hard, tight body had only gotten harder once Thomas had revealed his reward. How he'd managed to keep his mind on preparing a packed lunch for Thomas, he'd never know. And of course, what made it a million times worse was that he had the sneaking suspicion Thomas was laughing at him, albeit in his head. Did the man *know* how hard he was? Probably. Sir knew everything.

He stopped on the landing, confronted by his two choices. Which was it to be? Peter wanted to enjoy this, to savor it. That made it easier. *Bed.* He thought about the clean bedding. *In that case, you're gonna have to be careful. You can't change the sheets twice in one day.* For once, his niggling inner voice had it spot-on. He entered the room, and something caught his eye immediately—several somethings, actually. An unopened bottle of lube lying on his pillow. A towel spread out on the bed. And on top of the chest of drawers, a portable TV with built-in DVD player had miraculously appeared. Next to it lay two or three DVDs, along with a brief note. Burning with curiosity, Peter picked it up and read it.

"A selection for all tastes. Enjoy."

Sir certainly knows how to reward a sub. Peter looked at the titles and cover images with a grin. He wouldn't be needing those.

He glanced back at the towel, and suddenly a thought occurred to him. Sir had spread it over the bed. Yep, the man was *definitely* laughing at him.

Peter undressed slowly, painfully aware of how little it would take to have him coming. His cock sprang up with a bounce as he slid his briefs down and off. Nude, he stretched out on his back with the towel beneath him and opened the bottle of lube. After coating his palm in the silky liquid, he wrapped his hand around his length with a long-drawn-out sigh. *I can't remember the last time I did this.* He tugged gently, pulling at the velvety soft skin, which slid over a core of steel. *God, that feels so good.* He reached lower to cup his balls and rolled them in his fingers, enjoying the texture of the soft skin. He tightened his grip around the base and pushed up with his hips, loving the feel of his hard flesh as it squeezed through the tight circle of his fist. He released his balls and ran his hand up over his chest. Tweaking his nipples only served to arouse him further. He touched the hair, which was only just starting to appear once more.

It took him back to the upper room. Thomas shaving him. The sound of the razor as it scraped over his skin. Thomas shaving his balls, his crack, the base of his cock. And all with the same expression on his face. As though he were performing the most delicate task, which needed infinite care and painstaking precision.

His thoughts shifted to Thomas on his back and Thomas's tumescent cock rising into the air, long and thick. He imagined grasping that cock and holding it steady while he brought his lips to meet it and kissed the tip reverently. Peter closed his eyes and slid his hand faster as he worked his length. In his mind he heard Thomas's gasp as Peter took him into his mouth, heard the groan as Peter deep-throated him. He imagined how Sir's cock would taste, the flavor rich and pure male. His hand quickened as he watched Thomas starting to tremble, as Peter bobbed up and down on the man's dick, taking him deep again and again.

Too close. Almost at the point of coming, Peter backed off, opening his eyes, deliberately banishing the images from his head. He eased down, moving slowly, leisurely now, as he rubbed over the head, twisting the foreskin slightly with each downward stroke and releasing it on the upstroke. He caressed his balls and pulled lightly on his sac. *That's it. Slowly does it.* He kept up the regular movements as he tried to stave off his climax.

He closed his eyes, and there was Thomas, standing beside the bed, gazing over the length of Peter's body and focusing finally on his cock.

"That's mine, boy." Thomas reached down and grasped his dick. His hand slid from root to head, and the movement grew more urgent. He tightened his grip, and Peter pushed up as the lube eased his cock's passage. "That's it, boy, fuck my hand."

Peter began to moan, unable to keep the sounds from pouring out of him, incapable of doing anything but obeying his Sir. He bucked, pumping faster as Thomas knelt down beside him, keeping his eyes fixed on Peter's face as he squeezed tighter. Peter held his breath as Thomas came closer, edging lower toward him until their lips were almost touching.

"Sir," he begged, wanting to feel those lips on his, aching for his kiss. Thomas's breath was warm and sweet as his mouth claimed Peter's in a kiss that had him moaning softly, a sound swallowed as Thomas's lips met his over and over again. Peter reached for him, cupped his face, and stroked the gray hair at his temples as he lost himself in the kiss. And all the while, that hand never ceased its sensual motion, dragging him closer to the edge.

Thomas broke away and met Peter's gaze. "Come."

Peter stared into those green eyes, which saw him, saw *all* of him, and he came.

Peter howled as his orgasm crashed into him with all the force of a Mack truck. Come jetted over his belly as he arched up from the bed. Tremors shook his body as he succumbed to the sensations that had so long been absent from his existence. His thighs trembled. For a while he lay there shaking as he gradually came down from wherever the hell his climax had taken him. He only knew it had been a very long time since he'd come so hard and felt this good.

Peter wiped away the evidence with the towel and then dropped back onto the bed. The last tremors dissipated, until finally he lay quiescent, luxuriating in the afterglow. A sensation of well-being flowed through him, as though filling every vein with rich cream.

"Well, you said to make it a good one, Sir," he said aloud, addressing the absent Dom. And then he laughed, a sound of sheer joy that tumbled out into the quiet room and bounced off the walls. The surfeit of happiness took him by surprise, and he couldn't contain the grin that spread across his face. Warmth radiated throughout his body, and the one emotion that filled him was gratitude. And the words wouldn't be contained either.

"Thank you, Sir."

Fourteen

Contract

"PETER, can you come into the kitchen, please?"

Peter put down the book he'd been in the middle of cataloging. A swift glance around the library brought a satisfied expression to his face.

It had taken the better part of a month, but the room was looking beautiful. There only remained one crate to be emptied, and then he would type up his handwritten notes into some semblance of order. Sir would have a definitive list of every book he possessed and where it could be found. Definitely a job well done.

He entered the kitchen and found Thomas standing by the sink, coffee mug in hand as he looked out over the garden. Spring had most definitely arrived. Daffodils had sprung up everywhere, and the trees were hiding their branches under a new coat of greenery. Easter had come and gone, taking the last of the unseasonably cold weather with it.

"Yes, Sir?" Peter waited by the table to be acknowledged. Thomas turned to face him, and his expression seemed unusually serious. *Oh God, what have I done?* The thought raced through his mind with alarming speed before he realized he was overreacting. *You haven't done anything, stupid.*

"Sit down, boy. I need to talk to you."

Peter pulled back a chair and sat, keeping his eyes on Thomas. He waited in silence with his hands on the table in front of him, fingers laced. Thomas regarded him thoughtfully.

"Are you happy here, boy?"

The question took him by surprise, but his reply was immediate. "Yes, Sir." And it was the truth. Peter had never felt happier. He loved his life in the quiet Victorian house. Serving Thomas satisfied him completely. It filled him with pride to look around the house and know that he played a major part in its smooth running. He looked forward to Alex's weekly visits, which were always filled with laughter. And as for living with Thomas, Peter had gotten used to the man's ways. There were occasions when the thought of having to leave him intruded into Peter's peaceful existence, but he did his best to push such thoughts aside. Peter concentrated on serving Thomas as best he could. There was, however, one thing that preoccupied his mind. He wanted more. He was ready for more. But he trusted Thomas would know when the time was right to take things further.

That one word resonated with him. Trust. The Dom had proved to him time and time again that Peter could trust him. These last three months had given Peter a whole new outlook on life, and he was eager to take further steps.

"I'm going to repeat a question I asked you back in January."

"Yes, Sir."

"Do you still want to pursue the D/s lifestyle?" Thomas watched him intently.

Hell, yes! Peter's heart leapt in his chest. "Oh yes, Sir," he breathed. "More than anything."

Thomas's eyes lit up, and his face relaxed into a smile. "Well, that was fairly emphatic." Peter returned his smile. "Our initial contract was up a few weeks ago, lad, so we need to think about a new one. But I've been giving some thought to your training. Or rather, the form your training will take."

Peter said nothing but waited expectantly.

Thomas rubbed his chin. "There's something I'd like to do, a kind of experiment, if you like, before I make any decisions." That thoughtful expression was back. "Apart from going to your appointments with Dr. Herne and to the salon, you haven't set foot outside the house."

Peter stiffened. Thomas had found his Achilles' heel with one dart.

Thomas was watching him carefully. "So you and I are going out for lunch today, to a bar not far from my club. We won't be going to the club, however."

Peter swallowed. "Yes, Sir."

Thomas's expression softened. "It's not torture, boy. It's lunch."

Try telling that to my stomach, Peter thought. *'Cause right now it feels as though there's a bowling ball in it.* He tried to tell himself he would be safe with Thomas, that it was getting easier to be outside. Unfortunately, not all of him was listening. For a start, he'd just lost his appetite.

WELL, at least I have my answer, Thomas thought. It was as he'd feared. The Peter who had emerged during the last three months, the efficient sub who had slotted into his life with such ease, had been submerged in a young man who visibly trembled in a bar full of strangers. This was the boy when he'd first arrived, skittish and nervous. *Damn it, I don't have to be right* all *the time.* Just for once, Thomas would love to have got it wrong.

Peter had hardly touched his food. Every few seconds he glanced around anxiously toward anyone who came near him. The bar, Via Fossa, was relatively quiet. Thomas had deliberately chosen to come here at lunchtime to avoid the evening crowds, but in the end, it had made little difference. If Peter couldn't cope with a half-empty bar, there was no way Thomas was letting him anywhere near the club. Training him there would be counterproductive. And that left only one option.

"Come on, lad. Let's go home."

Peter's head jerked up in surprise, but he recovered and responded with alacrity.

"Yes, Sir." The boy was on his feet in seconds. Thomas let out a wry chuckle and stood up, leading the way to the door. Out on the street, however, Thomas's manner changed, as he was constantly on the lookout for Curtis or his associate. It hadn't been that long since the man had appeared at the club, and Thomas wasn't inclined to think he'd given up his search for Peter. Peter didn't notice, thank God, but then the lad was far too busy jumping at shadows to notice Thomas attentively scanning the street as they headed for the car.

THOMAS dropped his keys onto the hall table and went into the kitchen. His mind was made up, but he could really do with some advice. He was about to enter new territory, and the prospect was a little daunting, to say the least. He put on the kettle and went to the cupboard. The situation called for something less stimulating than coffee. He found Peter's favorite green tea and some chamomile for himself. Peter had followed him in, and Thomas sensed him hovering in the doorway, clearly still rattled from the field trip.

"Come and sit down, boy," Thomas said without turning, concentrating on the task in front of him. He heard the scrape of the chair across the stone floor as Peter sat. The only sounds to be heard in the kitchen were the bubbling of the water boiling in the kettle and the birdsong that drifted in through the open window. Once the tea had infused, Thomas brought the two mugs of tea to the table. Peter sniffed appreciatively.

"Thank you, Sir," he murmured. He sank back into the chair, expelling his breath in a long exhale as he wrapped both hands around the warm mug.

"Better now that you're home?" As if he needed to ask. Thomas could see the tension melt away.

Peter's gaze was frank. "Yes, Sir." A shiver ran through him. His brow creased into a frown. "Sir, may I ask something? Why did we go there? It wasn't to have lunch, was it?"

Thomas cocked an eyebrow at the intuitive remark. It was time for truth.

"Peter, I usually train submissives at my club, Collars & Cuffs. I've done that for a great many years now. It's a safe environment with good facilities. However, my concern was that you wouldn't be at ease there, and if that were the case, you would find it difficult to concentrate on your training."

Peter's face fell. "And look how I coped with being in a bar, let alone your club." He lowered his eyes to the table. "You're not going to train me, are you, Sir?"

Thomas reached across the table and grasped Peter's hand. "I said that's where I *usually* train submissives. I've only had the club for the past ten years, lad, and I've been training subs for a damn sight longer than that." Peter's gaze was on him at once. He winked at the boy and was relieved to see a hopeful look appear in his beautiful green eyes. "Would you like to see where I sometimes used to train subs before that?"

Peter nodded eagerly. Thomas released his hand and stood up. "Then come with me, boy." He led Peter through the hall and up the stairs until they were standing on the landing. Peter looked around in confusion. There were four bedrooms and a bathroom on the first floor, and Peter was well acquainted with them all. Thomas gave a brief flick of his head upward and watched as Peter glanced at the ceiling. Above their heads was the access hatch to the loft.

"Up there."

PETER stared at Thomas incredulously. "In the loft?"

Thomas appeared excited. "I warn you, it's going to need some sorting out before it can resume its original purpose, but yes, that's my playroom up there." He disappeared into the bedroom and returned a moment later with a long stick with a hook at the end. Thomas reached up and hooked the small handle that protruded from the hatch. A squeaking of hinges accompanied the hatch opening toward them and a set of wooden steps descending. It was surprisingly light up there. Peter was intrigued.

"Up you go, lad."

Holding on to the steps higher up, Peter carefully made his way into the loft, making good use of the rail as his head emerged above the hatch. He stood upright in the loft, aware of Thomas behind him. Peter's jaw dropped.

"Oh, wow."

Peter was standing in a wide room with a polished wooden floor. Large windows were set into the roof, and light spilled into the room, giving it an airy feel. Everywhere he looked there was a layer of dust. A black sling hung from hooks in the huge oak beams that stretched out between roof trusses. The beams were about six inches above Thomas's head. Peter could reach them if he stretched. A low, angled bench stood to one side, along with a long, low sofa with wide cushions.

Peter coughed as the dust got to his throat. "When were you last up here, Sir?" He blinked as motes of dust danced in the sunlight around him.

Thomas chuckled. "D'you know, I don't honestly remember, it's been so long." He startled Peter by jumping once, as though testing the floor's ability to sustain their weight. Peter gave him an anxious glance, and he grinned. "Don't worry, lad. It's quite safe." Thomas gazed around him. "I'd forgotten how little I'd left up here."

He gestured toward the cupboard to the rear of the playroom. "I emptied that when the club opened. That's where all the equipment went." He shook his head. "This is going to take some cleaning before we can use it."

Peter didn't care. He liked the room immediately. And if it was a choice between training at the club or here….

"Then I'd better get started right away, hadn't I, Sir?" He beamed at Thomas, who laughed.

"Bless you, lad. I love the way you think. But let's go down to the kitchen first. I want you to eat something. You didn't exactly stuff yourself in the bar."

Peter reddened. "I'm sorry, Sir. I… I wasn't hungry." His stomach chose that moment to growl, and Thomas smirked.

"Let's get you fed, and then I want to pop to the club. While I'm gone, you can make a start up here. How does that sound?"

Peter thought it sounded like a great idea. He was dying to get rid of all the dust and restore the playroom to its former glory before Thomas returned. He couldn't wait to see his face.

"Sounds good, Sir."

"CAN we talk?" Thomas poked his head around the office door. Leo glanced up guiltily and hurriedly stuffed the book he'd been reading into the desk drawer. Thomas grinned. "And what are you reading, Mr. Hart? Not more of your favorite erotic gay romances, surely."

Ever since Leo had revealed his liking for gay fiction, Thomas loved to tease the man now and again. Leo took it in his stride, but it was the first time Thomas had caught him in the act.

Leo huffed. "I was on a break."

Thomas came into the office and pushed the door shut. He sat in the worn leather chair that faced the desk and pretended to peer at the desk as if trying to see what Leo had hidden away from view. Leo glared at him, but Thomas could see he wasn't serious.

"I thought you were spending the day with Peter." Leo got up to pour them both a coffee.

"So I was, but something happened, and I need your advice."

"Go on."

Thomas told him about the visit to the bar and Peter's reaction. He then informed Leo of his plan to train the boy in his playroom.

Leo chortled. "Good God, man, when was the last time you used it?"

"So long ago that I don't care to remember," Thomas replied ruefully. "Peter is cleaning it as we speak." The memory of the boy's eagerness brought a fond smile to his face. "He'll probably have it spotless by the time I get home."

Leo handed Thomas his mug and then sat, sipping his coffee. "So why do you need my advice? Sounds like you've got everything covered."

Thomas got up and went to the filing cabinet. He pulled out the manila folder that contained the contracts and removed one. Once he replaced the folder and sat down again, he waved the contract at Leo.

"It's time for a new contract with the lad, and I'll be honest, I'm not sure what to do."

Leo straightened. "This isn't like you. What's on your mind?" His brow wrinkled.

Thomas opened the contract and perused its contents thoughtfully. "For a start, I'm going to forgo any training on how to behave around others. I'm not thinking about taking him anywhere near the club. He can't cope with that. I'll train him how to speak to me, not make eye contact, sure. Stances, responses, I don't have a problem with those. What does concern me is I'll have to avoid anything that inflicts pain. No whips, canes, floggers, paddles." His eyes clouded over. "You saw his scars, right?" Leo nodded. "That boy has had enough pain in his life." A brief shudder ran through him, and he composed himself quickly. "I'm also going to avoid using humiliation. And if I'm training him at the house, there will be no public scenes, either."

Leo's expression was equally thoughtful. "So, no pain, no humiliation, no public scenes. Fine. What's the problem, then?"

Thomas stared at him. "Leo, I've spent my whole life as a Dom training submissives so that they're used to everything their future Master may throw at them. What exactly can I use to train Peter if I cut out all the instruments of our lifestyle? How is that going to help him?"

Leo returned his stare. "Thomas, you've always done really well when it came to matching our subs up with the perfect Dom for them. Peter is going to require a very special Dom, that's all, and it may take a bit of research on your part. It will have to be someone who is fully aware of his history, and who is happy to play in a different way. Look at Jonathon and Dillon, for goodness' sake. When do you see Jonathon using whips or anything like that on Dillon? Never. Jonathon's main focus is to make his boy fly, but he doesn't do it through pain, because Dillon isn't built like that."

Thomas thought about the relationship between Jonathon and his submissive. He thought about the times he'd seen the two men in a scene. And suddenly it hit him.

"Toys."

"Excuse me?"

Thomas grinned. "Toys. Dildos. Vibrators. Prostate massagers. Sounds. Gloves. Cock rings. Cages. Sling." He beamed at Leo. "You've hit the nail on the head. Peter needs to fly. He's had four years of God knows what at the hands of Curtis Rogers, and I'd be willing to bet that in all those years, no one gave Peter the chance to fly. Bloody hell, Leo, the boy was almost in subspace just from being shaved. Did you see that?" Leo nodded. "Peter's going to need a Dom who gets off on seeing his sub fly. That boy was made to soar, lad." He could barely contain his excitement.

Leo was grinning too. Apparently Thomas's mood was infectious.

"It sounds to me like you need to go shopping. That's quite a list you've got."

Now *there* was an idea. Suddenly Thomas couldn't wait to get home.

PETER was *seriously* dusty. There was dust on his clothes and in his hair, what little he had of it. Sir's playroom, however, was looking great.

It had taken longer than he'd anticipated to get up all the dust, which had meant *very* carefully making several trips up and down the steps to get buckets of clean water and dry cloths, but at last the room was looking clean. Now that the task was completed, Peter had time to take a really good look around. He eyed the sling with great interest. He'd wiped the leather down with soapy water and then dried it with a clean cloth. Apart from the sling bed, which was attached to chains at each corner, stirrups had been fastened to the chains at one end. He placed a hand on the leather sling and stroked it, tentatively pressing down on it as though testing whether it would take the weight of a man.

Trusting Thomas

Peter couldn't begin to imagine how it would feel to lie in the sling with his legs in the stirrups, suspended in the air. He shivered. He deliberately turned away from the enticing object and looked at the most intriguing item in the loft. It was a bench of sorts, as it had padded surfaces, but it looked for all the world like a letter *P* lying flat on its back. There were several points around the tubular frame where rings protruded. Peter stared at the object for several long seconds, trying to work out its function. He supposed the lowest part of the bench was for kneeling on, which meant the upper part, comprised of two padded surfaces, was for lying over.

"It's a spanking bench, boy."

Peter gave a start. He'd been so lost in his thoughts, he hadn't even heard Sir come into the house. He turned to face Thomas, his cheeks flushed.

Thomas was grinning at him as he poked his head above the loft hatch. He glanced around the playroom with an expression of delight across his face. "You've done wonders!" Peter gave him a shy smile. "If you're done up here, come down to the kitchen. I have something to discuss with you." One last satisfied gaze around his playroom and Thomas's head disappeared from view.

Peter grabbed his buckets and cloths and made his way down the steps. He left the steps as they were, unsure if Thomas meant to return there later, and raced down the stairs. Thomas was in the kitchen, preparing two mugs of tea. Peter's mouth fell open at the sight of the documents that lay on the table. A contract. His heart began to beat faster.

"Sit down, lad." Thomas placed the mugs on the table and sat. His eyes were sparkling as he tapped the contract with a forefinger. "You know what this is."

"Yes, Sir." Peter tried to compose himself, but his pulse was racing, and all of a sudden his mouth was dry. Thomas arched his brows, and Peter blushed. Of course Sir knew what was going on inside his head.

"You know about limits and safewords from one of our previous discussions. Have you given any thought to what your safewords would be?" Thomas gazed at him inquiringly.

Peter had been giving the matter some thought ever since he realized Thomas would insist on him having them. "I'd like *razor* for my red word, Sir. The one that stops everything. And *beanie* for my yellow." He liked the amused glint in Thomas's eyes. "If that's all right, Sir."

173

"Perfectly acceptable." Thomas's expression changed. "But you and I need to discuss limits."

Peter swallowed. He'd been nervous about this part. He knew Thomas had talked about hard and soft limits, but Peter was sure the Dom might disagree with some of the thoughts in his head right now.

"I've been thinking a lot about this," Thomas continued, "and I have a suggestion or two." Peter said nothing, but waited. Surprisingly, Thomas got up from his chair and moved around to the empty seat next to Peter, who suddenly noticed there were two contracts on the table. Thomas picked up one of them and opened it. "Take a look, lad. This is what a contract usually looks like."

Peter was confused. Why two contracts? He pushed the thought aside to glance at the typewritten document. His heart nearly stopped when he read the heading *Pain*, and below it a list of implements that could be used. Cold spread through his body. He was dizzy. Thomas's warm hand on his steadied him.

"Easy now, boy. You're panicking. This isn't your contract."

THOMAS cursed himself. Why had he shown the boy the original?

Because you wanted to be honest with him. That much was true. But it was all too clear from Peter's reaction that it had been a mistake.

"Peter. *Peter.*" At last his words seemed to filter through the panic. Peter met his gaze. His breathing grew less erratic. Thomas nodded in approval. "That's it, lad." Swiftly, he reached for the other contract. "*This* is *your* contract, Peter." He waited as the boy opened it slowly. Thomas couldn't miss the catch in his breath as Peter read it. This contract was unique. Thomas had removed the entire section on pain, along with a few other things. What was left was a considerably shorter contract, but hopefully one that aroused Peter's interest.

Peter looked down the list, eyes growing rounder. "I... I don't understand, Sir."

Thomas pointed to the different sections. "These are normally what you'd find in a contract. Bondage. Toys. Marks. Safewords. Sex." He noted the sudden flush to Peter's cheeks. "But there is no section on Pain. I removed it." He sat back and awaited Peter's reaction. He didn't have to wait long. He could see the boy's muscles release their tension immediately, and a shaky laugh burst from Peter's lips. Tears appeared at the corners of his eyes.

Thomas couldn't contain his response. He hugged the boy to him. Thomas's heart beat faster as Peter slipped two slim arms around him and held him tight. He kissed the boy's forehead tenderly. Peter held on to him, his eyes closed. Thomas let go with one arm to wipe the lad's eyes gently, and came away with his fingers damp.

"No more tears, lad," he whispered. "Okay?" He broke the embrace and sat back, anxiously regarding his boy. Peter straightened and looked him in the eye, calm once more.

"Yes, Sir."

Thomas tapped the contract. "We can talk about this later. Right now, you and I have something *much* more entertaining to do." Peter cocked his head, and Thomas winked conspiratorially.

"Have you ever shopped online for sex toys?"

Fifteen

Time for Truth

PETER'S brain only registered one word—sex—and then it started. His heart began to hammer in his chest, and suddenly his mouth was as dry as the Sahara. He knew he was breathing too rapidly, and he tried to follow Dr. Herne's suggestions, but his body wasn't playing ball. He couldn't swallow. Nausea threatened to overwhelm him. Thomas's voice seemed to be coming from a long way off, and all of a sudden Peter was overcome by the urge to get out of there, right *now*.

He got to his feet and pushed back the chair before heading for the kitchen door, dimly aware of Thomas following him. The front door loomed ahead of him at the end of the hallway, and he shrank back. The sound of his heartbeat pounding filled his ears. He darted into the lounge, looking around in desperation, not even sure what he was looking for. Peter threw himself onto the sofa and curled up into a tight ball. He felt his limbs tremble. He closed his eyes tight, shutting out the world. He heard Thomas drop to his knees beside the sofa. Thomas's words barely made it through the fog of panic.

"Peter, *Peter.* I'm right here. What can I do to help, boy?"

He strained desperately to find his voice. "Get me... to... to count breaths, Sir. Count for me." He panted, trying to control his breathing. Thomas's deep voice filtered through.

"Okay, boy, breathe in... and out.... That's it, breathe in... and out...." Peter clung to the sound of Sir's voice as he fought to regulate his breathing. "Breathe in for the count of two, then out for two."

Thomas spoke calmly, and Peter tried to relax his tensed muscles, fixed on each command as Thomas got him to hold each breath for slightly longer. The nausea receded, and finally there was enough saliva to moisten his mouth. Thomas continued to count steadily, and Peter could hear him breathing in time, their patterns synchronized.

"Good boy, that's it." The words of praise flowed over him, calming him. Peter concentrated on Thomas's voice as at last the tremors died away. He straightened himself out on the sofa. The muscles in his legs and arms protested as he unwound them from his fetal position. "Just lie there quietly for a while. Let the blood flow." He felt Thomas's large, warm hands rub his legs briskly, then his arms. "I don't want you getting cramps." The pounding in his ears faded away until he lay quiescent, physically and mentally exhausted.

Thomas withdrew his hands, and Peter opened his eyes. Sir knelt beside the sofa with his eyes fixed on Peter. He said nothing, but the look of concern in his eyes was plain enough. The last thing Peter had wanted was for Sir to see him like this. It was bad enough when it happened with Dr. Herne. Their conversation of several weeks ago rang in his head.

"You will *have to tell him, you know. What if it happens at home? How will you explain that you've kept this from him?"*

He knew that was the submissive in her talking. He also knew it made sense for Thomas to be aware of what happened and to know how to deal with it.

"I can't," he said, hating the whine in his voice. *"Please, don't ask me to."*

Her voice softened. "Of course I won't. It's your decision. But I do believe you need to think about it."

"Peter? Can you sit up?"

Thomas's words pulled him sharply back into the present. Peter sat up slowly, blinking. Thomas was watching him carefully.

"Are you all right now?"

Peter gave a slow nod. "Yes, Sir." It was true. His breathing was still slightly fast, but he had it under control. He waited for Thomas's next words.

"So unless I've got it wrong, that was a panic attack." Thomas spoke quietly. "And obviously not your first."

Peter took a deep breath. *No use denying it any longer.* "Yes, Sir. I mean, no, Sir."

Thomas nodded once and then got to his feet. "I'm going to get you a glass of water, and when I come back, you and I are going to talk, okay?" Peter bobbed his head, swallowing nervously. Thomas gazed at him for a second or two and then copied his movement. When he left the room, Peter dragged in several deep gulps of air. He listened to the sound of the tap running in the kitchen, followed by Thomas's firm footsteps through the hall.

Thomas entered the room and stood for a moment regarding Peter, his brow creased into a slight frown. He handed Peter the glass before speaking. Peter took a long drink.

"Okay, boy, I'd like to try something different. Stand up, please."

Surprised, Peter got to his feet and watched as Thomas came around him to pick up some floor cushions from beneath the bay window. He placed them in front of the sofa and then sat down carefully, leaning back against it. He spread his legs wide and then gestured to the floor cushion in front of him.

"Sit here, boy, with your back to me."

Peter didn't have a clue what was going on, but he obeyed, keeping tight hold of his glass.

"Now, I want you to lean back against me, knees bent." Peter stretched out and placed the glass on the small table near the armchair before leaning back gingerly. "That's it, lad. Sit back, give me your weight." Peter complied. His head came to rest on Thomas's shoulder as he sagged back against him. Thomas slipped both arms around him, caging him as his hands came to rest on Peter's chest. Then he pressed his knees against Peter's, and there Peter was, surrounded by Thomas.

"I have you, boy." Warm breath tickled his ear. "We're going to talk just like this. You don't have to look at me, which might make it easier. But this way, I can feel how your body reacts without you saying a word. You're safe."

Safe. Peter focused on the word. In that moment, the world outside didn't exist. He felt Thomas all around him, felt the warmth of his body, heard the regular sound of his breathing, and simply let go.

"That's it, lad. Relax." Thomas stroked his chest and rubbed his belly. The movements were soothing. "Okay, I take it Dr. Herne knows about these attacks? Is she helping you cope more easily with them?"

"Yes, Sir. The counting helps. It was one of her first suggestions, but it really works. Once the panic sets it, I find it hard to breathe, and that just gets me hyperventilated. Learning to control my breathing has made things a lot better." He squeezed Thomas's hand slightly. "It also helps to have someone count for me. Thank you, Sir." Thomas briefly returned his squeeze. Peter dropped his hand back into his lap.

"Was it a panic attack when you were in the bar?" Peter stilled. "Boy?"

Peter sighed. "Kind of, Sir."

Thomas's arms tightened around him. "Kind of?" Peter held his breath. "Talk to me, boy. There's something you're not telling me."

Peter inhaled slowly, letting the air fill his lungs, and then expelled it in one long sigh.

"I'm agoraphobic, Sir." Thomas was right; it was easier talking when he couldn't see his face.

He heard the catch in Thomas's breathing. "Fear of public places? Well, that explains why you don't like leaving the house."

Peter shook his head. "It's not just that, Sir. It's situations when I have to go somewhere new and I don't know what's going to happen, especially if it's something I have no control over. And that starts off a panic attack."

He felt Thomas nodding. "Ah, I understand." He resumed stroking Peter's belly and chest. "How long have you known you're agoraphobic?"

"I'm not sure, Sir. The panic attacks started when I was about twenty-one. Dr. Herne says that's not unusual in sufferers. They got worse after I… I left home."

"Why the hesitation, lad? What is it you're not saying?" Thomas shifted, and then his voice sounded closer to Peter's ear. "This is the time for truth, boy. And I wish you'd been open with me from the start. We could have been working on this together. I could have been *helping* you." At the earnest tone of his voice, Peter dropped his chin to his chest. To his surprise, Thomas kissed the back of his head. "It's all right, boy. At least you're telling me now. But I want the truth."

Peter sucked in a breath. He smiled gratefully as Thomas took hold of his hands and held them tight.

"Thank you, Sir." *Now, where to begin?* "My parents threw me out when I was eighteen, Sir, when I told them I was gay. I went to live with my grandmother, who was already in her late eighties at the time. I looked after her for about two years until she died."

"I'm sorry, boy. Were you close?"

"Yes, Sir. She was a lovely lady, and although she never really came to grips with me being gay, she never judged me, she always supported me. It was a difficult time for me when she died." Peter closed his eyes, seeing in his mind his grandmother in her last days, surrounded by her precious things while the unseen cancer ate away at her.

"What did you do then?"

"I had already done my training to be a masseur when she died, and I had a job in the local leisure center, working with another masseur. We shared an apartment, actually, the top floor of an old house not far from the center. It was fine. We got on—in spite of the fact that Braden was forever bringing a constant stream of different girls to the flat." Peter let out a small chuckle. "And he wasn't quiet, if you get my meaning."

He felt Thomas's laugh reverberate through him. "Oh, you poor boy. Then what?"

"The panic attacks started, mildly at first. I'm not sure what triggered them, but I know they got worse once I went to live with—"

Thomas interrupted him. "I can do the math, boy. With Curtis Rogers?"

Peter bobbed his head, swallowing. He wasn't sure how much he would be able to share, despite Thomas's request for honesty.

"How did you come to move in with Curtis?"

Peter told him about his first visit to the BDSM club and meeting Curtis. He was shocked to hear a low growl from Thomas.

"He was certainly a fast mover, wasn't he?" Suddenly Thomas stiffened. "Wait a minute; we're getting off the point. What can I do to help you when you have an attack?"

Peter smiled. "Sir, what you did was just right. You stayed calm, you counted my breaths, you didn't leave me on my own. Dr. Herne will be proud of you." Thomas's chuckle shook him. "Actually, she says my life here is a big help."

"How so?"

"Well, I serve you. All the things I do around the house keep my mind occupied. It's a distraction. I don't have time to dwell on things when I'm focusing on running the house."

"Has she prescribed any medication?"

Peter shook his head. "She wanted to, but I don't want to take pills, so she's been looking at alternative treatments." He felt Thomas shift behind him.

"What's wrong with taking pills, if they help you?"

Peter swallowed. "Sir, Curtis…. We used to go to the club, and it wasn't unusual to get an attack, and then he'd get really pissed off with me. Sometimes he made me take pills, and things always got kinda fuzzy after. And I'm sure stuff happened that I couldn't remember. I… I don't want to take pills, Sir. Any."

There was a brief silence as Thomas obviously took in what he'd said. Peter waited, biting his lower lip.

"I understand, boy. Tell me about some of these alternative treatments."

Peter couldn't help letting out a tiny sigh of relief. "Well, if I start to get panicky, she gets me to visualize something in my head. Something calming, like a secluded beach on a sunny day, or standing in the middle of a field, with nothing but countryside for miles and miles."

"Does visualization work?"

"Yes, Sir. We've only been using that technique during the last month or so, but it really helps, especially the beach one."

"I'm glad. Hang on, though. I'm missing something here. What triggered this last attack? You were fine. Well, okay, maybe not exactly *fine*, but that was my fault for showing you the normal contract. We were about to order sex toys, for goodness' sake."

Peter froze. He couldn't help it.

"Peter, turn around, please. Look at me."

Peter sat up and turned himself until he was seated on the cushion, staring at Thomas, who was regarding him anxiously.

"Tell me what I did, boy. What did I do or say to trigger this?" He speared Peter with his gaze. "The truth, lad."

Peter swallowed. "Sir, you said you don't have sex with your submissives."

"Correct."

"Then why do you want to buy sex toys?" The words rushed out of him. He wanted to believe Thomas. This last month had brought with it such a feeling of hope. He *trusted* him.

Thomas looked at the floor, and Peter's heart sank. *Way to go, Peter.* After a few nerve-wracking moments Thomas looked up.

"Peter, for some submissives, the D/s lifestyle is all about boundaries. They set their limits, and then their Dom pushes a little, trying to get them to experience more. And yes, for a lot of subs, their focus is taking more pain for their master, more discomfort, because they know that once they do that, their master will reward them. Pain can be erotic, but no, it's not for every sub. Rewards can be erotic too. Our rewards tend to involve sexual pleasure. Speaking as a Dom, it feels good to give a sub pleasure, to see him soar to new heights. To be the one who gives him that is a very heady experience indeed."

He leveled a forthright gaze at Peter. "I want you to soar, Peter. I thought using sex toys would be the way to go forward. It's something we could work on together, not something that I would be doing *to* you. And after this conversation, I think it would be something else for you to focus on." He paused, looking down at his hands before lifting his gaze to meet Peter's. His eyes looked distinctly troubled. "But I must admit, I'm working in the dark here. Maybe my decision not to read your diary was the wrong one, because I have no idea what your experience of sex has been to this point. It strikes me this is as good a time as any to ask, though." He locked eyes with Peter. "Can you talk about it?"

Peter gulped. "Sir…." His mouth dried up and he reached for the glass of water and drained it. He focused on the empty glass. Thomas sat very still.

Keeping his eyes on the glass, Peter began to speak in a low voice.

"You said pain can be erotic, Sir. I'm sorry, but that's not been my experience. Curtis was into pain. With whips, canes, floggers, anything he felt like using. And sex? Sex was pain. He thought nothing of fucking me dry. Sex toys? I don't really suppose you'd class a broom handle as a sex toy, would you?" His smile was bitter. "Or how about the neck of a bottle? Or a gun barrel?" He heard Thomas's sharp intake of breath. "I repeat, sex was pain. And I had no way to say no. No safewords." Peter grimaced. "I haven't even mentioned his associates yet. Whenever one came to the house, I was required to service him. Curtis-speak for being taken to Curtis's playroom and blowing him, before being tied down and fucked. I was a hole, Sir, nothing more."

He clenched his fists. "The worst was when he had parties. Lots of men, some gay, some straight, but all lining up to fuck me, sometimes three at a time. Some were considerate—they used condoms. Most didn't. And he would stand by and watch it all. If someone complained that I didn't seem to be enjoying the experience, out came a whip or a cane. You can be sure I made all the right noises after that." Tears welled up behind his eyelids, spilling out onto his cheeks.

He raised wet eyes to Thomas. "And what makes it worse? He was my fucking first! The night we met, I was a virgin. I knew nothing beyond what I'd seen on the Internet." He wiped his eyes angrily, determined not to cry any more. "Don't get me wrong, I'd seen BDSM videos, I knew what to expect, but my first time? I'm not even going to go there. And he fucking *knew* it was my first time too."

Thomas stared at him, horror etched across his face.

"Why didn't you leave, lad?"

"Because I thought that was the way it was supposed to be!" Peter screamed. "I didn't know! And then, when—" He broke off, unwilling to say any more. Keeping quiet had kept him safe so far.

"What, boy?" Thomas's voice was unexpectedly gentle.

Peter shivered. "I'm sorry, Sir, but I can't. I've been honest with you, really, but...." Inside his head he was willing Thomas to call a halt to the whole dreadful conversation. Tremors rippled through his body, and the tears he'd fought to suppress spilled down his face in torrents. "Please, Sir, no more."

THOMAS reacted swiftly. He pulled the boy into his arms and cradled him. Peter's head rested against Thomas's shoulder.

"Hush, lad, I have you. No more talking." Bitter sobs racked Peter's body, and Thomas held him tightly, feeling hot tears soak into his shirt. His boy was crying his heart out, and Thomas wanted to cry with him. Sorrow filled him when he thought of what Peter had shared with him. He was convinced there was more to come, but he wasn't about to push the lad. Right now all he wanted was for his boy to have some peace. He waited until the sobs had begun to recede before speaking.

"Peter, let's get you upstairs. You're worn out, boy."

Peter raised his head to meet his gaze, his cheeks streaked with the tracks of his tears, and nodded. Together they got up from the floor, and Thomas led the way up the stairs to Peter's room. He pulled back the duvet and gestured for Peter to lie down. After pulling off Peter's trainers, Thomas covered him with the duvet.

"Rest, lad, for a little while at least."

Peter's hand shot out to grab his arm. His eyes were full of pain.

"Please, Sir, don't... don't leave me." The plaintive note in his boy's voice was more than he could bear. Thomas nodded, and Peter's grip weakened. Peter rolled onto his side, facing toward the wardrobe, and Thomas lay down on top of the duvet, curling up to Peter's back. He stroked the silky hair that was still so short. Thomas did his best to massage the boy's temples. Peter lay rigid below the duvet. Small hiccups and sniffles escaped now and again. Thomas kept up the soothing motion, listening as Peter's breathing became more regular, until at last he knew the boy was asleep.

Thomas lay still. His arm was draped protectively across Peter as he slept. Now and again he heard a soft whimper, but Thomas snuggled up closer, warming the boy with his body. In his head he replayed their conversation until the words were burned into his brain. He tried not to dwell on the images that forced their way into his mind. He kept seeing Peter, held down, helpless as numerous faceless men abused him. By not giving Peter the use of a safeword, what those men had done amounted to nothing less than rape, not that he would ever use that word in Peter's hearing. But doubtless it had crossed his mind.

Thomas watched the daylight fade outside. Where to go from here was what preoccupied his mind. Peter had no idea how good sex could be. True, it had been a long time since Thomas had taken anyone to his bed, but he would never forget the joy of being balls deep inside his lover, pleasuring him, bringing him to ecstasy.... That Peter had never known such joy was something that made Thomas's heart ache. The sated, happy look on Peter's face when Thomas had come home that evening after giving him permission to jerk off had been wonderful to behold. The lad obviously had no problem giving himself pleasure. And Thomas wanted to be the one to give him that joy. *The boy needs to fly.* The words hammered in his head until it started to ache.

I know, he told his stubborn inner voice. *I'll make it happen.* He just wasn't sure how.

Sixteen

First time

PETER awoke before the alarm clock and rolled onto his back to gaze up at the ceiling. Last night had been… well, strange. He'd awoken to find Thomas curled up around him, fast asleep. His arm had been across Peter's waist. Peter had lain there, enjoying the body warmth he could feel radiating through the duvet. It felt so good, Sir snugged up against him protectively. All too soon, however, Thomas had stirred and opened his eyes. He hadn't spoken of their earlier conversation, but surprised Peter by saying he would sort out dinner and for Peter to come downstairs when he was ready. Peter listened to the thud of his footsteps on the stairs, followed seconds later by the sound of the front door opening and closing. *What the hell?*

By the time Peter made it downstairs, Thomas had come back carrying two parcels wrapped in white paper, and the glorious smell emanating from them made his mouth water.

"Fish and chips? Whatever happened to eating healthily?" Then he'd clamped his lips shut in horror that he'd had the nerve to speak like that to Thomas.

To his relief, Thomas had merely chuckled and hurried into the kitchen, shouting back to him, "Come on, lad, or they'll get cold." They sat at the table, eating the delicious meal straight from the paper. Maybe it was a combination of the mouthwatering odor and the lightening of Peter's spirit since his confession, but food had never tasted so good. After dinner, they sat in the lounge, listening to the music that played softly in the background while Thomas read and Peter gazed into the fire, lost in his own thoughts. Thomas didn't question him further but left him alone, and Peter was grateful. All his previous tensions had fled, and his tears had left him feeling cleansed. His only regret was that Thomas was seated in his favorite armchair, instead of next to him on the sofa. Peter wanted to lean up against him once more and let the man's calm and warmth seep into his very bones.

Peter glanced at the clock. Ten more minutes before he needed to wake Sir. He pulled the duvet up around him and snuggled into its softness as he reflected on yesterday's conversation. The sense of relief that filled him was overwhelming. Sir *knew* about the agoraphobia and the panic attacks, along with what Curtis and his cronies had subjected him to. Peter felt so light, he could have floated up to the ceiling. Okay, so Thomas didn't know the whole story, and Peter wasn't naive enough to think he would never find out, but Peter knew his silence protected them both. Because once Sir knew, he'd want to do something about it, and on that road lay danger.

Peter felt shame at the way he'd behaved when Thomas mentioned sex toys. It had been a knee-jerk reaction, one that didn't take into account his newfound trust in the Dom. And now that he'd had time to think on it, what Thomas was proposing wasn't exactly *torture*, was it? Furthermore, it would be Thomas there with him, Thomas, who'd already admitted that he wanted Peter to soar. *Soar? How good can it be?* Because, he had to concede, it was something he had little experience of, and he wanted to find out more.

Eagerly, he pushed back the duvet and leapt out of bed. After grabbing his robe from the back of the door, he slipped quietly into the bathroom and did a quick washup before returning to his room and pulling on his jeans and sweater. No sound came from Thomas's room as he crept down the stairs and into the kitchen to make the tea. He shifted from one foot to another as he waited for the kettle to boil.

Back upstairs, after placing the cup of tea on the nightstand, he knelt down by the bed and waited. When Thomas showed no signs of waking immediately, Peter impatiently fanned the air over the teacup, wafting the odor of freshly made tea toward the bed. For a fraction of a second it crossed his mind that he looked vaguely ridiculous doing this, and he was grateful Thomas couldn't see him. But when Thomas stirred beneath the covers, Peter hastily pulled back his hand and assumed his normal position. He fixed his gaze on the floor.

No sooner had Thomas rolled over to face him than he began.

"Sir, I've been thinking about what you said. I—"

"Is this how we usually start our day?" Thomas sounded gruff, not properly awake, but his Dom-head seemed to be in full working order. Peter closed his mouth shut with a snap. "Better." Thomas sat up in bed and reached for his tea. He sipped it and sighed with satisfaction. Peter took a sneaky peek and was relieved to notice the amused twinkle in his eyes. "Okay, let's start again, shall we?"

"Permission to speak, Sir?" Peter lowered his gaze to the floor once more.

"Speak, lad. Whatever it is you're so desperate to tell me, let's have it." There was no disguising the note of barely contained mirth. Sir was trying not to laugh at him. A wave of affection for the man rolled through Peter.

"Sir," he began again, this time with considerably less haste, "I was thinking about what you said last night. Can we discuss it? Because I think I'd like to try it, Sir. With you."

The silence that greeted his words had him raising his gaze from the rug beside the bed to peer with concern at Thomas. The Dom was regarding him with an expression of mild surprise.

"Just so that I am completely clear what *it* is that you're referring to…," Thomas began. His brow was faintly creased.

Peter jumped in eagerly. "Sex toys, Sir." He met Thomas's eyes and swallowed. "I… I want to soar, Sir."

A lovely, gentle smile spread across Thomas's face. "What changed your mind?"

"You, Sir," he replied promptly. "I trust you."

THOMAS was briefly rendered speechless. He'd been mentally prepared to wait for as long as it took until Peter settled down once more. Last night had been a revelation, and the boy had clearly been overwrought. To be faced with this keen, bright-eyed sub after such a night was nothing short of miraculous. And Thomas wasn't about to look a gift horse in the mouth.

He sat up and gestured toward the small walnut-veneered table by his bedroom door.

"Bring me my laptop, boy, and then come and sit here." He patted the empty space beside him. Peter's eyes grew round, and Thomas let out a gleeful chortle. "No time like the present, after all."

Peter responded with a speed just short of joyful and grabbed the laptop. He brought it to Thomas and then clambered onto the bed and sat back against the pillows, hugging his knees while Thomas fired it up. Peter peered eagerly at the screen.

"Do you do this often, Sir?"

Thomas burst out laughing. "No, lad. In fact, Leo is the one in charge of ordering for the club. I do know where he shops, though." He winked, and Peter let out a smothered giggle. Thomas looked away from the screen for a moment to regard his sub. "I have to say something here, boy. It's about our conversation last night." Peter sobered immediately, but he said nothing.

Thomas drew in a deep breath. "One of the things that saddened me most was how sex and pain seemed to be irrevocably linked in your mind." He locked eyes with Peter. "It doesn't have to be like that, boy."

Peter dipped his chin and spoke in a whisper. "I believe you, Sir."

Thomas pressed on, anxious to get out the words. "Sex is pleasure. Sex is intense feelings, intense sensations, something to be enjoyed. Sex is a natural high, boy." He peered at Peter intently. "The other day when I left you alone to have your reward"—Peter blushed profusely—"did you enjoy your orgasm?"

The blush deepened. "Yes, Sir, of course I did."

"And that is what I want to give you more of, if you are willing. As long as you are aware that the *only* things to penetrate your body will be of *your* choosing." He weighted his words carefully. Peter gazed back at him with those beautiful green eyes. "Are we clear on that point?"

"Yes, Sir." It was an emphatic reply.

"In that case, let's go shopping."

PETER stared in frank amazement at the screen. He'd never expected there to be *so many* different toys to choose from. In his mind he'd imagined maybe a dildo or two, but *this*? Neither could he get over how much was *already* in their basket. Butt plugs in various sizes, cock rings in stretchy plastic and metal, a couple of dildos, including one which was so thick and long, it made his hole clench just *looking* at it. Thomas laughed to see his reaction.

"We'll work up to that one," he said with a wink. "By the way, did you know it vibrates?" That innocent look wasn't fooling Peter for an instant.

What drew his attention was the curved toy with a battery inserted at one end. The curve was smooth, but at the battery end, there were little bumps. He must have looked puzzled because Thomas felt the need to explain.

"The curve goes inside you and massages your prostate, and the bumpy bit goes outside and massages your perineum. Best of all, it's hands free. I could have that buzzing away merrily inside and out while I torture your cock."

Peter's eyes went wide. "T-torture?"

Thomas clicked on a link to bring up several items that resembled black flashlights, except they were made of some kind of fleshy sleeve, and at one end there was a curved, flesh-colored part that looked like a mouth or an arse. Peter was quick on the uptake.

"Can you imagine how that would feel? All those sensations at once?" Thomas's voice was low and intense.

Peter gulped. "You're trying to kill me, aren't you, Sir? I can see my headstone now... *Peter Nicholson, Death by Orgasm.*"

Thomas's sudden peal of delighted laughter was wonderful to hear.

"Oops, I nearly forgot the anal beads." Thomas clicked to add a set to the basket. Peter swallowed as he saw the size of the largest ball. Yeah, Sir was trying to kill him all right. "Now, is there anything else we've forgotten?"

Peter chuckled. "Sir, I think we have plenty, don't you?"

Thomas shrugged. "Well, we can always go shopping again." He quickly paid for their items and shut down the laptop. "That lot will be here on Monday." He affected a stern expression. "Er, isn't it time for breakfast, now we've got all the fun stuff out of the way?"

Peter hastily climbed off the bed and headed for the door. "I'll put the coffee on, Sir."

AS PETER was drying the breakfast plates, Thomas came into the kitchen.

"Something else occurred to me after last night." He came to Peter's side and held out his hands to take the breadboard.

"Yes, Sir?" Peter handed it to him and hung up the tea towel.

"Now that I know a little more about your past, I think it would be a good idea to get you to our club doc, Dennis Yelland, for a checkup. Specifically, a check for STDs and HIV." He saw the shudder that ran through his boy. "Just to be on the safe side, lad." Ever since Peter had told him of multiple partners and bareback sex, it had been preying on Thomas's mind.

"Yes, Sir." His reply was a whisper. "You're right, of course."

"I'll arrange it for as soon as possible. I'll get my regular test done at the same time." He couldn't fail to notice the change in Peter's expression. In that instant Thomas wanted more than anything to give Peter something else on which to focus. And then it occurred to him. *Why wait to play?*

"But that can wait. We have a far more pleasurable way of spending our Saturday."

He watched the hopeful light dawn in his boy's eyes. "We do, Sir?"

Thomas nodded slowly. "How about we go up to the playroom?"

Peter held himself so still. "Really?" he breathed. Thomas was gratified to see the eager expression that transformed his face.

"Yes, boy, really. I think it's high time you and I shared a scene, don't you?"

Peter's eyes were shining. "Yes, Sir."

PETER stood in the middle of the playroom, watching as Thomas looked around, clearly deep in thought. Peter kept his hands by his sides, back straight, eyes down. He tried hard to project an aura of calm, although inside he was quivering with excitement. It was finally going to happen. He had no idea what Thomas had planned, having expected their first scene to occur once the toys had been delivered. All Thomas brought up with him were a couple of towels and a bottle of lube. Peter eyed the lube in surprise.

"When you are in this room, you will only answer when addressed. Is that clear?"

Peter caught his breath. The authoritative note in Thomas's voice was compelling. He didn't know how to react. Had he just been given permission to speak?

"You may answer, boy."

Peter exhaled shakily. "Yes, Sir." He stayed immobile as Thomas approached him slowly. Peter straightened up further, not meeting the Dom's eyes.

"And when you are in this room, whether I am present or whether I have sent you up here to get things ready, you will be naked." He gazed at Peter expectantly.

Peter hesitated. *He means* now, *stupid!* His pulse raced. *Come on, Peter, this is Thomas. Do as he says.* His brain decided to listen, finally, and he began to undress slowly and place his clothes in a neat pile on the floor. Thomas's eyes never left him. Peter stood up straight, trying not to feel self-conscious. The temperature in the room was pleasant, thank goodness.

"Hands by your sides, boy."

Peter realized he had been fidgeting. He obeyed. What he hadn't counted on was how arousing it was to have Thomas speak to him in that tone, to be naked while Thomas was clothed. His cock was already at half-mast.

"No need to ask if you're enjoying this, is there?"

Oh shit, he's noticed. Peter's heart skipped a beat when Thomas moved closer and slipped a large, warm hand around his cock, which hardened further. Thomas ran his hand along his length, and Peter shivered.

"This is mine. Every inch of you is mine. And you do not touch without permission." Peter gulped. "And my rule still stands. You do not come without permission."

"Y-yes, Sir." That gentle stroking was making it very difficult to concentrate. And then it came to an abrupt halt. Peter let out an involuntary whimper.

"I want you in the sling, boy."

Whatever Peter had been expecting, that wasn't it. He walked over to the sling as if in a dream and gazed at it for several seconds, trying to figure out how best to get into it.

"Today, boy."

Even though the note of amusement was obvious, Peter hastily climbed into the sling. His legs dangled awkwardly.

"Get yourself comfortable. You're going to be there for a while. Feet in the stirrups, and hold on to the chains."

Peter adjusted his body until he felt totally comfortable—well, as comfortable as he was going to get, in the circumstances—and gripped the chains. Placing his feet in the stirrups meant that his legs were spread, his knees falling apart, and he tried not to let the feeling of being vulnerable overwhelm him. He was with Sir. When his breathing started to become more rapid, he focused on that one thought.

"Good boy." The words of praise warmed him through. He watched as Thomas walked to the chair where he'd left the towels and lube. Thomas brought the chair over to where the sling was hanging from the rafters and then slipped his hand between the towels, withdrawing something black. He held it up so that Peter could see. A blindfold. *Oh fuck.* Just seeing it was enough to have Peter's cock pointing up to the roof, twitching in anticipation.

Thomas chuckled. "Oh, now there's something *crying out* to be played with."

Peter's cheeks were bright red. Thomas leaned over him. His eyes were focused on Peter's face.

"I'm going to put the blindfold on you now, boy. You'll be able to hear me. I won't move away from you without telling you what I'm doing, all right?" Peter nodded, unable to tear his eyes away from Thomas's face. Thomas gave him an approving look before slipping the elasticized blindfold over his eyes. It was as soft as velvet and shut out the light completely.

Peter lay in total blackness and assessed his situation. It was weird, almost as if he were floating. He could hear the sound of Sir breathing steadily, and it soothed him.

"Are you comfortable?"

"Yes, Sir." The sling supported him well.

"Then let's begin."

Peter held his breath, unsure of what was about to happen. He let out a soft gasp as he felt Thomas's hand stroke across his chest, pausing to tweak his nipples—which drew another gasp—before caressing his abs. The muscles twitched as Thomas slowly, lightly brushed his hand across Peter's skin, traveling lower to trail his fingers over Peter's haunches. Peter inhaled sharply as Thomas rubbed the firm valley between his hips. He pushed up, wanting more, and mewled in disappointment as Thomas's hand pressed him firmly back into the sling.

"No, boy. Your task is to lie there and accept what I'm doing. Keep still. When I want you to move, I'll tell you."

Peter forced himself to lie still as the warm hand slid along his thigh, the touch light and sensual. With his sight gone, it was easier to focus on the sensations occurring in his body. He found himself eagerly anticipating each stroke, holding his breath as he waited for that hand to caress him. On and on it went, each new brush of Thomas's fingers more sensuous than the previous, until it was all he knew.

When Thomas's hand renewed its acquaintance with his cock, Peter gasped.

"Like that, boy?" Fingers gripped his length deftly, slowly sliding the silky foreskin and squeezing and tugging at his shaft, which grew ever more rigid. The hand paused in its sensual motion, and Peter heard a faint click. He shuddered as cool lube dripped onto the heated flesh, and then that hand recommenced its erotic task, sliding and curling around the hot column of Peter's cock.

"That's better." Peter could hear the note of satisfaction in Thomas's voice. "Does it feel good, boy? You can answer me now. I want to hear you. Every noise, every whimper. Give me your sounds. *Give* them to me."

Peter moaned, and the sound was low and earnest. "Oh, Sir, it feels so good." Thomas's hand increased its speed, and Peter groaned. "Oh yes, yes, Sir!" He was lost in it all: the sensation of floating in midair, the sensuality of Thomas's touch, heat pooling in his groin as his climax approached. He tried to dial back his arousal, not wanting this to be over. And besides, he couldn't come. Not without Sir's say-so.

The hand flogging his cock came to a halt. Peter caught his breath, relieved to have a moment's respite.

"Peter? I'd like to try something. Do you trust me?"

Peter inhaled deeply. "Yes, Sir." And it was true. In that moment he was totally in Thomas's hands.

"Then I'm going to ask you to trust me now, boy."

Peter didn't have time to dwell on the meaning behind Thomas's words before he felt a finger trail over his balls and down to his hole, which tightened involuntarily.

"Relax, boy. I won't hurt you. You have my word. Focus on what your body is feeling."

Peter forced himself to relax and gasped when that finger slid across his hole, pressing lightly against it. A shudder ran through him as lube dribbled down his crease. When the finger slid into him, Peter arched his back and groaned, unable to stop himself. He was already close.

"Sir, I'm going to come." He panted in his effort to hold it back.

"No, boy. Not until I say so." And then, wickedly, Thomas pushed his finger deeper into his arse, and Peter cried out as it connected with his gland.

"Oh, God, Sir!" The cry forced its way out of him, leaving him moaning as Thomas stroked over his prostate again and again. "Oh please, Sir, please." In reply, Thomas wrapped his hand once more around Peter's steel length, and Peter quailed beneath the double assault.

"Does it feel good, boy?" Thomas demanded, thrusting his finger in faster, nudging Peter's gland every time. The motion moved the sling with each penetration until a rhythm had been established. Peter had no words to tell him just how good it was. His orgasm was gathering speed, hovering, ready to bulldoze over him as soon as Thomas gave the word.

Peter arched his back and screamed up to the ceiling. "Oh, God, Sir, it's so good! Please, Sir, please, let me come!" He sobbed from the effort of holding back. Never had he felt so alive, as if every cell in his body was vibrating. He rocked, pushing down on the finger that explored him and thrusting his cock through that tight, lubed fist. The motion of the sling merely added to the sensations.

Thomas's hands sped up their erotic onslaught until Peter thought he was about to die from the feelings that threatened to overwhelm him, and then finally those blessed words rang out.

"Come for me, boy."

Peter howled as he jetted come over Thomas's hand. His anal muscles clamped down on the Dom's finger as his body tightened around it. Pleasure rolled over him in waves, and he took it all, shuddering with ecstasy. At last his body released Thomas, who wiped a soft towel over his spent cock, making him shiver. Thomas stroked him soothingly as aftershocks jolted him every now and then.

"That's it, let it flow through you. It feels good, doesn't it?"

Peter struggled to speak, to say what was in his thoughts. "Oh, Sir." He couldn't manage any more. His brain refused to cooperate.

Thomas let out a rough chuckle. "Run out of words, boy? Have I scrambled your brain?"

Peter finally had the presence of mind to respond. "Yes, Sir, but in a really good way."

Thomas laughed. "Then I've done my job." Peter felt him lean over. "I'm going to remove the blindfold. Open your eyes slowly. Let them get accustomed to the light." Thomas removed the blindfold, and Peter blinked in the sunlight that filled his vision. Gradually, he could see more, and Thomas's face loomed above him. "Better now?" Those expressive green eyes regarded him steadily. Thomas was grinning.

A huge smile stretched over Peter's face. "Oh, yes, Sir." In all kinds of ways.

Seventeen

Lies and Epiphanies

"THAT was definitely a happy sigh."

Peter glanced over his shoulder at Alex, who was standing in the kitchen doorway. "I don't know what you're talking about." He returned his attention to washing the dishes from lunch, biting back a smile. "Why would washing the dishes make anyone happy?"

Alex snorted. "Don't give me that. You're happy. And personally, I think it's great. It's a good look on you." He walked over to Peter and peered over his shoulder. "Can I help?"

Peter nodded toward the tea towel. "You can dry, seeing as you're in a helpful mood."

Alex chuckled as he reached for a plate. He was silent for only a few seconds before the pleading started. "Oh, go on, Peter, you *know* you want to tell me." He fluttered his long eyelashes, and Peter laughed.

"Go flash your big puppy eyes at someone else," he said with a grin. Alex kept it up for several seconds longer and then apparently gave up and concentrated on the task at hand, albeit with a cute pout. Within minutes they'd finished, and Peter put on the kettle to make them some tea. Soon the smell of the green tea with jasmine that he'd put on the shopping list specifically with Alex in mind had Alex forgetting his sulk and sniffing the air in appreciation.

"Ooh, nice."

Peter placed the mugs on the table and sat down. He'd already made the quiche for that evening's dinner, and the salad would be quick to prepare. The house was spotless and the laundry dried and put away. He could afford to spend some quality time with Alex.

Peter loved their weekly get-togethers. Alex was easy to talk to, and he always made Peter laugh. Sometimes they would watch a DVD with a bowl of popcorn nestled between them, or Alex would bring along his PS3 and they'd play for a while. Mostly, their time together was spent discussing Peter's recent experiences.

Alex sat back in his chair. "So, I take it everything's going well with you and Thomas." This was uttered innocently enough, but Peter knew by now that his fellow submissive was angling for gossip. He decided to take pity on him.

"Yeah, everything's great," he admitted with a shy smile, but then he paused. "Except...."

Alex sat bolt upright. "What did you do?"

Peter was indignant. "How do you know I did anything?"

Another snort. "Because I know you. Come on, 'fess up." His eyes bored into Peter, who sighed.

"I got caught doing something I shouldn't." His cheeks heated up at the memory.

Alex giggled gleefully. "Ooh, what?"

"Sir caught me jacking off. In the shower." He mumbled the words. His whole face was now hot.

Alex whistled. "Oh boy. What did he do?" After a second or two, he arched his eyebrows and added, "And what was Thomas doing in the bathroom while you were showering, anyway?"

"He was looking for something, I forget what, and he just stuck his head around the door to ask me about it. It was only for a second or two, but long enough to see what I was doing."

Alex chortled. "Well, I hope it was a good one till that point." When Peter's cheeks flamed even further, Alex's eyes narrowed. "There's more to this, isn't there?" He tilted his head. "What were you thinking of while you were spanking the monkey?"

Peter grimaced at the term, but he met Alex's gaze. "I was... I was thinking about Sir."

Alex's eyes grew round. "No kidding." His mouth dropped open.

Peter didn't know what to think of this reaction. "What?"

Alex shrugged noncommittally. "Nothing, it's just...." His words trailed off.

"No, come on, out with it," Peter demanded. "It's not like you to hold back from speaking your mind."

Alex's face twisted into an anxious grimace. "Does... does his age not bother you?"

Peter stiffened, but Alex's expression told him he wasn't saying it out of malice. He genuinely seemed to want to know. And God knows it had surprised Peter when he'd found himself jerking off to a memory of Thomas fucking him with a new glass dildo. Apparently his *brain* didn't find Thomas's age a concern.

"There's only twenty-nine years' difference," he retorted, but then he stopped and thought. *No, make that thirty years: it was Sir's birthday last week, remember?*

Alex's expression softened. "I'm sorry, I shouldn't have said anything." He looked so uncomfortable that Peter stretched his hand out across the table and seized Alex's hand in a tight squeeze.

"It's okay." He gazed down at the table. "It's just that.... When I think of Sir, I...." Words failed him.

Alex's hand closed around his. "Peter, it's okay if you think your Dom is hot, really." He smiled. "It's understandable, if you think about it. Thomas sees you at your most vulnerable. You obviously trust him implicitly. I mean, the man makes you *come*, for God's sake! In your head, Thomas, sex, orgasms—they're all connected. So it does make sense." Peter nodded. His cheeks burned. "But you still haven't told me. What punishment did he set you?"

Peter grimaced. "He made me wear a cage. All day and all night."

Alex's face contorted. "Ouch!"

Peter grinned at him. "Remember what you said all those months ago, about how Doms like it when you take their punishments without complaint?"

Alex nodded. "The next day in the playroom...." Peter rolled his eyes teasingly.

Alex pulled his hand free with a groan. "You're not gonna tell me, are you?"

Peter shook his head, laughing. There were some things Alex definitely *didn't* get to hear about. Peter loved their scenes in the playroom. Thomas had brought a joy to his life that fulfilled him, and it kept getting better and better. Now if he could just deal with the more pressing problem of his next appointment, he'd be a happy bunny.

"What did you just think about?" Alex quizzed. "It wasn't Sir, that's for sure. Your face changed."

Peter heaved a huge sigh. "Tomorrow's appointment with Dr. Herne."

Alex frowned. "But I thought the sessions were going really well?" Peter had told Alex about the agoraphobia and the panic attacks not long after he'd revealed all to Sir. *Was that only a month ago?* Time was flying these days, and Peter wished fervently that he could slow it down somehow. The end of their contract was almost in sight. Thomas had suggested a limit of three months, and Peter had agreed, the theory being that they would either renegotiate after that, or else Thomas would start looking for a suitable Dom for Peter. The thought of leaving Thomas made his heart ache.

"Sir wants me to go to the appointment without him." When Alex's face darkened slightly, Peter hastened to defend Thomas. "It's not what you think. A taxi has been arranged to pick me up here, drop me off at the car park near St. Ann's square, and wait for me there after the appointment to bring me home."

Alex's face cleared. "Ah, so you'll only have a short distance to go on your own."

Peter nodded. It was still a big step. It had been so long since he'd gone *anywhere* on his own that his gut tightened at the mere thought. He'd listened as Thomas made the suggestion, knowing instinctively that the Dom wouldn't push him. It would have to be Peter's decision, ultimately. But Peter wanted to do it for Thomas. It would be such an achievement.

Alex had clearly come to the same conclusion. "Wow." And then he grinned. "Just think of the rewards for getting through *that* for the first time." He winked salaciously, and Peter's blush surged once more into existence. Not that the thought hadn't crossed his mind too.

"ALL ready for tomorrow, boy?"

Thomas's words broke through Peter's internal meanderings. He looked up from the book he'd been trying to read for the last half hour and gave Thomas a hopefully reassuring smile.

"Yes, Sir."

Thomas made a low sound of approval and went back to his book. The light was just beginning to fade, and Peter stretched out to turn on the lamp beside the sofa. Warm light spilled into the room, and Thomas glanced up at the clock with a sigh.

"I love it when the evenings get lighter," he said quietly. "It makes me feel summer is nearly here." He gazed at Peter and his eyes twinkled. "How about if you and I go to a beach this summer? A really deserted beach, like the one you picture in your head when you're trying to relax?"

Peter could have kissed him for the thought. Keeping his face straight, he shrugged. "I can't see many beaches being deserted in the summer, Sir." *And besides,* he thought, *who's to say I'll still be your boy when summer finally gets here?* The thought left him feeling hollow inside.

"You leave that to me, boy," replied Thomas with a wink, and then he went back to his book. Peter studied the Dom as he read, his book balanced on his knee. In the quiet of his heart, Peter could be honest with himself. He was falling for Sir. He thought of Thomas, bare-chested in the playroom, eyes fixed on Peter as he played him with all the precision of a virtuoso, whether pushing him to control the urge to climax or pulling him over the edge into another heart-stopping orgasm that made him soar heavenward. And it wasn't a case of mere lust. The man engendered in him such a deep-seated feeling of trust and affection that at times Peter would look at him and be lost for words to describe exactly how he felt. Affection? No, it was more than that. How much more, Peter wasn't prepared to admit even to himself.

Peter forced himself to go back to his book. No use indulging in self torture like this. He wasn't about to let Sir know how he felt, and he'd already seen how one person reacted when thinking of the difference in their ages. It wasn't going to happen, so he might as well let it go. He snuck a quick peek at Thomas once more. Peter had never been in love, so he had nothing with which to compare his present feelings. There was Dan Forrester at high school, when they were both eighteen, but he'd known it for what it was: an adolescent crush, nothing more. And Thomas made him ache in a way Dan had never done. The thoughts that ran through Peter's head when Thomas touched him would have made *Alex* blush. Then again, maybe not.

Let it go, hammered his stupid inner voice. *You were right the first time. It's. Not. Going. To. Happen.*

I can dream, Peter thought wistfully. He gazed across the room at the man who was oblivious to Peter's yearnings for him. *And when I'm in my bed tonight, I know exactly* who *I'll be dreaming about. If I'm lucky.*

"ANY plans for this evening?" Dr. Herne asked him as he picked up his jacket from the chair.

Peter grinned. "Playroom tonight." He'd been looking forward to it all day.

Laura Herne laughed. "Ooh, no wonder you've seemed anxious for our session to finish. If I were going home to a scene with Master Thomas, I'd be the same, believe me." She winked, and Peter blushed. "By the way, well done. This was your first time alone, wasn't it?"

Peter tried to push the praise aside modestly. "The taxi's only in the car park around the corner," he protested weakly, but his wide grin belied his words. He'd done it. He'd found it difficult to contain his smile throughout the session. Sir was going to be *so* proud of him.

"Don't denigrate your achievement, Peter," Dr. Herne said, her expression serious. "It's the first step to beating this." She leveled a forthright stare at him until he acknowledged her words with a brief dip of his chin. She beamed. "Then I'll see you next week. Have fun tonight." Her eyes danced with wicked glee.

Laughing, Peter left the office and made his way down the stairs, feeling as though he were walking on air. He'd panicked a little when he walked out of the car park into the bright afternoon sunshine, but he'd kept repeating his mantra in his head, focusing on that instead of the crowds who swarmed around him, all going about their busy lives, oblivious to his inner turmoil. *You can do this. You can* do *this.* The relief when he'd arrived at the doctor's door had almost made him sob out loud, but with each step his heart felt lighter.

He hesitated in the dim hallway for a second or two before pushing open the solid wooden door and stepping outside. The bright sunlight hurt his eyes, and he squinted against the glare. Keeping his head tucked down, he walked purposefully toward the car park. It was definitely something that got easier the more he did it. By the time he reached the taxi in the darkened interior of the car park, his heart was singing. *I can do this.* He couldn't wait to see Sir's reaction.

PETER was pleased to be home. The taxi had departed, and he was feeling happy and light. He reached into his pocket for his door key. As he withdrew it, it caught on the edge of the pocket and he fumbled to keep hold of it, only to have it fall to the ground. He bent down and picked it up, then inserted it into the lock. As he turned the key, a voice from behind him froze him in his tracks.

"Peter?"

He turned to see Christian standing by the gate. Peter quickly looked up and down the street, anxiously scanning the faces of the passersby, but there was no sign of Curtis. The sub was regarding him nervously.

"Christian? What are you doing here?" Peter was dismayed to hear the quaver in his own voice. "And how did you find me?"

"I saw you in the city center, and I followed you in my car." He gestured toward a banged-up Ford Mondeo, which was parked in front of the house.

Peter paled. "Why? Why would you do that?" Another swift glance around him confirmed that Curtis was nowhere in sight.

Christian reddened. "I saw you for the first time a few weeks ago. I've been watching out for you ever since."

"Does Curtis know you've seen me?" The words came out as a whisper, as though merely saying the man's name out loud would somehow bring him there, large as life and twice as dangerous.

"Curtis is the one who sent me."

Peter blanched. "What?"

"He wants to meet with you. To clear the air, he said. He's been going out of his mind since you disappeared."

Yeah, I'll bet. And I know why. Peter pushed the thought aside. "I'm sorry, Christian, but I don't want to see him. Can you pass that message on to him, please?" He hesitated briefly before turning toward the front door. "Bye, Christian." All of a sudden he desperately wanted to be on the other side of the door.

As his hand reconnected once more with the key, he was startled by the sound of a car door being flung open and loud footsteps behind him. A large hand grabbed his shoulder and yanked him back.

"Where do you think *you're* going?"

Peter was whirled around violently and came face to face with Curtis. His face was mottled with fury.

"Pleased to see me, boy?" Curtis spoke in an undertone, his voice dripping with menace. "I've come to collect you and bring you home, where you belong."

Peter's heart began to hammer inside his chest, and his throat tightened up, making it almost impossible to breathe. He stood frozen to the spot.

"He sent me to collect you." Curtis gave an evil leer. Despite his increasing panic, Peter frowned, and Curtis's nasty smile grew wider. "Thomas Williams? That Dom who you're living with?" Curtis leaned in close, and Peter shuddered as his hot, stale breath wafted over his face. "He doesn't want you anymore. He's sending you back to me. How else would I have known where you were?" Curtis laughed, and the sound sent ice tripping down Peter's spine.

Beyond Curtis, Christian was watching the scene with a look of absolute horror etched across his face. In a burst of clarity, Peter realized the sub knew nothing of Curtis's real intentions. Then he realized what Curtis had said. Sir had sent him? He wouldn't believe it. Not Sir. Sir wouldn't do that.

Something of his disbelief must have shown in Peter's expression, which evidently angered Curtis. He thumped Peter in the belly, and all the breath left his lungs in a whoosh. He collapsed onto the front path, fighting to drag air into his body. Yet in spite of his terror, he somehow found the strength and enough breath to answer back.

"Don't... don't believe... you."

Curtis's face contorted into such an expression of fury that Peter recoiled, trying desperately to edge away on the ground, but Curtis seized his jacket in two tight fists and hauled him up, pinning him once more against the front wall of the house.

"What have you told him? *What have you told him?*" Curtis shrieked, and Peter prayed that *someone* heard that. Voices came nearer. People. Help.

You need Thomas, his inner voice clamored, and Peter heard it as clear as a bell. A sudden rush of rage flooded through him, and never had the term *fight or flight* seemed so appropriate. Because right now it was time for both.

"*Nothing!*" he screamed, and jerking his knee upward with as much force as he could muster, he connected with Curtis's balls. Curtis let out an agonized howl and promptly let go of Peter, dropping to the ground and grabbing his sac. Peter darted past him for the door, narrowly dodging the huge hand that grabbed for him but missed. Peter yanked his key out of the lock and spilled through the door. He pushed it shut as fast as he could and dragged the bolt across with trembling fingers before sinking to the floor in a crumpled heap on the doormat. Fists pounded against the door, and Peter held his breath, his eyes tight shut as he waited for the glass to break and that huge hand to slide through and grab him, but then the pounding stopped abruptly. Outside, he could hear raised voices. Some passersby had obviously seen Curtis's actions. Heart pounding, chest heaving, Peter listened as car doors slammed, followed by the screeching of tires. Curtis had fled the scene.

Peter didn't sit up but remained on the floor. His heart was beating so fast he was sure a heart attack was imminent. He tried to breathe, but the counting technique was long past working. One thought hammered in his brain, and he focused on that.

Thomas. I need Thomas.

"THERE'S a time and a place, you know," Thomas said with mock severity as he came into the office and found Leo with his arms around Alex, kissing him softly on the lips. Alex immediately broke free of Leo's embrace and tried to back away. His cheeks were tinged with pink, but Leo laughed.

"Your timing stinks, my friend," he said with a chuckle.

Thomas merely arched his brows. "Too bad. Now clear out of here, you two, and take your passionate making out somewhere else. *Some* of us have applications to vet."

His phone rang on the desk, where he'd left it, and Thomas peered at it, puzzled. Home. He answered and was dismayed to hear rapid breathing and sobs from the other end. "Peter! What's wrong?" Leo and Alex stared at him in alarm.

He could barely make out the garbled words. Peter seemed to be in a blind panic. But when he caught "Curtis," "here," "come home," and "need you," it was enough to send him heading for the door.

"I'm on my way! You hear me, boy? I'm coming to get you." He grabbed his jacket. "Come with me, you two. I think Curtis Rogers is at my house!" They didn't hesitate. The three men ran through the club to the exit, heading for Thomas's car. One thought was burning into Thomas's brain.

My boy needs me.

THOMAS ran up to the house, and Leo and Alex were only seconds behind him. There was no sign of Curtis, but the door wouldn't budge.

"He's bolted the door," exclaimed Thomas. His pulse raced. "Let's go around the back. Hopefully the back door isn't bolted and we can get in through the garage." He led the way around the house as panic gripped his heart. With shaking hands he unlocked the garage door and groaned with relief when it opened. After repeating the maneuver with the back door, he dashed into the house and looked around feverishly.

"Peter! Where are you, boy?"

A whimper pierced the silent house, and Thomas knew immediately where it came from. He ran to the hall cupboard and wrenched open the door, spotting the boy on the floor, curled up in a tight ball, hugging himself. Peter's face was ashen. Thomas crouched down and held his arms wide.

"Come here, boy."

Peter hurled himself into Thomas's arms, and Thomas pulled him close and kissed him on his head, his cheek, his neck, softly murmuring between kisses, "I've got you, boy. I've got you." When Peter raised frightened eyes to stare at him, Thomas brushed his fingers through his short length of hair and kissed his forehead. He kissed him once more on his cheek before moving his lips to kiss the soft skin of his neck. He held Peter tightly against his body, feeling Peter's heartbeat slowly return to normal. He cradled the boy in his arms until at last Peter was calm.

Thomas glanced into the kitchen to where Leo and Alex were standing. Their eyes were fixed on the scene before them. Thomas turned his attention back to Peter.

"Boy, I want you to go upstairs with Alex for a while, all right? Take a shower if you need to, change your clothes, whatever you want. I'll be up shortly, okay?" He caught Alex's eyes. "Alex will stay with you until I get there." Alex nodded and stepped forward to help Peter to his feet. Thomas stood up with him and let him go with one last brush of his fingers through Peter's hair. Peter gave him a grateful smile and then leaned on Alex's arm. The two men went toward the stairs. Thomas listened until they reached the top and then let out his breath in a long, shaky exhale.

"I need a drink." He went into the lounge and poured himself a small brandy, then downed it in one gulp. He gasped as the fiery liquid burned the back of his throat.

"What was that?" Leo said quietly as he came into the lounge and pulled the door closed behind him.

"I don't know what happened. I'll find out when I go and talk to him." Thomas resisted the temptation to pour another.

Leo shook his head. "That's not what I mean, and you know it." His eyes bored into Thomas. "The way you kissed him, Thomas. You clearly have feelings for the boy."

Thomas opened his mouth to retort, but the words died on his tongue. He faced his friend and sought the words to make him understand.

"Yes. He *needs* me, Leo. Do you know how long it's been since someone needed me? In fact, when has *anyone* ever needed me, beyond needing me to train them, only to pass them along to someone else?" He shook his head. "I've been fighting this... this *attraction* for a while now. I keep telling myself to ignore it."

"Why?" Leo demanded.

"Because it can't go anywhere!"

"Why not?" Leo said, his voice unexpectedly gentle.

Thomas laughed bitterly. "Oh, come now. We're neither of us *that* naive, surely. He's twenty-six, I'm fifty-six."

"So? What's wrong with that? You have feelings for him. He obviously feels the same for you."

"What?"

Leo laughed softly. "Old man, you can't be that blind. Of course he has feelings for you. I haven't seen Peter for a few weeks, and even I'm surprised I missed it this long. You only have to look at how he reacted to you just now." Leo walked across the room and took Thomas's hands. "Thomas, the age difference doesn't matter. It clearly doesn't matter to Peter. And there's *nothing wrong* with it." Thomas could hear how earnest his friend was. "But right now, it's not me you should be talking to. Go upstairs and talk to your boy. He needs you. You're right about that." He released Thomas's hands and flicked his head toward the door. "Go on, then. Send Alex down to me. We'll still be here when you finish talking to Peter."

Thomas took a deep breath and then nodded. He opened the lounge door and made his way up the stairs, listening to the quiet murmur of voices from Peter's room. When he got to the door, Alex was hugging Peter. Peter looked much calmer, and Thomas sent Alex a grateful glance. Alex gave Peter one last squeeze and got up from the bed, smiling shyly at Thomas as he passed by him to leave the room. Thomas pushed the door closed and sat down on the bed. Peter sat back against a pile of pillows, looking pale but calm.

"Alex helped me through the last of the attack, Sir."

Thomas held out his arms, and Peter crawled on all fours from his position on the bed to fold himself into Thomas's embrace. Thomas held him close, with Peter's head tucked under his chin.

"What happened, boy?"

Peter spoke into Thomas's chest. "Curtis came for me, Sir. He was here." He paused. His breathing grew slightly more erratic.

"What is it?" Thomas waited for the boy to continue.

"Curtis told me you didn't want me anymore. He said you were giving me back to him."

Thomas pushed him away to look the boy in the eye. "Did you believe him?"

Clear eyes shone back at him. "No, Sir. Not for a second." Sincerity rang out of every syllable.

"Good boy. Good boy." He pulled Peter once more into a tight embrace. The two men were intertwined as Peter reached up to hold Thomas, no words needing to be said.

He needs me. Thomas felt the warmth of his boy radiate through the thin layers of clothing and remembered the look of absolute trust in his eyes. He wanted to hold on to this moment and never let it go.

And then the reality of the situation washed over him, leaving him cold in its wake.

Wake up, old man, he told himself angrily. *This is not one of Leo's gay romances. This is real life. And in real life, sometimes you have to make painful decisions. Like now.*

Thomas hated his inner voice sometimes, but never more than in that moment. Because he knew what had to be done. He just didn't want to do it.

Eighteen

Revelations

THOMAS looked up as Leo came out into the garden. Thomas was sitting on one of the stone benches around the fire pit. He felt the warmth of the late afternoon sun on his back as he contemplated the fragile beauty of the spring flowers around him.

"Where are the boys?"

Leo smirked. "Enjoying a puppy pile on the sofa. I told them to snuggle up and watch a movie if they wanted." His expression grew sober. "Did he tell you what happened?"

Thomas nodded. "Eventually." They'd held each other for what felt like a long while, until it seemed their hearts were beating in unison. When he knew beyond a doubt that Peter was totally calm, Thomas had sat back against the pillows and held him while Peter recounted exactly what had happened. Thomas had fought hard to swallow his anger, not wishing to upset the boy any further. He could feel it surging through him even now as he thought about what had taken place. He gave Leo a quick summation.

Leo regarded him anxiously. "Are *you* all right, Thomas?"

Thomas raised his eyebrows in surprise. "Me?"

Leo nodded. "I was watching you through the kitchen window before I came out here. You were obviously deep in thought about something, and from what I could see of your facial expression, it clearly wasn't good. Want to share?"

Thomas opened his mouth to refuse the offer, but at the last second he changed his mind. He'd done his best to ignore the thought that had prodded and poked him for the last hour, but it wasn't giving up that easily. He stared at the ground under his feet.

"I want you to start looking for a Dom for Peter," he said at last. He kept his gaze lowered, deliberately ignoring Leo's sharp intake of breath. "He can't stay here with me, not now. Curtis knows about me—though how, I have no idea—and it's not safe. We've got enough contacts up and down the country to find a Dom who's suitable. Just make sure whoever you pick is aware of Peter's needs and history. There must be *someone* out there who—"

"Will you just *stop*?"

Thomas snapped his head up. Leo was staring at him in astonishment.

"What are you doing?" Leo demanded loudly. "Sending him away? *Why*, for God's sake?"

"You heard me. It's not safe here." Thomas gazed back at him stubbornly.

"Oh, I heard you. I just don't believe you." Leo was glaring at him. "That boy cares for you, goddammit. Why would you want to throw that away?"

"What would you have me do?" Thomas got to his feet. His hands were clenched at his sides. "He's thirty years my junior, Leo!"

"And?" Leo advanced on him. His chin jutted out. "I've already given you my opinion on that. It doesn't matter."

"Maybe now it doesn't, but what about in twenty or so years' time, when he's forty-six and I'm *seventy-six*?" He paused to catch his breath and noticed Leo's faint smile. "What?"

Leo's eyes were kind. "You can already see yourself being with him for that long, can you?" Thomas opened his mouth to deny it, but the words wouldn't come. "Thomas, *talk* to me. What's really behind this?"

Thomas sank down onto the bench. "Leo, in all the years we've known each other, can you ever remember me having a partner?"

Leo's brow creased. "I don't understand."

Thomas sighed patiently. "Leo, I'm crap at relationships. Oh, I'm good with *you* and the club members. In fact, with the world in general. And I'm good with the subs, because each one knows it's a short-term thing. But when it comes to having a relationship with one special person? I suck, big-time."

He craned his neck upward to peer at Leo. "Don't get me wrong. I've had lovers, but I'm crap at picking the right guy. I seem to excel at finding men who want me for my dick and nothing else. No one ever seemed to want to stick around for long." He got to his feet and walked over to the flower bed where his fragrant roses grew. He bent over to cup a peach-colored rose in his palm and sniffed it, enjoying its heavenly scent.

Thomas straightened. "I got used to the idea long ago that I was meant to be on my own. I *liked* being on my own. Pottering around in this old house that's really far too big for just me. Shutting out the world, save for the occasional visit from you. I threw myself into the training and then the club, and that was great. That was my life."

Leo was watching him with an affectionate expression.

"Then in walks that boy, into my house and slap-bang into my life. And now it's like he's a part of me. He's the first thing I see in the morning. I see his touch everywhere I look. He's in here," he said, touching his temple, "but somehow he found his way into *here*." His hand came to rest lightly over his heart. "And he needs me, Leo. Like no one has ever needed me before."

"So you've said. But there has to be more to it than that." All of a sudden Leo's eyes widened. "You want him. And I mean physically."

Thomas jerked his head up in surprise.

Leo grinned. "You do, don't you?"

Thomas shook his head angrily. "It doesn't matter if I want him or not. The point is, I can't have him, not now."

"Then it won't hurt to answer the question, will it?" Leo speared him with an intense gaze. "Do. You. Want. Him?"

"Yes!" Thomas cried out. "All right? Yes! Do you want to hear about those times when he's naked, vulnerable, so beautiful it hurts me to look at him, and I'm touching him, caressing him? Those times when my fingers are inside him?" Leo stared at him openmouthed. "What else do you want to know? Do you want to hear how sometimes I've dreamed of him, of making love to him?" Thomas wiped at his eyes where tears pricked under his lids. "But I'll be damned if I'll saddle him with a man old enough to be his father. He deserves better."

Thomas sat down once more on the bench. His elbows came to rest on his knees, and he put his head in his hands. He heard Leo step closer and sit beside him. Leo's strong hand rested lightly on his knee.

"I'm sorry, Thomas." There was such love in his voice that Thomas turned his head to look at him. Leo's icy-blue eyes shimmered with unshed tears. That was more than Thomas could bear. He straightened his back and cleared his throat roughly.

"And now you need to forget this whole conversation and do as I asked. Start looking for a Dom for my... for Peter." He swallowed. His mouth was suddenly dry. "Will you do that for me, lad?" He placed his hand over Leo's and squeezed. Leo nodded.

They turned to head indoors, only to find Alex standing in the doorway, gazing at the ground.

"Did you want something, boy? I thought you were watching a movie with Peter."

"That didn't quite pan out as planned, Sir." Alex raised his head. "Sir, I think you and Master Thomas need to come into the house. Peter wants to talk to you, and it's important." He exchanged a brief but intense look with Leo, who nodded. Alex stepped back into the house.

"Did I miss something?" Thomas inquired, composed once more. "The way he looked at you."

Leo sighed. "'Important' would seem to be an understatement. I think that's what Alex is trying to tell me."

Thomas exhaled and met Leo's gaze. "Then let's get in there."

WHEN Thomas and Leo entered the lounge, Peter was pacing, scraping his fingers through his hair. He came to a standstill when he became aware of their presence. His hands clenched and released at his sides. Leo sat in the armchair and dropped a cushion on the floor for Alex, who quickly went over to him and sat at his feet, leaning against Leo's long legs. Leo reached for his hand.

"Sir, remember how we were sitting when I told you about the panic attacks?" Peter was pale. His face was drawn and his hands fidgeted restlessly.

Thomas took hold of them and held them still. "Yes, boy."

"Could... could we sit like that now?" His eyes pleaded with Thomas.

213

There was a fragility about the boy in that moment that touched Thomas deeply. Without a word, he put cushions in front of the sofa and sat, and Peter nestled in between his legs.

"Are you sure you want us to stay, Peter?" Leo asked.

Peter dipped his chin once and exchanged a look with Alex, who gave him a brief nod of encouragement.

"Okay, boy, talk to us." Thomas held him still with arms and legs. He could feel Peter's heart beating rapidly beneath his ribs. "You're safe, lad." In that moment it didn't matter that he'd asked Leo to start the search for a Dom, which would ultimately lead to Peter's departure from his house and his life. Peter was still his boy, and Thomas would take care of him—for however much time they had left together.

Thomas breathed slowly and steadily, knowing that Peter would mimic his breathing. Sure enough, before long they were synchronized and Peter's calm was restored.

"Curtis owns a major part of the club, St. Andrew's," Peter began. "But what most people don't know is that he bought his way in with money gained illegally."

"You know this for certain?" Thomas asked sharply. Peter nodded. "How?"

Peter swallowed. "Curtis is a… a drug dealer." All three men gazed in shock. "I know this because he and his associates"—he spat out the word—"held their meetings at Curtis's house. And at the club. Where they also sold their stuff."

"There is drug dealing actually taking place at the club?" Leo was incredulous.

Peter nodded. "And this is exactly what he did at his last three clubs. He buys his way in, throws what looks like a lot of money at the place—which in reality is peanuts compared to what he and his cronies are making from the drugs and other… other activities—and then people turn a blind eye to him." Peter was gaining confidence. "No one dares to say a word if he's too rough with the subs and knocks them about."

"Back up a minute," Leo said, leaning forward. "You said 'other activities.' What other activities, exactly?"

Thomas felt Peter stiffen in his arms. He rubbed down Peter's sides and chest. "Tell us, boy," he said gently. Peter turned his head to meet his gaze,

214

and Thomas could see the pain in those eyes. "It's okay. You're among friends." Peter bowed his head once in acknowledgment, and Thomas couldn't stop himself from placing a tender kiss on top of his head. Peter leaned back once more. Thomas tried to avoid Leo's gaze. For the first time, he felt naked before his business partner. *Why couldn't I just keep my mouth shut?*

His inner voice was quick to reply. *Because it's Leo, and he loves you, old man.*

Peter squeezed Thomas's hand tightly and pulled him back into the present.

"Curtis also ran a prostitution ring out of the club."

Leo and Alex stared at him, their eyes huge. Thomas could feel Peter's heartbeat increase.

Leo was on his feet in seconds. "How long has this been going on?" he demanded.

Thomas could hear the misery in Peter's voice. "At St. Andrew's? Ever since he arrived back in June last year. But he did the same thing at other clubs around the city. I…." Peter broke off and lowered his head. His cheeks were flushed.

Thomas pressed his mouth close to Peter's ear. "I have you, boy."

After a minute of silence, Peter lifted his chin. "Curtis sold my services, at the club and at home. From the time I went to live with him until the day Steven Drummond grabbed me. I'm not going to tell you what they made me do during these past four years. You have to understand, I'm not that Peter anymore." Stunned silence greeted his words. Tears streaked his cheeks.

Alex left his position at Leo's feet and crawled over to Peter. He grabbed his hand and squeezed it tightly, then kissed Peter impulsively on the cheek before returning to Leo and tugging at him to sit down once more. His expression betrayed his emotions, however. Alex was clearly unhappy about what had been done to his friend.

Thomas kissed Peter's head and murmured into his ear. "You're right, boy. You're not that Peter anymore. We left him behind in the upper room of Darren's salon."

Peter turned to look at him, and Thomas kissed his cheek softly. Peter's eyes glowed in the lamplight.

"Are we talking male prostitutes only here?" Leo asked. Peter turned to face him and nodded. "How many?"

"I'm not sure of the exact number, but I know how much money they brought in. With the drug money and the gains from the prostitution racket, Curtis and his associates are looking set for life. You should see Curtis's house." He gave a bitter smile. "It was my prison."

"Now I understand what you meant when you told me Curtis wouldn't let you leave." Thomas shook his head as all the pieces slotted into place. "You know too much, don't you, boy?"

"Yes, Sir." Peter said quietly. "I kept my mouth shut. It was safer that way." He hesitated for a second or two. "I think there's more, but I can't be sure."

"Tell us," urged Thomas.

Peter bit his lower lip. "I could have sworn I heard the word 'auction' once or twice. And I'm pretty sure they were talking about the boys."

"You think rent boys were being auctioned off?" Leo looked horrified. Thomas could understand that. He hated to think this was all going on under the guise of a BDSM club.

Peter nodded. "I'm assuming that Curtis's sub before me, Ethan, was also a prostitute. One day he was there. The next? Gone, along with all his stuff. Maybe he saw too much and they sold him off. That would be my guess, anyway."

Leo was on his feet again and pacing the room, shaking his head. He stopped abruptly and turned to face Thomas.

"You *do* know we can't sit on this information, don't you? We have to go to the police."

Thomas nodded. His arms tightened around Peter. He leaned close to the shivering sub. "He's right, boy. Besides, Curtis knows where you are. We have to do something, and soon."

Peter turned in his arms and faced him. "I know, Sir. That's why I had to tell you. There was no point keeping quiet anymore." Suddenly his stomach growled, and Peter reddened. "Sorry, Sir. I must be hungrier than I thought."

In that instant Thomas was aware of an empty feeling in his middle. "Okay, let's all go into the kitchen and sort out some dinner. Peter—no cooking for you tonight, boy. You leave that to us." Peter made as if to protest, but Thomas shook his head. "We are more than capable, boy. You're looking at two Doms, for goodness' sake, plus a sub who works in an Italian restaurant. I'm sure that between us, we can come up with something that is both substantial *and* edible." He winked, trying to lighten the mood, and was relieved when Peter managed a weak smile. "But I would love a cup of coffee, if you wouldn't mind."

Peter scrambled to his feet. "Of course, Sir." He held out a hand to help Thomas to his feet and hoisted him up vigorously. Together the four men headed for the kitchen.

"WELL, Alex, if you ever decide to become a chef instead of a waiter, Sev would be mad to turn you down for a job."

Alex beamed with pride at Thomas's words of praise. He collected the dishes and began to fill the bowl with soapy water. Thomas glanced at Peter. The boy had been quiet throughout dinner.

"You all right, lad?"

Peter smiled at him reassuringly. "I'm fine, Sir. Understandably, I'm anxious for all this to be over."

"My thoughts exactly," echoed Leo. "And I've been thinking."

"Oh, I wondered what that burning smell was," remarked Alex cheekily. "Don't overdo it, Sir."

Leo walked slowly to stand behind his submissive and leaned in close. "And do I have to remind you what happens to bad little subs who cheek their masters?" He slid a hand down Alex's spine to caress his arse fondly. "Your cheeks, my hand. Later." He winked at Thomas as he walked back to the kitchen table. Thomas had to bite back a laugh as he watched Alex turn to Peter and pump his fist into the air, mouthing the word "Yes!" Thomas shook his head. Leo certainly had his hands full with Alex.

Leo sat down facing Thomas. "You remember when the police took me in for questioning when Alex's mother reported that I'd assaulted him?"

Thomas snorted. "As if I'd forget two detectives turning up at Severino's to take you down to the police station. What of it?"

Leo got out his wallet. "I think I might contact the detective inspector who questioned me. He struck me as a decent man. In fact, I liked him." He searched through the compartments in his wallet. "I'm sure I have his card." He gave a triumphant shout and withdrew a card. "Yes. DI Mark Saunders." He glanced at his watch. "It's still early. I'll give him a call. Do you want him to come here, or shall we go to the station?"

Thomas knew without looking that Peter had stiffened in his chair. He didn't have to say a word, however. Leo caught Peter's reaction and paled.

"I didn't think. Of course he will come here."

Thomas gave Leo a grateful look. Leo got up and walked out of the kitchen to make his call. Peter left his chair and started to set up the coffee machine while Alex finished the dishes. Thomas could hear Leo's quiet murmurs from the lounge. Peter glanced over his shoulder toward the kitchen door.

Now that Thomas knew the whole story, he could understand why the boy had been so frightened on his arrival at the house. Steven couldn't have known that by saving the boy from an abusive master, he was also putting him in danger. One day Thomas would make sure Steven knew everything.

Leo appeared in the doorway. "Saunders is on his way."

Thomas frowned. "Now?" Beside him Peter froze, and Thomas placed a protective hand on his shoulder, squeezing lightly.

Leo nodded. His expression grew sober. "When I told him what this was about, he got very animated. Said he'd be here within thirty minutes." Leo gave his sub a quick glance and then met Thomas's gaze. "Do you want us to leave?"

"No," Thomas replied emphatically. "I'd prefer it if you stayed." He looked swiftly at Peter to gauge the boy's reaction. Peter was nodding. His eyes were on Alex. "Let's have some coffee while we wait." Peter got up and went to the coffee machine, moving almost automatically. Thomas was relieved. Routine helped the boy take his mind off the present situation.

It seemed like no time at all before they heard the sound of a car pulling up outside the house. They were all in the lounge, and Leo went to peer cautiously through the window. He let out a sigh of relief.

"He's here."

Thomas went to let him in. He greeted the detective, shook his hand, and then led him into the lounge. Peter and Alex got to their feet when Mark entered. Mark gave Alex a nod of recognition and then smiled at Leo.

"Good to see you again, Mr. Hart." He crossed the room and shook Leo's hand. "I'm glad to see you two are still together." Leo beamed at that. Mark turned to face Thomas and Peter. "And this must be Peter." He acknowledged him with a brief nod. Peter bowed his head once.

Thomas indicated one of the two armchairs. "Have a seat, DI Saunders." Everyone sat down.

Mark took a notepad from the inner pocket of his black leather jacket.

"Thanks, but Mark will do just fine." He looked expectantly at Peter. His expression was kind. "Do you want to tell me what you told them earlier?"

Peter flicked a brief glance at Thomas.

"It's okay, boy." Thomas held his hand reassuringly. "I'm right here."

Peter took a deep breath and sat upright. He began to talk, hesitantly at first but with increasing confidence as his tale unfolded. Mark's face showed no reaction when Peter spoke of being forced into prostitution. He wrote copious notes, nodding every now and then to show Peter he was following every word. Occasionally he asked questions. The only sounds in the room were Peter's quiet voice and the ticking of the clock on the mantelpiece.

At last Peter finished speaking. Thomas hugged him and whispered into his ear, "Well done, boy. I'm proud of you." Peter's face lit up in a tired smile, and then he sagged back into the sofa.

Mark was reading through his notes, his brow creased by a deep frown. He looked up at Thomas and Peter.

"What I'm about to say may surprise you." Thomas arched his brows at this unexpected opening line. "This isn't the first time I've heard about Curtis Rogers's activities." Mark focused his gaze on Peter. "In fact, what you've just told me is almost word-for-word what someone else reported to me four years ago."

Leo's face contorted. "Then why was nothing done about it?"

Mark closed his notepad and leaned back into the chair. "That's a good question. Actually, it's the question I asked myself at the time."

"Who came to you with this?" Thomas demanded.

Mark fell silent for a moment, clearly deliberating what to say next. Then he peered intently at Peter.

"Does the name Ethan Samuels ring a bell?"

Nineteen

Plans

PETER gave a jolt. "E-Ethan? Ethan came to you?" A shiver ran through him, and he was glad when Thomas's hand tightened around his.

Mark nodded. His eyes never left Peter. "You're right, by the way. Ethan claimed that Curtis auctions off boys who either get to know too much or who he figures will fetch a good price. But I suspect Curtis is only part of a much larger ring. And there's more." Mark paused, scraping his hand through his hair. "Ethan claimed some of the boys were being used as mules."

"He was forcing them to run drugs too?" Peter was horrified.

Leo was shaking his head. "Hang on. I still don't get it. This Ethan comes to you *four years ago* and nothing was done? What the hell is going on?"

Mark got to his feet and began pacing the lounge. The man looked frustrated.

"All I know is, Ethan reported all this to me four years ago. I reported it to my superiors. It was about to be passed on to SOCA—the Serious Organized Crimes Agency. Then all of a sudden I'm told there's no evidence to support any of it, and that's as far as it got."

Leo's eyes narrowed. "Someone was paid to bury this. We're talking police corruption here."

Mark looked very unhappy. "That would be my guess too. I always thought it was weird how everything just got swept under the rug. And then Ethan simply up and vanished."

"I thought maybe Ethan found out stuff like I had, and Curtis had him shipped off somewhere." Peter couldn't keep quiet. He'd always thought there was something suspect about Ethan's sudden departure. "Perhaps Curtis found out that he'd been to the police." He shuddered. "That's why I kept my mouth shut. I figured it was safer that way."

Mark was nodding enthusiastically. "You did the right thing, Peter."

Peter swallowed. "I-I want to help you stop Curtis."

Both Mark and Thomas stared at him openmouthed. Mark leaned forward. "Are you sure? I couldn't ask you to do that. You're a civilian." He rubbed his chin. "But really, if I could think of *some* way in which you could help, you'd do it?"

Peter leaned forward to reply, but Thomas laid a hand on his knee and squeezed.

"I think that depends entirely on what it is you're proposing." There was a hard edge to Thomas's voice.

Mark shifted uncomfortably. "Peter, would you be willing to help us trap Curtis?"

Peter was taken aback by the speed with which Thomas got to his feet.

"Absolutely not." Thomas's jaw was set. "You will *not* endanger the boy like that."

Peter reached across and grasped Thomas's hand. Thomas looked down at him. His eyes were full of fire.

"Sir, let me do this." He gazed up at the Dom, trying to let him see just how important this was.

Thomas shook his head vigorously. "No. No *way*. I will not have you put in danger. Forget it. It's not going to happen."

Peter pulled Thomas to sit down beside him and grabbed his hands.

"Please, Sir, I need to do this."

"Why, lad? Let the police handle it," Thomas implored.

Peter gave him a sweet smile. "You told me I was yours to protect. You're mine too." Thomas stared at him. "But we need to stop Curtis from doing this to others. Think of all those lives he's destroying, Sir. The drugs. Those poor boys. Let me do this." He locked eyes with Thomas. "Sir, I need to do this for *me*."

He watched as Thomas rubbed his jaw, grimacing. Peter knew Thomas was protecting him, but he also knew this was the right thing to do. Even if the thought of it scared the hell out of him.

Thomas's expression softened, and he pulled his hand free to cup Peter's cheek tenderly.

"Very well, boy." The words were barely a whisper. Thomas released him and turned to Mark. "I want guarantees Peter will be protected." Peter couldn't see Thomas's expression, but he saw Mark pull himself upright and swallow. Thomas had that effect on a lot of people.

"I will do everything in my power to ensure he stays safe," Mark assured him. "Starting with moving the two of you to a hotel, right now." He pulled out his phone.

"What?" Thomas reacted swiftly. "Why?"

Mark grimaced. "Curtis knows where you live. It's not safe for you to stay here. He's already made one attempt to grab Peter. I don't intend to wait around for him to try it again. We'll organize a safe location for both of you, but tonight we'll find you a hotel."

THOMAS suddenly noticed the crease between Peter's eyes. He cupped his face.

"Would you feel better if we went to a hotel tonight?"

Peter appeared aghast at the suggestion. "No, Sir! This is my... our home. I won't be run out of it. And besides...." He paused and reached up to place his hand over Thomas's. "You're going to protect me. Just like you have been doing up to now. Right?" The overwhelming expression of trust in those green eyes almost floored him with its depth.

"Yes, boy." Thomas couldn't hold back his reaction. He brought his face closer to Peter's and kissed him lightly on the lips. Those eyes grew large and round, and Thomas wondered if he'd gone too far. But when a look of utter peace crossed Peter's face, he let out the breath he'd been holding. He stepped back and let the boy sit down. He couldn't miss Leo's happy expression as he watched them. Thomas leveled a warning stare in his direction, and Leo gave an innocent shrug, which didn't fool Thomas for a second.

Mark cleared his throat. "If you insist on staying here, then I need to get you some protection. I'll arrange for a couple of undercover detectives to stay outside all night. I don't want to risk leaving you alone. If he was desperate enough to try to grab Peter in the street right outside the house in broad daylight, I wouldn't put it past him to come back at night." He gave Thomas a quick glance. "Is that acceptable?"

Thomas gave a brisk nod, and Mark walked out of the room to make the call.

Leo got up, walked to the window, and peered out into the street. "I have to say, this whole business is worrying me to death." He turned toward them. "Police guarding you all night? Using Peter to trap Curtis?" Leo shook his head, scowling.

Thomas let out a sigh. "I think you two need to go home."

Alex looked at Leo beseechingly from his position on the floor. "Leo, can't we stay until the police arrive? I don't feel right about us leaving them alone here." Leo left the window and went to his sub. He knelt down and kissed him, holding Alex's face gently. Thomas watched the two men connect. In that tender moment, they were no longer master and submissive, but lovers reaching out to one another. It made his heart ache to see it, and for the first time he envied his business partner. *I want that too.*

Leo broke the kiss and sat back on his haunches. He turned toward Thomas.

"We'll stay until your protection arrives." He glared at Thomas. "No arguments, old man."

Thomas's sigh brought a chuckle to Leo's lips. A slight hand wrapped around Thomas's, and he turned to look at his boy. Peter's expression made it plain he was happy to have the two men here. Thomas wasn't about to argue.

"THE house is ours once more," Thomas announced as he closed the front door and bolted it. Leo and Alex had left once the police car turned up at ten. Mark Saunders stayed until then too. He and Leo had been in the kitchen, discussing something in very earnest tones. Thomas kept out of their way. He stayed in the lounge with Peter and Alex, who were stretched out on the floor on cushions, watching TV. Alex looked relaxed enough, but there was a noticeable tension to Peter. Thomas could see it in his shoulders, the hands that clenched and unfurled, the odd shiver that rippled through him when he thought Thomas wasn't looking. Mark intended to return in the morning. He'd gone back to the police station to put together some kind of a plan for dealing with Curtis. Perhaps that was what he and Leo had been discussing. They certainly talked for long enough.

He glanced up the hall to find Peter hovering in the kitchen doorway. The boy looked drawn. Thomas had an idea.

"How about you and I make some popcorn, snuggle under the throw on the sofa, and watch *Return of the Jedi*?" he suggested. Peter's eyes lit up, and that flash of a smile was the best thing Thomas had seen all evening.

Within ten minutes they were on the sofa under the throw. Thomas balanced the bowl of buttered popcorn in his lap, and Peter snugged up against him, an arm across his belly. His head rested on Thomas's chest. Thomas relaxed into the sofa and tried to concentrate on the movie, but he was acutely aware of Peter's body heat seeping into him as he held him close. The smell of Peter's citrus shampoo filled his nostrils, and underlying it all was the warm aroma that was pure Peter. Thomas closed his eyes and let the boy's presence fill his senses.

Just for a minute or two, Thomas allowed himself to imagine a life with the boy at his side. Evenings like this, enjoying being close. Days spent together, engaged in varied pursuits. Long nights with the boy in his arms, in his bed. A line from an Elton John song came abruptly to mind.

Rolling like thunder under the covers.

His heart ached with the thought of what he was about to throw away.

He deserves better. You said so.

Thomas could strangle that voice sometimes. *I can dream, can't I?* The wistful thought wouldn't be denied. He pulled his arm tighter around the boy and kept his eyes closed. The soundtrack of the movie may have been in his ears, but in his head was the wonderful fantasy of a life with Peter.

Let me hold onto my dream for a little while longer, he pleaded with whoever was listening. Peter stirred slightly against him and let out a barely perceptible sigh.

The inner voice remained blessedly silent.

"WELL, I've talked it over with some of my colleagues, and we think we've come up with a plan."

Peter couldn't help but notice how tired and drawn Mark Saunders seemed. The detective looked like he hadn't slept a wink. Peter got up from his chair and poured a mug of coffee. He placed it in front of Mark, who flashed him a grateful smile.

Thomas was sitting beside him. From the look of him when Peter entered his bedroom that morning, Peter could tell how little sleep he'd gotten. Thomas was already awake, lying on his back, staring up at the ceiling. Peter could understand that. He'd tossed and turned all night. His dreams had been a fragmented mess of Curtis, his associates, Thomas, Leo…. It had been a relief to hear his alarm clock going off.

There was steel in Thomas's voice. "Before you launch into this plan, I have a question. Who *exactly* did you discuss this with? I'm remembering what you said yesterday. Who's to know if one of your colleagues is on Curtis's payroll?"

Mark smiled. "You're a smart man. I only spoke about it with one colleague, a detective constable who I've known since I first became a police officer. I'd trust Bill Stephens with my life. Bill suggested that I contact SOCA directly, without reporting it to my superiors." He grimaced. "Now *that* was an interesting conversation. They weren't happy about me not going through the official channels, but once I explained why, they soon got over it. I've discussed this with a SOCA officer, and he's happy for me to go ahead and work out the details with you."

Peter swallowed. Thomas gave his hand a quick reassuring squeeze and then turned his attention back to Mark.

"We're going to go on the assumption that either Curtis or someone working for him will be watching the house." Mark sipped the coffee and gave a low moan. "Now I know why my son Josh is always banging on at me to get a coffee machine. This is delicious."

"So what's the plan?" demanded Thomas, a touch of impatience clearly evident in his voice.

Mark addressed Peter. "Mr. Hart told me about your agoraphobia last night. He felt it was something I needed to be aware of."

Peter felt a wave of affection for the absent Dom. Leo was looking out for him too.

"Now, I know you've just started going on your own to your appointments with"—Mark consulted his notepad—"Dr. Herne." Peter nodded. "We'd like you to carry on with this routine."

Thomas's eyes went wide. "You want Curtis to grab him, don't you?"

Mark nodded. "We'd have Peter under surveillance the whole time. Plus, he'd be wired. We would always know exactly where he was."

"'We'?"

"A team of SOCA undercover officers," Mark explained.

"Would he be able to take a taxi to and from the city center?"

Mark shook his head. "If he does that, you're cutting down the number of opportunities Curtis will have to grab him. The whole point of this is we *want* Curtis to grab him. No, Peter would have to make his own way there and back." He focused his gaze on Peter. "You realize that for this to work, it has to be this way, don't you?"

Peter swallowed hard. He wasn't ready. It was too much to ask of him. *I can't do this.* A quick glance at Thomas showed him the Dom was close to protesting. Peter looked at the man who had become his whole world. And then it struck him. *Sir has given me* everything. *How can I let him down?* Thomas was staring at him, clearly waiting for him to refuse. But Peter couldn't. He focused on Thomas's gorgeous green eyes, the creases around them that deepened when he laughed, the firm line of his jaw, those lips that had brushed so softly against his last night. *He's kept me safe. Now it's my turn to do the same thing for* him.

Peter took a deep, calming breath and met Mark's anxious gaze.

"I understand." He turned to Thomas. "I can do this, Sir. I *will* do this."

THOMAS was torn between horror at what Peter would have to go through and overwhelming pride in his boy.

"You're sure?" There was no way he would let Peter undertake something of this magnitude unless the boy was one hundred percent certain. Peter raised his head and looked him in the eye.

"Yes, Sir."

Thomas studied him for a moment or two, but Peter didn't waver. Reluctantly, Thomas nodded toward Mark. "Okay, what's the plan?"

Mark addressed himself to Peter. "The aim of this whole operation is to collect evidence of Curtis's involvement and to gain more information about his associates. For this to happen, we need Curtis to admit what he's been up to. We want him to make a grab for you, and then we'll track you to wherever they take you. Once there, it'll be your job to get Curtis talking." He tilted his head. "You lived with him for four years. Is he the kind of man who would be likely to want to brag about his exploits?"

Peter laughed bitterly. "Oh yes. Getting him to talk shouldn't be a problem."

Mark let out a sigh of relief. "Thank God for that." He flashed Thomas a quick glance. "We'll need to fit Peter with microtransmitters. Wearing a wire is out of the question. We can swap a button on his jacket for a transmitter, but that assumes he doesn't take it off." Mark swallowed and suddenly looked distinctly nervous. "There is also a possibility that we have to consider. Once Curtis has Peter, he's not going to take any chances. My SOCA colleague thinks the likelihood is that Curtis will try to find out if Peter's told the police anything, and then get rid of him."

Peter blanched, and his breathing sped up. Thomas reacted swiftly.

"Breathe, lad, breathe through it, that's it." He held the boy's hand and glared at Mark. "Did you have to say that?"

Mark paled. "Oh God, no, you misunderstand me. I don't mean… oh hell…." He wiped his brow. "SOCA thinks they'll try to sell Peter, probably to someone out of the country. I didn't mean to imply for a second—"

"Shut up for a minute, Mark, please, and let me calm him down," Thomas interjected harshly. He focused on Peter, noting with relief that Mark's latest statement appeared to have allayed Peter's fears. The boy was breathing easier. He waited until Peter was calm before addressing Mark.

"Sorry about that," he said gruffly, "but you scared the boy half to death." He kept tight hold of Peter's hand. "So what's the backup plan?"

Mark exhaled shakily before continuing. "If they do decide to auction him, they'll probably strip him. Then all transmitters will be useless. We can still use the button on his jacket to give us his location, but we won't be able to pick up any conversations between Peter and Curtis if it's not close enough. We need Peter to wear something that they're not likely to remove. Jewelry would be too obvious. They're going to be looking for transmitters, remember." Mark fell silent.

Thomas regarded him thoughtfully. "I take it you haven't been able to come up with anything?"

"No," Mark replied gloomily. "We were tossing ideas back and forth all night. No luck."

Thomas stared at the table for several seconds. "Mark, what's the smallest listening bug you can get your hands on?"

Mark snickered. "Thomas, I've been given a GSM spy bug. That thing is *seriously* tiny."

"How does it work?" Thomas had the germ of an idea, but its success would depend on two things—the size of this bug, and whether or not Mark would go for his plan. From the look on Peter's face, the boy was interested too.

"It has a slot for a tiny SIM card. You click it into place and that's it. When you want to activate it, you call it from a mobile phone, and that activates the microphone. It can pick up sounds from up to forty feet away. And you can call it from anywhere in the world."

Thomas barked out a laugh. "That's amazing." He thought furiously for a second. "Mark, I have an idea, but I have to warn you, it's a little radical."

Mark groaned. "*Anything.* I'm desperate, here!"

Thomas got up from the table. "Back in a moment." He exited the kitchen and went up the stairs to his bedroom. He rummaged in the bottom of his chest of drawers until he found the object of his search. He pounced on it triumphantly. Mark was going to have a fit when he saw this.

He hurried down the stairs two at a time and into the kitchen. "Got it." He dropped the item in front of Mark and retook his seat, biting back a smile as Mark's eyes widened.

"What the hell," the detective exclaimed softly. He looked up at Thomas. "Is that what I think it is?" He picked it up and turned it, shaking his head slowly.

Thomas chuckled. "Something occurred to me. We left BDSM out of the equation. It had to be something that wouldn't seem out of place on a submissive."

Mark burst into laughter. "Sure, but a cock ring?"

He gazed at the object in frank amazement. It was a metal cuff in two different colors, curved like an almost-closed letter *C*. The cock ring was almost two inches in depth and nearly half an inch thick. Mark fingered the edge of the metal.

"You might have something here," he said thoughtfully. "If this part could be hollowed out, we might just be able to insert the bug. If the microphone end points downward, it would be less noticeable. We could even fabricate our own cock ring with the bug built into it."

Mark got to his feet and grabbed his jacket. Thomas and Peter stared in surprise. Mark noticed their expressions and chuckled. "Sorry, but I've got to get this to the SOCA lab so they can play around with the idea, see what they can come up with. And seeing as time is of the essence, I'd better get a move on." He reached the kitchen door and stopped. "Oh. Can I have one of Peter's jackets? Let's see if we can sew another bug into it. Think of it as Plan B just in case the jacket stays close enough to pick up the conversation."

"Good idea." Thomas grabbed Peter's denim jacket from the cupboard under the stairs and handed it to Mark.

"Perfect."

"I'll see you out." Thomas followed Mark along the hallway to the front door. "Will we still have guests outside tonight?" He held open the door.

Mark paused at the threshold. "Yes. And they're going to be a permanent feature until this is finished." He indicated Peter, who stood behind Thomas. "Can you accompany Peter to his appointments until we're ready to run with this?"

"Certainly." Thomas shook his hand. "Thank you for all you're doing."

"It's my job, Thomas," Mark said simply. Then he shook his head, laughing. "A cock ring. Now *that's* ingenious." He was still laughing as he climbed into his car and drove away.

Thomas noted the car parked across the road. Its two occupants were watching him. Thomas gave them a brief smile as he closed the door. Peter was standing by the foot of the stairs, and Thomas could see immediately that all was not well. The boy looked jittery. Luckily Thomas had the perfect solution for a jittery boy.

"How about you go upstairs to our playroom and get ready, boy? I think you and I need to do something to take our minds off all this. What do you think?"

Peter's face was transformed as he smiled.

"That sounds perfect, Sir." And he bounded up the stairs without another word.

Thomas laughed to himself as he followed Peter at a more sedate pace. Sometimes he had great ideas, and spending time with his boy ranked up there with the best of them.

Twenty

Stepping out of the comfort zone

"PLEASE, Sir, let me come!" Peter made another impassioned plea as Thomas turned up the speed on the vibrator, pushed it slowly into him, and nudged his gland repeatedly. Peter arched his back as if trying to escape from the sensations that pulsed through his body, assaulting him at every turn.

"Soon, boy. Hold it back just a little longer for me." Thomas was watching him intently. He had one hand on his cock, pulling it gently while he stroked the vibrator in and out, sending shudders through Peter. Sir had brought him to the brink of orgasm several times already, only to back off each time, changing toys, varying the speed of his hand on Peter's cock, or sliding a finger or two into him. Each time Sir reduced the degree of intensity, Peter could have screamed, desperate to come. With each change, Peter's level of arousal increased, until he was at the point where he thought he would pass out.

"Ready, boy?" Thomas released his cock and turned up the vibrations.

Peter wailed. "Oh God, Sir, I can't take it anymore! Please, Sir, I beg you!" He gazed intently at Thomas and focused on those green eyes, which shone. Thomas stroked his hand softly down Peter's cheek and became still.

"Come, boy. Come now." Thomas slid in the vibrator to nudge his gland. "Let go, boy. Let it out."

Peter howled in ecstasy as come began to pump out of his cock and over his abs and chest. His whole body shook as the orgasm hit him at full force. He barely felt Thomas withdraw the vibrator, he was so focused on the sensations that flowed through him.

And suddenly Peter felt himself let go as a sense of well-being filled him, surging through his body to permeate every cell. It was as if he were floating, having left the world behind him. Peter could only describe it as sheer bliss. He felt safe. Warm. Utterly content. Loved. Peter felt like he was flying. He exulted in this beautiful state, the real world blissfully lost to him.

Little by little the world began to creep back into focus. Peter grew aware of strong arms around him, lips pressed against his forehead in a tender kiss. *Sir.* He lay in Thomas's arms, reveling in soft touches and gentle caresses, hyperaware of Thomas's comforting presence, which seeped into him, warming him.

"I've got you, boy. That's it, come back to me."

He focused on that voice he loved so much, feeling it pull him back into the sunlit playroom. Tiny specks of dust danced their ballet in the light that poured in from the huge windows. Thomas cradled him in his arms among the soft cushions that surrounded them both. Green eyes regarded him with affection and something else—joy.

"Sir, that was…." Words failed him. He couldn't begin to describe how he'd felt.

Thomas smiled at him. "Welcome back, boy."

Peter stared at him in surprise. "What… where… have I been somewhere?" A wonderful lassitude filled him, but it was more than that. For some reason, he felt a profound connection with Thomas, something he couldn't quite account for.

Thomas chuckled, a sound of pure delight. "In a manner of speaking, yes. Can you sit up?"

Peter assessed his present situation. "I think so." If anything, he felt great. Carefully, Thomas pulled him into an upright position on the sofa, placing cushions behind him before sitting next to him. Peter gazed questioningly at his Dom. "What was that?"

"Did it feel good?"

Peter couldn't begin to quantify it. "Oh, Sir, it felt…." He stared at the floor for a moment, searching for the right words. No. Wasn't going to happen. "Yes, Sir. It was wonderful. I feel so… so awake, like I'm hyperaware of every little thing."

Thomas's smile grew exponentially. "That's the adrenaline. You were in subspace." Peter tilted his head. "It's an altered state of being that occurs when a submissive achieves an orgasmic state. It can be a very emotional experience, but a physical one too. Did you feel floaty at all?" Peter nodded. "Your body was flooded with endorphins." The light in Thomas's eyes was truly beautiful as he gazed intently at Peter. "I promised to make you soar, boy."

Impulsively, Peter launched himself at Thomas and wrapped his arms around him. Thomas took a second before placing his hands on Peter's back and gently stroking up and down his spine.

"Thank you, Sir." Gratitude bubbled up out of him. "Thank you." He spoke fervently, murmuring his words against Thomas's chest. Thomas's arms suddenly tightened around him.

"You're welcome, my boy."

Warmth radiated throughout his body. His heart swelled with love of his Dom for giving him this wonderful gift. Peter wanted the moment never to end.

"ANY news yet from that detective inspector?" Alex was frowning.

Peter shook his head. It had been three days since Mark Saunders had taken his jacket—and Thomas's cock ring—back to the police station. Peter still couldn't believe Thomas had suggested bugging a *cock ring*. He hadn't mentioned *that* part to Alex; the sub would die laughing. DI Saunders had been in touch with Thomas by phone and said that it wouldn't be long before they would be in a position to begin the operation. But since then, not a word.

He passed a mug of green tea to Alex. The house was quiet. Thomas hadn't left his side since Mark's visit, but this morning something had happened at the club that demanded his presence, and he'd reluctantly left for a few hours. Peter didn't mind. The police car and its occupants were still a permanent feature, and besides, it was Alex's day to come by.

"If it were me, I'd have been going crazy with worry these last few days." Alex regarded him critically. "But you seem so calm. How on earth do you manage it?"

Peter hid a smile. He knew exactly what had kept him focused—the playroom. He and Thomas had shared a few scenes over the last two or three days. Since that first encounter with subspace, Peter had been eager to experience it again. Their times together in the playroom had filled him with a sense of joy and fulfillment he hadn't dreamed possible.

"I'm so happy, Alex," Peter admitted quietly. "Even though the thought of what's coming scares me to death, right now I just feel... content."

Alex beamed. "Oh, Peter, that's great." A crease appeared between his eyes. "I have to say, you're coping with this much better than I thought you would."

Peter gazed at his mug. "To be honest, I'm trying not to think about it. There's no point dwelling on it until they're ready for the operation to take place. I'm just going to get on with life and keep myself immersed in my tasks here."

The crease deepened. "I wasn't talking about the police operation. I meant, I thought you'd have been.... I thought you and Master Thomas...." Alex broke off, looking flustered.

Peter frowned. "What are you talking about, Alex? What about me and Sir?" He blinked. Alex was avoiding making eye contact. "Alex?"

Alex sighed. "I really thought you and Master Thomas were a good fit. Especially after you told me you, er...." His cheeks reddened. "I know you fantasize about him, and it's plain when you're together that you care for each other. I honestly thought he would make it a permanent contract."

Peter was flummoxed. "Alex, I don't understand."

Alex met his eyes. There was a sadness in them that made Peter catch his breath.

"I know, Peter. You don't have to pretend. I heard him asking Leo to find another Dom for you. The day you told us about Curtis."

The world stopped. Peter gazed at Alex incredulously. He shook his head.

"He... we...." Suddenly it was difficult to breathe. Sir didn't want him. Sir was going to pass him on to another Dom. Okay, so he'd always said that was what he was going to do, but Peter had hoped, especially in the last few days, that things had changed.

Alex's eyes widened in alarm. "Oh my God. You didn't know. I thought he would have told you." Alex left his chair and came around the table to kneel in front of Peter. His hands were on Peter's thighs, rubbing gently. "Are you okay?" Anxious eyes regarded him.

Peter breathed evenly, counting silently in his head, willing himself to calm down before the panic that bubbled below the surface erupted. Alex was staring at him. His eyes were full of concern. Peter felt the panic recede until at last he was calm once more.

He gave Alex a weak smile. "I'm okay."

Alex's lips pressed into a fine line, and he arched his eyebrows.

"No, really," Peter reassured him. The strange thing was, it was true. It was as though he was watching himself from a distance, assessing his emotions. How he was *able* to remain this calm, however, was a mystery.

He took a long sip of his tea and met Alex's gaze. "He didn't lie to me, Alex. He always said this would happen. I just didn't expect it to happen so soon." He curled his hands around the mug. Suddenly they felt so cold. "But it doesn't change anything. I'm still going through with this. Curtis has to be stopped, and right now, it's not only me that's in danger, but Sir too. I have to protect him." His chin trembled. He would do anything in his power to protect the Dom.

Alex's mouth fell open, and he became still. "Oh my God," he said softly. "You're in love with him." The expression on his face was kind.

Peter jerked his chin up. "No," he protested feebly, "I—"

"It's all right, Peter, I won't say a word. Not even to Leo." Peter could hear the sincerity in every word. The warm hand clasped around his, the soothing quality in his voice…. Peter couldn't hold back any longer.

"Yes, I love him." It was a relief to utter the words aloud. He pulled himself upright.

"He doesn't know, does he?" Alex stroked the back of his hand with gentle fingers. Peter shook his head. "Maybe if he knew—"

"No." Peter locked eyes with him, noting the sub's reluctance to meet his gaze. "That would be putting pressure on him, and I won't do that." He grabbed Alex's hand, squeezing it tightly. "And I want your promise, Alex."

"I promise. Not a word."

The phone in the lounge shrilled out its strident tone. Alex got to his feet, and Peter stepped around him to walk hurriedly into the lounge and pick up the handset.

Before he could say a word, Thomas's voice came down the line.

"Peter, I'm coming home. DI Saunders is on his way to the house. He should be with you in about ten minutes." Thomas sounded breathless. "Looks like we're in business."

"Yes, Sir." Peter's heart began to beat more rapidly.

"Boy." Thomas spoke quietly. "Breathe."

Peter's heart swelled with love for the Dom. "Yes, Sir. I'll try to remember to do that." He could hear Thomas's chuckle.

"Home soon, boy. Have coffee on."

Peter said good-bye and hung up the phone.

Alex was standing in the doorway. "Shall I leave?"

Peter smiled. "You can stay until Sir gets here. How's that?" His friend beamed. "But I'd better get the machine on. DI Saunders is coming, and he likes my coffee." He winked at Alex, affecting more calm than he was actually feeling inside. Alex snorted and turned to head back into the kitchen. Peter followed behind him. Inside his head, he kept up a litany. *You can do this. You can do this. For Sir.* He pushed aside his heartache. Right now he was Sir's boy. Peter was going to make the most of every second they had left together.

"I'VE been in contact with Dr. Herne," Mark said, after taking a long drink of his coffee. "She's agreed to go back to three sessions per week until Curtis makes his move. We want to give him as many chances as possible to make a grab for Peter."

"She knows about Curtis, Sir," Peter admitted.

Thomas was relieved that the lad had been able to share with Laura. He gave a brisk nod of approval before focusing his full attention on Mark.

"So, what happens now?"

"Well, seeing as tomorrow is Monday, we'd like Peter to attend his appointment as we discussed." Mark looked keenly at Peter. "Are you still okay with this?"

Peter bobbed his head and met Mark's gaze, appearing calm, but Thomas knew the boy too well. He noticed the slight tremor that rippled through the lad. Peter was putting on a brave face for the detective. Pride surged through Thomas.

"Any luck with the bugging device?" Thomas was dying to see what the police had come up with.

Mark's face broke into a broad smile. "I was wondering when you would ask about that." He took two plain brown packets from his jacket pocket and handed one to Thomas. "I'm returning your cock ring."

Thomas's face fell. "It wasn't a viable option?" *Damn.*

Mark grinned. "Actually, it was a great idea. But the one you gave me didn't lend itself well to our purpose. So we came up with this." He emptied the contents of the remaining packet carefully onto the kitchen table. Thomas let out a low, appreciative gasp.

"That's amazing. It's got a bug in it?" He picked up the item.

Mark nodded. "We were able to hollow out the end of the ring, which is made of a strong, flexible rubber. It took some doing, however, to get the internal working of the device to fit. The SIM card is already in place. Obviously we had to do that before we finished off the piece."

Thomas was nodding absently, but his attention was claimed by the beautiful item in his hand. It was a cock ring fabricated from black rubber, thick and sturdy looking, cylindrical in section. The ends overlapped at the front, and two loops of silver allowed the ring to be pulled tighter and then held in place. What drew his admiration, however, were the silver dragon heads that adorned each end. The dragons were open-jawed, with a slender forked tongue snaking out over delicate, sharp teeth.

"Did you have this specially made?" Thomas was impressed.

Mark blushed. "Actually, no. This was given to me by one of my son Josh's housemates. I spoke to Josh about trying to come up with a unique way to house a listening device, and the next thing I knew, his housemate Daniel volunteered this." Thomas lifted his brows, and Mark's blush deepened. He coughed and reached for the cock ring. "The microphone is in this end," he said, pointing to one of the dragons. "And no, he doesn't want it back when we've finished. He was tickled that we were able to use it, to be honest."

"It's hard to believe there's a bug in it," Peter said softly.

Mark placed it in Peter's hand. "Take good care of it." Peter nodded. He couldn't take his eyes off it.

"I need to know what your plans are," said Thomas decisively. "What will happen once Peter leaves the house?"

Mark straightened immediately and pulled out his notepad. "Peter will be shadowed all the way to his appointment. We will have undercover officers at different stages along the route—which we will go over now, by the way—so at no point will Peter be unobserved. I will be keeping in touch with you the whole time by mobile. I'll inform you when he makes it to Dr. Herne's and when he leaves."

Thomas nodded. He let loose small noises of approval. This was exactly what he wanted to hear, that Peter would be protected. "Should I stay at home?"

"No." Mark replied straightaway. "Keep your life as normal as possible. I'll be in contact with you immediately if something happens. So go to the club if you want." Mark was regarding him earnestly. "This is no small operation," he stressed. "A lot of man-hours are going into this. We want to catch this bastard, him and his associates." His eyes gleamed. "Peter's safety is our number one priority, I promise you."

Thomas had heard enough. "Okay, then it's full steam ahead tomorrow morning?"

Mark nodded and reached behind him for Peter's jacket, which he'd placed on the back of his chair. "This has two transmitters hidden in it, one for tracking Peter and another listening bug." Thomas took it and examined the buttons carefully. "You shouldn't be able to tell which button is the transmitter."

Thomas couldn't. "This is very impressive technology, Mark." He narrowed his eyes. "You're sure your superiors don't know what you're up to?"

Mark was quick to respond. "Absolutely. They think I'm working on a spate of gay bashings in the village. There's a false paper trail for them to follow if anyone gets too interested. SOCA was *very* helpful on that score." He turned to Peter, who had been watching quietly. "You know what you have to do, right?"

Peter nodded. "Get Curtis talking. That won't be a problem. I'll do my best to make sure he provides you with what you need."

Mark's eyes glittered approvingly. "Good boy." Peter bowed his head. His cheeks were flushed. Mark addressed Thomas. "We don't expect them to snatch Peter tomorrow. They're going to be too wary to do that. It might take them a few days, maybe even weeks, to work out his routine. We'll just have to be patient. But it doesn't matter how long it takes. We'll be there, watching." His tone was grim. "Now, let's work out that route, shall we?"

PETER sat on the bus. His back was rigid. He knew his shirt was soaked with perspiration beneath the denim jacket, but it was a cold sweat. The short walk to the bus stop had been fraught with anxiety. Every time someone passed within a few feet of him, he tensed, anticipating a sudden move to grab him. Logic told him that grabbing him in the middle of a busy street was not part of their game plan, but right now his brain wasn't listening. He tried to breathe deeply, but there was a pain in his chest, and he felt dizzy, his legs shaky and weak. When he saw the bus arrive, he almost wept with relief. After paying his fare, he sank down gratefully into his seat, doing his best to control his breathing.

At this rate you'll give yourself a heart attack, he told himself sternly. Counting wasn't helping. He needed to focus on something to take his mind off the rising panic that sent his heartbeat racing to the point where the blood was pounding in his ears. He closed his eyes and tried to picture his beach. It wouldn't come. *Oh fuck, I'm screwed*. His first time out on his own in years, and he wasn't going to make it. Sir would be so disappointed in him.

Sir. He pictured the Dom in his mind, focusing on those expressive green eyes. He thought of Thomas holding him in his arms as he came down from subspace. Thomas with his arm around him, holding him close as they watched a movie together. Thomas shaving him so carefully. The brush of Thomas's lips against his.

His heartbeat slowed, and his breathing became less erratic. Tears welled up behind his eyelids, and a sudden lightness suffused his whole being. Peter exhaled, expelling his tension as he blinked away the tears of relief. Of all the techniques Dr. Herne had come up with, why had she never thought of this one? For the remainder of the journey, he shut out the world around him and focused on Sir, dwelling on the times when he had felt closest to the Dom. It didn't matter that soon he would belong to someone else. Thomas would always be there in his heart. The man had changed his life, and Peter would always be grateful to him for that.

At last the bus arrived in the city center, and Peter got off. He'd been so wrapped up in his own thoughts that he hadn't even tried to look around at his fellow passengers to see if he could spot the undercover cops. Then again, he reasoned, as his brain finally got into gear once more, if you could spot them, they wouldn't be very good, would they? He walked briskly through the busy streets. He kept his head down, totally focused on his destination. He imagined Thomas holding his hand tightly, walking with him every step of the way. The thought warmed him, dispersing the fog of panic that had been frightening in its intensity. As he caught sight of the bright-blue door across the square that led to Dr. Herne's office, he let out a shuddering sigh of relief. *Made it*. The one thought that filled his head as he headed for the door was that Sir was going to be so proud of him.

THOMAS sat with his arm around the boy, holding him closely as they watched TV. He took a moment or two to enjoy the closeness and tranquility of their time together. Sitting like this had become a pleasant habit, one he was going to miss dreadfully when the boy moved on. Thomas tried not to dwell on such thoughts. Each time he considered Peter's imminent departure there was that small voice at the back of his mind. *You want to lose this? When are you going to admit how much the boy means to you?* Thomas didn't have an answer.

The day had been fraught with tension. Thomas had been unable to concentrate on the applications that had demanded his attention. Every few minutes he'd gazed at the phone, willing it to ring so Mark could tell him his boy was still safe. By the time that first call arrived to tell him Peter had reached his appointment, Thomas had felt close to the breaking point.

Leo wanted to send him home, but that would have been infinitely worse. Alone in that quiet house, seeing the boy everywhere he looked? Thomas was better off where he was. Not that Leo had agreed, of course. The man grumbled every time Thomas cast a glance in the phone's direction. When Peter called to say he was home, Thomas couldn't take any more. He announced he was going home, and Leo heaved a sigh of relief.

"So proud of you today, boy," Thomas said in a hushed tone. He cupped Peter's chin and looked at him with concern. "Was it so bad?"

Peter shrugged. "I got through it, Sir. That's all that matters. The next time will be easier. I learned a new technique today that really helped stave off the panic."

Thomas beamed. "That's wonderful." He waited for Peter to tell him more, but the boy simply snuggled closer. Thomas drank in the sensation of having a warm body pressed close to his, and tried to push aside that nagging thought that continued to torment him.

Why should the age gap matter to you when you're in love with him?

Because it does, Thomas told himself stubbornly.

Inside his head, he swore he heard a snort.

Twenty-One

Checkmate

PETER wiped his eyes with a paper tissue. "Why is it I always end up crying in our sessions?" He scowled. "God, I swear I must seem like such a girl to you sometimes."

Dr. Herne smiled. "Is that because real men don't cry?"

"Yes!" Peter felt like such a basket case.

"Peter, tears are very therapeutic. Believe me, I would be more concerned if you *didn't* cry."

"Really?" He sniffled and blinked at her in surprise. She nodded. "So you're good at reducing grown men to tears, huh?" Dr. Herne smothered a giggle. "Trust me, if I didn't already know you were a sub...."

She cleared her throat. "Back to my question. Did it feel good to admit to Alex that you love Thomas?"

Peter gave his eyes a final wipe. No more tears today. "Yeah, actually, it did. What surprised me most was how calmly I took it when he told me what he overheard. At first I was upset, but then.... It was strange." He looked his psychologist in the eye. "I hope you don't mind, but I don't want to discuss this right now. Besides, our time is about up, isn't it?" He didn't want to talk about Thomas. It hurt too much, not that he would admit that to her.

She glanced at the clock. "Pretty much." Dr. Herne gave him a forthright look. "Is it getting to you? After all, we've had six sessions now and no sign of Curtis. It must be stressing you out."

Peter shrugged. "I'm coping better than I'd anticipated. I still panic, but I'm dealing with it. But yeah, all this waiting around for him to make his move is starting to get to me." He glanced down at his hands clasped together in his lap. "Sir is looking tired. I try not to think it's my fault, but I know he's worried about me." He huffed. "I just wish Curtis would get it over with. I want this to be finished."

Dr. Herne closed her notebook. "You know what they say. Be careful what you wish for."

Peter smiled. "In that case, I'll wish harder." He stood up. "Thanks, doc. I'll see you on Monday morning." He picked up his denim jacket and headed for the door. At the threshold he turned. "Have a good weekend."

Dr. Herne gave him a wide smile. "You too, Peter. Give my regards to Master Thomas."

He nodded in acknowledgment and left the office. He paused at the heavy main door, taking a deep breath. Okay, so maybe he *was* coping better. That hadn't been a lie. But that didn't mean he no longer suffered from the initial feeling of panic that always stole over him every time he went to step out of his comfort zone and into the outside world. And although visualizing Thomas helped to clamp down on the rising tide of panic as he made his way to and from the doctor's office, it was always there, like molten lava that threatened to burst through the surface at any moment.

Peter pulled open the door and stepped into the late-afternoon sunshine. Walking briskly, head down, shoulders hunched, he followed his usual route, not deviating from it for an instant. He had yet to spot anyone following him, despite quick surreptitious glances now and again. Mark's men must be really good at their jobs, he surmised, and this thought comforted him. He hurried up pedestrianized Market Street and heaved a sigh of relief when he finally emerged into Piccadilly. The bus station was in sight.

As he rounded the corner, he noticed a car parked in the street in front of McDonald's. Raised voices emanated from the vehicle through the open windows. The occupants appeared to be two men.

"Yeah, like I'm going to listen to *you*. It was *your* directions that got us lost in the first place!" The voice was deep and gruff.

"I could've sworn the sign said turn left." The passenger's voice had a plaintive edge to it.

"Give me the map." The driver was definitely sounding more and more pissed off.

"I can do it! Just give me a minute, all right? Christ, you're so impatient!"

"Well, we're not supposed to park here. This is a bus zone. We're gonna get pinched if we stay here much longer!"

Peter chuckled. He wondered briefly if they were a couple. They sure bickered like one.

The passenger door was thrown open, and out got a squat man with a crew cut. He strode around the front of the car and pulled at the door. "Get out. *I'll* drive, *you* can direct us."

Driver guy snorted. "Yeah, *riiiiight*, like I'm gonna let *you* drive."

Passenger guy caught sight of Peter and gave a sigh of relief. "Oh, thank God. Excuse me, can you help us? We're really lost here."

Driver guy wound down the window fully. He twisted to look at Peter. "It's okay, mate, we don't need your help." He glared at Passenger guy. "We are *not* asking for directions."

Passenger guy pouted. "Well, maybe if we'd asked that little old lady when I suggested it ten minutes ago, *we wouldn't be lost right now*!" His eyes blazed.

Peter couldn't help but smile. "Where are you trying to get to?" He stepped closer to the car. Passenger guy thrust his hand through the open window.

"Give me the map."

Driver guy grumbled and handed it over with extreme reluctance. Passenger guy snatched it and spread it out over the hood of the car, where he began examining it closely.

"Okay, where the hell *are* we on this thing?"

Peter leaned over the map and quickly located Piccadilly, stabbing it with his forefinger. "We're here. Where are you heading?" His eyes widened in surprise as he felt a sudden sharp prick just above his elbow, and he opened his mouth to cry out, but Passenger guy slid a large, meaty hand across his mouth. Peter moaned in horror, but the sound was smothered.

"Get him in the back, quick!" hissed Driver guy, as Peter felt his legs start to give way from under him. Passenger guy seized his arms and fumbled with the rear door, then flung Peter onto the backseat. Peter tried to get up, but a wave of dizziness hit, and then the world fuzzed out.

THOMAS was staring at his computer screen, but the e-mail he was trying to read just wasn't getting through. His thoughts were focused on Peter.

"Thomas, it's Friday afternoon. Leave that and go home, for goodness' sake." Leo sounded gruff. Thomas looked up from the monitor and regarded his partner for a second. "Look, if it makes you feel any better, I'm going home too. Alex is waiting for me outside, and Miles is doing the stint in the public room tonight. Jonathon will be manning the office." Leo stood and reached for Thomas's leather jacket. He held it out to him.

Thomas sighed and gave up. "Okay, let's call it a day." His phone warbled and he picked it up, unlocking it hastily when he saw Mark Saunders's number. "Mark."

"They've got him."

Thomas felt as though all the air had been dragged from his lungs. "When?"

"About five minutes ago. We're tracking them. I'll call you back when we figure out where they are. Gotta go." Mark rang off abruptly.

Thomas dropped the phone onto the desk and sagged into his leather chair.

"Thomas? What's happened?"

Thomas stared at the wall beyond Leo. "They've got Peter." All of a sudden his limbs felt shaky and his heartbeat raced. Everything seemed to have got really loud around him. He was dimly aware of Leo's hand on his arm.

"We'll take you home."

Thomas nodded numbly and got up to follow Leo from the office. One thought reverberated through his feverish brain. *They've got my boy.* Talking about it, planning it, was one thing. Dealing with it when it actually happened was quite another.

He didn't remember getting into his car and handing Leo the keys. It was as if he were moving through fog: everything was indistinct. Outside the car, the world flashed by in a blur. The phone's warble cut through the haze like a razor blade. It was Mark again.

"Okay, they've stopped. We know where they are, and the team is on their way. The microphone is working perfectly." He paused.

Thomas reacted instantly. "Is Peter all right?"

"We haven't heard him yet. The officer who saw them take him thinks he's been drugged."

The world was suddenly very sparkly. Thomas blinked rapidly.

"Thomas? Did you hear me? He'll be fine. They need him alive to find out if he's told anyone." Mark spoke urgently.

"Where... where is he?"

"I'm sorry, I can't tell you that. The state you're in—and don't deny it, I can hear it in your voice—you'd want to go round there and charge in, guns blazing. Leave it to us, Thomas. Let us do our job. I promise you, I'll ring when there's more news." He rang off.

Thomas stared at the phone in his hand. All he could do now was wait—and pray.

SOUNDS filtered through to register in Peter's brain. Voices. Several voices. He shook his head slowly, as though trying to dispel the heaviness that enveloped him. A hand shook him roughly.

"Come on, wake up."

Peter knew that voice.

He opened his eyes and looked around, recognizing the location immediately. He was in one of the private rooms at St. Andrew's club. He glanced down. His eyes widened when he realized he was naked. He looked around wildly, but his clothes were nowhere in sight. Thank goodness the cock ring was still in place.

Peter blinked at the strong lights that glared at him. Three lighting units, like the ones used on film sets, were set up beyond a chair that sat in front of him. Curtis sat in the chair, leaning forward, gazing at Peter with malevolence.

"About fucking time." Curtis had his arm on the table beside him. His hand rested lightly on a gun that lay there. The barrel pointed toward Peter. Peter felt the hair lift on the nape of his neck.

Curtis gave an evil smile. "Yeah, you remember my gun, don't you, boy?"

Peter swallowed. "Intimately." He tried to straighten up in his seat, but his arms were tied to the back of the chair.

Curtis curled his hand around the grip. "You refer to me as Master, boy." His low voice dripped with menace. Cold blue eyes bored into Peter. "You seem to have forgotten how you speak to me."

Peter felt as if his heart was about to explode, but he met Curtis's gaze bravely.

"You are not my Master." He ground out the words through gritted teeth. "You are just a sadistic bastard who beat me, whipped me, tortured me, and made my life hell for four years. You sold me to men to be fucked." Peter couldn't believe what he was saying, but the words were pouring out of him. "Why am I here? I told you at the house, I've said nothing." He stuck out his chin, but his heart was quaking all the while.

Curtis bounced to his feet and advanced on Peter. He held the gun aloft, as though he were about to backhand him with it. Peter closed his eyes and waited. Nothing happened. Cautiously, he opened one eye, and all the air fled his lungs as Curtis punched him in the stomach, driving his fist forcefully into his abs. Peter gasped for air as Curtis backed away and retook his seat.

Curtis gripped the gun tighter. "Don't you fucking speak to me like that, you little shit. You've caused me a load of trouble, disappearing like that. Made a lot of people very nervous. Not to mention the money I lost." He snorted. "Not that you ever made me much on that score. You were fucking useless as a sex slave. Who wants to fuck someone who doesn't even *act* like he's enjoying it? And as for you not telling anyone, why should I believe you? You know far too much. So you have to go." He waved the gun in Peter's direction. Peter gulped. His stomach muscles ached.

"What are you going to do?" Peter whispered. All the fight was gone out of him. "And why am I naked? Are you going to kill me?"

Curtis guffawed and gestured to the lights. "You're about to be auctioned." Now Peter could make out the webcam on the desk beside Curtis. "We have some overseas clients who'll hopefully pay a good price for you."

He leered at Peter. "Looks like I might make some money from you after all." He looked down to Peter's flaccid dick. "Nice cock ring."

"Doesn't selling drugs earn you enough? I thought you and your associates would be set up for life by now." Peter tried to keep Curtis focused. He knew what the listening officers needed to hear.

Curtis scowled. "There's no such thing as enough, not when it comes to money. Yeah, the drugs bring in plenty, but selling off the rent boys is proving very lucrative indeed." His eyes gleamed. "There's definitely a market out there."

"Did they have any choice in it, the boys you sold off?"

Curtis rolled his eyes. "Yeah, 'course they did. Be sold, or end up like Ethan."

An icy fist curled around Peter's heart. "What happened to Ethan?" The words came out as a whisper.

A cruel smile twisted Curtis's features. "He had an 'accident.'" He crooked his fingers into quotation marks.

Peter felt as though he'd been punched in the gut again. "You killed him?"

Curtis growled. "The little fucktard gave me no choice. He knew everything. I thought he wanted in, wanted to be part of my project, but he screwed me over. He apparently developed a conscience or something and ran to the cops. Have you any *idea* how much it cost me to get that investigation quashed? When I confronted him about it, he told me, 'Curtis, I love you, but I can't be a part of this.'" Curtis sneered. "The little shit thought I loved him. He became a liability and had to be dealt with. Then, luckily for me, you came along."

Despite the fear that rampaged through him, Peter's heart leapt to hear Curtis's words. Thank God the man couldn't keep his mouth shut.

Curtis eyed him with distaste. "So now you know what happened to the last sub who blabbed. I learned from Ethan. I kept you in the dark about a lot of things. Even if you had told the cops, they still wouldn't have known everything. I got my fingers in a lot of pies. That's why I got Christian. Figured sooner or later, I'd have to get rid of you too."

Peter prayed silently that the police had heard enough.

The door opened, and Peter's heart skipped a beat. He recognized the three men who entered. They were Curtis's associates. All wore business suits. The men stood around the edge of the room. Two of them looked Peter up and down, leering at him. He shivered. One looked at Curtis and tapped his watch. Curtis nodded.

"Untie him." The words were directed above Peter's head, and suddenly hands grabbed his upper arms roughly. His wrists were freed, and then he was hauled to his feet. He got a glimpse of the two men who flanked him. The guys from the car.

Curtis gestured with the gun. "You're gonna stand over there and keep your mouth shut. We're ready for the auction to start." His gaze dropped to take in Peter's limp cock. "Pity you're not hard. That cock ring shows off the package well enough, though. I'm not gonna make a lot off you, but it'll be enough to make it worth my while." He leered at Peter and then addressed the two men who held Peter. "Move him."

Peter's heart began to beat faster, and his legs were shaking as the two men pulled him into position while Curtis adjusted the webcam. In his head he kept up a constant litany. *Now, now, come and get me now.*

All the men looked up in alarm as muffled noises intruded from the corridor. Suddenly, the door burst inward, splintering at its hinges. Eight uniformed police officers in black body armor poured in through the door so quickly that the occupants had little time to react. The officers aimed rifles at the men, who raised their hands above their heads immediately. Curtis dropped the gun and winced as an officer seized his hands and pulled them behind his back. Peter watched as all the men were read their rights and then cuffed.

Curtis met Peter's gaze. "Looks like I might have underestimated you." His eyes were glacial.

Peter said nothing, but watched his exit from the room under escort. Once Curtis had gone, Peter's legs gave way, and he collapsed in a heap on the floor, trembling. He heard footsteps and then a familiar voice.

"Peter, it's okay, it's over." Mark Saunders knelt on the floor beside him, holding out a blanket, which he draped around Peter's shoulders. Peter's teeth chattered.

"C-c-can't s-stop sh-shaking,"

"That's the adrenaline rush," explained Mark, helping him to his feet. "It'll pass. I've got a car waiting outside to take you to the police station. The police surgeon will make sure you're okay, and you'll have to make a statement, of course."

Peter nodded. His limbs were still shaking.

"Peter." Peter looked at Mark's face. "I've rung Thomas. He's coming to the station to get you."

Peter could have kissed him. Sir would be there. Sir was waiting for him. But then his heart sank. Thomas wouldn't be Peter's Sir for much longer. In that moment Peter vowed to hold on to every precious minute they had left together.

Mark slipped an arm protectively around his shoulders. "Let's get you back to your Sir." Mark's cheeks reddened, and despite the tremors in his body Peter smiled to see this adorable reaction. He leaned gratefully against Mark as the detective led him from the room and out through the club to the waiting car. A noisy crowd of onlookers had gathered outside the club. Mark pushed through with his arm still around Peter's shoulders. Peter kept his head lowered in an attempt to shut out the stares. He pulled the blanket tightly around his body and shivered.

An officer helped Peter into the back of the police car, and Mark went around the other side to climb in next to him. Peter was grateful to have him there. He leaned his head back against the rest and closed his eyes. *On my way to Sir.*

THOMAS couldn't keep still. His eyes were trained on the door that led from the reception area of the police station to the restricted areas. There was a line of plastic chairs, two of which already held Leo and Alex, who were regarding him anxiously.

"Sit down, Thomas." Leo spoke in a low voice. "A watched pot... remember?"

Thomas couldn't help it. He wanted his boy. Mark Saunders had told him it wouldn't be long, and Thomas hadn't taken his eyes off the door since. He was dimly aware of Leo talking to him earnestly. He tried to focus on what Leo was saying, but his gaze kept moving back to the door. His thoughts were firmly focused on Peter.

"Thomas? Have you been listening to me?"

Thomas turned his attention back to Leo. "I'm sorry, I zoned out. What did you say?"

"I said I've finally found the perfect Dom for Peter. He's smart, understands the boy's special needs, and is equipped to handle them."

Thomas swallowed harshly. Telling Leo to find someone was one thing. Leo informing him that he'd done just that was apparently another. Thomas pushed down his feelings of regret. *This is for Peter.*

"That sounds good. What can you tell me about him?"

"He's well versed in subs. He's trained many of them throughout the years. We've spoken about Peter, and I can tell he really wants to get to know more about the boy."

Thomas winced at the thought of losing Peter. "I want to meet him before I commit to anything. I need to know that I can trust him to care for my... for the boy."

Leo laughed. "Thomas, my friend, that Dom is you. You're exactly what the boy needs."

Thomas narrowed his eyes at Leo. "We've already had the conversation about the difference in our ages, right?"

Leo smiled. "Yes, and you know what I think about that." His gaze traveled beyond Thomas and he smiled. "That boy cares for you."

Thomas turned his attention back to the door and finally noticed Peter, accompanied by Mark Saunders. Peter quickly glanced away and focused on Mark once again, but not before Thomas caught the way Peter's eyes lit up when he saw him. Thomas could see the blush in the young man's cheeks. He wore an unfamiliar pair of jeans and a T-shirt.

Leo's voice sounded in his ear. "Look at him, Thomas. He's in love with you. He wants to belong to you."

Thomas gazed at the boy and let the words sink in. His heart soared. *Can it be true?* He watched as Peter shook Mark's hand and then trudged over toward them. Mark raised a hand to Thomas and gave him a grateful smile. Thomas returned it.

"What did they say, boy?" Leo asked.

Peter may have been answering Leo's question, but his eyes never left Thomas. "They got them all, sir. And they have all the evidence they need." And still those eyes didn't shift from their exploration of Thomas's face.

Leo smiled. "Peter? What would you say if I told you we've found the perfect Dom for you?"

Peter blanched. His gaze dropped to the floor. He swallowed. "That's great, Master Leo."

Thomas's heart constricted to hear the boy's lifeless tone.

"Then what would you say if I told you I think Thomas is the one you should be with?"

Peter's head jerked up.

"Really?" That hopeful expression in his boy's eyes was more than Thomas could bear. In those beautiful green eyes lay the answer to his question of a few seconds ago. Peter cared for him. He opened his arms wide, and Peter simply walked into them. His head came to rest against Thomas's shoulder. Thomas enveloped the boy in his arms and held him close, conscious of Peter's heart beating so strongly, Peter's body fitting perfectly against him. He brought his mouth close to Peter's ear.

"Let's go home, boy."

Twenty-Two

Finding Joy

"PLEASE thank Peter again for me."

Thomas chortled. It was the third time Mark had said it.

"I take it things went okay with your superiors?"

He heard Mark's intake of breath. "Eventually. At first I fully expected them to tear me a new arsehole—they were that furious. There was talk of disciplinary action, demotion, endangering a civilian.... I tell you, Thomas, I was scared I was about to lose my job. Thank God for SOCA."

"Did they smooth things over?"

"Better than that. They gave me a letter of recommendation. And once I explained *why* I left my superiors out of the loop, the Chief Constable himself got on the phone to thank me and tell me that an investigation had already been launched into discovering who was taking bribes from Curtis Rogers."

"Fantastic!" Thomas was delighted. The detective had gone out on a limb for Peter, and if this got him some well-deserved recognition, so much the better.

He looked across the lounge at Peter, who was stretched out on the sofa under the throw. His eyes were closed. The boy hadn't spoken a great deal in the two or three hours since they'd returned from the police station. Maybe it was time for a talk.

"Mark, sorry, but I have to go."

Mark reacted swiftly. "No, I'm sorry for taking up your time. I should've realized you'd want to spend time with Peter. I'll let you go. Thanks again, Thomas, for everything. I'll be in touch."

"Mark." There was something Thomas needed to say before he let the detective finish the call. "Thank you for protecting my boy."

He could hear the smile in Mark's voice. "You're welcome. Say hi to Peter for me."

Thomas hung up the phone and regarded the boy thoughtfully. Dinner had involved reheating some of Peter's homemade soup and chunks of bread, and both men had eaten in silence. Peter seemed almost dazed. Thomas had no idea what the lad had gone through, but he didn't push. Peter would talk when he was ready.

"Would you like to watch a movie, Peter?" Thomas asked, although a cursory glance at the clock on the mantelpiece told him it was perhaps too late for this.

Peter opened his eyes and looked at Thomas. The boy looked tired.

"Actually, Sir, would you mind if I went to bed? I feel exhausted."

Thomas wasn't surprised. Today must have been draining, both physically and mentally. *You can talk to the boy tomorrow*, he reasoned with himself.

"Certainly, lad. A good night's sleep is just what you need." He locked eyes with the boy. "We can talk tomorrow." He waited for Peter's reaction.

Peter gazed back at him. His expression lightened for a second or two. "I look forward to it, Sir," he said softly. He got up from the sofa and walked over to Thomas, lifting his chin to meet Thomas's gaze. "Good night, Sir."

Thomas couldn't resist. He cupped the boy's face gently with both hands and kissed him on the lips. Peter closed his eyes, and as Thomas pulled away, there was the faintest smile in evidence.

"Good night, boy." He kissed the top of Peter's head. "Sleep well."

Peter bowed his head slightly in acknowledgment and exited the lounge. Thomas listened to the sound of his feet on the stairs. And after that, he stood fixed to the spot, straining to pick up the sounds that told him Peter was getting washed.

Is that it? You're just going to let him go to bed?

What else would I be doing?

How about going to bed with him? It's not like you don't want to.

And Thomas did want. The thought of taking the boy into his bed had crossed his mind more than once that evening. But each time the idea occurred to him, the muscles in his abdomen quivered and there was a fluttery feeling in his stomach. He knew why his body reacted in this way. It had been far too long since Thomas had been with anyone, and he was nervous. No matter how many times he tried to tell himself that Peter wasn't about to rate him on his sexual prowess, the nerves wouldn't desist.

Give it time. Peter's not ready. Thomas almost laughed aloud. Neither, it would seem, was he.

THOMAS stood outside St. Andrew's club, watching as the uniformed police dragged away Curtis Rogers and friends. Anxiously, he eyed the doorway, waiting for Mark to emerge with his boy. His heart gave a jolt as the paramedics came through the door, pulling a trolley between them, on which was a black body bag. Mark Saunders accompanied it. His hand rested on the bag, and his eyes were full of pain. As the paramedics carefully placed their precious cargo into the ambulance, Mark looked up and caught sight of Thomas. That expression didn't change one iota as he walked slowly toward Thomas. Mark held out his hand toward him, the same hand that had lain so protectively on the body bag.

Thomas could just make out what Mark was saying.

"Thomas, I'm so very, very sorry."

Blood pounded in Thomas's ears, and the world started to gray out, becoming distorted. Mark was still speaking, although now in slow motion, and his words made no sense. Mark reached him in time to grab him as the world began to spin....

GASPING for breath, Thomas sat bolt upright in bed, clutching his chest, which was bathed in perspiration. Christ, the dream felt so real. He sat there, waiting for his heartbeat to return to normal. The urge to check on Peter was overwhelming, hammering at him until he had to act. He threw back the duvet—and froze as he heard breathing coming from the floor near his bed.

"Sir?" Peter's voice came to him out of the darkness. Thomas reached across and switched on the lamp.

Peter lay curled up on the rug beside his bed. There was a pillow beneath his head and a single white sheet pulled over him. The boy sat up and rubbed his eyes. The sheet fell away to reveal his nude form underneath.

Thomas swallowed. The lad eyed him nervously, blinking in the lamplight.

"What are you doing here, boy?"

Peter's breath hitched. "I… I wanted to be near you, Sir." His eyes appeared so large and round in the warm glow from the lamp. He bit at his lower lip.

Thomas backed toward the center of the bed and held out a hand. "Get in bed, lad." He heard Peter's slight gasp. "Peter, I want you in my bed, now."

Peter got to his feet, naked and beautiful. And totally unaware of just how sexy he was in that moment. Slowly, he climbed into the bed and stretched out on his side. His eyes never left Thomas. He nestled his head in the dent where Thomas's head had rested moments before. Thomas lay down facing him and let his eyes feast upon the sight. Peter's lean body trembled.

"Are you cold?" Thomas reached for the duvet to cover him, but Peter laid a soft hand on his.

"No, Sir. I'm not cold, I… Sir, I… I need…." Peter shuddered.

"What do you need, boy?" The sight of the boy's nude form, his skin glowing in the lamplight, aroused Thomas. He felt his cock stiffen, jerking toward Peter with a life of its own. Peter's eyes grew larger, if that were possible.

"Would you hold me, Sir?"

Thomas groaned and pulled the boy to him, slipping his arm around to caress his back, moving gently over the raised skin of the lad's scars. Thomas gasped as their bodies met. The boy was warm. He pressed his hands against Thomas's chest and stroked the mat of graying hair that covered his pecs.

"I was so scared, Sir."

Thomas pulled the pillow across to cradle Peter's head and then another for himself. They lay there looking at each other in the warm light. Thomas stroked his fingers down Peter's cheek, loving the sound Peter made as he caught his breath.

"You were very, very brave today." At last he could say the words, the horror of the nightmare having receded slightly. Peter was alive, in his arms, in his bed.

"Do you want to know the one thing that went through my mind when Curtis had that gun trained on me?"

Thomas's heart gave a jolt as he heard the words. An icy cold hand danced along his spine. *Oh God, this day could have ended very differently.* He forced himself to remain calm. "Tell me."

Peter locked eyes with him. "That I was going to die before I had a chance to tell you...." He swallowed. Thomas cupped his cheek tenderly. Peter closed his eyes for a second and then opened them wide. "Before I had the chance to tell you that I love you, Sir," he whispered.

Thomas's breath quickened, and he was suddenly aware of his heart beating strongly.

"I love you too." At last he said it, words he hadn't dared to voice. Thomas gazed in wonder at the beautiful man who had found his way into Thomas's heart. He felt the need to reassure the boy. "And although I've said the words before, many years ago now, never have they meant as much to me as they do in this moment." He felt his eyes grow moist. "I speak the truth, boy."

"Oh, Sir." Peter's lips parted, and he edged closer. Thomas could feel heat pouring off the lad. Peter's chest was flushed, and his eyes shone. "I know I dreamed of hearing you say that, but I never once imagined—"

Thomas silenced him with a single finger laid across his lips. "Boy, you're talking too much." And then he kissed him.

PETER responded hungrily as Thomas claimed his mouth in a kiss that grew in intensity. Thomas's tongue licked along the seam of his lips and slid inside, causing Peter to open for him. He moaned softly as Thomas's hand curled around his nape and pulled Peter to him, deepening the kiss. This was how he *wanted* to be kissed, how no one had ever kissed him before. Thomas rolled him onto his back and leaned over him, pressing Peter into the mattress, never breaking the kiss once. There was an urgency to his kisses that sent the blood rushing to Peter's dick. He could feel Sir's cock, heavy and full against his thigh, and the thought of touching it made his hands clench briefly against Thomas's back.

Thomas broke the kiss only to begin again at Peter's neck, licking and sucking at the warm skin until Peter was trembling all over. "Yes, Sir." When Thomas dipped his tongue into the crevices of his collarbone, Peter shivered violently. The sensation was unlike anything he'd felt before. Thomas nuzzled the skin, and now Peter became aware of him rubbing that thick cock against his thigh. The motion grew more insistent. Peter didn't want it to stop. But *God*, he wanted to touch.

"Sir, can I…. Can I touch you?"

Thomas pulled back with a groan. "God, yes!" Peter moved his hand haltingly down Thomas's chest, moving slowly over the firm abs. He stroked the tight pubic curls before finally wrapping his hand around the thick base of his cock. Peter traced the heavy vein that ran from root to head with his fingers. Thomas let out another low moan. "Boy." The word was plainly an entreaty. Peter wrapped his hand around the thick column of flesh and pulled gently, loving the feel of Thomas's silky foreskin as it slid back to reveal the head, wide and flared. A drop of precome glistened invitingly at the slit. Peter licked his lips.

"Sir, I want to taste." The low sound that emanated from Thomas's parted lips left Peter in no doubt as to his Dom's reaction, and Peter eagerly scooted lower down the bed, pausing momentarily to take in the view of Sir's magnificent erection up close before tentatively sliding his tongue over the head, lapping up the clear nectar. The moan that burst from Thomas spurred him on, and he sucked him deep, loving the smell and the taste of the man. Thomas laid a hand lightly on the back of his head, and Peter tightened his lips around the shaft, pulling him deeper.

"God, boy, how deep can you take me?"

Peter grinned, took a deep breath, relaxed his throat—and swallowed Sir's cock.

THOMAS'S heart almost came to a shuddering stop as his dick was suddenly enveloped in hot, wet, tight heat. Peter reached around to grab his arse and pull him deeper, plunging him into the boy's willing mouth as the boy's head bobbed on his cock, the muscles of his throat tight around him. Peter began to hum, sounds that spoke in no uncertain terms of his pleasure. All too soon Thomas felt himself pushed perilously close to the edge. With a supreme effort, he pulled out of the boy's mouth and, grabbing Peter under his arms, hauled him up to retake that sweet mouth in a bruising kiss. Peter responded eagerly as Thomas rolled onto his back, taking the boy with him. Thomas could feel Peter's erection against his hip. Peter's hips undulated, and he moaned softly, sounds full of want and urgent need.

In that instant Thomas wanted the boy under him, pinned to the mattress with Thomas balls deep in him, and the thought brought him to a shuddering stop. Too fast, it was all going too fast. Thomas didn't want to fuck Peter in a mindless blaze of urgent passion. He wanted to take his time, to savor their first joining. Thomas wanted to make love to his boy. Now. Soon.

Peter clearly sensed the change in him. Tentative hands stroked his face. "Sir, is... is something wrong?"

Thomas kissed him, and their mouths met in a collision of eager lips and heartfelt sighs. Thomas rolled the boy onto his side and then faced him. His head rested on his arm. He ran his fingers lightly down Peter's side, noting the sharp intake of breath as he slid his hand around to squeeze the perfect globe of Peter's arse.

"Oh, God, Sir." Peter sounded breathless. "More, please."

Thomas stroked soft skin as he traced a path to the boy's crease with his fingers until he slid a finger down to skim over his hole. Peter shuddered as Thomas pressed lightly against it. Peter pushed back against the welcome intrusion. Thomas stretched to the bedside drawer, pulled out his bottle of lube, and pumped a few drops onto his fingers before dropping the bottle onto the mattress. He pulled the boy to him, and their lips met in a kiss full of need as Thomas sought out his prize once more. He slid his finger into the boy's heat, moaning as he felt Peter tighten up around him. Peter responded more urgently to his kiss. He bucked now as he pushed back, clearly wanting to get more of Thomas inside him.

Thomas stroked into him, the motion both familiar and new. He loved how Peter shuddered when he nudged his gland. The times they had done this before sent Peter into paroxysms of ecstasy, and now Thomas wanted to send him soaring once more. Slowly, he pushed a second finger into him, loving

Peter's groan at the fuller sensation. Thomas deepened the kiss and slid his fingers into the boy again and again, making sure to hit his prostate with each penetration.

Gasping, Peter broke away, and Thomas's fingers slipped from his body. "Sir, please, Sir, I need you inside me." He reached down to grasp Thomas's cock, which was so hard it ached. "Sir, I want this inside me."

Relief flooded through Thomas. The boy wanted this. Thomas could have laughed, his heart felt so light. But then Thomas became still as logic took over. "Boy, I don't have any condoms." Any condoms lurking in a drawer in *this* house would have expired many moons ago. He stroked the boy's sweet face.

"Sir, may I ask... we were both tested. We're both clean." Peter sucked in a breath before continuing. "I... I don't want anything between us." His eyes beseeched Thomas. "Please, Sir?"

Thomas wanted this, wanted it with his whole being. But there was still that tiny part of his brain that protested. He had to be sure. He said aloud what was in his thoughts, and his voice was hoarse with arousal.

"Peter, are you sure you want us to do this? We don't have to. Christ, boy, after everything you've been through, I'd—"

Peter silenced him with a kiss. When he broke it, his gaze locked on Thomas.

"Sir, I'm not that boy, remember? We left him behind that day. So I'm a new Peter." He sucked in a deep breath. "And this Peter is a virgin."

Thomas stilled as he thought about the enormity of Peter's gift. He loved the idea. This was a virginal Peter, untouched by any man, free of the horrors Curtis had inflicted upon him.

"Sir, be my first? Please, Sir?"

The words humbled Thomas. "Yes, boy. I am going to be your first. And for as long as you'll have me, your last." He watched as his words registered. Peter stared at him. A look of fierce joy was etched on his face.

"I'm your boy? For always?"

Thomas's heart danced. "For always. Tomorrow I would like to renegotiate a permanent contract." Peter's eyes lit up, and his smile made Thomas's legs go weak. "But tonight? I want to be inside my boy."

PETER'S chest tightened. Sir wanted him. He couldn't tear his eyes away as Thomas pushed him gently but firmly onto his back and placed warm hands on his thighs to spread him wide.

"Grab hold, boy. Let me see how beautiful you are."

Peter grabbed his legs behind the knees and pulled them up toward his chest, revealing himself. He shivered as he watched Thomas's gaze drift lower, until at last he was staring at Peter's most intimate of places. Peter wasn't nervous. This was Sir, who knew his body so well. There wasn't an inch of Peter that Thomas hadn't touched or caressed. Thomas knelt between his parted thighs and leaned over him, kissing him tenderly before dropping down to kiss the tip of his cock, which rose up to greet him, hard and aching. The intimate gesture made Peter catch his breath. He gazed at Thomas in admiration. Sir was his. That lean, hard body was all his. Then that thought was driven from his mind as Thomas's tongue circled his hole.

He cried out as Thomas fluttered his tongue over Peter's entrance, teasing it as he pressed into him. The sensations were unbelievable. Peter was no stranger to sex, but, *fuck*, it had never felt so good. He recalled Thomas saying that sex was about intense feelings and sensations, and a laugh of sheer joy burst from him. This was all those things and more. This was heaven.

Thomas stopped to gaze at him with a look, and Peter let go of his legs to hold his arms wide. Thomas crawled up his body to lie on top of him. He placed his arms on either side of Peter's head and then moved closer, closer, until Peter could feel Sir's breath on his lips.

"Kiss me, Sir," he whispered, and whimpered as Thomas took his mouth in a kiss scorching in its intensity. He felt Thomas's hips roll, pushing that long, heavy cock over Peter's hard dick, and he moaned, desperate to feel that rigid length push inside him. When Thomas shifted and his cock slipped down to rub against his hole, sliding over it repeatedly, Peter couldn't take any more.

"Sir, now, please, *now!*"

Thomas dripped lube liberally onto his thick cock. His eyes were fixed on Peter as he slicked it, and his length glistened in the lamplight. Peter started to roll himself onto his belly, but Thomas laid a firm hand on his thigh. He shook his head slowly.

"No, boy. I want you to watch me when I enter you. I want you to see who is making love to you."

Thomas's description of the act they were about to perform sent Peter's heart soaring. They were going to make love.

"Yes, Sir. I want to see you." He grabbed his thighs once more and revealed himself. "Make love to me, Sir." He fixed his eyes on his Dom's face, loving the expression of joy that appeared there.

Thomas grabbed a pillow, and after folding it in two, he pushed it under Peter's hips and then scooted forward until Peter could feel the blunt head of his cock press against his hole. Thomas clasped Peter's hand, and their fingers interlaced as he slowly pushed into him. Peter felt the muscle resist at first, but finally it gave way. Peter's eyes widened at the sensation. *Oh God, he's so thick!* He let out a small whimper as Thomas inched his way inside him, until at last he felt the tickle of Thomas's pubic hair against his arse.

Thomas stilled, gazing down at him. "Fuck, boy, you're tight." There was a look of dazed wonder in his eyes.

It was as if Peter could feel every vein in his cock as Thomas began to move slowly in and out, rocking gently. Peter couldn't hold back. He rolled his hips up from the bed and met Thomas's thrusts, causing him to cry out softly.

"Peter." Hearing his name on Sir's lips as the Dom slid deeply into him was so erotic. Thomas stroked his cock in and out with increased speed, and his hips began to buck faster now. Much as Peter wanted to prolong their first time together, in that instant he knew it wasn't going to happen. He was barely hanging on, and Thomas seemed to be just as close. Suddenly he yearned to feel Thomas's skin against his.

Peter released his thighs and reached for Thomas, who responded immediately, stretching out on top of Peter. His cock pistoned into him as their mouths fused once more in a series of urgent, heated kisses. Peter wrapped his legs around Thomas's waist and pushed at his buttocks with his heels, propelling him deeper inside him. He clutched at Thomas's back, holding on tightly as Thomas gathered speed. The air was filled with the sounds of their lovemaking: sighs, whispers, murmured words of love. When the head of Thomas's cock connected with his gland, Peter let out a cry.

All too soon, Peter felt his orgasm approach. "Thomas. Thomas, I'm close."

Thomas locked eyes with him. "Peter, I'm already there. Come, come for me." He reached down to grasp Peter's cock, but Peter brushed his hand away.

"Don't need that," he gasped hoarsely. "Just don't stop." Thomas sped up, and his rhythm grew more erratic as he slammed into Peter's body, hitting his prostate with every thrust. "Oh God, Thomas, I'm coming!" Peter arched as the orgasm hit, and he grabbed Thomas's shoulders, digging into the muscles as he shot his load between their bodies.

"Peter… love you." Thomas thrust deeply into Peter and froze, his body curved around him. Peter gave a low moan as he felt Thomas's heat fill him. They clung to each other, slick with perspiration, shuddering through their climax as their lips met in kiss after tender kiss.

"Thomas." Peter whispered his name as he lay in Thomas's arms. He ran his hands over Thomas's chest before sliding them up to curl around his nape, and pulled him down into another kiss. Peter was addicted to his kisses. When Thomas stroked gently down his back, skimming over his scars, Peter caught his breath and looked at Thomas in wonder. "They really don't bother you, do they?"

Thomas looked at him. He raised his eyebrows in a look of honest puzzlement.

"The scars are part of you, Peter. I hate what you suffered, what you went through that led to them, but I don't hate *them*. I love every inch of you." Thomas rolled Peter onto his belly and proceeded to plant tender kisses on every single scar, murmuring softly as he worked his way from Peter's shoulders down to the swell of his arse. Peter lay there, and tears pricked his eyes as each scar was adored by Thomas's lips and tongue. Peter gasped as Thomas licked into his crease, lapping up his come as it trickled from Peter's hole. Thomas chuckled and rolled him onto his back.

"Does that answer your question?" His eyes shone with love. "I have one for you. Does the difference in our ages bother you?"

Peter laughed. "Not even for a second." He cupped Thomas's cheek and pulled him down into another long, lingering kiss. When the kiss finished, he met Thomas's gaze. "Does it bother *you*?"

Thomas gave him a sheepish grin. "It did, but not anymore." He leaned over and kissed him. Peter sighed with pleasure. "I count myself very fortunate to have a young lover who fills my heart with joy, my days with his presence, and my bed every night." He fixed Peter with a firm stare. "Your place is here, boy, with me. In my life, in my bed. Is that acceptable?"

Peter's face lit up with joy. "Oh, yes, Sir."

Epilogue

THOMAS dressed himself quickly and cast a furtive glance at the clock next to his… *their* bed. He smiled to himself. That would take some getting used to. The feeling he had upon waking up that Saturday morning to find Peter asleep and curled up in his arms was something that would never grow old. The ghost of a smile played about Peter's face. And as for what followed…. Thomas had abandoned the joys of having a weekend lie-in years ago, but it seemed some things were never truly forgotten. Such as the joy of bringing a beautiful boy to climax with his mouth, or the heavenly feeling of coming inside his young lover while the morning sun spilled through the curtains. Thomas sighed happily. He loved his life.

Peter was standing by the door, watching him dress. Thomas had promised to do a couple of hours at the club that evening, although he had to admit, leaving Peter was a real wrench. Theirs had been a day filled with kisses and caresses. He couldn't stop kissing the boy, and judging by the number of times Peter turned those big green eyes onto him, silently pleading for yet another kiss, Peter had no wish for him to stop anytime soon.

"Sir? Can I go with you to the club?"

Thomas came to a dead stop. It was the last thing he expected to hear from the boy's lips. He regarded him speculatively. "Do you think you're ready for that, boy?" Peter immediately opened his mouth to reply, but Thomas held up a hand in warning. "Remember, nothing but honesty between us." It was one of the things they'd discussed that morning when lovemaking was finished and they lay in each other's arms, hearts full and minds clear.

Peter looked down at the floor. "No, Sir." He raised his gaze to look imploringly at Thomas. "I want to do it for *you*."

Thomas's heart leapt in his chest. "You do me a great honor, boy, but I want this to be something we will enjoy together." He crossed the room swiftly and cupped the boy's face tenderly. "You've made such great progress, Peter. Think what you've achieved already. One day you'll be ready, and we can walk in together so I can show everyone how perfect my boy is." Peter's cheeks flushed. "But until that day? I think we will continue to work it out together." He leaned closer and kissed Peter. It started as a gentle brushing of lips but quickly deepened. Sighing reluctantly, Thomas broke the kiss. His boy was definitely addictive. He fixed the lad once more with his gaze. "Is that fair enough?"

Peter's smile was so wide, his cheeks must have been hurting.

"Yes, Sir. I think it's a wonderful idea."

THE club was busy, as was common on a Saturday night. The air was already filled with the usual sounds as members enjoyed varied scenes—loud and soft cries, along with the swish of various whips, floggers, and crops—not to mention the sound of a paddle striking flesh. Matt was on duty in the public room, and Thomas had already caught sight of Dorian in full force, eagerly sucking off one Dom while his back was still red and marked from a session with another. Thomas shook his head. That boy needed taking in hand.

As he made his way through the main floor of the club, a young man approached him cautiously.

"Are you Thomas Williams?"

Thomas glanced down quickly to look at the boy's wrist. A lime-green wristband adorned it, telling him the lad was here checking out the club. Or more specifically, it seemed, checking out *him*.

"Yes, I'm Thomas Williams. And you are...?"

The lad's cheeks reddened. "My name is Christian Prenton."

Thomas stiffened at the name. "Christian.... You were Curtis's sub." Thomas suddenly had a sour taste in his mouth. "What do you want?" His words were cold, but he couldn't help his reaction. According to Peter, Christian had led Curtis to his house.

Christian trembled. "Look, I don't blame you for thinking badly of me. That's why I had to come here, to tell you the truth… and to find out if Peter is okay."

Seeing the boy tremble forced Thomas to calm himself. He spotted an empty table at the far end of the bar. "Let's sit down," he suggested. He led the way to the corner, and Christian followed close behind him. The boy perched awkwardly on the edge of his seat, and his gaze darted around the club.

Thomas folded his arms. "All right, talk to me."

Christian sucked in a deep breath. "The police interviewed me about Curtis. When they told me what he'd been arrested for, I was horrified. I *swear*, I had no idea. I haven't been his sub for very long, and as for all that shit he's involved in…." Christian shuddered.

Thomas wasn't interested. "Tell me how Curtis Rogers found out where Peter was living."

Christian paled. "That was my fault. I saw Peter once in St. Ann's square, coming out of an office building, and I told Ma… Curtis. He made out like he was delighted, and he said he'd been worried to death. He told me to go back the same time the following week to see if I could see Peter again."

"Which you did."

"Yes! I thought I was helping! And when he suggested coming with me, and then us following Peter to see where he was…." He scowled. "He said he wanted to check that Peter was safe, that he hadn't fallen in with a bad crowd or something." Tears welled up in his eyes. "I should have known he was up to something when he told me not to tell Peter he was in the car. And when he punched him…." The tears fell freely now, and Thomas felt a jolt of guilt. "I'm so, *so* sorry for what happened. Tell Peter if there's ever anything, *anything* I can do for him, he only has to ask." Christian wiped at his eyes savagely with the back of his hand. "I was such an idiot."

Thomas laid a hand on the lad's arm. "Don't be so hard on yourself." He waited until the boy had composed himself. "Is that all you came here for? To speak to me?"

Christian managed a watery smile. "Well, yeah." He sniffed. "Thank you for your time." He got up to leave, but Thomas asked him to hold on for a moment.

"What are you going to do now?"

Christian's brow furrowed. "I'm not sure I understand."

"Curtis is gone. Who is taking care of you?"

Christian shook his head. "Right now, I'm on my own. I'm not ready for a new master. And even after one brief look around here, I'm beginning to doubt just how authentic Curtis's training was." He grimaced. "If you could call it that. They've closed down St. Andrew's, for which I'm grateful. I'll just be happy to find a club that I can fit into."

Thomas gave him a reassuring smile. "Feel free to check out the club. And I will pass on your message to Peter tonight."

Christian's eyes grew wide. "Are you definitely going to be his Dom now?" Thomas gave a short nod. Christian's face broke into a happy smile. "I'm glad. He needs someone like you." Christian got to his feet and held out his hand. Thomas shook it. "Thank you for hearing me out."

Thomas flashed that reassuring smile once more. "Don't mention it. And I hope you decide to stay. There are some good Doms here." He winked. "Maybe one who's just right for you. Good-bye—and good luck." Thomas watched the boy as he walked off to inspect the club. He sighed. He hoped Christian would stay. The boy needed to see what the D/s life was really like. Thank goodness he hadn't spent much time with Curtis.

Thomas spied a familiar face at the bar and hastened to greet his friend. Steven Drummond was perched on a stool next to a new Dom, his friend Alan Marchant, who'd joined at the same time. Both men were deep in conversation with Ben, the barman, and all three were laughing.

"Nice to see you making yourself at home, Steven."

Steven's face creased into a huge smile. "I've hardly seen you since we joined. Where have you been keeping yourself?"

Behind the bar, Ben grinned. "In the arms of a younger man, by all accounts. Lucky sod." He winked at Thomas, who waved a warning finger at him. "Sorry, Thomas, couldn't resist."

Steven's smile widened. "That wouldn't be a certain younger man by the name of Peter, would it?" He waggled his eyebrows. "Remember, you're only as old as the man you feel. And if you're feeling up a twenty-six-year-old…." He laughed.

Ben joined him in his laughter. "Yeah, come to think of it, Thomas, you're looking awfully pleased with yourself tonight. A definite spring in your step." He winked again. "Did we have a good night?"

"Yes, *we* did," Thomas said with a snort. "Glad my love life gives you something interesting to talk about, Ben."

"Well, at least you *have* a love life." Ben's face fell. "Mine's virtually nonexistent these days." He met Thomas's gaze and smirked. "Maybe I need to find myself a younger man. Seems to work wonders for you." He grinned.

Thomas ignored him for the moment and turned to greet Alan. "Are you enjoying your time here so far, Alan?"

Alan nodded enthusiastically. "This is a fantastic club. I'm so pleased Steven recommended it." He glanced around the club. "I've already had some great scenes with some of the subs. They're certainly well trained."

Steven smirked. "Told you," he said smugly.

Alan smiled. "There are a few subs who've approached me to do scenes with them. Really, I'm spoiled for choice. They seem to be vying for my attention at the moment."

Thomas sighed, hand over heart. "Ah, the joy of being the newbie." They all laughed. "Then you must have met Dorian. I think Dorian has done scenes with every single Dom who ever passed through those doors. And I'm pretty sure he's carved notches on every whip, cane, and paddle in the place."

Alan looked puzzled. Ben stepped in. "Dorian is our resident pain slut," he confided.

Alan's brow cleared. "Ah, now I understand. No, I've not met him." He scowled. "And it doesn't sound like I could teach him anything about taking pain."

Thomas gazed at him thoughtfully. "No, but if you like a challenge, you could try teaching him that there *are* other ways to fly." He smiled. "Do you like a bit of a challenge?"

Alan returned his smile. "Love them." His eyes gleamed.

Leo appeared at Thomas's side. "Do you think you and I might have a word in the office at some point tonight?"

"Certainly." Thomas caught Ben's attention. "But first I need a brief word with Ben. In the office?" Ben gave him a brisk nod. "Leo, can you man the bar for a few minutes? We shouldn't be long."

"No problem."

Ben followed him into the office, pulling the door shut after him. "Is there a problem, Thomas?" A crease appeared between his eyes.

Thomas leaned back against the desk. "Not as such. I just wanted you to know that I'm not going to be able to continue with your training for a while. In fact, probably not for the foreseeable future."

Ben looked relieved. "Oh, that's all right. I mean, I know you've got a lot on your plate right now, what with Peter." Thomas lifted his brows, and Ben flushed. "Word gets around," he said sheepishly. He gazed earnestly at Thomas. "Do you think I'm ready to take on my first submissive?"

Thomas considered the question. "I don't see why not. Is there a sub at the club who you'd like to work with?"

Ben shook his head. "No, not really." He gave Thomas a frank look. "Actually, Thomas, it's great news about Peter. I'm so pleased for you. You deserve to have a special someone in your life."

Thomas smiled. "We all deserve that, Ben. But thank you. You might get to meet him, one day."

The barman gave a lopsided grin. "I look forward to it."

There was a light knock at the door, and Leo stuck his head around it. "Safe to come in?"

Thomas laughed. "Get in here, lad. Thanks, Ben." Ben bobbed his head and exited the office. "Right, what was so urgent?" Thomas sat down in his chair and regarded his desk, piled high with paperwork. Who knew that running a successful BDSM club required so much work? He caught sight of a small photo frame near the keyboard. It was Leo and Alex, and it had obviously been taken in bed. Both men were bare-chested, staring up at the camera and laughing. Thomas looked at it thoughtfully. Maybe the desk needed a new photo.

"Earth to Thomas, come in, Thomas." Leo was grinning at him from across the desk.

Thomas folded his arms. "Out with it, lad."

Leo cleared his throat. "I want to talk to you about the number of hours you're working in the club," he began.

Thomas straightened instantly. "Look, I know I've not been doing my fair share around the place, but—"

Leo cut him off. "Actually, that's not what I meant. We've coped for the last six months with your reduced hours. The club is still successful. Everything functions." He gave Thomas a hard stare. "The place hasn't collapsed without you." Thomas chuckled.

But Leo hadn't finished. "So, why not continue with the way things are?" His expression grew sober. "Thomas, you're not a single man any more. You have a young lover, a submissive, who needs you. You need to spend time with each other. Let's face it, old man. I'm thirty-eight, you're fifty-six. *One* of us should be thinking about early retirement."

When Thomas opened his mouth to retort, Leo held up a hand. "I'm not advocating giving up the club entirely. You still own half of it, same as me, *but* maybe you could be more of a stay-at-home partner." His expression softened. "For the first time in your life, you're in a relationship, Thomas. You're in love. Take time to enjoy it."

Thomas stared at him in silence for a few seconds. "You're right. Okay, I accept." Leo's mouth dropped open, and Thomas smirked. "Why would I want to argue with flawless logic like that?"

Leo's face cracked into a delighted smile. "That's fantastic. I thought I was going to have a real battle on my hands to make you see sense."

Thomas gave him a gentle smile. "Let's just say my priorities have changed somewhat in the last day or so. Life is too short, lad."

Leo stared at him, his eyes full of understanding. Then his expression cleared. "Go home. It's Saturday night. Go spend time with your boy." He tilted his head. "You two worked out a permanent contract yet?"

"That was the plan for tonight."

Leo shook his head. "The contract can wait until tomorrow. Spend tonight with Peter in your arms." He unfolded himself from his chair and walked toward the office door, pausing before he pulled it open. "Want to know the best thing about having a younger lover? It keeps you young." He winked. "And my *God*, it improves your staying power!" With that, he left.

Still shaking his head, Thomas got out his phone and dialed his home. Within two rings Peter picked up.

"Good evening, Sir. I hope everything is going well at the club." Thomas could hear the smile in his voice.

Thomas's heart leapt at the thought of that sweet face greeting him as he walked through his front door, upturned expectantly to receive his kiss. Thomas grinned.

"Boy, I'm coming home."

Born and raised in the north-west of England, K.C.WELLS always loved writing. Words were important. Full stop. However, when childhood gave way to adulthood, the writing ceased, as life got in the way. K.C. discovered erotic fiction in 2009, where the purchase of a ménage storyline led to the startling discovery that reading about men in love was damn hot. In 2012, arriving at a really low point in life led to the desperate need to do something creative. An even bigger discovery waited in the wings–writing about men in love was even hotter....

The laptop still has no idea of what hit it... it only knows that it wants a rest, please.

K.C. can be reached via e-mail: k.c.wells@btinternet.com, on Facebook: http://www.facebook.com/KCWellsWorld, or through comments at the K.C.Wells web site: http://www.kcwellsworld.com. K.C. loves to hear from readers.

Collars & Cuffs Stories from K.C. WELLS

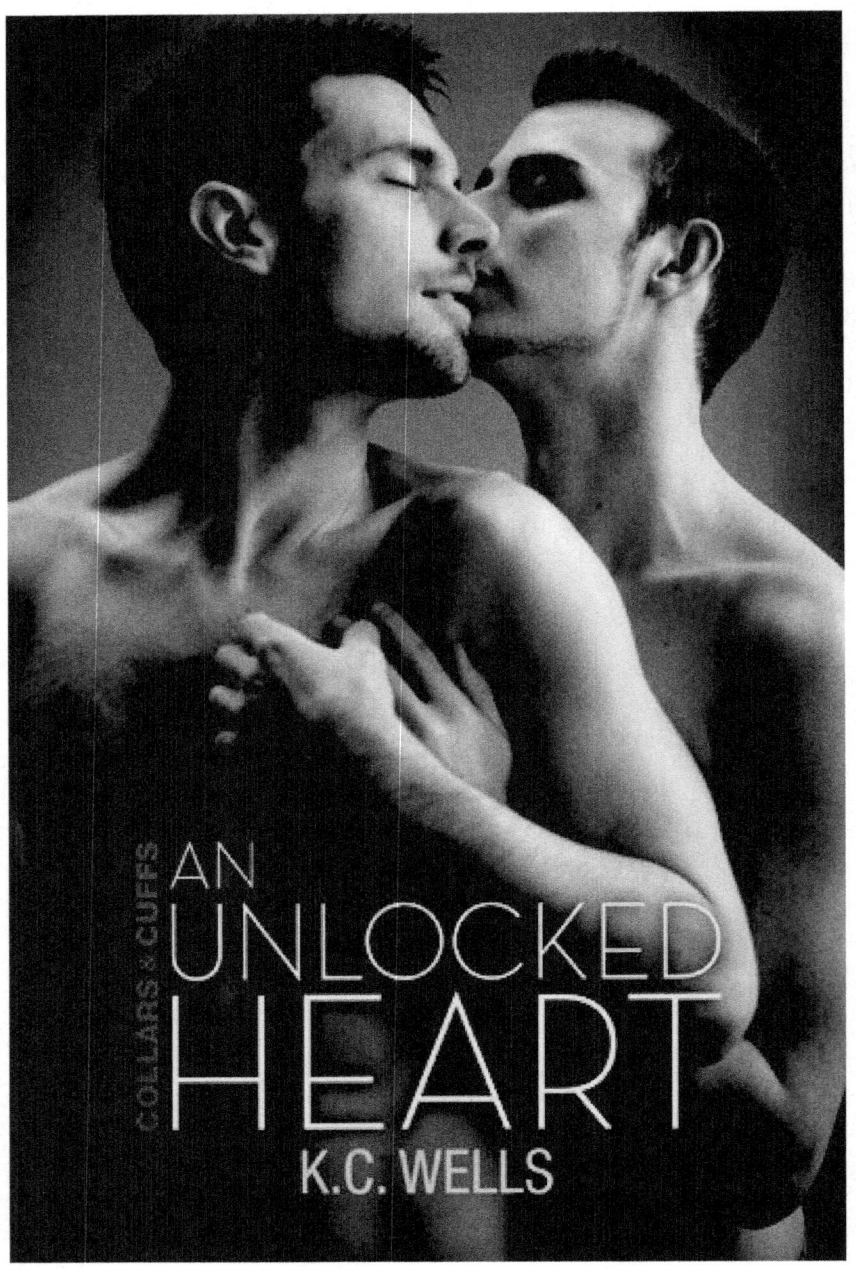

COLLARS & CUFFS
AN
UNLOCKED
HEART
K.C. WELLS

http://www.dreamspinnerpress.com

Learning to Love Series from K.C. WELLS

LEARNING TO LOVE:
Michael & Sean

K.C. Wells

http://www.dreamspinnerpress.com

Learning to Love Series from K.C. WELLS

LEARNING TO LOVE:
Evan
&
Daniel

K.C. Wells

http://www.dreamspinnerpress.com

Learning to Love Series from K.C. WELLS

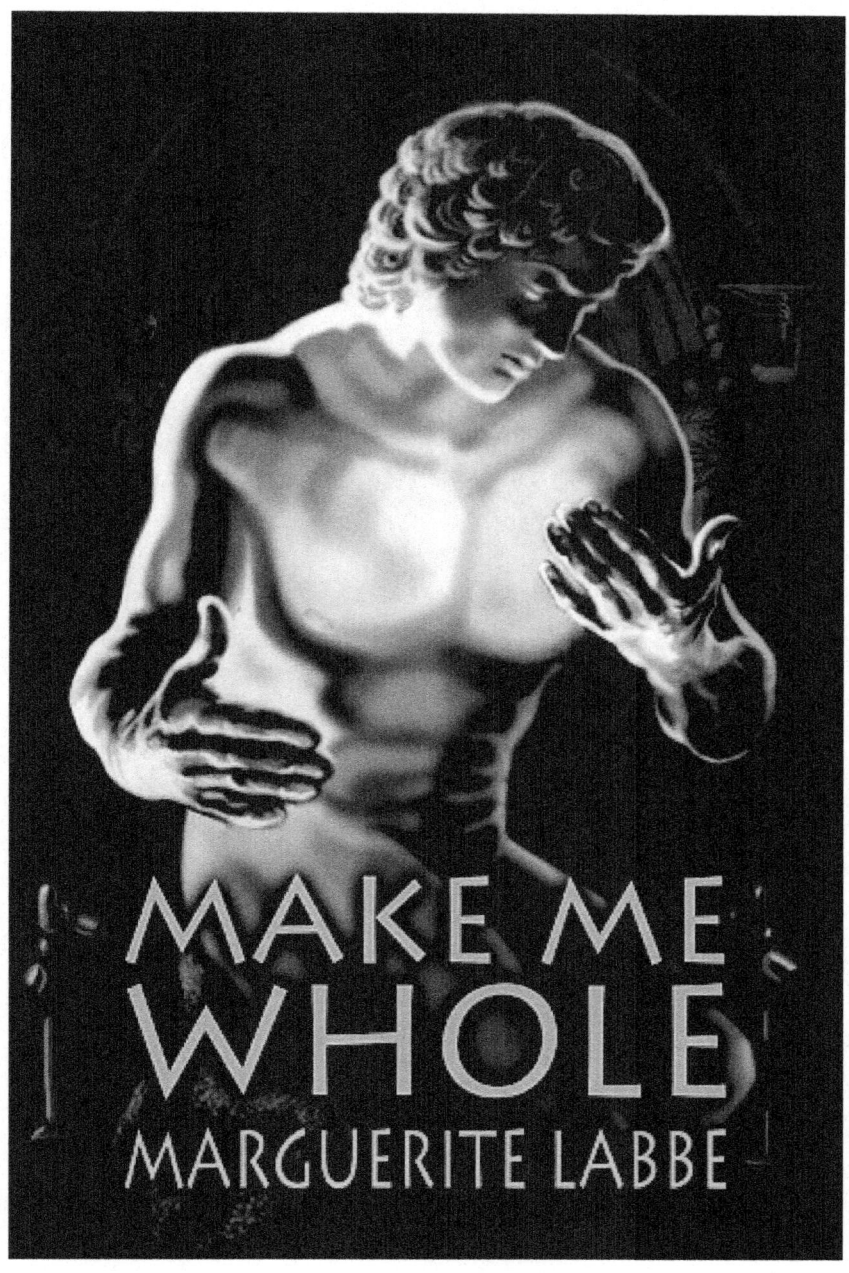

MAKE ME
WHOLE
MARGUERITE LABBE